92 Park Street · Adams, MA 01220
phone · 413 743-8345

** DID I READ THIS ALREADY? **

Place your initials or unique symbol in a
square as a reminder to you that you have
read this title.

B. M	A J	B		Mill

Barbecue *and* Bad News

Center Point
Large Print

Also by Nancy Naigle and available from
Center Point Large Print:

The Adams Grove Series:
Sweet Tea and Secrets
Out of Focus
Wedding Cake and Big Mistakes
Pecan Pie and Deadly Lies
Mint Juleps and Justice

**This Large Print Book carries the
Seal of Approval of N.A.V.H.**

Barbecue *and* Bad News

AN ADAMS GROVE NOVEL

NANCY NAIGLE

CENTER POINT LARGE PRINT
THORNDIKE, MAINE

Pub 36

This Center Point Large Print edition is published
in the year 2017 by arrangement with
Amazon Publishing, www.apub.com.

The text of this Large Print edition is unabridged.
In other aspects, this book may vary
from the original edition.
Printed in the United States of America
on permanent paper.
Set in 16-point Times New Roman type.

ISBN: 978-1-68324-278-9

Library of Congress Cataloging-in-Publication Data

Names: Naigle, Nancy.
Title: Barbecue and bad news : an Adams Grove novel / Nancy
Naigle.
Description: Center Point Large Print edition. | Thorndike, Maine :
Center Point Large Print, 2017.
Identifiers: LCCN 2016049567 | ISBN 9781683242789
    (hardcover : alk. paper)
Subjects: LCSH: Divorced women—Fiction. | Large type books.
Classification: LCC PS3614.A545 B37 2017 | DDC 813/.6—dc23
LC record available at https://lccn.loc.gov/2016049567

To anyone who has ever been so focused on a goal that they've forgotten to stop, take a breath, and embrace the moment that's happening right now.

The best moments are usually unplanned. Never be too busy to experience them.

Barbecue *and* Bad News

Welcome to the small town of Adams Grove, Virginia

Chapter ONE

"What now?" Savannah pulled her gaze from the flashing blue lights in her rearview mirror back to the speedometer. "Seven over. Seriously?"

Traffic heading south out of DC had been a nightmare. Not that it was ever good, but today had been worse than normal. Or maybe it just seemed that way because she was headed where she didn't want to go. She hadn't been back to her hometown in . . . well, a long time . . . and that had been just fine by her. There wasn't anything she needed back there. She'd been perfectly happy leaving all those memories back in Belles Corner. But when Aunt Cathy called out of the blue, hearing her voice—sounding like the old Aunt Cathy who used to be like a second mom to Savannah before everything went haywire in Belles Corner—had made it hard to say no to her request that she come back for the wedding.

If she was going to have to be there, she had every intention of making a good impression. There was no changing the past—or who her ex-husband was marrying—but the future was all hers. At least that was what Evelyn Biggens, her best friend and her boss at GetItNowNews.com, was always telling her.

Savannah had padded her travel time by two hours to compensate for the summer traffic. Once the interstate exits had started getting farther and farther apart, the traffic had thinned out too, and she'd thought it was going to be smooth sailing all the way to Belles Corner, North Carolina.

Fat chance.

The hustle of the city might be miles behind her, but getting stopped for a ticket would eat up her head start, and that cop car behind her didn't look like it was going to zip around her to nab one of the other cars that she'd been keeping pace with.

"Please keep going," she said as she eased off to the shoulder.

No such luck.

What had seemed like a pretty sure plan this morning was suddenly at risk.

Traffic sped past her southbound on I-95, all except that car with the bright blue blinking lights. He pulled to a stop right behind her.

"My lucky day," she said with a groan. Savannah pressed the button to lower the window. She pasted her best wide-eyed I'm-not-pissed-off look on her face. Momma had said you catch more flies with honey, and that was a lesson she'd never forgotten. Lord knows, she got enough practice using this sweet expression at the office these days as she hid her real activity from everyone at GetItNowNews.

Only Evelyn and two others at the online paper

knew she was the talent behind the witty, snarky, and at times downright shocking Advice from Van column on GetItNowNews. Speculation was that the person behind the column was a man. That had amused Savannah in the beginning, but she sure was tired of that gig now, even if it had garnered her an office, one of the few in cubicle world. It was small, but it came with one heck of a view, since it was just outside Evelyn's office. It was no fun to get zero credit for the top-rated column, though. Since Van's identity was kept on the down-low even from her coworkers, everyone assumed that Savannah was Evelyn's assistant. At this rate, it might always look that way.

Who else would have such bad luck that an April Fool's prank would end up with them in a two-year commitment? She should've known better than to go toe-to-toe with Evelyn. That woman was as savvy as they came, and Savannah knew she was lucky to be under her mentorship.

She still hadn't figured out what exactly she would tell all those people back home in Belles Corner. Even if the gig wasn't top secret and she *could* tell them about it, the people from her hometown wouldn't be too impressed with her for writing that column.

Every kook and crazy across the nation had come out of the woodwork asking for advice on topics better left unmentioned. It was like their goal in life was to shock her, and since she'd started out as unshakable, she was getting a run for her money.

That's what had her running late today. Her nine-to-five was always creeping into her private time and even weekends, and she was getting darned sick of it.

But as cranky as she was feeling, she had to admit that her mood just brightened a smidgen as she watched the officer approach her car. Probably about her age or not much older. Good-looking. *Really* good-looking. In fact, strangely familiar. She leaned out the window, then tugged her glasses off at just the moment he glanced down at her.

Sound innocent, get a warning, and get back on the road. "Good morning. Something wrong, officer?" Her lead foot had given her plenty of practice in this, and usually it worked.

"License and registration, please."

So you're going to be like that? Fine. "Yes, sir." She smiled. He didn't. She tugged the paperwork from the console and handed it his way.

"License?"

"Right." She leaned toward the passenger seat and rummaged through her purse, coming up with everything but her driver's license. She slipped a piece of gum from a pack and popped it into her mouth. "Gum?"

He didn't look amused. "Do you have a license, ma'am?"

Lighten up, man. "Yes. Yes, of course I have a license." Finally, she laid her hand on her wallet. "Right here." She snatched her driver's license from its slot and handed it over.

As he took the license, she still had that I've-seen-this-guy-before feeling and just had to ask. "Do I know you?"

He glanced down at her license. "Being as you're from Washington, DC, I don't know how our paths would've crossed."

"Oh." His tone really said, "I've heard all this before." Why did her mouth always act before her brain gave it permission?

His brows lifted and he gave her a little nod, as if he agreed with the thought running through her head. Was he some kind of mind reader?

"Thank you. I'll be just a moment."

She couldn't pull her gaze from that side mirror as he walked away. Nice walk. Athletic types with light-blond coloring usually turned her head, but there was something about this brown-haired guy in a uniform that held her attention. Was it attraction, or more that he seemed familiar?

An insistent little *boing* came from the dashboard. LOW FUEL flashed on the display.

Why had she thought things would work out okay today?

At this rate she'd never make it to Belles Corner.

If only that were true. She wasn't even halfway there yet, and the trip was making her more

13

anxious by the mile. As if having to attend her ex-husband's wedding wasn't already bad enough.

Aunt Cathy had convinced her that it was important for her to be there when Tripp got remarried, or else people would talk. But that wasn't what made her give in. It was that Aunt Cathy had apologized. After all these years, she'd said she was so sorry she hadn't been there for Savannah when all that stuff happened with her parents. More importantly, she'd said she'd never blamed her. Aunt Cathy had always been her favorite, but when things went bad, everything she'd known in that town was different. Everybody. Everything.

If she went back, it would certainly slow down the rumor mill. At least for a little while. That was one thing you could count on in a small town. If they didn't know the truth, they'd make up something that made sense to them, and somehow that always wound up worse. So she'd made peace with going back and showing her face after all these years.

The thought of that made her feel a little sick. Or maybe it was just the ticket. Or maybe the ticket was a sign of more trouble to come. It was bad news no matter how you looked at it.

Regrets. She had plenty, and now agreeing to make the hometown visit was inching toward the top of the list.

Think positive. Don't put any negativity out into

the universe and the universe won't serve any up.

Evelyn was always preaching that to her.

Maybe enough time had passed that people wouldn't remember the reason she'd left town.

Doubtful, but one could hope. Maybe they wouldn't even notice her; then she could just say her hellos, dole out a few hugs, and get the heck out of Dodge. It'd been so long they might not even recognize her.

That was a laugh. If she believed that for even half a second, she wouldn't have spent the better part of the week getting herself pulled together for this brief reunion. The time she'd spent on hair, nails, makeup, even waxing—which would go to waste—added up to more than she had spent on primping the whole time she was married to Tripp Cassidy. Which admittedly wasn't much, since the marriage had lasted less than a year.

The officer tapped on the top of her car with the back of his hand.

Startled, she nearly choked on her gum as she left dreamland.

"Thank you, Ms. Dey. Do you know why I stopped you?" He barely gave her a glance as he handed back her license and registration.

"Not really."

"Speeding."

"Only seven over," she said apologetically.

He lifted a brow. "Well, then you do know."

"Don't we get five or ten . . . like an unspoken rule or something?" She giggled, but even that didn't raise a smile from the man wearing the badge.

"Uh, no. The sign says speed *limit*. That means the limit. At least around here."

"Speed trap," she mumbled.

"The speed limit is strictly enforced. The limit is clearly marked on the signs. It's for your own safety, and for that of others traveling the highway."

Blah, blah, blah. She sucked in a breath to keep any more smarty-pants remarks from escaping her lips, but she still straightened in the leather seat, feeling ready to argue. That seldom worked out in situations like this. She swallowed back the sarcasm and gave in. "Look. I'm having an awful day. I'm late. I'm headed to Carolina to watch my ex-husband get remarried, because I don't have a choice. He's marrying my cousin. Younger cousin. Much younger cousin, and my whole family thinks I need to be there to show my support. It sucks, and I don't want to do it. But here I am doing the right thing. And now this. And look. Look at that." She stabbed a finger toward the dash. "I'm running out of gas. Literally and figuratively, as we speak." She closed her eyes to keep the tears of frustration from escaping. "I know you don't care. But it's a bad day."

"Your ex is marrying your cousin?" The officer

tucked his book under his arm and crossed his arms. A smile spread across his face, showing a row of perfectly white teeth, forcing tiny wrinkles —like rays of sunshine—from the corners of his eyes. "You really *are* having a bad day."

"Yes. Yes. I'm aware of that." She forced herself to look him in the eye. He looked amused. Heck, they probably married cousins around here. And was that a smirk? She'd probably just offended him. Great. "She's not a real cousin. A stepcousin by marriage. And why am I even telling you all of this? I'm sorry. Just give me the ticket. I earned it."

"I guess when I mention your back tire looks low, it's not going to make your day any better."

"Please tell me you're kidding."

He tugged on his hat. "I never kid about safety, ma'am."

She pushed the car door open and leaned out to look. She let out an audible groan and slammed the door. "Great. Just . . ."

"Sounds to me like you *just* could use a little break." He pointed straight ahead. "Take that next exit to get gas. There's a service station on your right, the Adams Grove Garage. You can't miss it. Let Bobby take a quick look at that tire while you're there. Just up Main Street on the right-hand side. I'll follow you."

"No ticket?"

He hesitated, but then he smiled. "No ticket. For

the record, it was that whole ex-husband–cousin thing that saved you. That prom queen smile and sultry stuff . . . that doesn't fly with me."

So he had noticed. *I haven't lost it.*

"Buckle up and get going before you run out of gas."

She turned to say thank you, but he was already walking away.

Suddenly, the day looked a little brighter, even if he had called her out on her efforts. She idled up the emergency lane in her Mini Cooper until there was a break in the traffic and then pulled back onto the highway toward the next exit. *Sultry? Never thought of myself as sultry before. I was just going for a little flirty.*

As she approached the exit, he was still right behind her. She knew she should appreciate him following her to safety, but there was something about small-town cops, even after all these years, that still sent her nerves into fight-or-flight mode.

The exit dumped her just about a mile away from anything except for a dilapidated old feed store. Quite frankly, if he hadn't been following her, she might have thought she'd taken the wrong exit.

Almost a mile up the road, a brightly painted sign in the median read WELCOME TO ADAMS GROVE.

It had been a while since she'd been to a small

town like this. In fact, this one didn't seem so different from the one she'd grown up in.

Finally, just ahead she saw a canary-yellow service station canopy. ADAMS GROVE GARAGE stretched end-to-end in bold red letters across the front of the building.

She pulled up to the nearest pump, thankful that she'd made it without further incident.

A salt-and-pepper-haired man sauntered out of the building. "Good morning."

"Good morning." Savannah got out of the car, but the man was already popping open the gas tank door.

"Fill it up?"

She eyed him suspiciously. Bobby was the name embroidered on the patch on the left pocket of his uniform. "I can pump it myself."

"Costs the same either way. May as well let me do it."

It took her a second to decipher the deep Southern accent. Strangely Southern to still be right here in Virginia. "Um, okay." Caught off guard, she did a goofy forward-back step like a bad cha-cha, trying to decide what the heck to do with herself. "My tire is low." She pointed to the rear driver's-side tire. "Hopefully, it just needs some air. Can you check that too?"

"Sure thing." He pulled the handle from the pump and tugged a red shop rag from his back pocket.

"I'm kind of in a hurry." He didn't seem like he knew more than one speed, though.

"Won't take long."

Even his short response took longer than necessary.

"You just passin' through?"

"I am. Is there a restroom inside?"

"On the side, but the key is next to the front counter. Help yourself." He gave her an exaggerated wink and went about his business. "And welcome to Adams Grove."

"Yeah. Thanks." Wasn't he sweet for an old guy. Under the circumstances, it felt a little tacky to grab her keys from the ignition and lock the car.

Besides, if the car got stolen, she'd have a good excuse not to go to the wedding.

Bright side to everything. Evelyn's words echoed in her head.

It wasn't hard to spot the bathroom key once she walked inside the building. Below a plank of wood that someone had branded BATHROOM into hung two Virginia license plates—vanity tags at that—reading BOSSMAN. One painted pink, the other blue.

She wrangled the pink one from the hook. Upon closer inspection, the license plate had been bedazzled. Was that even legal?

She lugged the supersized key chain with her to the side of the building, wondering just how much of a boss a man could be with pink glitter polka dots. She struggled with the awkward key chain as she worked the key in the heavy metal door. The dented condition of the door didn't give her high hopes for what she was getting ready to enter. She poked her head in, bracing herself for the worst . . . but to her surprise it was quite clean. Someone had even put up pictures and added a silk flower arrangement. A little tacky but definitely clean. Maybe her luck was about to turn for the better.

She stepped out of the restroom and checked her watch again. She'd lost that head start, but she'd still be on time. She looked to the left. To the right. Her car was nowhere in sight.

A wave of panic hit. *God, I was just kidding about an excuse to miss the wedding. They'll talk about me if I'm not there, and I do* not *want to be the talk of that town again.*

She ran to the front of the building, then slowed and swallowed back the hissy fit she was just getting ready to throw as she saw her car rising into the air on the lift.

"Is all that necessary?" she called out as she approached.

"You picked up a screw. Need to plug the tire. Won't take long."

"Just my luck," she muttered under her breath. *Stay calm and make the best of it.* Evelyn was always saying that too. "Is there somewhere I can grab something to eat?"

"Sure. Up the block, but I'd make it quick if I was you, or you'll get caught in the parade traffic. That wouldn't be good, seeing how you're in a hurry and all."

"I am, but a girl's got to eat." Multitasking. She was the queen of it. "I'm sure I'll be back before you're done." Parade traffic? That was a laugh. No more than a dozen cars had driven by since she pulled onto the man's lot. She lived in DC; she knew what real traffic looked like. Heck, she knew what real *parades* looked like.

"Suit yourself," he said with a shrug.

She hitched her purse up on her shoulder and set out up the street with the sound of his tools ringing in the air behind her. After sitting in the car for a couple of hours it felt good to stretch her legs. The blue sky reminded her of those childhood vacations on the Carolina shore with only a few fluffy clouds floating by. All that was missing was the waves crashing and the smell of suntan lotion. The heat waves modulated off the pavement, but the air wasn't sticky like it could be this time of year. One of those days that begged for outdoor activities. It was just that perfect of a day. Leave it to her family to find a way to ruin it.

Out of habit, she checked her watch again. A quick bite wouldn't set her too far behind. There was no sidewalk, so she kept close to the shoulder of the road on the slight incline toward the center of town. A big bronze sign boasted that Adams Grove had been one of the major crossroads between the North and the South since 1887. The buildings here had become the oldest residents— the structures rich with history and begging to tell their stories.

Adams Grove was bigger than Belles Corner, for sure, but it was still a small town, and small towns still conjured up negative memories . . . even after all this time. On the next block a row of buildings and a sidewalk led to the small town's merchant area. Shopkeepers busied themselves in front of their stores, setting up tables of sale items. Families claimed their spots on what was apparently the parade route, and people made small talk and even eye contact with one another as they moved through the streets.

Brick and stone structures nestled tightly next to tiny shops and lined each side of the lazy street like a welcome committee with jewel-toned awnings and fancy lettering. Bright-teal banners hanging from the lampposts did more bragging about the history of the town. Flowers around each of those lampposts added a rainbow of colors and textures, like a wild Picasso in the middle of a wall of landscapes.

She followed an irresistibly sweet aroma right to the bright-blue awning of Mac's Bakery. A string of brass bells tinkled as she stepped inside. There was barely standing room, and she found herself jockeying for a view of the glass case filled with freshly baked goodies.

How do you pick just one? The only time she bought pastries or doughnuts at home was for the office. At least then she could use the excuse of buying for the large group that she worked with at GetItNowNews to fill up two boxes with all the prettiest and yummiest-looking stuff. Then, deciding on just one was so much easier in front of everyone.

She stood there eyeing the assortment, her brain quizzing her with silly and untimely questions: Which one would least blow her calorie count for the day? Which would be the most filling? Should she pick the biggest or smallest? She'd managed to get up early enough to get her treadmill time in this morning, so what was the harm anyway, really?

Her mind was changing as quickly as the line moved.

"The bear claw."

"Excuse me?" She spun around at the slight touch on the back of her arm. "Oh, hi again, Officer—" She let the word hang. The officer who had so kindly given her a break was standing just behind her.

"Sheriff," he corrected her. "Sheriff Scott Calvin."

"Ah. I stand corrected." *La-dee-dah. Sheriff.* Arrogant enough to think he could give out tickets and still get elected? Good thing she didn't vote in this town. But he would get the cute vote. What a waste of a great body.

"Mac's known for his bear claws. I highly recommend them."

"Well, then I guess I can't leave Adams Grove without trying one, can I?" Darned if his eyes didn't sparkle . . . even in here, under the fluorescents.

Someone behind them cleared his throat and she realized she was holding up the line. "Sorry." She quickly stepped to the counter with the sheriff at her side.

The man behind the counter handed the sheriff a glossy white bakery bag and a large cup of coffee. "Here ya go. The usual. On your tab."

"Thanks, Mac." Scott turned to leave, then leaned toward Savannah. "Safe travels," he said, then in one quick movement, he was out the door.

Savannah caught herself watching for a moment too long, then turned back to the counter. "I'll have what he had," she said, thumbing toward the door, then turning one more time . . . catching herself smiling as she saw him jog across the street. Maybe a speeding ticket wouldn't have been so bad if it meant coming back to face him in court. Or not. Last thing she needed was another ticket, or another man.

Mac's Bakery only had a few stools at the counter and a couple of small tables, so Savannah took her cup of coffee and still-warm-from-the-oven bear claw outside to one of the benches that lined Main Street to enjoy the sunshine. The rich smell of the cinnamon evoked fond memories of being with Momma in the kitchen. As she tugged on the outer edge of the bear claw, the flaky crust gave way to a sumptuous middle and the gooey lace of icing clung to her fingertips. It was every bit as good as Sheriff Scott Calvin had promised.

Despite her attempt to appear aloof sitting on the bench all alone sipping her coffee, almost every single person who walked by smiled and said hello, or at least nodded. It gave her an odd sense of belonging that she'd never felt back home in DC, and she'd lived there, in the same neighborhood, for over seven years now. For one fleeting moment, she wondered if it would have been like this had she stayed back in Belles Corner.

Even though her tummy was satisfied, she couldn't help but notice the diner across the street, filled to the brim. That would have been a much healthier choice, but not nearly as fun. Too late now. She chased the sweet pastry down with the last of her coffee. Her car should be ready by now; she'd be late if she didn't get a move on. She licked the sugary icing from her thumb and forefinger, then tucked the sticky bakery paper into her empty coffee cup. Heading back to the garage, she dropped her trash in the waste can in front of a florist's shop called Floral and Hardy.

The storefront window sparkled with more twinkle lights than an entire galaxy. Even in the daylight it was pretty darn dazzling. Inside, a cute blonde girl scurried around the store and a handsome man tucked fresh flowers into a cobalt-blue vase, fiddling with an arrangement that was sure to make someone's day.

Another old building had been given a new life with a coat of bright-orange paint. It would have reminded her of a pumpkin, except that the yoga studio had accented it with island-like melon and turquoise that gave it a playfully serene look. Inside, rows of people stretched so gracefully that they probably felt like they were on island time. Not that island time was a feeling she'd ever experienced, other than on the Travel Channel. Someday, though.

In that instant, she let go of the image of all those stretching yogis and her eyes transfixed on the old bank building. Stone columns ran the length of the three stories on each side of the entry. Shiny gold letters graced the fairy-tale tall wooden-and-glass doors in a way that said "Come on in," and darn if she wasn't tempted. She double-timed it across the street. A lawyers' office. Someone had bought the old bank and set up an office. Too bad. She'd have loved to go inside, but browsing in a lawyers' office wasn't likely to be allowed. A sign tucked in the corner of the glass front gave her cause for pause.

OFFICE FOR RENT
INCLUDES FURNISHED STUDIO APARTMENT

It tugged at Savannah's sensibilities. The small blue block letters read 2ND STORY OFFICE/ APARTMENT $450 PER MONTH, followed by a phone number.

A parking space and a tiny storage unit in DC cost her that. She craned her neck to the second story—it had to have twelve-foot ceilings. Bright marigolds peeked over window boxes upstairs. She could almost picture herself working from up there, looking out over the throng of locals getting ready to enjoy their little parade.

Turning to leave, she paused, then swung back around and snapped a picture of the building and that sign. She texted the image to Evelyn with a note that read Why can't we get deals like this in DC?

Technically, she could work from anywhere. She had options, but why was she even day-dreaming about living in that old building? She loved the city.

Why had she let herself lollygag like that? Now she really was going to be late. She double-stepped it back down the hill to the garage. Her car was parked out front at last, but both the entrance and the exit were barricaded off with bright-orange sawhorses spanning both drive-ways.

Savannah waved to Bobby. "Hey, are you getting ready to close for the day?"

"No. Why?"

"The barricades. I just assumed. Never mind. It doesn't matter. What do I owe you?" She tugged her wallet out of her purse.

"Forty-two dollars."

"That's it? For the gas and the tire?"

"Yes, ma'am." She pulled a fifty out of her wallet and handed it to him. "Keep the change. Thanks for everything. I better hit the road."

"You're welcome, but you can slow down. You won't be going anywhere for at least an hour."

"What? Why? Is there something else wrong with the car?"

"This is the parade route. You can't leave."

The sound of an almost-in-tune version of "Soul Man" filled the air, followed by an equally aggressive thumping on a bass drum. "Is that the Blues Brothers song?"

Bobby guffawed. "Yep. Band director did the best Blues Brothers karaoke around back in high school. He loves that song. Everyone around here gets a pretty good kick out of hearing it too."

"I bet." That's the way it was around small towns. People never forgot anything.

"By the way, didn't you hear some scraping coming from your car? Your brakes are shot."

She *had* heard something when the radio was

off, now that he mentioned it. "Is that what that was?"

"You should get that taken care of soon. Gal works down at the diner let hers go so long, we had to replace the whole rotor. Cost her a month of tips, I'm sure. You don't want to do that."

Just as she suspected. No one's business was their own in a small town. She glanced at her watch. "Fine. I promise I will, but can't you just let me slip out on the road between a couple of the floats?"

"Sorry. Can't do it. Traffic rules."

"But . . ."

But he'd already turned away.

She called Evelyn.

Evelyn didn't even bother to say hello. "Are you already back home?"

"Heavens, no."

"Just where are you that they rent offices with furnished apartments for just four hundred and fifty dollars? That's got to be weekly, right?"

Savannah was more than happy to have the chance to unload on Evelyn about her crazy day, and it wasn't even lunchtime yet. "No. That's four-fifty a month. I'm in a little town called Adams Grove off of I-95 near the North Carolina border."

"I've heard of that place. Why have I heard of it?"

Savannah could picture Evelyn pondering.

They'd been friends long enough that she could even see that wrinkle between Evelyn's eyes when she furrowed her brow at times like this.

"I have no idea why you'd know of this place," Savannah said. "Unless maybe you got a ticket here. I almost got a speeding ticket for going seven miles over the speed limit. They take that stuff serious around here. Not only that, but now I'm stuck here until their little parade is over."

"Parade? It's not a holiday weekend. Why are they having a parade?"

"Who knows? All I know is that I'm being held hostage for an hour in this one-horse town."

"Lucky you."

"Bad luck," she said with a snicker.

"I don't know why you're complaining, Savannah. You just got the perfect excuse to not go to that wedding handed to you on a silver platter. Text them a picture of that small-town parade and plead innocent . . . then buy a corn dog and enjoy the day."

"A corn dog. You sure know how to hit a girl when she's down." She didn't bother explaining that she'd already used up today and tomorrow's calories on the best bear claw she'd ever tasted. "I wish it was that easy. They'll talk smack about me if I don't show up."

"Who cares? That's really not reason enough to put yourself through this. Everything happens for a reason."

31

"That's what you always say," Savannah said.

"And you know that I'm right. So let's talk about something that matters. Tell me about the cop. Handsome?"

"Very."

"Makes it less painful."

"I'm not so sure I agree with you on that, but he looked so familiar. I even asked him if we'd met previously."

Evelyn laughed out loud. "Like he hadn't heard that one before."

"Maybe, but as soon as I laid eyes on him it was like I recognized him." Then it struck her where she'd seen him. Well, not him, but why he looked so familiar. "Oh, my gosh. He looks just like Matthew McConaughey. Well, his hair is a little bit darker, and he's taller. Maybe not like him at all, but he reminded me of him. Not like in that last movie where he was all skinny either, but more like the really hot one in that movie with—"

"Pacino. Say no more. I know exactly which movie you're talking about. Tell me again why you're hightailing it out of that town? If you need more reason than that handsome cop and a parade to skip that wedding, you need more than just a day off!"

"You're probably right. I haven't taken a vacation in how long?" Her mood lightened. "He was cute."

"You're right. You do need a vacation. In fact, you deserve one."

"I know that tone in your voice." Savannah had heard Evelyn use that soft, singsong way of getting what she wanted a hundred times over the years they'd worked together.

"I have an offer for you."

"Why do I have a bad feeling about this?"

"Oh, stop it, Savannah. You're going to love this idea. Write me a small-town piece about that cute cop that didn't give you a ticket for seven miles over. You haven't written a fun piece like that for GINN in . . ."

"Since you made me take on the Advice from Van column full-time." GINN, better known as GetItNowNews, had become a soaring success under the keen command of Evelyn Biggens. When her husband died, she'd inherited all his newspapers across the country. Most of them were failing, but she'd been smart enough to revamp a couple of the good ones and then collapse all the others into one huge online company that no one else had been able to match. "I hate that column, you know."

"Don't you complain to me. You brought that on yourself." Evelyn's voice didn't hold a bit of compassion. "I've compensated you well for it too."

"It's not that I'm not grateful. I am. It's been a wonderful opportunity for someone with so little experience, but I'm ready to move on to something new. Something I can tell people about."

"I know you're chomping at the bit for something else. Write that article for me. Folks will get a kick out of that kind of story. We need something light to balance all the heavy stuff going on these days. Plus it might be fun. Stick around there a couple of days and consider it a vacation. When you get back we can talk about your assignment."

Savannah would do just about anything to get out of that Advice from Van gig, but hanging out in a little town didn't seem much like a vacation, and she had some serious doubts that Evelyn was going to let her off the hook completely. "I'll have to get back to you on that." But her mind was already looking for a story angle. If she couldn't get out of the column, maybe a break from it would do her good.

"Yeah. You do that, dear."

And when wasn't Evelyn right?

Chapter TWO

Scott Calvin jumped into his car and set his coffee in the cup holder. It was time to check that all the barricades were in place so the parade could start on time. Just as he dropped his sunglasses from his head to his nose and pulled his cruiser out onto Main Street, that pretty brunette walked out of the bakery. He pressed his foot on the brake, watching as she took a seat on one of the benches in front of Mac's. She balanced her coffee next to her and laid the bag of goodies in her lap. She had to be warm in that sweater set.

Savannah Dey.

Sounded more like a description of something, or a pop song, than a name. And why the heck did he even remember it?

She was cute, but he knew lots of cute girls. It was rare that he ran radar, so what were the odds he'd pick a speeder who looked like her? Maybe there was a correlation between fast cars and pretty girls. And who the heck knew a Mini Cooper could go that fast? Not that it mattered.

She'd looked taller sitting in that little blue car, but standing in line at the bakery she'd barely come up to his shoulder. And her chestnut hair was longer than he'd realized. Pretty girl. Not cute. Definitely pretty.

He pressed the gas pedal and turned onto the street, nodding to the volunteers as he slowly passed the corner. He glanced in his rearview mirror, then pushed the whole mirror up and out of the way to resist the temptation to look back at that girl again.

Waste of time. Every girl he picked out was the wrong girl. That guy who said there is a match out there for everyone hadn't met him, because he'd rolled the dice on a lot of women and not one of them had worked out. It had to be him. He slowly made his way down the entire parade route to confirm everyone was ready to go.

His eye was surveying the progress, but his mind was still on that woman. Odd name.

Who would name their kid that? Maybe Ms. Savannah Dey was one of those people who changed her name to make some point. But then again, her driver's license said she lived in DC. It had to be her parents who had been the creative types. *That's got to be it.* His own laugh caught him off guard. *That girl was definitely more jet-set than flower child.*

Of course she was jet-set. Wasn't every woman he ever found attractive a big-city kind of girl?

It was his fatal flaw and what would probably ensure him a life of bachelorhood. Not that being a bachelor was so bad. Maybe somewhere in the deep recesses of his mind he wanted to be alone and that was why he was attracted to the wrong kind of woman.

He knew from firsthand experience that a girl in love with the city life would not, could not, live in Adams Grove. At least not for long.

Okay, so maybe Kasey had adapted just fine to the small town, but still . . . that relationship hadn't worked out for him. And darn if Ruth hadn't seemed perfect until they started spending more time in Adams Grove. The town was too slow and a shopping mall short of her happy place. His type and his life were just a total mismatch. How many times would it take for him to get that lesson through his thick skull?

Children waved frantically in his direction. At that age anything on the street seemed like a parade. He flipped on the lights and let the siren wail. The kids' faces lit up. These moments touched his heart. He loved kids. Wouldn't mind having a couple of his own, but at this rate, that wasn't likely to happen.

Maybe that was part of why not winning Kasey had been so hard. He'd lost not only her, but Jake too. Although technically, he'd lost nothing at all. Once they got past the awkwardness, they'd repaired the friendship. Scott still regretted acting like such an ass when it became apparent that Cody Tuggle was stealing her heart. It had been a tough pill to swallow, but watching her and seeing how the two of them treated each other . . . even he had to admit they were a good match.

Mom was about to drive him crazy with all the grandchild talk, though.

He'd kept her at bay with his black lab, Maggie, and her puppies for a while, but that whole granddog thing was losing its charm pretty quickly. She kept encouraging him to settle down with one of the local girls. The problem with that was that he'd known those girls his whole darn life, and that just felt a little like getting close with a sister, and that put out the spark every time.

Impossible.

Chaz Huckaby waved a giant orange flag as if Scott was crossing an imaginary finish line. Even on a hot day like today, that guy's hair never moved. Those Captain Kangaroo bangs would withstand a hurricane. Chaz's job was to keep the parade entries spaced far enough apart that the bands didn't drown each other out and there was time for everyone to see all the hard work that had gone into each of the floats. Since he didn't hear too well, Chaz didn't mind being right there next to the booming music as they started down the parade route.

Scott made a quick U-turn and headed for the high school parking lot. All the entrants were lined up in the order they would go down the route, and they looked ready to roll.

Deputy Taylor had already pulled his car catty-corner along the right lane of the road to block any traffic, and the first float was at the ready to kick things off. All that needed to happen now was for Chaz to drop the flag for the first band to get to steppin', and it looked like that would happen in about two minutes.

Right on time.

About six floats back, a flatbed trailer had been decked out to match the purple silks worn by the Hillcrest Joyful Kixx jockey the day of the Kentucky Derby.

It had been a day of surprises, not all good ones.

The celebration had been meant for Rick Joyner and Jenny Herndon becoming part owners of the fancy racehorse. The Derby-themed party was like nothing this little town had ever seen, and then to top it off, Rick had surprised them all by proposing to Jenny in the middle of it all. But then everything went to hell . . . literally.

As in the guy behind the Goto Hell murder that had shaken this state all those years ago had come back, and in his plot for revenge against the man who had put him away, he'd abducted Brooke Justice. Thank goodness for the quick actions of Mike Hartman that night.

Scott's jaw pulsed. That night would hang over this town for a long time. This parade was an attempt to soften that blow by shifting the memories of the day to the good ones that happened on that date.

Hillcrest Joyful Kixx had won the Kentucky Derby that day. This parade, in honor of that win, not only shifted the emotion of the town, but was also giving the ladies another chance to wear those hats they'd created for the party.

Ladies from the garden club sat in white Adirondack chairs, poised in their Sunday finest, ready to give their friends and family their best parade waves. His mom was one of them. He could hear her now. "Elbow, wrist. Elbow, wrist." She fancied herself quite the waver ever since her homecoming days in this town. Lord, he'd heard that story five hundred times if he'd heard it once.

Ted Hardy, the owner of Floral and Hardy, had re-created a huge Kentucky Derby winner's circle flower arrangement for the float representing his shop. Scott couldn't imagine how many fresh flowers it had taken to fill up that monstrosity of an arrangement. While others used metallic floral sheeting, balloons, and crepe paper, Ted always used flowers. Oodles of them. But it wasn't like he could recycle that gigantic forty-pound blanket of roses draped across a four-foot-tall horseshoe covered in peanut hulls by taking it to the hospital or the old folks' home. Heck, it was too big to fit in a car. They'd had to make arrangements to use the ambulance to deliver it. Now he could see why.

The members of the marching band from the

neighboring town just north, Hale's Vineyard, let out snippets of the chorus of "Camptown Races" as they nervously prepared to represent their town in the big celebration.

Hillcrest Joyful Kixx, the guest of honor, stood regally in a makeshift holding pen that the local farm supply dealer had created out of red pole gates decorated in purple that matched the jockey's silks. The Thoroughbred looked way more relaxed among the hustle and bustle than most of the kids lined up. In fact, the horse was about the only one who looked relaxed in the whole darn group.

Funny too, since the horse had been the biggest point of difficulty in planning the parade that he'd ended up being the least of the trouble. The town held three meetings to get approval to have that horse in the parade. It wasn't like they'd never had an animal in one of these events. Heck, Rick had even ridden that darned camel he rescued from the circus in one, but then again that camel wasn't worth a plug nickel.

The town council was worried to death that something would happen and they'd get the bill. The rest of the town was mad that there was even consideration of having a parade in honor of the horse's big win without allowing the horse in it.

It had become downright comical that they were that worried about a horse when Scott could barely get them to listen about the safety of the people coming to watch the parade.

But eventually Cody Tuggle's mom, Denise Hill, had been able to reassure the committee that the horse would be fine and filed the appropriate papers to be sure the town would not be held accountable if there was an accident or injury. After all, now that she was moving her operation here to Adams Grove, in Kasey Phillips's old place, she was one of them.

Just to be sure though, part of the deal was for Scott to drive his patrol car behind the horse to keep watch on the situation.

There'd been discussion of a float with Cody Tuggle on it, but thank goodness he turned down that idea and offered to do a free concert later in the evening instead. Part of that offer had been so that Cody would have a chance to showcase a new young talent he'd taken on since the death of his agent, Arty Max. That worked to Scott's favor. Fans would've just made the parade route crazier, and even though Scott had made his peace with Kasey being with Cody, he'd be lying if he didn't admit that if he'd had to cruise the whole parade with Cody and Kasey in his rearview mirror looking like the most adored couple in America, it would have been the worst.

Scott gave Chaz the nod, and Chaz dropped his flag to get the first float on its way down the parade route.

●●●

Music filled the air, and the low boom and perfectly timed rim clicks of a bass drum made the children bounce with excitement. Savannah had to admit she too was beginning to feel anxious about the parade. Her mood was ten times more cheerful than it had been just a short while ago when she was cruising down the interstate.

Savannah raised her iPhone and snapped a picture of one of the floats. Evelyn had never steered her wrong before, and her advice to take advantage of the parade to skip that dreaded wedding was feeling like a pretty good idea.

She'd hesitated only a minute before taking Evelyn's suggestion. One more click and the picture would go to Aunt Cathy; Savannah's cousin, the bride, Winnie; and motormouth Monica, Savannah's best friend all through high school, who was sure to spread the word as fast as the torque from that mechanic's air tools had removed the lug nuts from her wheel.

She typed, Car trouble and now stuck behind a parade in Adams Grove, VA. Sorry, I'm not going to make it. All my best on this special day. Love, Savannah. That would have to do.

Sucking in a breath, she hit Send.

The sound of the text zipping out into the world made her stomach spin in a very uncomfortable way that reminded her of the tilt-a-whirl at the county fair. Old feelings from the last time she was in that small town she grew up in still haunted her way too many years after she'd fled the darned place. Belles Corner. It sounded so charming, but boy, could it put her stomach in a knot.

She hiked back up Main Street, nearly catching up with the first float that had passed by when she was down at Adams Grove Garage. She wasn't sure what it was powered by, but whatever it was, it was struggling. She could just picture a rusted VW bug underneath the cardboard-looking float covered in streamers and what looked like Easter grass. Too bad forty clowns couldn't jump out of it and push the thing. It would surely move faster.

Joining the locals along the sidewalk settled her uneasiness some. She'd just begun to relax when her phone indicated someone had texted her back. Her knee-jerk reaction was to grab for her phone, but she stopped short and decided to just pretend to be out of range. That felt rather like a victory in itself.

She slipped out of her sweater and tied it around her waist, then leaned against the lamppost and watched another float go by. How many years had it been since she actually stopped and watched a parade? Except for the occasional glimpse of the Macy's Thanksgiving Day Parade . . . never, since she left Belles Corner. Her hometown was so small the only parade they ever had wasn't a parade at all, but rather just a convoy of pickup trucks on the opening day of hunting season. It had been a tradition for as long as she could remember. She wondered if they still did it.

DC had its share of parades, but comparing the big-city parades to ones like this was like comparing movies to slide shows.

She'd only been to one parade in DC, and that was only because she'd had to be in it. Right after she'd taken the job with Evelyn, all the writers at the paper rode on a float sponsored by GetItNowNews in the Christmas parade right past the Capitol building. She was still pretty sure they'd tricked her into drawing that short straw that forced her to be the newspaper's stupid mascot. As if it wasn't bad enough being the only woman, she had to be the one wearing a rolled-up-newspaper costume, which really made no sense at all, since they didn't even have a physical paper anymore. Everything was online. Someone must have dragged that musty thing out of an old storage closet. The guys had spent the better part of the next year begging her to swat them for being naughty.

The timing of that parade had been less than perfect while she'd been trying to make a good first impression and be taken seriously in a man's world like the newsroom. None of them had wanted to be in that parade, but Evelyn had made it mandatory. They'd all been half-drunk by the time the float started edging its way down

Pennsylvania Avenue. To her benefit, at least no one could see her face in that costume.

The unmistakable clip-clop of horse hooves against the pavement grabbed her attention. There'd been a time when riding was one of the only things she could still find joy in. It had been years since she'd even been around horses, but the one walking by wasn't your everyday trail horse.

The beauty of this horse was undeniable.

The sheen from the animal's coat glimmered almost like it was wet, and his muscles screamed athlete, even with the bright-purple saddle towel and decorative tack. The jockey sat astride the horse in matching bright-purple-and-white silks.

Cheers and hushed whispers from the crowd filled the air. This wasn't just any horse. This was Hillcrest Joyful Kixx, the Kentucky Derby winner. From what she was overhearing, he was being moved out here to a local farm. His win had been big news; in fact, if she remembered correctly, Evelyn had lost a bundle on that race because this horse won.

Too bad she hadn't placed a bet. She probably would've picked this horse—purple was her favorite color.

A police car followed closely behind the horse, probably more for safety precautions for the high-dollar athlete than for parade reasons.

Savannah pulled her phone out of her purse

and snapped a picture, then texted it to Evelyn with the message, Look.

Evelyn: Who's the hot guy in the cop car? That your cop?

Savannah: The picture is of the horse. The Derby winner. And yes. That is the cop who pulled me over.

Evelyn: He's hot. The cop. That horse cost me 5k.

Savannah: ;)

Evelyn: This little gig is going to be more fun for you than I thought.

Savannah: I didn't agree to that gig.

Evelyn: One more thing. Hang on a second.

That woman ran at ninety miles an hour all day long. Her mind was always spinning up the next big thing. Too bad Savannah hadn't considered that *before* she'd tried to play that silly April Fool's joke on Evelyn. That joke had backfired on her big time. Evelyn hated advice columns. She made no bones about that, so Savannah had slipped a fake advice column tagged Advice from Van in the GetItNowNews upload to run on April 1.

In the Dear Abby format, she'd posted a question with a snarky answer. Evelyn was the only one who'd ever called Savannah *Van,* so she'd know exactly who was behind it, and it had seemed the perfect prank at the time. She'd thought they'd get a big laugh and it would be over. The problem was, the readers loved it.

Questions came pouring in, and Evelyn, being the shrewd businesswoman she was, knew a good thing when it was in front of her and wasn't about to let Savannah get away with not finishing what she'd started.

An advice column was not her idea of being a writer, and it sure as heck wasn't something she could write home about. Especially since it wasn't done with a real remedy in mind. The answers poked fun, making light of what really were some serious issues.

The paper had decided early on that part of the viral aspect would be to keep the columnist under wraps, which was easy to do since so few people knew about it to begin with.

So there she was, stuck getting no credit for all the hard work she'd put in and not sure she'd really be proud of it if she did.

She glanced down at her phone. Nothing back from Evelyn yet, and that just made her nervous.

She dreaded the one-more-hoop that Evelyn was always putting in front of her. Why was there always one more hurdle before Savannah could get off of that darn advice column? Change takes time. Patience just never was one of her strong suits.

Float after float went by. Good thing she'd decided to skip the wedding, because Bobby's estimate of an hour had long passed. These people were serious about their parading!

The music drifted as the parade disappeared around the corner, and the locals started peeling back from the curb. Some gymnast in an animal costume went bouncing by, cartwheeling and carrying a sign that said HAPPY DAY Y'ALL! on it.

She wasn't sure if it was the parade, getting out of going back to her hometown, or the possibility that she might really get off the Advice from Van assignment making her feel so good, but whatever it was, she wasn't about to question it.

Savannah maneuvered between the people who had stalled to talk and catch up, then waited to cross the street with the others as cars filed out of a church parking lot.

To the mechanic's credit, he was right; there was a significant amount of traffic once the barricades were pulled back. Of course, now she wasn't in as big of a hurry.

First things first: she checked the text to her aunt and cousin. Aunt Cathy had responded with just a simple FINE, which was never fine at all, but then maybe that was just one more reason to be happy she wasn't going home. Home. Just thinking about it was enough to make the bear claw do a somersault inside her gut. Winnie had sent back a selfie of her in her gown. She really did look beautiful.

Savannah tucked the phone into her purse. "Excuse me, ma'am," she said to a woman walking down the street, holding the hand of a small boy. "Is there a hotel in town?"

"Well, there was, but it closed down a few months ago. But the Markham B and B is right up the block there." The woman pointed in the opposite direction of the gas station. "It's much nicer, anyway."

"Thank you." Staying at a bed-and-breakfast wouldn't be so bad. Although if she got right down to work, she could probably get her research done and knock out the article in a few hours. She could do that from the diner. Then she could just go home and relax. Whoever said a vacation had to be away from home?

But since she was here, it wouldn't hurt to check out the B and B. It didn't take but a few minutes' walk before she spotted the hand-painted wooden sign swinging from chains in front of a huge Victorian.

Savannah pushed the old wrought-iron gate open. It creaked and closed behind her with a loud clang, but no one came outside. As she walked up the sidewalk to the front porch, she noticed an older gentleman in a rocking chair.

"Excuse me, sir?"

He flew to an upright position. "Right here." Then he settled his gaze on her. "Hello. Can I help you?"

"I was hoping to rent a room."

"You could, but my wife isn't here right now. I'm Mr. Markham."

"Nice to meet you. Is there a room available?"

"I think so. Fifty dollars a night. But it's two hundred dollars a week, so you may as well stay the whole week, if you ask me. That includes your breakfast." He rocked forward. "And the bed, of course."

"Internet connection?"

He rolled his eyes, sending his bushy eyebrows on what looked like a caterpillar race across his forehead. "No. Although my daughter says you can piggyback on the wireless signal over at the library from here, if you know what any of that means."

"Good to know."

"Only TV is down here in the living room, but my wife probably has some suggestions for you. She knows everything around here. Everyone is up at the park for the big concert. Why aren't you over there, come to think of it?"

"I'm not from around here. What concert?"

"Cody Tuggle and some other loud guitar-playing guy. Dustin something. Anyway, big celebration here in town today because of the Derby. Lady that owns the horse is moving to Adams Grove."

"I saw the horse. He's a beauty." The old man didn't flinch, not a blink, not a wiggle. Could he even hear her? "In the parade," she added a little louder.

"Yep. That's the one."

"Kind of a celebrity for y'all, huh?"

"I guess. Hell, country stars, horses. I don't know what else is coming to our town, but things are changin'."

"Can I walk there from here?"

"Where?"

"The concert."

"Well, you could, but you'd be tuckered out and probably miss the whole darn thing if you tried to walk all that way."

"Hmm. Okay, well I guess I'll go back down to the garage and pick up my car, then."

"Your car down at Bobby's?"

"Yes, sir."

"Just keep heading north and you'll see all the signs. Probably hear the racket. No one plays good music anymore. Not since Sinatra. Even Tony Bennett has abandoned the good ranks, doing duets with those pop stars. What the hell is that all about?"

She stifled a laugh at the ol' curmudgeon. "Probably just trying to stay relevant in changing times."

"Change. Someone ought to ban that word from the dictionary. Nothing good can come of change."

She sure hoped he was wrong, because she was ready for a change. A big one.

Evelyn: IDEA! Call me now.

The day Evelyn became text savvy had been a bad day for Savannah.

The woman was relentless with the number of text messages she sent out. It hadn't taken Savannah long to learn that Evelyn considered everything an emergency. When she'd first started working for her, Savannah would drop everything and practically fling herself on the phone to respond to Evelyn's call-me-now requests. Not anymore. Now she'd known her long enough to know that she could respond when it was convenient . . . no matter how urgent it sounded. If it was really an emergency, Evelyn would put a #911 on the text.

Savannah pressed the button on her phone to speed-dial Evelyn. "What's up?"

"I just had the best idea."

"Uh-oh. Your ideas always mean more work for me."

"It's only because you're the best, dear. Take it as the compliment it's meant to be."

"Mm-hmm."

"I need that filler piece, but we need more than just one little story."

"The one I didn't agree to yet, you mean?"

"Oh, you'll do it. Quit being hard to get along with. You write that story about your seven-over speeding ticket by that amazingly hot piece of ass. It'll be funny. People love to hate cops. You know I'm right. Then, follow up with maybe a series that I can run once a week about small-town mishaps."

"Look, I'm so over the Advice from Van thing that I want to poke my eyes out rather than read another e-mail to that account. You promised you'd get me off of that assignment."

"Maybe this will be your chance, and you just might score a nice date with that cute man behind the badge if you try hard enough in that little town. Where are you again?"

"Adams Grove. And you know I don't want a date."

"Oh, live a little, girl. You don't have to marry the guy. Just have a little fun. You can't just work all the time."

"Why not? You do."

"And I'm old enough to be your mother's older sister. Much older. Besides, I already had the love of my life. I outlived him, but there won't be another like him. This is a choice I've made. You don't even have a social life."

"I have a social life." Savannah didn't like having this conversation with Evelyn. It wasn't the first time they'd had it.

"Uh-huh. Going out for drinks once in a while and playing cards with the guys once a month is not a social life."

Savannah pushed up her sleeves, biting back any argument. Problem was, Evelyn was half-right, but she really liked it the way it was.

Evelyn's voice held that don't-be-a-fool tone. "You're too young to not find true love."

"I'm making a choice too, and I'm happy with it. I'd be happier if you'd get me off the Van column, though."

"Anyway . . . here's what I've got for you."

Savannah could hear the papers shuffling on Evelyn's desk. She was on speaker—as usual.

"While you were watching the parade, I made contact with a very nice man. His name is . . . here it is. Connor Buckham. He's the guy at the phone number on that little sign you texted me. I just paid for you to live and work there for the week. Any other expenses can go on the corporate card."

"Evelyn, I don—"

"I don't want to hear it. This is a well-deserved semi-vacation on my dime. You get me that story. And a few more too. There's bound to be some fun stuff to write about there. We need something fresh in the news right now. You can do this. Get your head together, and when you get back, I'll give you that Senior Associate promotion we've been talking about and reassign the Van page to someone else permanently."

"Are you serious?"

"I already contacted Jones to fill in for you. He's thrilled."

"Jones?" Was she kidding? Savannah felt doubt creep in. She'd wanted off the Van column for months, but it was too big of an income stream for GetItNowNews. Evelyn had refused to let her ditch it, instead dangling one carrot after another to keep her going. But this time Evelyn had someone covering for her. She'd never done that before. Maybe the timing was finally in her favor. She couldn't imagine Jones being the voice of Van, and it took about everything in her to not say so . . . but after all, this might be her only chance off that darn assignment. "Do you promise?"

"I promise. This little series will have folks on a high from all the feel-good crap. They'll gobble it up."

"Series?"

"Give me at least three stories. That way they'll be so distracted in your fun small town stories they won't even realize there's a new Advice from Van voice."

"That makes me sound extra special."

"Can't have it both ways, my dear. Do you want out or not?"

"I want out."

"See, I told you everything happens for a reason."

Savannah's mood brightened as she got closer to the bank building. One innocent text of a picture of the tiny sign in the window had just forced her life into a new direction. She paused in front of the huge window.

Be careful what you wish for rang from her past. But this was what she wanted. A new chance to show her writing chops in real news articles.

Okay, so it wasn't real news, more like fluff, but it was a step in the right direction. And she'd get her own name on the work. That's what she wanted.

She also couldn't deny she could use the break. It had been way too long since she'd taken time for herself. Not that this was totally for herself. She'd be writing those stories for Evelyn, but a little downtime in a small town with no drama sounded pretty good right now.

Suddenly, the sign was plucked from the window.

Had it all been a marvelous daydream?

But then a redheaded man walked outside. "Were you interested in the space?"

"Me?" She swallowed back the urge to say *Yes! Yes! Yes!* "Hi. Do you work here?"

"Yes." He extended his hand. "I'm Connor Buckham. I own the building. There are two offices and apartments on the top floor. Sorry, I just rented the vacant one."

"I know. I mean, Evelyn Biggens rented it for me." She pushed her hand out in his direction. "I'm Savannah Dey."

"Nice to meet you. Welcome to Adams Grove."

"Thanks. You know, I'd give anything to get a tour of the old bank. Please tell me the original vault is still in place. Those things are so cool."

"It is, and I'd be happy to take you on the ten-cent tour." He pulled the door open and motioned her inside. "Come on in. I'll show you the apartment too."

"Just four hundred and fifty dollars a month? What's the catch?"

Connor laughed. His blue eyes danced as he gave her a wink. "No catch. It's a small town and there's not a whole lot of demand for rentals. Where you from?"

"DC."

"Not too far. I used to live up in Chicago."

"And you moved here? On purpose?" *Don't offend him before you even get to know him.* Doggone that mouth. She needed a piece of tape!

He laughed. "I grew up here."

"And after living in Chicago, you still wanted to come back?" She knew what it was like to be a kid wanting to get out of a small town, but she'd never once looked back.

"Actually, my mom got sick and I came back to take care of her, but I knew I was ready to come home. The city just wasn't for me. Even under the stress of Mom being sick, I was happier here in Adams Grove than I'd been up there." He eyed her carefully. "What do you do?"

"You mean for work?"

"Yeah. Evelyn is your boss. What do you do?"

And just how was she supposed to answer that question without lying to the nice man? "I'm a writer."

"Well, then this just might be my lucky day. One of my clients owns the local newspaper. As luck would have it, the woman that covers the police blotter down at the paper, her grandniece, Anna, just went into labor. Early. Bee had to drop everything to get there. She's a dear friend of the family. They could sure use your help. Won't pay much. Paper goes out twice a week these days, so it won't take too long either. It would be a huge help if you could cover it while you're here."

Now what on God's green earth would make him think any old writer could do a police blotter? For all he knew she could write advertising copy, or personal ads. "I don't know if that's a good idea. You know that my boss is the one paying for my stay. I'd have to clear it with my editor. Besides, I'll only be here for a week—"

"Any help you could give would be appreciated. It'll ease the burden that she has to get right back home. At her age, she's too old to be missing out on important family events. Consider it a good deed. They're really good people. Jack and his sister have kept that paper going on a shoestring just to stay in business. They're a cornerstone of this community."

How could she say no to that?

He must've sensed her hesitation because he kept rambling on, selling her, as it were. "It's interesting. The police blotter stuff. You'll see all the cases come through . . ."

Well, now that he put it that way, it could potentially work to her benefit. The police blotter? Seriously? It *would* help with the stories that Evelyn wanted her to write. It would be like getting paid to do research. And it was only for a week. She knew Evelyn wouldn't care. It wasn't like this little paper was any competition for GINN.

She leveled a stare into Connor's pleading blue eyes. All she really wanted was to chill out. She needed the break, and she needed to figure out what the heck she was going to do if Evelyn didn't make good on her promise to take her off the Advice from Van column.

"And it won't take long," he said.

"Fine. I'll do it. How much time could it take? Besides, how could I say no without sounding like an awful and uncaring person?"

"My thoughts exactly," Connor said.

"Like I said, I'll have to clear it with my editor, but I don't think it will be a problem."

"Excellent. I'll let them know you'll stop by and chat with him first thing Monday morning. That work for you?" His eyes twinkled with satisfaction.

He was probably a pretty good lawyer, because she'd just agreed to do something she'd had no intention of doing just moments ago. How had that happened? "Fine. Who do I talk to?"

"Jack over at the *County Gazette*. Thanks for

doing this. You really have no idea how big of a help it is."

"Good timing, I guess." And she really did kind of look forward to seeing how the small-town paper worked. It would be interesting to compare it to the huge conglomerate of GetItNowNews.

Connor moved toward the door. "Let me show you around, and then I'll show you the apartment. I've got the key right here."

"Sounds like a plan."

"Follow me." He led her through the old bank building's main floor. The wooden teller stations still spanned the front room, and the vault door was like a piece of artwork with the brass shined to a luster as lovely as gold. "What do you think?"

She ran her fingers along the fine wood railing. "This place is great."

"Yeah. I fell in love with this building when I was a kid. It was empty back then. A safety hazard, really, but I was always drawn to it. I'd imagine bank robbers racing down the street and good guys capturing them, tying them up, and then locking them in the vault until the sheriff came and carted them off to jail."

"You have a good imagination."

"I guess locking up bad guys in the vault *with* the money wasn't that brilliant of a plan, but it worked in my head at the time. It was a part of my childhood, and when I moved back and found out that the town had put this old building up for sale, I couldn't believe I was going to be able to actually own it." She followed him up the stairs.

He pushed a key into the lock and swung open the door. "I used to live in this apartment. That's why it's furnished."

"Nice." It definitely lacked a feminine touch, with the oversized furniture in three colors of leather and pictures hung way too high for any woman to have hung them, but overall it was comfortable and clean. The light coming through the long floor-to-ceiling windows was almost magical. The original glass panes made it seem to swim across the pine flooring.

"Over here there's an office, and . . . well, you can see the rest."

"I can."

Connor punched at his iPhone and then raised a finger as he spoke into the phone. "Hey, Jack, yeah, you still need someone to run down the police blotter stuff for the paper?" He nodded and gave her a wink. "Yeah, I've got someone that can help you out temporarily."

An hour later she had the key to her new apartment, had landed a job doing the police blotter, and had accepted an invitation to join Connor and his wife, Carolanne, the next day for some kind of Sunday cookout at the artisan center just outside of town.

By the time Savannah got back down to Adams Grove Garage, Bobby had already locked up and headed out. She drove back to her temporary home and parked around back where Connor had told her. The back entrance looked bright and cheery, with planters of bright orange and yellow marigolds, just like the ones in the window boxes on the front. The flower boxes flanked a shiny burgundy door.

With her laptop and the dry cleaner bag with her party dress in it over her shoulder, she rolled her suitcase over the threshold toward the stairwell. The narrow staircase to the second floor was pretty steep, so rather than risk a tumble, she dragged the suitcase, clunking it on each stair tread, one at a time, as she made her way up.

Connor hadn't bothered to lock the door, but she tested her key once just to be sure. One quick twist and she was in the apartment. She hung the dress she'd spent weeks picking out for the wedding in the oversized armoire in the bedroom, then unpacked her clothes. The kitchen was twice as big as her one at home, and all the appliances she'd need for her stay looked to be there. Rather than set up her computer in the office space, she set it on the antique table near the window. The light was much better there.

She pulled a notepad from her purse and made a quick list of the facts she knew to get started on the article. Scanning the list, she was impressed with just how much she already had. Now that she had the inside track and access to the police blotter, this assignment should be a breeze.

Evelyn would be thrilled to hear the progress she'd made, and she was pretty happy with how things were going herself. Then again, if she made it sound like it was going too well, Evelyn might want the articles sooner. Maybe she'd wait and update her tomorrow.

Right now it was still early enough to make it out to the Cody Tuggle concert, and that sounded like a great way to get her impromptu vacation under way.

Scott Calvin sat behind his old metal-and-wood desk and pushed a fancy ivory-colored envelope to the side. There was something just not right about getting an engraved invitation to something that would probably cost more than he made in a year. Especially when they were giving him an award for something that was clearly in his job description.

He wanted to forget about that night when they took Frank Goto down, but somehow that case just wouldn't let go. Officially, it was closed, but inside he knew that this case left behind links to more . . . more he wished he could ignore.

He picked up the envelope and slid out the invitation. Mike Hartman had gotten one too, but he'd already declined. Getting recognized in a public forum wasn't Scott's cup of tea, especially when it was for keeping his community safe. That was what he was paid to do. When Frank Goto committed those crimes all those years ago it had shaken the whole state, no question about it, and it still blew his mind that the guy had been paroled at all. He'd love to know how that had happened on the down-low.

You'd think they'd have swept the whole case under the carpet rather than give out awards. It would only bring up more conversation and potentially stir up controversy or expose poor judgment on someone's part, which wasn't going to be good for anyone. Let the whole damn situation die on the vine, that's what they should do. The bad guy was dead and gone. Didn't make him proud to kill someone, but he'd really had no choice. The right thing had happened. He had to wonder, though . . . would they be making such a big deal out of this if it had happened in a city? Why was it that people thought because he was enforcing the law in a small town, it somehow made him less skilled than someone working in a highly populated area? He took his job seriously, and when others didn't, it had a way of getting right under his skin.

"Hey, Sheriff." Deputy Taylor leaned in the doorway.

Scott tucked the invitation into his desk drawer. "You headed out to the concert?"

"Yeah. Shortly. Just wanted to let you know that Jelly was in one of his moods again today during the parade."

Scott leaned forward. "He's harmless."

"I know, but I hate seeing him so worked up. He was begging people to come with him to see something that was evil. I think he was kind of freaking them out. I heard people complaining that he was drunk."

Scott knew that even if Jelly might look like a drunk, he wasn't one to take to the bottle. He'd been living down by the creek near the park for as many years as Scott could remember. In fact, Jelly had lived there before the park *was* the park. Guy must be every bit of sixty by now, maybe even closer to seventy. "Anyone file a formal complaint?"

"No. Not yet. Probably just a matter of time, though." Deputy Taylor looked genuinely worried. "I just wonder if he's kind of losing it." He tapped the side of his head. "Like dementia or something."

"I'll talk to him."

"Thanks," the deputy said with a look of relief. "I'm out of here."

"Have a good one." Scott's mind was all over the place today. He didn't need another thing on his plate, especially Jelly. He knew exactly what had Jelly all flustered. The old man had stopped him in the park and made him go to Happy

Balance and look at the mural in the men's locker room with him a couple of weeks ago. He'd thought the old guy would forget about that mural once they'd talked about it, since Scott had assured him he'd look into it, but it looked like he wasn't going to let it go.

Scott grabbed his hat and headed outside. He walked down Main Street and then crossed the road at the old bank building toward the park. It was unusually quiet in the park today. There were only a couple of joggers. It seemed that folks had cleared out and headed home after the parade.

Jelly's camp was more like a fort a kid would build out of scraps he'd gathered from his dad's garage. He didn't come into town often that anyone saw, but there was a clear-ish path down to his camp not five feet off the jogging trail at the 1.75-mile marker. All the locals knew where it was, but no one ever bothered him.

Scott ducked beneath a low-hanging branch and made his way through the trees. It was at least ten degrees cooler in the damp shade. He followed the slope of the land down toward the creek.

"Jelly?" Scott paused and listened. "Jelly? You out here, man?"

A slender man wearing a dirty blue-and-white-striped long-sleeve shirt that was so thin you could see through it popped up from behind a bright-yellow forsythia bush. "Heard you coming."

"Sorry. Didn't mean to scare you."

The old man shook his head. "You don't scare me. Just didn't know it was you. How ya doin', Sheriff?"

"Worried about you. Deputy Taylor said you seemed upset today. You okay?"

The wisp of a man started running his hands through his long, thinning hair. He turned his back on the sheriff and headed toward his camp. Then he spun and marched right up to Scott. "I told you before."

Scott nodded.

"It's evil." The man's eyes bugged out and his fists seemed to be grabbing for air. Jelly folded his arms across his chest and flopped his elbows up and down a couple of times in a way that made him look like some kind of crippled bird. His voice shook. "That painting tells a story. An ugly story. I seen it myself. You saw it. It needs to go away." Jelly turned and nearly sprinted to the creek.

Scott broke into a jog and caught up with him. "I don't want you to worry, Jelly. I'm going to take care of it. If there's something to it then we don't want to ruin the evidence, right? If we paint over it . . . then the story is gone."

The old man nodded his head so fast, it looked more like he was shaking than agreeing.

"Can you be patient with me?"

His eyes darted around. "I don't know what the story is, though. But it's bad. I know it's bad."

"I'm not sure what it means either, but trust me, Jelly. I'll figure it out. You trust me, right?" The old man looked so frail. He hated to see him afraid too.

Jelly dropped his hands to his sides. "Of course you will. You're a good boy." He shook his head. "I can't go back there until it's gone."

"I'll let you know what I find out. Until then, you can shower at the jailhouse like you used to instead of at the yoga studio."

He nodded. "Okay. I can do that."

Scott's heart went out to the guy. He didn't have anyone, and although he seemed to prefer the solitude, it worried Scott to see the guy so frazzled. "You can't be scaring folks. You need to keep this between us."

"I'm sorry. You promise you're looking into it?"

"I promise. Now, man, you're looking thin. Can I buy you a meal?"

Jelly shook his head. "I got plenty of rations. Plenty."

"More than bread and jellybeans?"

He gave a hearty laugh. "That's not true. I don't just eat jellybeans. I got other stuff too. I do like me some jellybeans, though."

"I know you do. Just not the green ones."

"That's right."

Jelly looked surprised, but it hadn't been all that hard for Scott to figure out. Around the campsite green jellybeans had been pitched into the dirt.

You didn't have to be a great detective to notice that evidence.

"You'll come to me if you need anything, right?"

Jelly wrung his hands together. "Yeah. I will."

Scott put his hand out and they shook. The guy still had a firm handshake. "I respect that. You take care of yourself, and I'll take care of the painting."

When Scott had first been elected sheriff in Adams Grove, one of the first things he'd tried to do was to help Jelly get some assistance and a place to live. It had never occurred to him that the man was living exactly the life he wanted to live. Jelly had once been a businessman with a family. Somewhere along the way his marriage failed and he blamed his job. He ended up leaving it all behind to just be alone. It was the kind of story you heard about but never really believed happened. But once Scott got to know him, it was clear the guy was happy with his life the way it was and was harmless. They'd come to a pretty quick agreement on letting things continue as they were with just a few ground rules. It had all worked out peacefully, until this mural thing came up. It seemed like Goto was determined to haunt this town—dead or alive.

Scott hiked through the trees and back onto the jogging path. It was a good day to be outside. Not too hot for mid-June. Perfect weather for the parade and the concert, which he needed to get to

70

now. His staff would already be there and in place, but with crowds this big it was all hands on deck.

He stopped in front of the yoga studio. A class was just finishing up, and people were peeling off in both directions to their cars. No one else even knew that the murals at Happy Balance had been painted by Frank Goto. Scott was relieved that Jenn, the owner, had agreed it was best kept under wraps.

Besides, the murals Goto had painted in the studio were peaceful and serene, nothing like the wicked scenes he'd painted on the house where he'd abducted the girl. No one would ever make the connection unless they'd been told. Or unless they saw the subtle imagery that seemed to taunt from beneath the peaceful image . . . but no one else seemed to notice that.

He wondered how long that would remain the case.

Savannah had worked her way through the crowds to the front of the stage. Cody Tuggle was giving an arena-worthy performance to this small town. He looked relaxed, like he was having fun, and every single person in Adams Grove must have come out to enjoy the free concert.

The crowd clapped in time to the music, and when Cody started playing just the first few chords of "A Mother's Love," everyone went wild. She was glad she'd thrown her good camera in her handbag for the wedding trip. She took a few pictures, then headed off to one of the concessions to get a sweet tea.

When she finally got to the front of the line at the refreshment stand, none other than Bobby from the garage was waiting on her.

"Hi," she said. "Remember me?"

"Flat tire. Bad brakes."

She laughed. "That's me. I'm staying the week. I might pop back in so you can take care of those brakes for me."

"Good plan. What can I get you?"

"Sweet tea, please."

Bobby slid a clear plastic cup of iced tea in her direction. "On the house."

She swept the cup up and nodded. "Thank you." This town was proving to be kind of good for her morale. A group of people had cleared out a section just to the right of the stage and were dancing. It had been forever since she'd been dancing. There was a time when people would stop and stare at her dancing with Tripp. There wasn't much two-stepping going on back in DC, though. She and Tripp had found a couple of fun country-music-night spots that they'd frequented, but work got busy and then he was gone, so it was short-lived.

Standing at the edge of the crowd, she sang along with the band and watched as the couples danced. A brown-haired man who couldn't have been more than twenty-three or so stepped in front of her, causing her to abandon the song she was singing off-key.

"Want to dance?"

"No, thank you." She shook her head. "I haven't danced in a long time."

"Awww, come on. It'll be fun."

"I'll step on your feet."

He grabbed her by the wrist. "I can take it." He tugged her hand in the air and spun her beneath it, then pulled her close and started moving around the dance floor.

The beat carried her back, and her two-steppin' feet were picking up right where they'd left off all those years ago. She couldn't contain herself. It was fun, and unexpected.

He gave her a nod. "You were sandbaggin'. You can dance, girl."

She shrugged.

He spun her and then dipped under her arm, shifting direction. "I have an eye for good dancers," he said. "I spotted you from all the way over there."

"Is that right?"

He gave her a wink. "Oh, yeah."

Seriously? He was a little too young for her, but who the heck cared? It was just for fun, and she was feeling like a million bucks about now. She smiled without a reply and kept up her steps.

• • •

Sheriff Calvin paced the front of the stage, keeping the fans at a reasonable distance. He glanced over at the crowd of folks who'd started dancing just off the stage area. Derek, Mac from the bakery's son, was dancing. He was a good dancer, everyone in town knew that, but the girl he was dancing with caught Scott's attention. Savannah Dey moved with the grace of a ballerina, light on her feet and with a smile that could light up the evening. He watched them move around the makeshift dance floor, and she was keeping up with Derek like a pro.

"Sheriff!" someone shouted from behind him.

He spun around to see two girls clambering onto the stage. They weren't locals.

One of his deputies was already escorting one of them off. That was the only problem with having a celebrity do these kinds of things locally. The locals respected Cody and his privacy, and appreciated the free concert, but fans always found out about their private events and showed up causing trouble.

He grabbed the second girl by the waist and set her down on the ground. "Calm down, young lady."

"I know him!" she screamed. "I love him. He wants me to come onstage."

"I'm sure he does. It just won't be tonight." Sheriff Calvin guided the half-drunk, scantily clad brunette to the edge of the stage and gave her a choice. "You can enjoy the rest of the show from right here, or I'd be happy to show you the way to the parking lot."

She started with a flurry of words that his momma wouldn't deem ladylike.

"Parking lot it is," he said.

Chapter THREE

When Savannah opened her eyes, the room was so dark that it was disorienting. The sun wasn't shining through the blue sheers of her bedroom window, and the city sounds of DC weren't ratcheting up like an alarm clock trying to nudge her awake along with the smell of coffee she'd set to perk the night before.

No, this morning the room was so dark she wasn't sure whether it was still night or her body had done its usual six o'clock ready-to-go like it did every other day.

She extended her arm, patting the air for a table and her phone. Finally she felt the rubbery case of her phone and picked it up. As soon as she pressed the thumbspot, the display cast a bright light in the room and showed the time: 6:00 a.m.

Like clockwork. That's me.

One fuzzy thought pushed in and she remembered she was in Adams Grove. In a rented apartment for some downtime. Or a semi-vacation, as Evelyn had put it. But seriously, wasn't vacationing like being pregnant? You either were or you weren't.

Then again, Evelyn was going to reassign the Advice from Van column, and that was enough to make her practically bounce right out of the bed. She didn't even care if it meant a pay cut. She'd been frugal with the pay increase from the column, treating it like a bonus rather than a long-term thing from the start. Who knew that joke would turn into a two-year commitment? She'd had a good run with it.

With no commute and no schedule, she felt like she had time to sleep in. An unusual feeling, but a nice change. Plus it was Sunday. But her body wouldn't cooperate with her brain.

She twisted the light switch on the bedside lamp, then slipped out of bed and into her yoga pants and a T-shirt. She hadn't planned to be in Belles Corner but one night, so her impromptu extended stay in Adams Grove left her with limited wardrobe choices.

Her notes and laptop lay on the table near the window. She grabbed them and sat down to write, but her attention kept drifting outside. Maybe the good view wasn't the best recipe for productivity. Finally she got up, took her laptop to the office, and settled into the oversized executive chair behind the ornate wooden desk.

She'd forgotten to ask Connor for the Wi-Fi login information, but she remembered what that old guy at the B and B had said. A quick glance down the short list of wireless connections and she was able to log in on the wireless network titled AG_Library. Sure enough, no password and no pass-through fee. A few clicks and she was on the GetItNowNews website and able to access her work e-mail at GINN, which was already stacking up. It hadn't been but a couple of days, but if she let it go, it would become unmanageable in a hurry. She did a quick scan of the long list of e-mails and deleted the ones she knew were junk, then closed out of it.

There was no sense in getting started on the story for Evelyn, since she'd just have to stop to meet up with Connor and Carolanne at the event down at the artisan center this afternoon. So she jotted down a couple of ideas for articles instead. Speed traps. Pumping your own gas. Small-town gossip. Diet differences. How many businesses does a town really need? Car choices—city versus rural. None of them seemed exciting, though.

She shifted gears and made a quick grocery list and a to-do list and arranged the desk to her liking. Maybe she'd pick up a few stronger story ideas while she was in town.

The small-town cops idea hit a little close to her discomfort zone, and Evelyn knew that, but the incident was funny, and Savannah knew she could turn that little speeding ticket story into something fun with nothing more than her imagination and memories from her hometown. Out of the few she'd brainstormed, that seemed to be the best one to start with. Besides, Evelyn already seemed to love that story and it would buy Savannah more time to figure out the others in the series.

Right now, though, the priority was coffee.

She shut the top of her laptop and headed downstairs to venture out. A quick cup of coffee and then a trip to the market to get the bare necessities should do it.

The morning air was warm, but a breeze made it pleasant. The air smelled of breakfast. Not bagels and coffee, but bacon and sausage. Even the food preferences of small-town folks were different. She'd grown up on eggs, bacon, and toast slathered in butter. Not refrigerated hard pats of butter either, but butter that had been left right out on the kitchen counter so it'd be soft enough to really glop it on good. Those were the days, but then if she still ate like that, she'd have to spend every afternoon in the gym burning calories. Nowadays, she might get an occasional doughnut, but more often than not breakfast was limited to just coffee, and on the rare occasion a yogurt or maybe a piece of fresh fruit.

She resisted the temptation to go back to Mac's for another one of those amazing pastries and crossed the street to Jacob's Diner. When she walked inside, the only seats left were at the counter. She slid into the chair closest to the door.

Was it her imagination or was everyone staring at her?

That feeling reminded her way too much of being back in Belles Corner. Rather than ignore it, she ordered two coffees to go and whole wheat toast, plain. Of course, the two coffees would probably get their tongues wagging. Who was she with? Was it one of their own? Blah-blah-blah.

Too late. She'd already placed the order, and sure as heck people were still looking her way.

She picked up the complimentary copy of the *County Gazette* from the counter and thumbed through it as she waited. The police blotter section caught her eye. She'd been bamboozled into that gig pretty quickly, but Connor seemed like a nice enough guy. How many lawyers would look out for their clients like that? Besides, she kind of hoped the police blotter would give her some more story ideas.

If she got these assignments done, she might just be lounging around on Evelyn's dime.

Of course, Evelyn probably knew that would never happen. Savannah hadn't taken a real vacation in the seven years they'd worked together. The busier she was, the better. She wasn't sure if it was real ambition or a safety net, but either way it meant she was focused on work . . . all the time. She didn't have time for friends or hobbies with the work schedule she kept. And she liked both better at arm's distance anyway, no matter what Evelyn had to say about it.

At least using the information from the blotter, she could limit her interaction with the people in town. Evelyn was always saying that it was never a good idea to get to know the subjects of your story too well. That could make it harder to write an unbiased article, and then she'd have a second small town wanting to run her out of it.

Not that anyone here would even read the articles. Most of them didn't look like the online-paper-reading type, and there was only local news in the *County Gazette*. She skimmed through the entire paper as she waited, and she didn't see even one news item picked up from the wire on all six pages of it. She flipped back to the police blotter.

The first report was "Resident on Valley Drive saw male duck."

Savannah stifled a giggle. *The quack-quack kind, or is there a peeping Tom in this small town?* The list of speeding tickets was collapsed into a table. In- and out-of-state offenders, speeding, equipment violations, and other. The only details were a list of the local infringements—only a total of eight of those. She'd be able to report this without too much effort.

As she set the paper back on the counter for the next patrons, a family walked inside. The tall waitress with LARA embroidered across her blouse whisked them over to a table that had just been cleared and poured coffee for them.

Savannah did a double take. Darned if it wasn't Cody Tuggle, and he was even hotter in person than he had been onstage. He was with a beautiful blonde and a little boy.

It was a nice diversion to feel like she wasn't the center of attention as the room's interest moved from her to the superstar and his little family.

She pretended to check the messages on her phone and snuck a couple of quick pictures of them. Couldn't hurt to have them tucked away for later. Maybe there was a story there to tell.

"Here you go." Lara came out with the two coffees and a bag full of condiments along with the toast. "I slipped in some of our apple butter for you to try. I know you said you wanted that toast plain, but we're known for our apple butter, and it's not even all that fattening. You've got room for the extra calories anyway."

Savannah shoved her phone into her pocket. "Thanks. I'll give it a try."

"You'll love it," Lara said with a quick squeeze of Savannah's arm.

"By the way, your nails look beautiful. Where do you get them done?"

"Nicole down at the Hair Station does them for me." She wiggled her long fingers to show off the shiny lacquered nail color. "She's the best.

They do nails on Tuesdays and Thursdays. While you're there, get Linda to wash your hair. Honey, that's better than a spa treatment. She'll scrub your head till you want to kick your leg like a coonhound. I swear." She tugged a pen from her apron pocket and jotted the number right across one of the coffee cups. "There ya go. Just give her a call and tell her Lara sent ya. She'll do you up right."

"I appreciate that." Savannah gathered the cups and bag. "And can you tell me where the nearest market is?"

Lara pointed behind them. "The Piggly Wiggly is right down that street."

"Perfect," Savannah said. They didn't have Piggly Wiggly up in DC, but they did back in Belles Corner. They'd always referred to the market as the Hoggly Woggly back home. Tripp had asked her out on their first date when he was bagging her groceries at the Hoggly Woggly. Momma had been more excited than Savannah had that day, insisting on stopping for Diet Coke floats on the way home to celebrate Savannah being asked out on her first real date. Momma had loved to celebrate every little thing.

One time Momma had pulled her right out of school and taken her shopping for what she decided to call MD Day. Mother-Daughter Day. They bought carnations to match their outfits and had lunch at a fancy tea shop.

Savannah balanced the diner bag in her arms.

"I thought you were in a hurry to get out of town yesterday."

She froze at the sound of the male voice. Was he going to pop up over her shoulder everywhere she went? She spun around and met Sheriff Calvin's gaze. Any other time her mouth ran in overdrive, but at this moment it opened and nothing happened. Not a hello or even a witty comeback. She blinked to break the lock from his hazel eyes. The flecks of gold didn't go unnoticed. She shook off a tickling feeling, like he had pulled her into his space without so much as the whisper of a touch.

Lara sauntered up with the coffeepot and a heavy ceramic mug. "Hey, Sheriff," she said, letting the words linger in the air. She filled the mug to the brim and pushed it his way on the counter.

Savannah felt her lips twinge a little as she smiled. Guilt? Maybe for the topic of the article she was getting ready to write. "Change of plans. I'm sticking around for a little while."

"Really? The parade was that impressive?"

"It was pretty good. Those bear claws are definitely worth a second look, though."

Did he just give her a nod, as if she was worth one too? Or was she imagining things? His scrutiny had her feeling as warm as the bacon sizzling next to a heaping mound of hash browns on the open grill.

"Lara, here, hooking you up with her famous apple butter?"

"Yeah, she is. Got my coffee to go." Why did she even say that?

"Can't start the day without my coffee either."

"I was just reading the police blotter while I was waiting. You've been busy. I had to laugh. It said . . . Wait a second." She reached for the paper and swung the page back. She ran her finger down to the spot. "Yeah. Here it is." She held it out in his direction. "See. Resident on Valley Drive saw male duck." She let out a hearty laugh. "That just cracked me up. I'm sure they meant a male subject ducked below a window or something, not a quack-quack duck." She laughed again, but he wasn't smiling. Clearly he didn't see the humor in it. He looked like she'd just said his momma wore combat boots or something. "Anyway, it's not that big of a deal that it wasn't clear." *I should have stuck to the weather.*

Sheriff Calvin looked rather stoic. "Actually, it's right just the way it is. Misty Johnson saw a male duck. As in waterfowl, or of the quack-quack persuasion, in your words."

"Oh." She pressed her lips together, unsure whether to apologize or just let it go.

"One of our 4-H'er's projects flew the coop, and Misty was reporting that she'd found it in her backyard."

"Sorry, I—"

"Yeah. We rescued the runaway duck. It's a small town. Everything is not peepers, perps, and bad guys around here, but it's all important to the people of this community."

"I didn't mean to—"

"I know what you think, but that kid would have lost out on the opportunity to show at the county fair if we hadn't helped locate that duck. I don't consider that a waste of resources. In fact, I'm glad this town has so little real crime that we have time to support our neighbors in things like that. It may not seem like newsworthy to read over your coffee, but it's important around here."

Geez. Had she hit a sore spot or something? She totally should've stuck to the weather. What a grump.

"My apologies for making light of your work." She slid to the side in an exaggerated manner, still clutching her bag with the two coffees and toast. "Maybe you should drink *your* coffee."

He tugged the hat from his head and took a sip from the mug.

Goodness gracious, he was just handing her the column on a silver platter. How do you even respond to a sheriff who is spending his time rescuing waterfowl?

"Well, all in a good day's work. Don't work too hard, Sheriff."

She turned to leave, and as she opened the door to exit, she heard him call after her.

"Scott. You can call me Scott."

Or not, she thought.

Who did that sheriff think he was, getting all indignant with her first thing in the morning? Man, and she thought she was cranky without coffee. She'd definitely get to the grocery store and pick up a few things this afternoon, including coffee, because starting each morning with a run-in with the sheriff could be a real mood spoiler.

Too bad too, because he seemed more handsome every time she saw him. "Looks can be deceiving," she mumbled. He had her so fired up that she headed straight back to the apartment to crank out that article while her mind was still buzzing with ideas. The market could wait.

What's that quote? Don't fight with someone who buys ink by the barrel. Something like that. Yeah, Sheriff Scott Calvin might want to get a little plaque of that one for his desk.

She ran up the stairs and didn't even bother locking the apartment door behind her. She pressed the Power button on her laptop, then spread out her breakfast next to it. She sat in the chair in front of the desk, but she was too darn short to sit and type for long. She got up and grabbed a pillow from the couch and tried again. Perfect.

Closing her eyes, she rolled her shoulders and then set her hands to the keyboard, counted to three, and began to type. It was her process. It felt good to be typing her own story. Not a response to some whack-job reader who wanted advice. She chomped on the toast and slugged back coffee between lines. Fueling the fire.

She typed and typed without even so much as a pause. A smile pulled at her lips as she transferred her recollection of the ticket yesterday and the run-in this morning onto the page. It had been a long time since she'd been able to sit down and write a real story—not an over-the-top answer to some amazingly out-there question, but an article from scratch. She was back in the zone . . . and it felt good.

She opened her eyes and leaned back in the chair. From here she could see most of the merchants up and down Main Street. No parking meters here. Strictly first come, first served. The sheriff had probably stopped in at the diner after marking tires as a way of enforcing those forty-five-minute maximum parking time signs along the curbs. Seems like that would be just his style.

She probably should have mentioned that she was going to be covering the police blotter for the *County Gazette* when she saw Scott at the diner, but under the circumstances there just hadn't seemed to be a good way to mention it. Especially after she'd stuck her foot in her mouth about that darn duck. Boy, was he touchy.

Hopefully, he wouldn't have to know, and she'd

be gone before they even crossed each other's paths again.

She pulled her feet into the chair and stared out the window. Main Street was quiet this morning. Maybe it was always quiet. It was so different from the view from her downtown condo in DC. It was never quiet there. Even when there was no traffic, there seemed to be a hum of energy in the air. Maybe it was nerves being pulled and the sizzle of the stress that came with the lifestyle in the city. She tapped her pen on the side of the desk, eager for a little noise in the space. As if on cue, music came through the wall of the other apartment. Good old classic rock.

She hadn't even thought to ask Connor about her neighbor. She'd seen the sign on the door that he was a private investigator. Her mind had jumped to the stereotype of a stodgy guy, like the ones in the old movies who somehow always seemed to have a cute, ditzy blonde working for them. Like that would ever happen in real life. Maybe he was an old fart, but he had good taste in music, and that was all she needed to hit her stride.

The sound of her nails tapping against the keyboard had a way of lulling her right back to work. By the time the third song finished, she had pretty much the whole story typed out. The facts, anyway. Now to turn it into something entertaining.

She plucked the laptop from its charger, went over to the couch, and reread the story.

This won't work at all.

She'd spent way too much time describing the handsome sheriff and not nearly enough on the fact that she had been going just seven miles over the speed limit. How had that happened? That was not what she was going for.

She turned on Track Changes and began electronically redlining the story. Only what she had left when she finished editing was pretty much a pile of red lines, like a tiger had slashed through the whole blessed thing.

The Guns N' Roses song "Welcome to the Jungle" started thrumming through the walls, and her neighbor must have kicked up the volume, because the thump-thump-thumping nearly vibrated the pine floors, which was fine by her. In fact, if she'd picked the song for her playlist personally, she couldn't have paired her story to a song more perfectly.

Her stomach growled. Maybe it was a good thing she had plans for lunch, because that toast wasn't doing it this morning.

But first things first. She put her fingers back on the keyboard and got down to business. A few facts from the police blotter, a couple of sly pokes at the sheriff for good measure, and she was done.

Rereading it start to finish made her chuckle,

and *she* already knew what had happened. Yeah, this would catch an eye or two.

"Writers don't get mad, they get even."

So she couldn't kill him off in a novel, but she sure did just fry his butt in that article . . . even if he'd never know it.

Payback. Karma. Call it what you like, but that cranky sheriff just got his dose.

One down, just a few to go. She clapped her hands, relieved to have already cranked out the first piece of her commitment. One quick e-mail to Evelyn asking if she minded Savannah helping out with the police blotter down at the local paper while she was here, with the article attached . . . and off it went.

"That felt good." She shut down her computer and tucked it into the drawer of the desk. A quick brush to her hair, a dab of mascara, and she was ready enough for a community cookout.

She locked the door behind her as she headed downstairs while her neighbor continued to rock on, probably totally unaware that she'd even moved in.

Maybe he'd be around when she got back. Her creative mind was kicking into gear, and suddenly that stodgy image of an out-of-shape PI was replaced by something more in line with a movie star with muscles, oh, and really nice lips. Maybe she'd start on that novel after all. That last thought had all the makings of a good hero.

Evelyn was right. She'd been all work and no play for way too long, and maybe, just maybe, there was a small-town love story here.

Then the cigarette-smelling, pudgy PI came in focus in her mind again. Yeah. That would be her luck. She grabbed her car keys and the directions to the artisan center, taking the stairs two at a time to the beat of the music.

Savannah loved her little blue Mini Cooper. She'd treated herself to the new wheels last year. It was so easy to park in the city, and it was fun to drive, but even she had to laugh at how tiny it looked sitting next to the big GMC pickup parked next to it behind the apartment. The monster of a 4x4 made her car look like a toy. The truck must belong to the PI, although the fire-engine red was anything but understated. But then neither were his music choices.

She popped the trunk on her car and pulled out a box wrapped in glossy white-and-silver paper. She'd wrapped up a couple of bottles of wine as a gift for the wedding festivities this weekend, so rather than let them go to waste, she figured she'd take one of them to thank Connor and Carolanne for inviting her to the cookout. Good wine would've gone to waste on her ex anyway. He was strictly a Miller Lite kind of guy, unless he'd changed, and that wasn't likely.

She ripped away the glossy paper, then retied the white tulle into a presentable bow around one of the bottles. Comfortable with the casual transformation, she placed the bottle in the passenger seat and then set the directions in her lap for the short drive to the artisan center. Why they hadn't just given her a street address that she could type into her GPS was beyond her, but the directions looked easy enough to follow.

There wasn't much traffic on Route 58, so it took less than ten minutes to get there. The artisan center was well marked and the building hard to miss with its bright-blue roof. She pulled her car into an open parking space on the side of the building where Connor had said they'd meet her. Connor had mentioned that he and Carolanne lived in the new neighborhood that backed up to the center, Bridle Path Estates. It looked like it was all Connor had described it as—homey, understated, and charming. Only a few houses dotted the landscape, although several plots were flagged off and ready for breaking ground on construction. Even so, the lots were large. A few acres at least. Neighborly with enough space for privacy. The best of both worlds.

She got out of her car to wait. Rainbow-colored tents lined the lawn near a pond. Lots of people were already milling around. A corn hole tournament was in full swing at one end, and some kids played good old-fashioned Frisbee near the pond. It looked like it could be fun, and the weather was perfect for it.

Connor pulled his car into the spot right next to her. "Hey there," he said as he got out. "Have you been here long?"

"No. I just got here."

A stunning redhead got out of the passenger seat. "It's so nice to meet you, Savannah. Connor told me that you're staying upstairs for a few days. Any trouble getting here?"

"None at all." Savannah handed her the bottle of wine. "Wasn't sure if this would be appropriate or not, but I wanted to at least thank you for inviting me."

"That was so nice of you." She twisted the bottle and read the label. "Made right here in Virginia. I can't wait to try it. That was so thoughtful of you." She put it in the backseat of the car. "You'll have to stop by and enjoy that with us while you're here. We live just across the way. You can see our place from here." She pointed across the pond.

"Lovely home."

"Thanks," Carolanne said. "Well, let's head on down. I promised Jill I'd help her if things were crazy this morning, but it looks like everything is running smoothly."

Savannah fell in step next to Connor and Carolanne, down the slope toward the activities.

Carolanne raised her arm in the air and waved to a couple across the way. "There's Jill and Garrett. They're great, you'll love them. Jill runs the Artisan Center."

"Great. It'll be nice to meet her," said Savannah. "This is all quite an accomplishment."

"Jill dreamed of building this center for as long as I can remember. We grew up here together. She lived with her grandmother after her parents died."

Savannah swallowed hard. She knew exactly how it felt to lose your parents. "The location is perfect," she said, trying to sound light.

"All of this land used to belong to her grandmother. When she died she left it to Jill and Garrett. Only they weren't together at the time. Long story short, Pearl Clemmons did a little matchmaking from beyond the grave and we all are living happily ever after."

"Pearl sounds like a gem."

"You got that right. She was the heart of this town. Jill is following in her footsteps. She's really done great things with this place in a short time. She and Garrett are the best team."

Carolanne and Jill hugged once they reached each other, and the guys disappeared almost as quickly to hunt down food from the assortment in the tents around them.

"We'll meet you back at the bar tent," Garrett said.

Savannah smiled, feeling a bit like an outsider . . . not that feeling like an outsider was so unusual for her. But then that was by her own choice. Once she'd left Belles Corner she'd found it hard to open up, and since she didn't go out often, on dates or with groups, when she did, she often felt this way. She didn't like it, but she could fake it like nobody's business.

"I can't wait to check out the artisan center, Jill. I'm Savannah. Nice to meet you."

"Thank you. I hope you find something you can't resist in there. You're new to the area?" Jill's grin was wide and her words bounced with excitement at just the mention of the place.

"Just passing through."

"How long are you visiting for?" Jill asked.

"Just a week or so. I'm getting a much-needed rest before I start a new job."

"You picked the right place for it. How did you and Carolanne meet?"

Savannah and Carolanne both laughed. "Well, actually . . . we met for the first time just a few minutes ago," Carolanne said.

"True." Savannah nodded. "I rented Connor's old apartment for a week and he invited me."

"Do you have family in the area?"

"No."

"Then what made you pick Adams Grove?" Carolanne gestured to the other girls to head toward the bar tent.

"A ticket." They looked confused by her evasive answer. "Where I'm from we get ten over. Doesn't everybody?"

"A speeding ticket. Oh, gosh. Not around here.

Even the locals can't get away with that," Carolanne said, but both she and Jill were shaking their heads.

"Well, I guess I should thank my lucky stars then, because he let me off with a warning."

Carolanne and Jill responded in chorus. "Seriously?"

"Yeah, but I think he only did it because he felt bad for me. I was supposed to be headed to my ex-husband's wedding, almost got that speeding ticket, was almost out of gas, and my tire was almost flat . . ."

"Oh, man. I feel bad for you too, and I wasn't even there. So you decided to almost stick around?" Jill said.

"Kind of like that." Savanna nodded.

Carolanne asked, "Who stopped you?"

"The sheriff," Savannah said. *Scott,* she thought. *"Call me Scott"* . . . *or not.* "Although I didn't realize he was the sheriff at the time."

"Scott Calvin?" Jill sounded unconvinced.

"Yeah. You know him?" Stupid question. Everyone probably knew everyone around here.

"We grew up with Scott," Carolanne said.

Jill waved a warning finger toward Savannah. "Careful, he met his last girlfriend on the side of the road. You could be next."

"I can assure you that will never happen in a million years," Savannah said. She'd been so hell-bent on keeping anyone from getting close all these years that she hadn't even hesitated with that well-practiced answer, but she had to admit that the cute lawman had caught her attention on the side of the road too.

"But I'm sure there's a good story there." Savannah added.

"Long story," Jill said. "Another time."

"He's really cute, but he was kind of cranky. I made a joke and he didn't even crack a smile!"

"Maybe you read him wrong because he'd stopped you," Carolanne said. "You have to admit getting stopped never makes for a good day."

"True, but he was pretty cranky this morning when I ran into him at the diner too."

"That's really not like him." Jill looked perplexed. "In fact, he's usually the fun one."

Carolanne nudged Jill. "Not as fun as he used to be since he became sheriff, though. He was half of the trouble in this town when we were growing up."

Jill nodded a confirmation. "She's right."

Savannah's interest perked right up. "Do tell."

Carolanne put her hand over her mouth as she started to laugh. "Remember the time—"

"You girls aren't talking about us, are you?" Garrett entered the bar tent with Connor on his heels.

"No," the girls said in unison.

"Uh-huh. That didn't sound suspicious," Connor said.

Carolanne said, "It's not always about you, hon. We were talking about Scott."

"Good guy," Connor said.

Garrett nodded. "Yep."

"Remember the time he painted that big Ford emblem on the side of the Chevy dealership in town?"

"Hey, that was art," Connor said.

"Says his partner in crime?" Carolanne shot Connor a look. "You're only taking up for him because you were handing him the spray cans he was using to tag the place."

"Who knew his uncle couldn't take a joke?" Connor shrugged. "Scott and I had to spend three weekends painting the side of the building white to cover it up . . . in August! That was the worst summer ever."

"Aren't you a bad boy," Savannah teased. "And you look so innocent."

"I was, like, thirteen at the time."

Jill elbowed Connor. "Not as bad as Scott's summer the year y'all turned sixteen."

"Oh, yeah. Poor guy."

"What?" Savannah was hungry for more details about the grumpy overseer of law and order of the county. Maybe story number two was going to be as easy as the first one.

Connor raised a hand and poured out the details. "He missed curfew one too many times and his dad grounded him from driving his car. Scott thought he was so smart taking the riding lawn-mower out instead, only his dad reported it stolen and he got arrested for joyriding."

Carolanne laughed so hard she snorted. "He had to cut all the yards on the whole street for the rest of that summer."

"I wasn't talking about that time," Jill said. "I was talking about the skinny-dipping incident at the pond."

"That was right through those woods," Connor said.

Carolanne waved an imaginary surrender flag. "Okay, y'all are going to give Savannah the wrong idea about our sheriff. We were kids back then. Scott's well respected around here. He was just a little bit of a hell-raiser in his day."

"I guess he's kind of the last guy you expected to run for sheriff," Savannah said.

"Not really. He was always the one leading the trouble, but he was also the one making sure we weren't in any real danger. It was all innocent horseplay. Guess it did prove his leadership skills, though," said Connor.

"He sounds like a lot of fun, nothing like the Scott I met more than once in this town," Savannah said. "Are you sure we're talking about the same guy?"

Garrett shrugged. "Probably just needs to get laid."

"Garrett!"

"What? We get grumpy when we go without."

"I swear he's not usually like this." Jill swatted at Garrett's arm.

"That's only because you keep me—"

Jill wagged her finger at Garrett. "Okay, that's enough out of you."

Garrett snickered and pulled Jill in front of him, resting his beer on her arm. "Scott's a good guy."

Carolanne's voice softened. "Scott just needs a little lovin'. It's like a country song. He's got the dog, the truck, and the small town. Now all he needs is the girl."

"Speaking of country music, I saw Cody Tuggle at the diner this morning," Savannah said. "He was there with his family when Scott came in."

"Maybe that explains his mood." Carolanne and Jill exchanged a glance. "Another long story," said Carolanne.

That old feeling that nothing was private in a small town nagged at her. Who knew the real story? Suddenly she felt a little bad for judging Scott. "I don't know how you do it. Living in a small town where everyone knows everything. Doesn't it make you crazy? Everyone knows the stuff you want to forget."

"It's not that bad," Jill said.

"It can be," Carolanne admitted. "I moved away because of that very reason."

That caught Savannah's interest. "But you came back."

"Yeah. Surprised the heck out of me too," Carolanne said.

"Made my day," Connor said.

Carolanne caressed his arm. "Turned out that the town was way more forgiving about the past than I was. I'd assumed everyone was hanging on to all the bad stuff. Turned out everyone else had moved on and it was just me living with those old woes."

Savannah wasn't sure she knew what Carolanne was trying to say, but somehow the sadness in the redhead's eyes kept her from pushing further, even though she had a feeling that there was definitely a story there.

"It's no secret, so you may as well know." Carolanne stepped closer to Savannah. "My dad, he was the town drunk. Not always, but after my mother died . . . losing her just tore him right out of the frame. My childhood here was a mess. If it hadn't been for Jill and her grandmother, I just don't even want to think about how bad it could have been."

Jill jumped in. "I loved you being at our house all the time."

"I know. I did too, and it doesn't matter now. It's in the past, but back then I couldn't get out of Adams Grove fast enough. Thank goodness for college scholarships. After college I moved to New York City to practice law. I honestly thought I'd never come back here."

"You practiced law in New York City?" Savannah spun toward Connor. "And you in Chicago? And y'all are both back here?"

"And not one single regret." Carolanne looked to Connor, who smiled in agreement. "You can't let the past drive your future."

That message hit home for Savannah, but then her situation was different.

Connor clapped his hands and rubbed them together. "This is supposed to be fun, and y'all are getting all serious. Let's eat. What's everyone want?"

"Just bring back a little of everything. We'll commandeer a table in the shade," Carolanne said.

Across the way someone had fired up a karaoke machine, and now that church was out, the grounds were filling up fast.

The guys came back with two cardboard box lids stacked high with food. Connor placed a paper plate filled with deviled eggs in the center of the table. "No one can pass those up," he said to Savannah.

Savannah lunged for one. "Oh, my gosh. It's been forever since I've had deviled eggs. My granny used to make the best."

"Well, be prepared to be wowed," Connor said. "I don't know where you're from, but here in Adams Grove, we think these are the best."

Savannah grabbed one and sank her teeth into it.

She hadn't felt that close to her granny in years. "It's perfect. I swear it has to be the same recipe as my granny's. No relish. Just a mix of fresh herbs and spices and her secret weapon—a dash of parmesan."

Jill's eyes went wide. "Don't let Miss Daphne hear you. If your granny's secret ingredient is the same as hers, she'll kill you for giving away the secret. Folks around here have been begging for it for years!"

"Oopsy. Don't rat me out," Savannah teased. "I don't want to be run out of town before I even get unpacked."

"We've got your back," Connor said, then turned to Carolanne. "Hey, babe, I'll get you another glass of wine. Savannah, you sure you don't want a glass of wine with your lunch?"

"No, thank you. I wouldn't want to drink and drive in this town. No telling what would happen if I got caught seven sips over the limit."

Everyone laughed, and Connor raised his beer in the air. "To new friends. Hope you'll stick around a while, Savannah."

Savannah raised her cup of sweet tea. "I'll drink to that."

An older woman in a bright-yellow top and a green apron, who looked like a team mascot for John Deere, joined them at the table. "How's everybody doing?"

Connor stepped over and hugged her. "We're

great, Miss Daphne. Meet our new friend, Savannah Dey. She's visiting from up near DC."

"I heard we had a new gal in town. Welcome, Savannah," Daphne said.

"Nice to meet you, Miss Daphne. I'm just visiting."

"You can just call me Daphne. They've known me since they were school-aged kids. I quit having birthdays ten years ago; the way I figure it, they'll be catching up with me soon and I'll be calling them miss and mister." The woman giggled, then pointed toward the center of the table. "Did you like those deviled eggs?"

"They were just as delicious as the ones my granny used to make for me. It was like being a teenager back at her house all over again."

Daphne beamed with pride. "My special recipe."

"You made those? They are absolutely delicious." Carolanne and Jill turned away, hiding their smiles. "Thank you for the memories. I haven't thought about those in years."

"You are welcome, dear. Nothing better than family." She patted Savannah's arm. "Connor tells me you're a writer. That's so interesting."

There was that small-town kudzu message-delivery service in full swing. Every town had one, but Connor worked fast! "Yes. Yes I am," Savannah said, but didn't offer anything further. The silence was awkward, but what could she say? She couldn't divulge that she was the person behind that infamous Advice from Van column making light of pretty serious issues. That probably wouldn't go over so well here, where people had each other's backs, and she sure couldn't say she'd just submitted a story about one of their local heroes that was probably less than flattering. Okay, no probably about it. It was totally less than flattering.

"Are you writing a book? I've always thought it would be so interesting to meet a real novelist."

What could she say? *"No, I answer questions from readers online in so cynical a way that I hide behind a pseudonym?"* One little white lie wouldn't hurt. "More like freelance work. About all kinds of topics." Daphne looked disappointed, and the storyteller in Savannah just sprang into action before she had a chance to think about it. "Don't let it get around, but I *am* working on a novel now. It's kind of a hush-hush project." She held her finger to her lips.

Daphne's eyes lit up. "Like a ghost writer. How exciting." She pretended to zip her lips and throw away the key. "Your secret is safe with me. I bet you're here getting some ideas. I'd love to sit and talk to you. I could probably even help you. Why don't you come join me for tea on Tuesday?"

Savannah looked to Jill for help, but clearly Jill misread the look. "Oh, Savannah. You'll love chatting with Miss Daphne. She's got a million stories. Tea with her is always amazing. Make her break out the butterfly tea set."

Daphne blushed. "It's my favorite too."

Jill leaned in. "Miss Daphne has the most amazing collection of teapots. She has at least fifty. Probably way more than that. One of these days we're going to talk her into opening that tearoom that she's always dreamed of."

"That would have been so neat." Daphne's wistful look told that this was still a dream with a glimmer of hope. "I had so many ideas perking about that, but I'm too old to do it now."

"You're never too old to follow your dreams," Savannah said. "A tearoom would be so fun to run. All those cute little sandwiches and pastries. I used to love spending time in the kitchen with my momma baking. She'd have loved the idea of opening a tearoom." She missed Momma like crazy, not that she allowed herself to think of her often. She prayed that the tears that usually came with those memories wouldn't show up now. She quickly focused on the tearoom. "You could serve tasty bites, and tea never goes out of style."

"You really think so?" Daphne's voice softened. "You're such a delightful young lady, Savannah. I'm so glad to meet you. Is your husband traveling with you?"

"Oh, no. I'm not married."

Daphne tsked. "No worries, sweet girl. The right

one will come along. Your one true love will always find his way to you."

How did you even know if he was the right one? Maybe Tripp had been it. She had more baggage than the Dulles airport. Who would want that? "I'm really not looking."

"That's what they all say. Until they find him." Daphne cast her glance to Carolanne. "Am I telling the truth?"

Carolanne nodded in agreement. "That was certainly true in my case."

Daphne turned her attention back to Savannah. "Will you come and visit while you're in town? I'd love to show you my collection, and I do serve a delightful afternoon tea, if I do say so myself."

Savannah couldn't deny how much Daphne reminded her of her mother, and that was hard to say no to. Besides, a little small-town tea and gossip couldn't hurt if she had stories to write, even if they weren't exactly for a novel. Why not? "I'd love to join you for tea on Tuesday."

Daphne squeezed Savannah's hand. "I'm so delighted. Could you come at one? One o'clock would work perfectly."

"Yes. Absolutely," Savannah said.

"Terrific, dear." Daphne pulled a slip of paper from her apron and scribbled down her address and phone number, then handed it to Savannah. "Carolanne can give you directions."

"Sure thing." Carolanne turned to Savannah. "It's really easy to find. Just two turns from our building."

"Well, I have to go help the kids sell their goods. I haven't missed an event with the 4-H kids since my boy was one." Miss Daphne hurried off back to the 4-H tent, waving over her shoulder as she did.

"She seems sweet," Savannah admitted.

"You'll love her. We all do."

After two hours Savannah had had enough of the picnic. She was getting antsy and was ready to get back and do some writing. Maybe she wasn't cut out for relaxing. It always felt so awkward to her. So she excused herself and promised to catch up with Carolanne the next day to get directions to Daphne's for tea on Tuesday if the address didn't come up on her GPS.

Just as she pulled out of the parking lot and sat at the intersection to turn onto Route 58, a guy in a baby-blue convertible classic Thunderbird turned in. With the top down, it was easy to see who was driving. It was Scott Calvin.

She pretended not to notice him, but his gaze drilled a hole in her direction. She flipped on her blinker and prayed he was going to the picnic and not about to hunt her down and make sure she didn't leave town without a ticket as a souvenir.

• • •

Scott Calvin parked his 1957 Thunderbird next to the 4-H tent so he could unload the coolers his mom had asked him to bring for her. He was late, but duty had called and there was nothing he could do about that. Not only would his mom probably be pacing like a penned-up panther, but apparently he'd missed a chance encounter with Savannah.

Of course, knowing Mom, she probably had her portable police scanner with her, even here, and knew exactly why he was late. She loved knowing his whereabouts, and had become rather obsessive about it since Dad had died. Sometimes it made him crazy, but she was a good ol' gal and he wouldn't do anything to disappoint her. All the attention she used to give Dad was just redirected to him; things could be worse.

As soon as he stepped out of the car, she ran out of the tent carrying two hot dogs with mustard and a deviled egg on a plate.

"Hey, Scott. You've got to be starving. You get those bicycle thieves all squared away?"

Just as he'd suspected. "Yes, ma'am." Her shirt was as bright yellow as the mustard on those dogs. Good thing he was still wearing his sunglasses.

"Kids?"

"Yes, ma'am."

"Whose were they?"

"Not tellin', Mom."

109

"Someone we know?"

He lowered his head, giving her the "really" look over the top of his sunglasses.

"Well, it doesn't matter. Got to nip those troublemakers in the bud early so they don't grow up to be problem adults."

Her selective memory made him laugh. It wasn't all that many years ago that he'd been the kid in trouble for much the same thing. "They were stealing back the bikes that had been stolen from them last month. Same kids, different day. They're good kids."

He picked up the deviled egg between two fingers and handed it back to her. "You know I'm not going to eat that."

"Oh, Scott. One of these days you will eat them again. You used to love them. Everyone else in town does."

"Not going to happen." The last time he'd eaten an egg he was dating Ruth. They had laying hens in the backyard then. She'd thought that would be fun, so he'd set up a little chicken coop for her. Only she wasn't really good about pulling the eggs every day. Evidently one morning she'd found some that one of the hens had been sitting on for a while, because he could hear her blood-curdling scream coming from the kitchen. He'd been in the backyard working on the weed whacker that Saturday morning. He'd dropped it so fast, it cracked the casing. When he got to the back door of the kitchen, she was screaming, "Save them. Save them!"

He had no idea what he was going to find when he made it inside, but it sure wasn't what he did find. Two half-formed chicks in a frying pan.

He'd turned off the burner and scooped them out with a spatula, then carried them out and given them a proper burial. He still to this day had no idea what exactly she thought he could do to save them, or why the heck she'd cracked the second egg without noticing the first one, but that memory had ruined him for eggs ever again. Hidden in a cake mix was fine, but anything that looked like an egg was an absolute no. Even chicken wings made him a bit queasy.

He bit into one of the hot dogs. "Thanks. This is good." He placed the plate on the hood of his car and lifted a cooler out of the back. As he toted it into the tent, he asked, "Where do y'all want this?"

Mom cleared a spot for it. "Right here, son. You got here just at the perfect time."

He slid the new tray into place, and his mom took the half a dozen or so remaining deviled eggs and nestled them in with the new batch. "I was afraid we were going to run out."

Scott held back a snicker. "I'd have probably gotten a 911 call if that had happened."

"I would never do that, but it could have darn near been a social emergency if we had," she mumbled.

Scott chatted with the 4-H'ers and even helped keep the line moving while his mom fussed with her eggs.

Once she had everything set up just the way she wanted, she wiped her hands on her apron and walked back over to him. "Are you going to be able to relax this afternoon?"

"At least for a little while."

"Good. You need a break. There's a good turnout too, especially for this early in the day."

"Looks like it." Truth was, now that they were holding a lot of these events at the artisan center, they pulled in some passersby, and frequent visitors of the center got mailings about them in the monthly newsletter. A plus for the town's revenue too.

"It'll be good for you to catch up with old friends. You work too hard."

He bit into the second hot dog. "I'm not complaining. So why should you?"

"Because I'm your mother and I want what's best for you."

He wasn't about to go down that path again. The two of them had gone round and round about him being an adult and her needing a hobby besides him.

She snapped her fingers. "Scott, I almost forgot, are you still going to take me to my eye appointment on Tuesday?"

"Yep. It's on my calendar and I've already got

Deputy Taylor covering for me so I can pick you up at two o'clock."

"Two o'clock. Yes, just as we'd planned. That will be perfect. Thank you."

Her eyes danced when she smiled like that. The problem was, that usually meant she was up to something.

"Is everything okay, Mom?"

"Of course. It's a gorgeous day. Couldn't be better."

The way she sang it, he wondered if the 4-H'ers might start jumping off the tables and doing a dance like those kids on *Glee*. Hopefully, he was just reading too much into her good mood.

Chapter FOUR

Savannah quickly realized that Monday mornings were Monday mornings whether you were in an office or not, but she sure as heck didn't need to be awake at six o'clock today. This whole relax-and-vacation thing might kill her. She just wasn't cut out for sitting still.

She rolled over and pulled the pillow over her head to try to sleep in. Isn't that what you were supposed to do on vacation?

But her mind was already chugging like a steam engine with a fresh load of fuel. She had those

113

other articles to write, and she was supposed to meet Jack over at the *County Gazette* to get the details on her assignment this morning.

Most people hated Mondays, but she looked forward to them. In fact, she was thankful she had this appointment. Doing nothing just didn't suit her well. They hadn't set a specific time to meet down at the paper, but she'd rather show up early and make a good impression, even if she was the one doing the favor.

Why she even cared what he'd think of her was a mystery. Just part of her DNA or something, because no matter how much she'd rather snuggle under the crisp sheets, she knew she would get up.

And she did.

She pondered how to make a decent outfit from the slim pickings packed for that wedding. The dress wasn't all *that* fancy, but it was black, and even with a scarf instead of jewelry it was too dressy for around here.

She pulled on her jeans and made do with the camisole of her nightie and the shrug she'd planned to wear with her dress to the wedding. It made for an eclectic but nice dressed-down look. It would just have to do.

Out on the street, the morning was already warm and sticky. Summer was bearing down on them, and if the weatherman was right, it would be a hot one. It was only a short walk to the newspaper, but the humidity had her wishing she'd driven.

Her hands slipped against the metal doorknob to the *County Gazette* office. She struggled to get a grip, then slung the door open. The metal blinds slapped against the door behind her.

A short gray-haired man popped to attention behind the counter. His eyebrows danced over his eyes like cotton balls after a hard rain. "You must be Savannah. Connor said you'd be by this morning. I'm Jack."

She stepped toward the counter and extended her hand. "Nice to meet you."

"So glad you can help us out. There's not much to it, really, but my sister and I have done it all forever and so there really isn't anyone else to help out when something happens. I'm so thankful for your help." He shuffled through papers and manila folders stacked at least seven inches high that teetered on the corner of the yellowed Formica counter. He plucked one out of the stack and passed it over. "Here are the last four issues of the police blotter. You can get an idea of the format from those."

Inside the folder were clippings of the blotter she'd already taken a look at in the diner as well as three others that looked like just a copy-and-paste job. Straightforward. Just a table and some bullet points. Piece of cake.

"My sister is the one who usually does this part. If you have any questions, we can call her. I'm sure she wouldn't mind."

Savannah shrugged. Jack had to be every bit of seventy, so she wondered just how old his sister was. She sure hoped she'd be retired by the time she was their age. "I think I can handle this just fine. It's pretty straightforward."

"Connor says you're from up DC way."

"I am."

"Haven't been there in years. Too much traffic for me. Loved the Smithsonian, though. That place was huge. You been there?"

"The Smithsonian? Yes. Several times."

"How you like livin' in the city?"

"I wouldn't have it any other way." It was none of his business that there was a time in her life when she lived in a town about the size of this one. Some things were better left where they were . . . in the past. The distant past.

"Y'all probably don't run a police blotter up there. Heck, it'd probably take all the pages in the paper to get all that crime in."

"It's not that bad, but now that you mention it . . . you might have a good point."

"Here, we summarize the traffic stuff."

No doubt, or it would take pages to cover *that!*

"And we use our judgment on the sensitive stuff like domestic abuse. If in doubt, come ask me and we can talk about it. My sister, Bee, has been doing this since she was a little girl helping Daddy out. She knows this town and the people like the back of her hand. She knows what's best left out. Or you could probably talk to the sheriff."

"Your dad used to own the paper?"

"Yes, and his dad, and his dad's dad. It's been in our family since its inception. My sister and I are the end of the line."

"That's too bad. It's quite a legacy to pass on."

"You're just being nice. We know that papers are struggling everywhere. It's a dying concept unless you put it all online. We were only putting the paper out twice a month until recently. We'd just restructured for twice a week when all of this happened and Bee had to leave. Probably not a great idea, but we had to try something. Once we go, that will probably be it, but we love keeping our town informed. The online stuff is the big buzz now, but Bee and I are just way too old to learn those new tricks."

"It's not as hard as it looks. The online stuff, I mean."

"I'll just take your word for that. We've been thinking about selling here recently. Anyway, if you need any help, just ask me . . . or Scott."

"I'm sure you can keep me on track."

"I'll do my best. Do you have a computer?"

"I do."

"Good. You can just e-mail me your write-up, when you're done, to this address." He took a card from a small metal holder and handed it to her. "If you don't have Word, then save it in RTF format."

"Will you e-mail me the police notes so I can pull them together for the next issue?"

"They're right here." He pulled a stack of papers from a mail sorter next to the front desk. "You can just stop by as you get caught up and pick up more. Bee always just typed them up each day. She said it was easier that way, but anything we can keep up while she's gone is appreciated." He handed her the stack. "Here you go. This will get you started."

Savannah stared at the handwritten pages from the log. Seriously? "Alrighty then. I'll get right on it." Lord have mercy, she'd be typing for an hour.

"I need the content by Wednesday at ten."

"No problem." This little favor was turning out to be less writing and more transcribing, but the sweet old guy needed her help. She knew she'd better turn around and skedaddle before he saw her snicker. It wouldn't do to hurt the poor guy's feelings. She waved the pages in the air and headed for the door. "You got it."

She hiked up to the next block and placed a to-go order at the diner. Then she headed back to her apartment to get down to work.

She juggled the flimsy chef salad container in one hand and a cup of sweet tea and the folder from Jack against her chest as she worked the key in the lock to the apartment.

Kicking the door closed with her foot, she

unloaded her arms on the desk and hit the Power button on her laptop.

One quick minute to scan her e-mail for anything critical while she'd been out was all she spent on it. Evelyn had responded to her note about filling in on the police blotter while she was here. She didn't mind. Savannah had known she wouldn't, since it would help with the articles she was working on for Evelyn anyway.

"Good deal." She opened the folder and started flipping through the handwritten pages of the police blotter notes. She'd give her right arm to get the whole story on each of the summarized events. Most of them were worded in a way that left a lot open to interpretation. She wondered if the vague nature of the content was on purpose. Did they mean to make it funny?

6/5 5:15 p.m. A grandson is continually breaking into his grandfather's locked cabinet and stealing his quarters for the laundry.

6/6 9:36 a.m. A fireman's ladder was reported stolen from the side of a house on Magnolia Street.

6/6 12:49 p.m. A dog was seen panting inside of a red Toyota in front of the Piggly Wiggly. It may be suffering. Turned out to be the taxidermy remains of the family pet.

6/6 12:57 p.m. A woman is trying to figure out what's behind an odd poem taped to her front door that says "Every door that opens is one closed for someone else." She found that the same poem had been left at houses all over her neighborhood. The neighborhood watch has engaged in an all-nighter.

6/6 3:23 p.m. A former mother-in-law was chagrined to receive a letter from her ex-daughter-in-law.

6/6 5:10 p.m. A woman reported that a homeless man was approaching people during the parade on Saturday preaching about a dangerous message in a painting at the yoga studio.

6/7 6:28 a.m. An injured cat was reported on Bleeker Street. When the officer arrived to check on its condition, the cat suddenly jumped up and climbed a tree. The fire department was dispatched to perform the rescue.

6/7 9:57 a.m. Mac's Bakery received two threats from an unknown female for making her fat with their bear claws.

6/7 10:18 a.m. Called out to Hunters Lane about a nuisance dog. New resident stated that the barking dog case has followed him all the way from Florida.

6/7 3:25 p.m. A man is getting around a trespassing order against him by making harassing phone calls to his ex-girlfriend.

6/7 8:42 p.m. A resident of Purdy Manor wants to complain to a neighbor about his barking dog, but the neighbor is never at home.

Since the paper only came out twice a week, she really would only have to spend an hour or so twice a week on the task, even with all the typing. It was actually proving to be pretty entertaining. She was nearly done with the stack when her phone whistled.

That was the sound she used for texts from Aunt Cathy. Like a cuckoo bird, which seemed fitting. Momma used to say Aunt Cathy was plumb crazy. Her momma would always follow it up with— "but the good kind." Was there really a good kind of crazy?

Momma had never meant it unkindly. She and her sister, Cathy, were so close it was like they were twins. When Momma and Dad died that night, the only thing nearly as bad as losing them was the fact that Aunt Cathy had withdrawn from Savannah so completely.

It had been a clear night, and there was no weather-related reason why Dad had lost control of the vehicle. Although Savannah had remembered the headlights of the oncoming car, there wasn't any evidence of it. Having no answers was hard for Aunt Cathy. She needed answers. She'd even asked Savannah if she'd been arguing with them when the car had gone off the road. She hadn't been, but the fact that her parents would have never been on the road if she hadn't been drinking that night made Savannah feel responsible anyway. She'd never been able to forgive herself, and she knew the town wouldn't either.

The sheriff had questioned her a thousand times over. So many that there was a point when she began to question what happened herself. In the end they called it an accident, but the tongues were already wagging. The damage was done.

Savannah grabbed the phone and absently thumbed in the code to check the message.

Pictures from the wedding.

She only recognized about half the people in the pictures. People changed a lot in eight years.

She could almost imagine the hushed whispers about her since she didn't attend the wedding. Maybe it was just as well that she didn't go. The stares. The questions. There'd still have been those "bless her heart" whispers even if she'd been there. You can't change the past.

Everyone in the pictures looked so happy.

She'd never even met her cousin Winnie. Technically, they weren't related at all. She was Uncle Stu's third wife's daughter. She hadn't even lived in Belles Corner when Savannah lived there. But they all probably accepted her more than they ever would Savannah after all that had happened. Aunt Cathy certainly had accepted her stepniece. That stung.

Tripp looked good. Really good. And happy.

The smiling faces she did recognize were people she'd gone to school with. Aunt Cathy had aged. A lot. Funny how in her mind everyone had stayed exactly the same as they were the day she'd left town . . . well, even younger than that, in a way.

She skipped back to the picture of Tripp. He'd been good to her. He deserved a wife who loved him more than she ever could. So why did it make her feel just a little bit jealous to see him so happy? It had been her idea to end the marriage. He was so miserable in northern Virginia, and she didn't really love him the way a wife should love her husband. Not that she realized it at the time. When her parents died, it was Tripp who was by her side. He shielded her, gave her reasons to live on while the whole community seemed to stare at her in pity, or blame, or . . . heck, she still wasn't sure. Even Monica, her very best friend, had seemed to get wrapped up in all the talk and speculation, and that made her dive even closer to Tripp.

He'd always said he wanted out of that town, so his dream became her rescue. She couldn't wait to go on his adventure, but when it came down to it, he hated the hustle and bustle of the big city. And when his dad got sick, it was all the excuse he needed to move back home to Belles Corner. He'd promised to come back, but she knew once he left, she needed to let him go.

Tripp had begged her to at least visit and try to work things out, but she just couldn't bring herself to go back. And maybe it wasn't even that she wanted to be in a big city. It was just that she needed to be out of that small town. She needed to leave that history behind.

He was married. She wasn't. He'd finally found happiness . . . and she was still afraid to even look for it.

Compromise had never been her strong suit. She dated, and she'd had plenty of opportunities for relationships, but she'd managed to keep all of them at arm's length ever since the divorce. Tripp had been the only one who had ever even gotten close to getting past the bulletproof shield she kept up in front of her heart.

It was probably best that way anyway. Especially for the last two years, as she continued to hide her connection to the Advice from Van column. That would have been nearly impossible if she'd had a spouse, or even a serious guy, in the picture.

The column wasn't that long, but it took an incredible amount of time to get through all the stuff to put it together. The amount of mail she got each week for that column was crazy. What didn't practically take down the server in the form of e-mails came in big tubs, sometimes even huge cotton USPS sacks, every single week. There were two people to pre-sort some of it, but she still went through the final review, because finding the letters that weren't from the true nut jobs, that had potential for the next column, was just easier to do on her own. They'd tried hiring interns in that role, but the letters had to spark something in her to make the humorous impact that folks had grown to expect.

Savannah's phone did a vibrating dance across the table, followed by the sound of clicking type-writer keys.

It wasn't a total surprise to hear Evelyn's ring-tone.

Even if it had been Evelyn's suggestion that she try to enjoy some downtime while writing those stories, it was highly unlikely that she'd be able to wait to hear how things were going. That woman never rested. They were alike in that way. She and Evelyn had gotten into such a routine of talking on the phone every morning that the line between friendship and employer/employee had blurred and stayed blurred.

Besides that, Evelyn had taken her under her wing when she first hit DC, and she was the closest thing Savannah had to a parent figure now. She'd never do anything to put that relationship at risk.

Savannah snagged the phone and punched the button to answer. "Tell me you absolutely adore that story I sent you yesterday."

Evelyn's bubbly laugh was enough to confirm her agreement. "I do adore it."

Savannah raised her hands in the air in a little happy dance. Evelyn never pulled a punch. Savannah always knew exactly where she stood and exactly what Evelyn was thinking. There was no candy coating. Savannah loved that about Evelyn. "Now tell me how awesome I am for knocking it out so quickly."

"Amazing *and* awesome."

"Thank you." Making Evelyn proud always felt good. "What's up?"

"Checking in. How're things going?"

"You got your story, didn't you? I'd say they're going well."

"Got any angles for the others yet?"

"No, but I'm having tea with a sweet old lady on Tuesday. She knows everyone and everything around here. I'm sure I'll get something good from that."

"Tomorrow?"

"Yep."

"What're you doing today?"

"I just met with the guy over at the paper about the police blotter. Thanks for letting me do that. It'll give me some good details for the articles, but they really needed the help too. It's just an old guy and his sister running the little paper down here. Nothing much else planned, but I'll maybe get my brakes checked out, but that won't take much time. Why?"

"Nothing big. I've got a courier on the way to your place."

"Here? In Adams Grove?" Whatever on earth for? Maybe she was sending a fruit basket or something.

"Yes, there. Wouldn't do me any good to send you stuff at your apartment up here."

"With what?"

"The Van letters."

"Ev—"

"Don't worry. I know what you're thinking. I'm going to hold up my end of the bargain, but if you'd seen Andrew's face when he saw all that mail . . . He didn't even know where to begin. I just need you to dig out a week's worth of good ones to get him started."

I'll never get rid of this. Andrew Jones will never pull it off.

"I promise that's the end. I told you we'd talk about it when you get back and we will."

She sure hoped so. She let out a sigh.

"I heard that. Don't get stressed out on me. I'll extend the lease on your little home away from home an extra week and throw in a little bonus of use of the Nats box seat tickets if you do."

Savannah loved a good hot dog at a Nats game. "Deal, if I can use the box seats this month *and* next month."

"Done," Evelyn said without even a second of hesitation. "He should be there shortly."

Of course he would. Evelyn wasn't calling to ask. She'd already set those wheels in motion hours ago. Heck, if Savannah knew Evelyn, she'd set it up during the parade!

It had been too long since she'd been to a Nats game. Evelyn was not a fan. Her husband had been, and one of his friends had gifted her those box seats in his honor when the team first came to DC. Evelyn mostly just dangled them as a bonus to inspire the behavior she wanted out of people. Call it manipulation, bargaining, whatever . . . it was what Evelyn did best. For just a tiny moment she allowed herself to imagine sitting in those box seats next to Dad. He probably wouldn't have been proud of her for the contents of the Advice from Van column, but he would have absolutely flat-out loved watching a pro ball game from those seats. He was the whole reason she'd ever fallen in love with the sport.

A loud knock on her door sent Savannah tumbling back to the present.

The courier.

She scrambled up from the couch, and without bothering to look through the peephole first, she swung open the door and said, "You can just put the boxes over there." She used a sweeping motion of her hand toward the sofa.

"Excuse me?"

Savannah peeked around the man standing in front of her. There were no boxes, although he'd have had no problems lugging some up the stairs with those arms.

"I'm your neighbor." He held out his hand. "Mike Hartman."

"Oh?" Savannah shrank back, embarrassed, then shook his hand. Well, he wasn't at all what she'd pictured him to be. He was about the farthest thing from an old, stodgy, cigarette-scented private investigator as you could get. His grip was firm, and that was no surprise by the curve of his bicep. This guy was in great shape, and if he had a vice, it was probably sit-ups, not cigarettes. "You've got great taste in music."

"Sorry about that." He looked embarrassed. "Connor didn't tell me anyone had moved in until this morning. I don't normally crank it up like that. I thought no one was around. Sorry."

"No worries. I enjoyed it."

"Glad you didn't hear me singing."

She laughed. "No. Can't say that I noticed. I guess the walls are better insulated than we

129

thought, or you can carry a tune pretty well. Trust me, if I had sung, you'd have known it. The dogs would've howled and the paramedics would have probably raced up to save me from myself."

His face relaxed into a smile.

"Well, I just wanted to introduce myself. If you need anything, let me know."

"I will. Thanks."

"And if I get too loud . . . just pound on the wall."

"I'm sure it will be fine." She meant it, but her attention was redirected at the sound of clomping up the stairway.

A familiar voice said, "Hey, girl. You had to be upstairs, didn't you."

She immediately recognized the guy carrying a wide corrugated USPS bin full of letters. This wasn't just any courier. It was the mailroom guy, and he had a GINN tote over each shoulder too. "George? She let you out for the day?"

"Yeah, thought it was a sweet deal until I realized how far away you were, and how heavy these are without a cart! Where do you want these?"

"How many are there?"

"Six."

She caught the scrunch of lines forming in Mike's forehead. How the heck would she play this off?

"Just drop them in the living room. I'll take care of them."

George turned sideways and shuffled past her. The bin dropped to the floor with a thud. Then he whisked past them and ran downstairs to get the rest, which she could now see he'd left stacked at the bottom of the stairs.

"Need help?" Mike called down after him.

"No!" Savannah grabbed his arm. "No. He's got them. He does this all the time."

"What is all that?"

"She's famous." George was huffing, but it sure wasn't stopping him from talking. She'd like to kill him about now. He knew it was supposed to be hush-hush.

"I'm not." She rolled her eyes, playing it down with her new neighbor. "He's kidding around."

Mike didn't look so convinced. "Fan mail?"

The courier busted out laughing.

She gave him the stink-eye and he immediately swallowed the rest of his hardy-har-harring.

She turned her back on George. "No. Not fan mail. It's just part of my . . . research."

Mike looked like he was trying to get a read on her. "Research?"

"Yeah." If she were researching what made people crazy-mad, sad, or just downright combative . . . She had about all she'd need to make one helluva graph out of all this data. Of course, she didn't really give two hoots about all that. She just did it for the paycheck, and for Evelyn. Evelyn had given her a chance at that

131

paper when she really had no right to even earn an unpaid internship. For some reason Evelyn had believed in the little country girl.

Savannah would never be able to repay Evelyn for all she'd done for her. She remembered the outfit she'd worn to that interview. It was actually the dress she'd worn to prom. Bright purple, her favorite color, and shiny. Aunt Cathy had cut it off to make it short so she could wear it to the Valentine's Day dance one year. It was the nicest dress she'd owned at the time. And entirely inappropriate for a business interview. But it must have touched Evelyn's heart because she'd hired her on the spot.

She'd even hired Tripp to do some handiwork around the old building when she heard he was out of work. Once Tripp left to go back to Belles Corner, Evelyn made quick work of moving Savannah out of the awful neighborhood they'd lived in, saying it was one thing when she was married and it was all they'd been able to afford, but no place for a young woman on her own.

Yes, Evelyn had been a true blessing for her. It just proved over and over again that moving to DC had been the right thing to do.

Mike leaned against the doorjamb. "That's an awful lot of mail. Sure seems to me that it would be easier to just do your research online."

He had no idea just how much baggage she

carried around, but she wasn't about to get into that with him.

George grunted as he repositioned the box to get a better grip. "Oh, there's four times this amount in the online log."

Mike's eyebrow shot up. "Really."

"He's exaggerating." Savannah dug a few dollars from her pocket and hurried George out the door before he helped her any more. She scrunched a GINN tote bag into a ball and shoved it into his stomach. Maybe Mike hadn't noticed the logo.

With George on his way, she turned back to Mike Hartman. He didn't look like he was ready to go anywhere. If Evelyn knew that George had practically blown the secret of who Van was, she'd fire him on the spot. Savannah sure didn't want that to happen. Not only for George's sake, but because she really didn't want it to be known that she was the snarky one behind all those letters. If George got fired he might not keep that secret. That could be a real career-limiting move.

Mike cleared his throat. "You going to give me any details?"

She shook her head. "Nope. Nothing to share."

A woof came from down the hall.

"You have a dog?"

"Yeah. I do." He smiled. "For research."

"Real funny."

"Makes about as much sense as your story."

They stood there, neither willing to budge. "I really have to get to work," she said.

He turned and started for the door, then turned back. "Don't get a paper cut."

"I'll be careful."

She closed the door, thankful that he was gone but quite certain she hadn't seen the last of him. If he was any kind of PI he'd probably have her figured out soon enough. She'd better get on his good side . . . and quick.

The next morning, Savannah stood outside the sheriff's office, waiting. It wasn't exactly how she'd planned to spend her morning. She'd thought it wouldn't take but a few minutes talking to Jack down at the paper to resolve her questions about the incidents on the police log. Unfortunately, he didn't have any answers and told her to deal directly with Scott on them.

Reluctantly, she'd headed down to the sheriff's office. That "staying behind the scenes and out of the sheriff's way" plan hadn't lasted long.

She'd already been standing here outside his office for the better part of ten minutes waiting too, and it wasn't easy to not eavesdrop, no matter how many times her mother had tried to drill into her head that eavesdropping was rude.

So he'd been a little grumpy Saturday; he really

hadn't done anything wrong. Maybe she was just overreacting. Or holding a grudge. Wouldn't be the first time she was accused of that.

People seemed to really like Scott. Carolanne and Jill sure thought he was a nice guy. So maybe deep down it was her, not him. Maybe her impression had more to do with her past with small-town cops than it had to do with him. Maybe she hadn't given him a fair shake.

She was prepared to give him a fresh shot at a first impression—in the attitude department anyway, because from a looks perspective, he sure didn't need a makeover.

Her gut still wrenched just a little when she thought about how information in the hands of a small-town cop could suddenly become public, though. The police blotter she held in her hand proved that too. Small towns were like self-appointed judge and jury, or the blasted gospel. There didn't seem to be a formula for who was protected and who was going to be the talk of the town at any given time.

She leaned against the wall, shifting her weight to her other leg and trying not to be so obvious about listening in. He'd been on the phone for as long as she'd been standing there, and he must have been able to see her in the hallway, but he hadn't acknowledged her.

He was young for a sheriff, not an old crony like Sheriff Pittman had been back home—back then, when her life had gone off the rails. He'd probably retired by now.

She and Scott had to be about the same age. She noticed the white bakery bag on his desk. If he ate those sweets every day, he must work out pretty faithfully, because there sure didn't appear to be any excess weight on him.

A lanky uniformed man nodded her way as he gave a quick double knock on the sheriff's open door and dropped off a stack of folders on his desk. As he walked out, he stopped and asked, "Can I help you with something?"

For a fleeting moment she considered avoiding the sheriff and getting this guy to answer her questions, but then Jack had been pretty clear about talking directly to Scott.

"No. I'm waiting for him." She pointed to the sheriff's office.

"Okay. I'm Deputy Taylor. If he takes too long, I'll be right down the hall. Just come get me. I'll be happy to try to help you."

"Thanks. I'm good." She turned her attention back to the deep voice coming from the office.

He'd been trying to get off that call for a good five minutes.

He said, "Thank you for the recognition. I really appreciate the award, but I was just doing my job."

Probably for top speeding-ticket-giver in the whole South, if she had to guess.

"I'm just not sure my schedule will allow me to attend." After a short pause, he answered. "Yes, yes. No. Mike Hartman has already declined. Yes. I'll keep that in mind. Right. Thursday night. Seven o'clock. Got it. Yes, thank you very much."

She heard the call end and him sigh.

She counted to three and poked her head around the corner.

"Excuse me." She gave another courtesy knock on the door. "You got a minute?"

"Sorry to keep you waiting." Scott motioned her into his office. "Why didn't you tell me you were filling in over at the paper when we talked Saturday?"

"Jack called you?"

"Yeah. He told me he was sending you over. You didn't mention—"

"I didn't know, then. I rented Connor Buckham's apartment. He asked if I could do them the favor over at the paper. Seemed like the right thing to do. Here I am."

"Nice of you. Have you ever done anything like that before?"

"Like what? Write an article?" It sure wasn't rocket science. A fourth grader could probably do this gig if the sheriff's folks could write a decently clear summary. "Yeah. I've got some experience."

"That what you do up in DC?"

She was definitely not going there. A change in subject was in order . . . right about now. "Was

137

that a sneer? What do you have against DC?"

"Nothing. I could have guessed you were from a city without even looking at your driver's license."

"Oh, really?"

"All the beautiful ladies I meet are city girls."

She smiled. "You think I'm beautiful? Is that why you didn't give me a speeding ticket?"

"Hardly."

Even when he was giving her a hard time he had a way of making her feel special in a weird sort of way. "How often do you let someone out of a ticket?"

"Never."

"Not never. You let me off."

"You were the exception. You caught me in a good mood. Parade day and all."

That parade had made for a good day for her too. "What is it with small towns and parades?"

"You got something against them?"

"No. Not really, but you actually closed down the streets. No one could even come into town and get gas. Didn't it occur to you that it would hurt the revenue stream?"

"The revenue stream was just fine. Everyone in town was right here, and money was spent while they were here. People from neighboring towns come to the parades to see their friends in them too. It works."

"Seems like overkill to me."

"It's a safety matter."

"Protect and serve and all that, I guess."

"Yep. Maybe you should try slowing down and just enjoying things for a change. Ya know . . . instead of speculating."

"You do have one heckuva parade wave. Guess you've done your share."

"I've done a few. It's fun. You should try it."

"Waving?"

"Having fun."

Ouch. She could be convinced to give it a try with him, though. "Well, I plan to slow down and have a little of that while I'm visiting your quaint town, but right this minute I need some clarification on this police blotter. The first being, why don't you automate this stuff? It was like a handwriting analysis class." She shoved the stack of papers toward him.

"We have all that online. It's just that Jack's sister isn't very computer savvy, so she likes it done the way she's always done it. We jot down the paper copies just for her."

"Tell me you're kidding."

"Nope."

She'd typed all those suckers in for nothing. "Can I get the files e-mailed while I'm helping out?"

"Absolutely."

"Cool. Well, that will probably answer several of the questions where I just wasn't even sure what the notes said. There are a couple that read kind of strange, though."

"Shoot."

"Here's the first one." She moved to his side of the desk and placed the paper in front of him as she read it aloud. " 'June sixth, 1:34 p.m. Some louse made unauthorized charges on a woman's credit card, causing a loss of three hundred and ninety-nine dollars.' "

She laughed. So did he. He had a nice laugh. "You don't really want me to print it in the paper that way, do you? You'll have a slander lawsuit for sure."

Scott said, "Well, actually, I do want it printed that way. That wording was intentional. You see, we know who the louse was. It was her ex-husband, only we can't prove it. But one thing we know about him is that he will hightail it up here when this hits the paper to file a complaint on his wife for calling him a louse. We'll be able to close that issue out."

"That's sneaky."

"It's not my first rodeo."

"I hear ya. Okay, well here's another one." She flipped to the next page. "How about this one? 'June seventh, 8:42 p.m. A resident of Purdy Manor wants to complain to a neighbor about his barking dog, but the neighbor is never at home.' " She laughed. "What? She can't leave him a note or something?"

"You're right. Let me help you with that one. I'd like you to add his address."

"The whole address?"

"Yep. That should pretty much take care of that little issue too."

"Sheriff Calvin, are you telling me that you use this police blotter to manipulate people?" Evelyn Biggens would have met her match with this guy—he did all this without even leaving his desk.

"It's Scott to you, and I wouldn't call it manipulating. I like to think of it more as helping gently persuade people to do the right thing."

"I see. Well, I bet this one will take some explaining. I didn't even type this one in. See?"

Scott read it out loud. " '12:16 a.m. Some adults were being overly noisy in a hot tub frolic.' " He gave her a sideways glance. "Just what is it you want to know about this one?"

"Some adults? Frolicking?"

"I really can't share those details."

"Now you get a conscience? Okay, fine. So that's accurate."

"Print it as is." He drummed his hands on his desk. "Next?"

"Just one more." She scanned her notes. "Here it is. It's the one about a drunk spreading rumors about a message in some painting down at the yoga studio."

Scott shook his head. "Scratch that one."

141

"Why?"

"I don't want to stir people up with rumors. That was a misunderstanding."

"Do you want me to just rephrase—"

His smile had faded, and so had the joking tone. "Nope. Scratch it entirely."

"Okay, fine. I won't include that one."

"Good."

There was that cranky mood again. "Well, it appears I wasted your precious time. I'm sorry about that."

"Don't be." He smiled and that dark cloud was gone as quickly as it had arrived. "I'm glad you came by." He pushed his chair back and stood next to her.

"Thanks for helping me get all the details right."

"Thank you for helping out with the police blotter. You stop by or call me anytime."

There was an awkward pause. He cleared his throat. "I mean, I'd rather be sure it's right. Don't go filling in the blanks on your own. Trust me, it's never going to be predictable."

"I'm beginning to see that." She started to leave, but that nosy side of her wouldn't let her leave well enough alone. "By the way, I heard you talking on the phone before I came in. You're getting some kind of an award?"

"Yep."

"You're not going?"

"No. I'm not a rubbery-chicken-eating, gripping-

and-grinning kind of a guy. Besides, it's up north in your neck of the woods."

"It's not such a bad place."

"Lots of traffic. Been there, done that. I don't need a plaque for doing my job."

"I could show you around. What's the award for?" *Perfect attendance? I could see skipping that.*

"Does it matter?"

"I'm curious."

"We had a case here not too long ago that struck a lot of nerves. They don't usually pay attention to anything we're doing down here."

"And?"

"They're honoring me and your neighbor, Mike Hartman, at a dinner up in Arlington. It's not just us. It's a whole night of recognition for various people in our field. Somehow our case got someone's attention up there for this year. Mike's already begged off. One of us has to go, and he left me with the short straw."

"Well, that ought to be front-page news in this town."

"I don't care about that stuff."

"You should. Folks around here will be thrilled that you got that kind of recognition. It's good for the town too. Hey, they might even throw *you* a parade if you play your cards right." His look told her he hadn't appreciated her little jab, so she quickly changed gears. "I'll let Jack down at the paper know about it. I'm sure he'll want to cover the event, or at least interview you for the details."

Scott handed her an invitation on high-quality vellum.

"Embossed. Nice." She scanned the details. "This is a big deal. You have to go. It would probably be good for your career too."

A line slashed across his forehead. "It *is* an election year."

"I wasn't thinking about the sheriff being a voted position. This could be a *very* big deal for you in an election year." She reread the invitation and committed the details to memory. That was always one of her strong suits. Served her well in the card games with the guys over the years too.

She handed the invitation back to Scott.

"Yeah, well, unless you're throwing me a parade, don't bother telling Jack. That kind of attention makes me uncomfortable."

"Well, then you better buckle up, Mr. Calvin."

Chapter FIVE

Savannah had already spent the better part of the morning on the Internet googling and making calls to get more details about the event that Scott had been invited to. Her curiosity always got the best of her. It was none of her business, but she just couldn't quit digging.

Normally, that kind of research would have only taken a few minutes, but the Internet speed in this town left something to be desired. Plus, this wasn't some little award ceremony. One link had led to another and another. It was going to be quite a shindig. The list of attendees was impressive too. Hmm.

Savannah: You sending anyone to cover the Gold Meritorious Safety Award presentation in Arlington?

Evelyn: Yes. Why?

Savannah: Sheriff here being recognized.

Evelyn: Name?

Savannah: Scott Calvin.

Savannah had no sooner typed out the name than her phone rang. She answered, but before she could even say hello, Evelyn was talking.

"Same guy in your article, Scott Calvin? Are you kidding me? Now I know why Adams Grove sounded so familiar. That's the small-town sheriff that killed that Frank Goto. The Goto Hell murderer."

The room seemed to swirl around her. She hadn't really thought of the sheriff as anything but a paper pusher who gave out some speeding tickets and a face for the county. Her mouth went dry. "I remember that story."

"It was hellish. No pun intended," Evelyn said. "You should write a series of stories on him!"

She shook her head. Not that Evelyn could see

her, or that she'd pay attention if she could. Evelyn was like that. When it was her idea, she thought it was a good idea and she never changed her mind.

"It's perfect. Those small-town stories can feed right into a series on that sheriff. We'd get a nice juxtaposition of small towns and big stories."

"One thing at a time, Evelyn." No one else had the nerve to tell Evelyn to chill out, but their friendship had been filter-free from day one.

"Fine."

But Savannah knew that Evelyn was thinking she'd get her way eventually, and she usually did. Even with Savannah. "I better get to work before you make this a two-year assignment too."

Evelyn's laugh bubbled across the line. "Get to work."

Savannah laid her phone aside and sat back in the chair, digesting the new information about Scott.

The *County Gazette* might be a small paper, but Jack needed to know that Scott was being recognized for his heroism and get the hometown angle. She pulled all her notes together to take them over to him, but first things first. She'd spent way too much time messing around on her computer. She had just enough time to jump in the shower and get dressed so she could be at Daphne's house for tea by one.

She'd stop by the paper after her visit.

• • •

It was only a couple of turns, but the address that Daphne had given her ended up being on the outskirts of town.

Savannah turned onto Nickel Creek Road. The trees, in all their summer glory, hung over the road like a canopy. The road was paved, but narrow and with no painted lines. She'd learned to drive on a road like this. Momma would cling to the door handle, swearing she was hugging the ditches. Dad had way more patience, and thank goodness, else she might never have learned to drive. She zipped around the next corner in her Mini Cooper, knowing her mom would have been terrified in that car. Momma had always driven a big car. She liked lots of metal around her, and she thought her daughter should be the same way, which was why when all her friends were getting their first cars, small economical rides, she was saddled with Momma's old Buick that only got, like, eleven miles to the gallon. She hadn't driven a big car since.

After nearly two miles of nothing but trees and fields of crops, a house came into view. White vinyl fencing marking off pastures that nestled right up to a white clapboard rancher with a red tin roof. The long porch ran the entire length of the house.

A sign sported the name ROCKING R, but the house number was still thousands off from the address Daphne had given her.

The houses seemed few and far between.

"Am I ever going to get there?"

Then the road came to a stop sign and right in front of her was a neat little brick rancher up on a rise. Bright-red geraniums overflowed from baskets that hung between the white columns on the front porch. On a cooler day, sitting out on the porch in those rockers would be so nice, but today was too hot for that.

Before Savannah even got out of her car, Daphne was out on the porch waving.

"Hi," Savannah called out. "I didn't have any trouble finding it, but that's one long road."

"Yes, it is. There's another way to get here quicker. Carolanne could have told you how to come that way, but the way you came is the easiest."

Savannah got out of the car. "What a lovely home."

"Thank you," Daphne said. "Come on in."

Savannah climbed the three stairs up to the porch and followed Daphne inside.

Tea was already set out on a table in the living room. "That tea set is exquisite." Savannah stooped to pick up one of the delicate cups. The soft pink china was edged in gold, and full cherry blossoms filled the sides of the cups and their saucers. "There's even a cherry blossom inside. I love those kinds of details."

"Thank you. I figured since you live near DC,

the cherry blossoms would make you smile. It's my favorite." Daphne tittered. "Who am I kidding? They're all my favorites. Let me pour our tea and then I'll show you my whole collection."

"That would be lovely." Savannah wondered where the heck that came from. She never talked that way, but somehow it seemed fitting with the formal tea setting and all.

Daphne poured the tea.

Savannah took a sip of the floral blend. It reminded her of her mother's favorite tea. "When I was a little girl my mother would have tea parties for me. All the girls in the neighborhood would put on their best Sunday dresses to come over—even the tomboys." Her nose tickled and her eyes felt glassy. "I remember being so excited that I wouldn't sleep the night before. Just the thought of everyone dressed up and using the real dining room and delicate china . . . it was so exciting. I can still remember the china pattern my mom had. A lovely mint green with delicate flowers in the center." Her heart ached, but it wasn't quite as painful as it used to be.

"Your mother shared her love of tea with you. That's very special, but it's not so much about the tea itself as much as it is the coming together with others and the time spent sharing. Having only a son, I never got to do that, but that sweet boy of mine did accompany me to high tea when we went to Bermuda."

"I bet that was fun. I've always wanted to go to the islands."

"You should. So lovely, and high tea British-style was quite an experience. But I'm not that snobby about teatime. Don't you think it's the people we share it with that makes it extra special?"

"I do." Savannah smiled. "Mom loved planning those afternoon tea parties for me. I loved it too. We'd bake all kinds of goodies and make finger sandwiches together. Those hours in the kitchen were great."

"You haven't done that in a while, have you?" Daphne's expression softened. "I can see it in your eyes."

Savannah lowered her gaze as she set her teacup down on the table. "No, ma'am. My mother passed away when I was eighteen."

"I'm so sorry. That must have been so hard. What was she like? Your mother."

"She was the best." Even now, after all these years, Savannah had to fight the tears. She never talked about her mom and dad. Never. It was still too hard, but somehow here, now, it felt right. "She was so beautiful, and she always seemed so happy. I don't think I ever saw her cry. Not once."

Daphne smiled gently. "It's okay to cry sometimes."

"Her smile could light up a room."

"Like yours."

"Thank you. She was a stay-at-home mom. I don't think she ever missed one single event. Not a homeroom party, a sporting event that I cheered, a softball game I played, or even a dance recital. Everyone loved Momma. You could talk to her about anything."

"Had she been ill?"

"No." Savannah sucked in a breath. "No. It was unexpected."

"Oh, goodness. Well, I'm so sorry to bring that up, but I'm sure she was a very beautiful woman, because you are quite stunning."

"Thank you."

"I'll be meeting up with some other gals on Friday to prepare some treats for a fund-raiser. I'd love it if you'd join us. We're going to meet up at the church."

Savannah started to say no. A knee-jerk response. But really, why wouldn't she help out? It wasn't like she had anything else to do. She enjoyed Daphne's company, and the thought of working side by side with a bunch of ladies in the kitchen had an unexpected appeal to it. Besides, she might find out some neat details. "I'd enjoy that."

"Great. Why don't I just pick you up? You're right on the way. Around six o'clock on Friday."

"Sounds like a plan. Thank you, Daphne." Savannah felt an overwhelming swirl of joy inside. Evelyn had been her protector, in a sense, since she hit DC, but their relationship was different. Just a few moments with this woman and she felt like she was with Momma. There was a soft kindness about her, slow and purposeful, that made Savannah feel like she'd just slowed down for a school crossing compared to her highway-speed life . . . and it felt good.

"We'll be baking cookies and brownies, that kind of thing. If you have a favorite recipe, bring it along. If not, I'll hand over one of mine for you to make. Of course, you'll have to promise to never share it with anyone."

"Of course. Your family secret will be safe with me." But her wheels were already turning. Could she remember how to make Momma's special shortbread cookies?

"Let's talk about something happy." Daphne patted Savannah on the leg.

Daphne sounded just like her mother. *Fill your space with happy and you will always be,* she'd say. "Let's. How about those teapots? Carolanne and Jill went on and on about your collection. I'd love to see it."

"Yes, I collect teapots like some girls shop for shoes. I adore them. It's silly. I should sell them. I started the collection years ago. I'd always said when my sweet Tom retired that I was going to open a tea shop in town. He bought me one for every occasion."

"What happened?"

"He died, and I just couldn't imagine doing it

without his help. He'd probably be disappointed that I didn't follow that dream. He'd always encouraged me to do it. Now I'm just getting too old."

"You are not too old. He must have really believed you'd be a success."

"Together he and I could have made anything work. He loved buying those teapots. I'm not sure if it was really because he wanted me to open that shop, or if it just made for an easy go-to gift for any occasion. You know how men are about buying gifts. If you tell them exactly what you want, you'll get exactly what you want. That's what I always say, but I never picked a single one of these out that he gave me. He did all the legwork to hunt them down. I haven't added any new ones in a while."

"I'm sorry for your loss."

Daphne reached out and squeezed Savannah's hand. "It's okay, dear. God has his own plan. Doesn't have to make sense to us."

Savannah knew about loss not making sense, and she wasn't sure if she would ever face God and ask why again.

Tears danced in Daphne's eyes. "I still miss him, though. It's been five years and it still feels like yesterday." Daphne's expression softened. "Tom used to love estate sales, so quite a few of these teapots had probably been in families for generations."

"I've never been to an estate sale, but I bet that would be fun."

"They have them all the time around here. Guess it's not really the kind of thing they do much of up there in the big city."

"Maybe. I don't really know."

"I can't wait to help you with your book. I guess you can really do that from about anywhere."

"Yes, I'm mixing in a little fun with work on this trip. That's a nice perk."

"It sure is." Daphne moved toward the dining room. "I'm glad you landed in Adams Grove."

"Me too." Savannah followed her. The dining room had wall-to-wall shelving with just a table in the center of the room. Each shelf displayed a tea set, or a few, in some cases. Some housed complete sets, others just the teapot.

"Oh. My. Goodness. Now this is a collection!"

"Thank you." Daphne's cheeks flushed.

"Not one speck of dust here either. You must spend all your extra time dusting."

Daphne let out a hearty chuckle. "They do require a little dusting now and then, but I don't mind. They all bring back such good memories. I just do a few each day and work my way around the room eventually."

Memories. Some memories were easier to just push aside.

Daphne lifted a small blue porcelain teapot from the shelf. "This one is extra special. Tom gave this to me on Mother's Day one year to thank me for our son." She hugged it to her chest like a treasure. "Isn't that so sweet? He'd think to thank me for giving him what's already the most precious gift in my life. Tom and I were so blessed to have that child." She stepped closer to Savannah. "See here. The pot has Romans 15:13 in gold on it. *May the God of hope fill you with all joy and peace.*"

"The cups have 'joy' and 'peace' on them." Savannah lifted the cup that had JOY scripted on it. "No wonder you love the set so much. What a great memory."

"It is. That's why it's so hard to pick a favorite. Each is tied to something just as special as the next."

"You and Tom were married a long time. Do you think that couples in small towns have longer marriages?"

Daphne thought for a moment. "You know, I wonder. I've never really thought about it, but I don't know many people who have been divorced. Maybe the small town does have an impact. Let me think about that. This is for your book, isn't it?"

"Yes, a little research," she said.

"How fun." She turned her attention back to her collection. "Do any of them strike you as extra special?"

"They're all so different." Savannah scanned the

155

shelves. "You're right. It is hard to pick one over the others, and I don't even know the stories behind them." She stopped and looked closer at a small teapot with a purplish base. The pretty purple swooped up the handle. On top of the handle was an intricately detailed butterfly lighting on wildflowers against a blue sky. "This one. This one might actually be my favorite."

"One of my favorites too. Tom got that for me on my fiftieth birthday. It's hand painted by the artisans of Franz. Look at the detail work on it."

"Stunning." The memories tied to the abundance of teapots of all shapes, sizes, and materials filled the room. She suddenly longed to have that many good memories in her life someday. She still had a storage unit back in Belles Corner with all of her parents' things. There was no way that she could deal with any of it back then, and ever since it seemed easier to push to the side. For sixty bucks a month she could just pretend her parents were traveling abroad, which was what she still told people when she didn't want to deal with the discussion.

Savannah felt her mood dip, and she really didn't want to ruin what was starting out as a good day, so she changed the subject. "I know those silver sets on the top shelves are a lot of work."

"Friends from church come over once a month and we put a little shine on them together. Everyone brings a dish to share and we make an afternoon of it. Makes fun work of it." Daphne bumped Savannah's arm playfully. "And it's a good time for all of us to catch up on what's been going on around town. You should join us next week."

"I'd like that. If I'm still in town I might take you up on that."

A timer sounded from the kitchen, and Daphne bounced to attention. "Oh, I made us some treats to go with our tea. Don't let me ramble on about those silly teapots. I could tell those stories all day."

"I love your stories." Daphne's memories touched Savannah in a way she hadn't expected. She was here trying to get more information about the town, something a little edgy she could use in her column, but instead she was being tugged to a place that she'd held at arm's length for a long time. A place like home. She followed Daphne to the kitchen, where Daphne pulled out a tray of mini quiches from the double wall oven.

The room filled with savory scents, and suddenly Savannah felt hungry.

Daphne tenderly plucked each bite-size morsel from the baking sheet and placed it just so on a serving dish. She picked up a covered plate with her other hand and headed out of the kitchen.

"Let me carry one of those," Savannah offered.

"I've got it. Will you grab the napkins and silverware from the counter?"

"Yes, ma'am." She swept the cloth napkins and silverware into her hand and followed Daphne into the living room.

Daphne lifted the tray to Savannah to offer her a quiche. "Please have one."

"If these are as good as those deviled eggs, I know I'll love them." She helped herself to one from the plate and took a bite. She was tempted to mention her granny's deviled egg recipe to Daphne. She suddenly felt very guilty that she might have given away the secret ingredient.

"Don't you worry. If you don't like it, I have some egg salad. Same recipe as those deviled eggs, although folks swear it's different. I put it on my homemade poppy seed rolls and everyone goes on and on about them. I think it's the roll that makes it taste different."

"That sounds good."

"Mac has been dying to get his hands on my poppy seed roll recipe. I might just have to leave it to him in my will!" Daphne grinned. "I'll pack you some to go. You can have them for lunch tomorrow."

"Oh, you don't have to go to that trouble."

"No trouble at all. I love doing stuff like that. Did you have any brothers or sisters, Savannah?"

"No. I was an only child."

"Do you want children?"

She picked up her teacup, resting the saucer in her lap and took a sip of her tea. "I haven't really thought about it much. I work a lot. I guess that probably means no."

"That doesn't mean a thing. You find the right special someone and you'll be thinking differently. People are starting families so much later these days. You have plenty of time."

"It's not really on my radar. A special someone or children."

Daphne patted her leg. "When the right one comes along, you'll know the answer to that question."

Savannah's whole body tingled under Daphne's gentle words and touch. To love like that was a gift, but it also came with a cost. When it was taken from you it was the worst sorrow imaginable. Nearly unbearable. She'd promised herself she'd never feel that way again. So far, she'd held love off. Keeping family and friends at a safe distance so she didn't risk falling into that trap. She wasn't going to break her lucky streak, no matter how appealing Daphne made it sound. But Daphne would never understand that. "Tell me more about the tearoom. You're an amazing cook. You have all the equipment and place settings; why haven't you done it?"

"My son always asks me the same thing. I think I've waited too long now. It's a lot of work for a woman my age. No one else has any interest in a tearoom."

"He sounds supportive. That's nice that y'all are

159

so close. I think it would be a blast to own a tearoom. Too bad I don't live here. I'd help you in a hot second."

Daphne's eyes danced, and Savannah felt warning flags snapping in the make-believe breeze.

Savannah righted the course of the conversation. "But then I'll be moving on in a week or so." She paused and took a sip of her tea to give that time to sink in. "You could always just be open four days a week. Maybe focus more on special planned events rather than daily hours. Whatever you can handle. I think you'd be a huge success. I bet those church gals who polish your silver would pitch in too."

"Really? Do you think young people would appreciate a nice tea?"

"There are several tearooms in the DC area. I think tea is one thing that never goes out of style. It's timeless."

"Timeless Tea!" Daphne practically screeched it.

"What?"

"Timeless Tea. That would be the perfect name for my shop. I'd never been able to come up with the right name. Not until right this second. You are an angel. Maybe this is a sign."

It was hard not to get caught up in her excitement. "Maybe it is. Good luck!"

"My son is going to be so excited for me. He's been on me to get busy on a project or hobby or something. He'll be so surprised."

"He sounds like an angel."

"He is. Handsome too." She gave Savannah a wink. "He's single, you know."

"Too bad I live so far away." How else do you politely tell a woman you have zero interest in a blind date with her perfect son, which was clearly what she was angling for? She scanned the room for pictures of him. In that moment, she realized there were no pictures out, but there were empty spaces where they had been, like on the mantel. And on the end table there was even a rectangular spot amid the dust where something had been plucked from its place. He was probably as ugly as all get out. Even his momma didn't want to scare her off. Now that *was* bad.

"Now dear, what's really holding you up there in Washington, DC? You said yourself you could work from anywhere."

"That's true. I could."

"Or you could do a different job. Maybe you should follow your dreams, just like you're telling me."

Savannah wasn't quite sure how to respond to that. The truth was, she'd never stopped—heck, even paused—long enough to consider what it was she really wanted out of life, or what her dreams even were. She'd just run full-speed ahead with the first thing she'd tried—working for the paper. There'd been a time when she and Momma had talked about her going to culinary school, but that hadn't seemed fun once Momma was gone. So she'd put her focus on the first work she landed. Anything to keep her days busy and herself so exhausted that she might sleep, because those nights when she lay there wide awake thinking about her parents, that was almost more than she could bear. And some nights it felt like just yesterday that God had snatched them from her life.

"What kind of jobs are there in a small town the size of Adams Grove?" Maybe there'd be a hook in that subject.

"A lot of people work over at the prison. And there's the plant. They used to employ a few hundred people there making chipboard, but they shut that down a while back. But we have probably all the same stuff you have in the city, just fewer of them. I mean, we have banks, and stores, and a newspaper and library. Everything a family needs."

"Not as many differences under the covers as you think at first glance between big cities and small towns, I guess."

Daphne pursed her lips. "Well, we don't have public transportation. Amtrak used to stop through here, but they canceled that stop. The bus station closed down on Main Street, so now they pick up over at the truck stop, but that's to go to other towns, not around here. You pretty much have to have a car to get around."

"I guess most everybody drives a car around here. In the city, public transportation is so easy."

"I've been to your fair city. It feels like another planet. Everything is so intense. The volume. Traffic, people, buildings, crime . . . everything multiplied by something." Daphne must have been bored with that conversation because she abandoned it pretty quickly, saying, "I'm so glad you accepted my invitation today. I felt a connection when we met."

"I really appreciate you spending your time with someone just passing through."

"You'll be back. I just know it. Did I tell you that I even have plans drawn up for my tearoom?"

"No, you didn't. You mean like a business plan or an architectural plan?"

"Professionally done by an architect. Sweet man. He lives on the other side of town. He and Tom were good friends. He heard me going on and on one night about the possibilities, and a week later he came back with these drawings. Want to see them?"

"I'd love to see them."

Daphne rushed down the hall and came back carrying a cardboard tube. "They're drawn based on the general shape and square footage of most of the buildings on Main Street. So I could pretty much make it work with any of those spaces without a lot of adjustments. They're pretty basic, but I love the way he did the artist's rendering with even the goodies on the tables and all."

She pried the end of the tube off and pulled out the plans. "Grab an end," she said to Savannah as they moved from the living room to the dining room. They spread the paper wide across the shiny wood of the dining table.

Daphne grabbed teacups from the shelf behind her and weighted the corners of the drawing.

"Oh, Daphne. You're right." Savannah reached out and ran her fingers across what looked like fine linen tablecloths, and there was the butterfly teapot they'd just been talking about. "I feel like I could step right into that shop and sit in that chair. It's gorgeous."

"Isn't it?"

"So many very detailed touches. The wooden drawers of tea are so elegant along that wall."

"Yes. My Tom was so handy. He could build anything. My son would be able to help with a lot of that too. Not building the furniture, like Tom did, but he can fix just about anything. Cooks a mean steak too. He gets that from me."

"You make him sound like Mr. Perfect."

"He is. He just hasn't found the right girl yet."

"Never?"

"He's had some serious relationships, but so far not that everlasting love that I know is out there for all of us."

Or he was a freak. If he hadn't settled down with the right girl yet, he was probably gay, kinky, or a player. No man was that perfect and still alone, but darn if Daphne wasn't a sweetheart. Maybe her son *was* just that perfect.

"I hate to spend his inheritance, but he keeps telling me that I should follow my dreams and open up the tearoom, and if I'm not going to do that, then I should spend it all traveling to all the wonderful tearooms around the world."

"That would be an amazing trip to take."

"It would, but not alone. Trips aren't about the places. They're about sharing those places with someone else. I almost opened the tearoom a couple years ago. I was so close. Mac was selling one of his buildings, but I dragged my feet too long and his girlfriend put a yoga studio in."

"Oh, I saw that. I love all the bright colors on the outside of that building."

"Not that one . . . same building, but different yoga center. Mac got mixed up with this gal from up near Hale's Vineyard. She was bad news. We all thought so, but then we all love Mac, so we might be a little protective of him. But we were right about her. She's serving time in prison for her wrongdoing now."

"Wow, that doesn't sound good." She wondered if that had anything to do with that item in the police blotter that Scott had told her to leave out.

"It wasn't. People always think nothing happens in a small town, but we just know how to keep our business within the town limits."

Savannah wondered how talking within the town limits made it any different. Gossip, news, call it what you want. It traveled.

"It was pretty heartbreaking for Mac, but he's recovered and the new gal that opened the yoga studio there is a transplant from Virginia Beach. Nice girl. A little New Age for folks around here, but I think it's done the town good to have a little dose of health on Main Street."

"To balance out Mac's tasty treats?"

"You've sampled the bear claws, I take it."

"Sampled? No. Inhaled? Maybe."

"They are good. His son makes amazing cakes too. It's been nice to have some new young folks come to town. We're so glad Jenny opened up that yoga studio. We need more young women to move here. Did you know our population is seventy percent men?"

Maybe that was the article she'd write. A town where the odds of finding a man are in the girl's favor. "Really? Now how many of those are of the available type?"

"I don't know, but I do know of a few good catches right off the top of my head."

"Well, it sure seems to be a great town to live in."

"It is."

"And a great town to live out your dream. So if you named the shop Timeless Tea, what would the menu look like?"

Daphne took the bait. She was off the subject of men and that perfect son of hers. This was way more fun anyway. Dreaming up ideas to spend someone else's money was always fun.

"I always thought I could just do a pretty chalkboard with the dailies on it and have the kind of ambiance where my servers share the menu verbally. After a while everyone would know what they wanted, or even better, just always count on me to surprise them."

"I love that idea."

Daphne rolled up the drawing and fit it back in the tube. "Sit down. Let me bring you your tea."

Savannah sat down at the dining room table. "I like the idea of the server bringing the personalized touch. Maybe you could even have local art in the tearoom. I heard someone talking about a painting in the yoga studio. What was it they were saying? I can't remember."

"I'm not even sure I've been in there yet. I'm a little old for twisting myself up like a pretzel. Once I got on the floor I'd likely never get up." Daphne placed both of the cups and saucers on the table.

A loud rap at the door was followed by a man's voice. "Hello, Mom?" The screen door slapped against the frame.

"In here," Daphne called out. She leaned to Savannah and whispered, "That's my son."

Savannah took a sip from her teacup, then lifted

her eyes and looked in the direction of the foot-steps, then almost choked.

Sheriff Scott Calvin strode toward her, pulling his aviator-style mirrored glasses off as he got closer.

Scott stifled a laugh when he saw Savannah practically spit tea across the room. For a second there he thought he might have to resuscitate her.

She recovered pretty quickly, but not without her teacup clanking against the saucer and her spoon hitting the floor. That blush that was rising on her pretty cheeks was about as bright as the sunset on a summer night.

He'd recognized her little blue Mini Cooper straight off. No one in this town owned one of those. He'd even contemplated just rolling on by, knowing full well Mom was up to no good. Again. Wouldn't be the first time, and he'd had that feeling on Sunday too.

Poor Savannah had no idea she was playing the starring role in a made-for-Lifetime movie written by none other than Daphne Calvin.

"Daphne is *your* mother?"

Savannah could've caught butterflies with her mouth dropped wide like that.

"Hi, Mom." He then nodded in Savannah's direction. "Hello to you, again."

Daphne ran her hand though her hair and practically stuttered. "Y'all ha-have met?" She looked confused.

Savannah stammered. "We have. W-we met by accident. Sort of."

"It was no accident. You were speeding."

She slanted her body away from him. "Just seven miles an hour over."

Daphne tilted her head and gave Savannah one of those shame-on-you looks. "Well, technically that is speeding, Savannah, and it *is* his job."

Mom took his job as seriously as he did. He'd grown accustomed to that shame-on-you look over the years, but he could see it was affecting Savannah just like it used to affect him back in the day.

His mother's expression softened, and she stepped closer, placing herself right between the two of them. She reached out to take one of their hands in each of her own, connecting them, and Scott wished he could lock his mom away in one of those jail cells when she got on these obsessions.

"So y'all have met. That's so wonderful. Scott, did you know that Savannah and her mother used to have tea parties? I can't believe I've met someone who loves tea as much as I do."

"No one could possibly be as crazy about tea and teapots as you are, Mom."

"I thought the same thing, but here she is."

Mom was up to no good. Wasn't the first time. Wouldn't be the last. If he was polite, maybe Savannah would take the cue and be on her way. "I know very little about our new visitor except that she seems to be crossing my path at every turn."

"Fate." Daphne smiled. "It could totally be fate. Hmm. Maybe Pearl Clemmons is doing a little angel matchmaking again."

"Pearl. I heard about Pearl," Savannah said. "She sounded like quite a lady."

"She was the best matchmaker this town ever had," Daphne explained. "You'd have loved Pearl Clemmons. She passed on a while back, but she's still in our hearts. You met her granddaughter."

"Jill?"

"Yes, Jill. Sweet girl, and her grandmother was the heart of this town. Still is, really. No one will ever forget that woman."

"She's not any more special than you are, Mom." He shot Savannah a smile.

"Mom, are you ready to go to your doctor appointment?"

"Oh, Scott. I'm so sorry. I forgot to call and let you know that they called and rescheduled my appointment just this morning. Dr. Bostic had some kind of emergency."

Sure he did. Just how much of a pushover did she think he was? "An eye exam emergency?"

"Well, of course not. Something else. Anyway, I'm so sorry I didn't call and tell you. But since you're here . . . I've got plenty of tea, and look, I even made your very favorite little ham-and-Swiss quiches."

His mom was already scurrying around, and it was quite clear that she'd invited him here at this time specifically with a little hookup with the new stranger in town in mind. Pearl wasn't the only matchmaker in Adams Grove.

Scott popped a baby quiche in his mouth and chewed in silence. His mom was still scurrying, but Savannah wasn't saying a word and as long as he kept popping quiches, he wouldn't have to either.

"Your mom is great."

He nodded, still chewing.

Savannah looked like she wanted to crawl under a table. "I'm sorry about this. I had no idea she was up to—"

"Don't apologize. I know she was the one behind it. It's fine. She's just anxious about grandchildren. I'm getting used to her trying to help me out in that department."

"It's sweet."

"It's a pain in the ass. Want to swap moms?" Something that looked a bit like panic flickered in Savannah's eyes. She looked so vulnerable in that fleeting moment that he wanted to pull her into his arms. Hold her. Tell her that whatever that was, it was only a memory. But that look disappeared as quickly as it had arrived. The wall was back up. It was like watching a windshield wiper sweep away the emotion.

"I wish." She lowered her eyes and her thick lashes seemed to touch her cheeks. He knew that

171

whatever he'd seen a moment ago was something she wasn't ready to talk about.

"Mom means well. I'll keep her."

Savannah smiled. "Did you decide if you're going to the award ceremony or not?"

He knew she'd change the subject. He was a skilled negotiator—he could take her right back there if he wanted to, but somehow he knew that was a painful place for her and he didn't want to be the one to escort her there. "I'm going. You're right. It's a good thing to do in an election year, and in a small town I have to pull from resources across the state all the time. It'll be good for me to renew some of those connections."

"Good. I'm glad you're going." She pursed her lips.

She was struggling to keep the conversation going and keep it off her. He let her wriggle in the silence for a moment. On a two count she'd be filling the space with words. He silently counted: one . . . two.

She said, "I hear that several of the large papers are going to be there."

"How did you hear that?"

She paused.

She was scrambling for an excuse. Years of being on this side of the law had sharpened his ability to read people. She was about to lie, or tell a half-truth.

"I did a little peek online. I was curious."

"Connor said you're writing a book."

She tilted her head in a nod but didn't offer up any details.

Daphne rushed back in with three crystal flutes filled with fresh fruit and whipped cream. "A little sweet something to balance the menu."

"Mom, I've got to run."

"But—"

"Sorry. Things are hectic down at the station today. I'll take a rain check." He grabbed a napkin and stuffed four baby quiches in it before turning and heading out the door.

He could hear his mom apologizing to Savannah as he pulled the door closed behind him.

The summer sun wasn't the only thing making him hot under the collar. She meant well, but he had a job to attend to. He didn't have time for this in the middle of the day.

He'd put his money on his mom not taking the matchmaker crown from Pearl Clemmons if this was the match she'd picked. This was a setup if he'd ever seen one, but he and this city girl had zero chance of working out.

Mom had good taste. Savannah was cute. Pretty, in fact, but that wasn't going to turn that city girl into a country girl, and he had no intention of ever leaving Adams Grove. This was his home.

Chapter SIX

After the visit with Daphne, Savannah couldn't wait to spend more time with her. Yet even though her heart was full of nostalgia, her head was telling her to run for the hills. She didn't need that kind of connection with someone she'd never see again after she left. It was a nice trek down memory lane, but getting lost in that kind of feeling again wasn't in the plan. It was a recipe for disaster, and yet she'd already agreed to help out on Friday. She couldn't back out on that.

Savannah couldn't stop thinking about Scott. He'd spoken softly, and darned if he didn't look sincere, talking to his mother. And taking her to her doctor's appointment. How sweet was that? Momma's voice echoed advice from long ago: *If he treats his momma right, he'll treat you right.*

Her impression of the sheriff softened by the day, and she wasn't sure if it was because she'd been wrong about him, or if meeting Daphne and feeling so at home with her had also had an impact on her opinion of him. That had been right tricky of Daphne to try to set them up. Not effective, but tricky. It sounded just like something Momma would've tried. In fact, that was how she'd met Tripp. Her mom played Bunco with his mom and she just knew they'd be a perfect match, because he seemed like the best catch in Belles Corner to her.

Good-looking. Good job. Scott was apparently pretty good at his job if he was getting an award, and his momma was an absolute sweetheart.

Everyone in Adams Grove seemed to think Sheriff Scott Calvin was the big catch in this town. And it really annoyed her that she couldn't deny that she was beginning to think so too.

She swung her car into an empty space behind the bank building. No sense driving to the news-paper when she could walk off the savory treats Daphne had served up. Besides, whenever she got all stirred up like this, it was best to burn off the anxiety with some exercise.

She must have put well over a thousand miles on her treadmill the year she lost her parents. If she hadn't, she might have had a heart attack from all the stress or died from her sadness. Something she prayed for some days, because Lord knows it would have been easier than dealing with that emptiness, but then who would make sure there were flowers on their graves?

She hopped out of her car and cut through the building to get out on Main Street. A bright-turquoise-colored flyer fluttered in the breeze on the lamppost just outside the law office. The two tacks at the top were working overtime to hang on to the piece of paper since the summer breeze had ripped it from the bottom two. The whole pole was full of old staples and tacks hammered so deep into the soft pine that you'd never get them out.

She stopped to read the flyer. New classes at the yoga studio. They were adding a meditation hour and a smoothie bar Scrabble night. She used to be a kick-butt Scrabble player.

The police blotter entry that Scott was so adamant about nagged at her. Maybe an hour of yoga would do her good, and just a little peek at that painting wouldn't hurt.

She tore one of the tabs with the phone number and details from the flyer and tucked it in her pocket, looking forward to stopping in the yoga studio to check things out. The first class started this afternoon.

Yoga had been on her to-do list for years, but she'd never tried it. If she gave it a whirl here, instead of at her gym at home, at least no one would know her if she looked like a fool trying it. Or maybe she'd be better off sticking to the smoothie night. She couldn't screw that up. When she stopped in the *County Gazette* office, Jack was just sinking his teeth into a huge slice of pizza. The whole room reeked of tomato sauce and pepperoni.

He ran his sleeve across his mouth and just nodded since his mouth was full.

"That pizza smells great!" She tossed the report folder on his desk. "All done."

"Hey. That was fast," he mumbled through that mouthful of pizza. "We have the best pizza joint around. You'll have to try it." He pushed the half-open box toward her. "Have a piece."

"Thanks, but I'm good." She grabbed the latest entries from the police blotter file for good measure. She figured it wasn't worth hurting his or his sister's feelings by telling him that she was getting the electronic version daily from Scott.

"You are fast!"

"We're all squared away, but I have some news for you about Scott Calvin."

"What's up?" He swallowed the mouthful of pizza and then took a slug from a glass of sweet tea that had sweated a pool of water on the desk. "Big bust or something?"

"Nope. The sheriff is being honored up in Arlington tomorrow night. They're presenting him with a pretty impressive award. He said it was for a recent case."

"Isn't that where you're from?"

"It is."

"Is that how you heard about it?"

"No. Actually, I overheard the sheriff on the phone talking about it while I was over there getting answers to some questions for the police blotter. It sounds like a very big deal."

"Ohhhh." Jack's eyes went wide. "I'm not

surprised. He captured the Goto Hell murderer. You had to hear about that one. Made national news." He leaned forward. "We tried to keep it real hush-hush, but some things get out anyway. The town is still in shock about it. It was pretty terrifying to know that a killer like that was making himself at home in our community. Walking right down our streets every day." He dropped his pizza like he'd just lost his appetite. "Sick man." The old man's eyes narrowed. "Frank Gotorow killed at least two women eight years ago. Rumor was there were more, but they couldn't prove it. They called it the Goto Hell Murders. Isn't it weird how some of those sickos just thrive on being famous for those awful things? Anyway, Scott helped catch him. Right here in Adams Grove."

Savannah tried for an over-the-top facial expression so that he'd think he was telling her something she didn't know, and to encourage him to keep filling in the blanks. Everyone had heard about the recapture of that crazy lunatic. Maybe he'd give her some details that hadn't been in the news.

"Mike Hartman and another guy from Virginia Beach had both lost their wives to that sorry excuse of a human. That Gotorow guy came back for revenge. He almost got it too. Mike's girlfriend was the target. With Scott's help, they took the guy down before he could succeed."

"Wow."

Jack's breathing got faster. "Yeah. That guy tried to cause trouble in the wrong town. Mike Hartman had just moved here after getting out of the Marines and his girlfriend had just transferred in as our new extension agent. Nice girl. She used to live in Virginia Beach. It was huge news. Just think. If it had happened somewhere else it could have ended so differently."

"I guess it could have. I can't imagine going through something like that."

Jack nodded toward the pizza box. "It wasn't without loss. I'm not talking about them killing him. That crazy guy deserved to die for all he did, but Goto killed one of the young guys who worked at the pizza joint." He pointed to his pizza. "Made it look like a fire and planted his information on him, so people would think it was him. Neighbors said that Goto had been staying in that boy's apartment for weeks. Heartless."

"No surprise they're recognizing your sheriff for that. If he hadn't stopped that madman, it could've been another string of murders."

"You got that right."

She chased a shiver, only this time she wasn't acting. It really did give her chills to think that someone that crazy had lived among these nice people, with the intent to do them harm. She needed to meet this girlfriend of her neighbor's. "Well, I figured you'd want to send someone to cover the story. So I wanted to get over here and let you know. Glad I did. It's an even bigger deal than I'd thought." She turned to leave, but before she could get to the door he was hollering her way.

"Wait! I don't have anyone to send." He gulped from his glass of tea. "You've got to do this for me."

"Me?"

"Yes. I can't go. I have to cover things here. Plus you're from up that way. You'll know how to get around in that town and act right around all that pomp and circumstance."

She laughed. "Look, I don't mind helping out with the police blotter. I can even watch things here at the office for you, but I have things I have to do. Plus, I'm not so sure my editor is going to like the idea of me covering actual stories." She put her hand on the doorknob.

"Please! Wait."

There was nothing worse than a man begging. But seriously, how do you say no to an old man? He looked so desperate. She was a marshmallow when it came to saying no.

"You have to help me out. I'll owe you one. I'll give you the full byline on the story and photo credits. You know how to take a picture, don't ya?"

"Of course I know how to take a . . . No . . . I'm not going to that award ceremony. I don't have a hotel reservation or anything."

"Well, then you may as well have not told me." He shoved the rest of the pizza straight into the trash can. Poor guy looked like she'd just about stabbed him in the heart by saying no. That pizza was the symbolic blood of her doings.

"Fine. Fine. I'll do it. If you pick up the cost of the room." She was sure that would be a deal breaker for the low-budget paper.

"Done! It'll be great. I'll call the sheriff and get all the details and make the reservations. The paper will pick up your room. Savannah, you really are saving the day."

"Whoa. No need to call the sheriff. I've got the details right there on that sheet with the police blotter stuff. I'll do it if you don't tell him I'll be the one there covering it."

He paled. "Why not?"

"He's kind of nervous about the whole thing and we don't want to freak him out." Besides that, the last thing she wanted was for him to think she was interested enough to make that kind of effort. She'd zip in, get the pictures and the story, and be done with it.

"Deal. Oh, wait." He dug around in the drawer and pulled out a huge antiquated digital camera. "Here. For the pictures."

She took the camera, but there wasn't any way on earth she planned on using that doggone thing. It had to be one of the first digital cameras ever manufactured. It was huge. She flipped it over and popped out the memory card. That sucker was, like, two inches square. Darn near a floppy disk! She'd use her phone before she'd pull that thing out in public.

"Savannah, I owe you for this. You've been a godsend."

"You're welcome." *Just don't throw me a doggone parade,* she thought. Now to break it to Evelyn, and keep it from Scott. No sense in him getting the wrong idea, like she was interested or something. That's all she needed.

She walked out of the *County Gazette* feeling good about helping Jack out . . . again. The good deeds were making her feel like part of the community, and that made her a little sad that she would be leaving in just a short while.

Savannah did a bicep curl with the camera. It had a neck strap, and needed one, as heavy as it was. She lifted it in the air over her head. It might weigh more than her laptop.

How had she let herself be talked into doing another favor for this town? What was it about these people that she got sucked into their issues so easily?

All the way back to the apartment she tried to figure out how she'd swing an outfit for the award ceremony. It was black tie, but her little black dress was a little too sexy for press credentials.

She'd have to shop or go home and change

there. She had plenty to choose from in her closet, and then she could pick up some casual clothes for the rest of her semi-vacation. She could probably drop off the letters she'd selected for the Van column to Evelyn while she was there too. That would please Evelyn to no end.

She'd insisted Jack pay for a hotel to try to get him to back off, but she could easily have stayed in her apartment. It wasn't but a forty-five-minute drive. The joke was on her . . . again. When would she learn that every time she tried to outwit someone, it backfired on her?

Her phone sounded off with that familiar ring of flying typewriter keys. "Hi, Evelyn. I was just thinking about you."

"Good. You getting ready to send me another story?"

"Soon. Actually, I think I'm going to come back up to the city, just for one night tomorrow."

"You're already bored in that little town? You haven't even given it a chance."

"No. That's not it. Well, maybe a little, but that's not why I'm coming back."

"What's up?"

Savannah tried to sound nonchalant. "Remember that big award ceremony in Arlington tomorrow night?"

"Where your cute sheriff is the guest of honor?"

Savannah felt her stomach flip. Why was she nervous all of a sudden? "The paper here wants me to cover the awards. Do you mind? I mean, I know you want me to write those stories on the sheriff, so I could use it for that too, but I also know it could be a conflict. I'd never—"

"That's fine with me, Savannah. Just be sure to use the time toward those other stories we talked about."

"I can do that. I'll send you a copy of my story too. Just so you know what I'm submitting."

"Good. Either way. I have Franklin covering that event for us. You sound good. Are you getting a chance to relax down there in Adams Grove?"

I would if everybody would quit adding to my to-do list. "A little."

"Chomping at the bit to get back yet?"

"No. Not yet, but I'm going to have to stop by my apartment to get something to wear. There's nowhere to shop for something like that here, and I'd only packed for the wedding. I need a few things for while I'm here anyway."

"Want to get together for dinner?"

"No." *Think fast . . . why not?* She sure couldn't tell her it was because she knew she was going to be frazzled about seeing Scott again. That would get Evelyn started for sure. She was always saying Savannah was too young to be single. The last thing Savannah needed was another cheerleader rooting for Scott Calvin. Daphne was enough to handle on that front. Nothing was going to come of it anyway. Plus, she was a little mad that Evelyn hadn't offered her the story for GINN. "We'll just talk about work if we do."

"That's true."

"I picked out some letters from what you sent over. I'll drop those off for you while I'm in town."

"Thanks. I appreciate you doing that. Maybe now Andrew can actually write something. I swear he's been sitting out there in that cube staring at the computer screen ever since you left. Not sure he's going to be cut out for this. Not your problem, though."

She hoped that would remain the case.

"Now get to work and write me those stories."

"I'm on it. Thought of an interesting angle yesterday about the ratio of men to women in small towns. Could be fun."

Evelyn let out a happy shriek. "Oh, my goodness. That could be great, like a twenty-first-century *Looking for Mr. Goodbar*, only more like looking for Mr. . . ."

"Mr. Feed and Seed?"

"That's hysterical."

Not talking stories was nearly impossible for the two of them.

"I've got to run. I'll drop that stuff off to you tomorrow."

Savannah hung up the phone. She and Franklin had never really gotten along. He was way too big for his britches. She'd found out the hard way when she'd given in and gone out on a date with him. Big mistake. He was always on shaky ground with Evelyn. He'd tried a couple of times to better his reputation by trying to sully hers. Thank goodness, Evelyn knew better. Savannah could do without his tacky come-ons too. The guy would never give up. Hopefully, she could stay out of his sights at the dinner.

He'd give his eyeteeth to be in Evelyn's good graces . . . or better yet, Savannah's eyeteeth!

Savannah worked on the second article for GINN for a little while, but the truth was she couldn't get her mind off that police blotter entry that Scott had told her to forget about. It kept nagging at her. She glanced at the clock. She had just enough time to get to that class over at Happy Balance. She was already in her yoga pants. She could totally still make it. Work, or research?

She didn't even need to flip a coin to decide. She jumped from her chair and got the rest of her clothes to match the pants, then ran down the stairs. Mike was just getting ready to climb the stairs when she hit the bottom step.

"Where are you off to in such a big hurry?"

She hopped to the landing. "I'm going to check out the yoga class."

"Oh, you'll probably like it. My girlfriend's best friend runs the place."

That caught Savannah's attention. "Really? What's her name?"

"Jenny. She and Brooke moved here from Virginia Beach not long ago."

Just as Jack had said. "I'll have to look for her."

"Good luck with that class. I went down there one night. I thought that slow yoga stuff would be for sissies, but I have to tell you it about kicked my ass."

"I'll let you know how it goes."

He grabbed the railing and began to head upstairs. "You do that."

She stepped out onto the sidewalk wondering if she should have stuck to the Scrabble smoothie plan.

It was only a short walk to the yoga studio, but she didn't know if she'd need to register, so she didn't dawdle. When she grabbed the handle of the heavy wooden storefront door, there must have been at least twenty people already there. A few sipped smoothies while the die-hards were already on their mats stretching or meditating. She wandered through the space, checking out the artwork on the walls. None of them seemed too extra special. In fact, most were just sayings and quotes with silhouettes of people in various poses. Unless you called the corpse pose a threat, she wasn't seeing anything to worry about. Maybe Scott was right. She shrugged off the nagging doubt and focused on the opportunity to give something new a try.

"Can I help you?" asked a pretty gal dressed in

black yoga pants and a nearly transparent flowing, colorful top over a black camisole. The top was so wispy it made her look as delicate as a butterfly.

"Yes. I'm just in town visiting. I've never done yoga, but always wanted to try. I thought I'd do that today. Here."

"Perfect! I'd love that. I'm Jenn. I own the place."

"Nice to meet you. I'm Savannah. You must be Brooke's best friend."

"You know Brooke?" Her face lit up.

"Not exactly. I'm renting the apartment next to her boyfriend. He mentioned it."

"Mike is amazing. Come with me. I'll show you the locker room so you can put your keys and stuff away. Then, we'll get you a mat, and trust me . . . you are going to love this. Don't over-extend, just move however your body lets you."

"I'm probably going to make a fool of myself."

"No! Oh, no. You just get into your zone. Trust me, the people around you just fall away when you get to the right place. No one is watching you. No one is judging you. I promise."

"I might have to live here then."

"I know what you mean."

Savannah cast a sweeping look around the space. "You've got some nice artwork in here."

Jenn looked around. "I wanted to create something peaceful and uplifting."

"You've accomplished that."

"Thanks." Jenn turned and backed into the door to the locker room, pushing it open with her rear end. "This is the locker room. All of the lockers have a key already in the lock for you. Just take one." Jenn dug a melon-colored wristband with her logo on it from her pocket. "You can just slip the key right into the little pocket on this. My gift to you just for showing up to try."

"Thank you. That's a great idea." Savannah slipped off her shoes and put them in the locker. "That mural is amazing." And this time it wasn't just small talk. The painting covered every square inch of the wall and extended right up to the ceiling into one of those sky murals that made you forget you were inside, like the ones at the Venetian in Vegas.

Jenn sucked in a breath. "Long story about that."

"Must have cost a fortune."

"Nope. Barely cost a thing, actually." Jenn scrunched her lips and stared at the mural. "That should have clued me in that something was wrong. I thought I was being a brilliant barterer. It is pretty, though. You should see the one in the men's locker room. You think this is amazing. That one is . . ." Her voice trailed off and she didn't even finish her sentence. "Come on." Jenn led the way to a rack full of yoga mats. "Pick one."

Savannah picked out a purple mat and followed

Jenn back out front. She wondered if the murals had anything to do with that message. She cursed herself for getting caught up in the idea that there was something behind that police blotter entry. Scott had already said it was nothing, and he sure did have his thumb on the pulse of this town.

"Do I need to fill out any paperwork or anything?"

Jenn shook her head. "No. Just enjoy your afternoon with us and catch up with me at the smoothie bar afterwards. Deal?"

"Deal."

"Class starts in about five minutes."

Savannah hung back. "I'll be right there. I just want to enjoy this painting for a moment."

Jenn gave her an awkward smile, then one of the other ladies grabbed her and they walked out of the locker room together talking about the intricacies of something that must have been a yoga move, because it wasn't anything she'd ever heard of before.

Leaning against her locker, Savannah examined the painting. It was truly beautiful art. There wasn't one evil thing about it that she could see. Even the colors were peaceful. Colorful hot air balloons filled a perfect sky. Different shapes and colors. There were the regular lightbulb-shaped ones, and fancy ones, like one that looked like a sunflower, another that looked like Darth Vader, and one that looked like a cabin that was so intricate that she wondered if they could really even fly a balloon with so many chambers.

As the room began to empty, Savannah headed out to the main room and took a spot in the far back corner.

An hour later Savannah felt like she'd had one of the best workouts she'd ever been through, and yet there hadn't been one pounding running move or one grunting lift. She hit the locker room, took a quick shower, and then memorized that mural as she toweled off. No matter how she tried to twist the bright colors or images into some sort of symbolism, it didn't make sense that this would upset anyone. Even the clouds were playful shapes. The one in the far right that had a stormy color to it looked like a squishy, soft stuffed bunny. She gathered her things and went out to the smoothie bar.

A huge container of cucumber water sat on the end of the brightly colored counter, where Jenn and another gal were pushing smoothies across to a few of the people who had been in the class and a couple of folks who seemed to have just stopped in for one.

Jenn waved to Savannah. "I made one of my special JB smoothies for you."

"JB?"

"Jenn's Balance." She winked as she handed the bright-purple concoction across the bar.

"What's the use of having your own business if you can't name some cool stuff after yourself?"

"Thanks," Savannah said, and took a sip from the neon pink straw. "Very good." She took another sip. "You know, I have an amazing recipe for a protein brownie. They'd be perfect for in here."

"Well, aren't you just a little Rachael Ray or something."

"No, but Momma would have given that little girl a run for her money. There was a time when my favorite thing was to be in that kitchen with my mom."

A short brunette walked into the studio wearing a pair of jeans and a suit jacket. "Hey." She joined them at the bar. "What's up?"

"Brooke, meet someone new in town. This is Savannah. She just moved in with your boyfriend."

Brooke's eyes went wide.

"Not like that," Savannah said, trying to stop the joke before it went too far, besides the writer in her would die to hear her side of the story of that abduction. Looking at the pretty girl, she couldn't even imagine something so awful happening to her. "You must be Mike's girlfriend. I'm renting the apartment next to his."

Brooke extended her hand. "Nice to meet you. We're pretty new to town still too."

"Oh, I didn't move here. I'm just renting the apartment for a week."

"Mike mentioned he had a neighbor and that

he'd kind of blasted you half out of the apartment your first morning there."

"It was no big deal. I was up; in fact, it was pretty good timing. I'd just been working and thinking I needed some music when he started rocking out. There wasn't a radio in there, so it worked out kind of nice actually."

Brooke winced. "He does love that classic rock."

"It was fine. I like my rock a little more Southern, but he happened to pick the right song for my mood that morning."

"Me too," Brooke said. "If you like country music, you ought to come down to the barn dance this weekend."

"You should come," Jenn said.

"Maybe I will."

"Everyone will be there." Brooke hopped up on one of the stools.

Savannah said, "A lot happens in this little town of yours. I was at the parade this weekend."

Jenn smiled wide. "Is Hillcrest Joyful Kixx not the most beautiful creature you've ever laid eyes on?"

Brooke nudged Jenn. "That's just because you own part of him."

"Really?" That piqued Savannah's interest. She'd always thought only the rich and famous owned racehorses. "I overheard someone saying y'all are moving him here to Adams Grove. That's pretty cool. Do you live on a farm nearby?"

Jenn poured a glass of water. "Oh, I live upstairs. No room for a racehorse here. I just own a piece of him. My boyfriend and I recently bought interest in him. Cody Tuggle's mother raised him. She has several racehorses. She's moving her whole operation here."

"A piece of a racehorse is still more than most people ever even dream of owning," Savannah said.

Jenn's lips pursed. "Come to think of it, maybe I should have asked which piece. I probably own an elbow or something."

"Maybe you're better off not knowing," Savannah said.

They all laughed, and Savannah was enjoying getting to know Brooke and Jenn. She really didn't have any girlfriends her age, and this had turned out to be relaxing and fun. Maybe it was the yoga that had her so chilled out.

"You mentioned you're new in town. How did you and Mike meet?" she asked Brooke.

"I was doing farm visits. I'm the extension agent here. Mike was watching over the farm where Cody's mom is going to be moving. There was an instant attraction." Brooke looked starry-eyed.

"I was talking to someone the other day who said there are way more men in this town than women. That must have worked out for you."

"For Jenn too. We both met guys since we've been here. Maybe you should stick around."

"Or not. I'm not sure I'm the relationship type. I've been married before."

Brooke nodded. "I know exactly what you mean. My first marriage was a disaster. I thought if I ever got out of it, I'd never even date again. But I guess you have to be careful about those 'never' statements. They have a way of biting you in the butt and proving you wrong."

"I don't think that will happen in my case," Savannah said. "But I won't say never . . . just so I don't jinx it."

"Good plan," Brooke said.

"So that was pretty lucky that your horse won the Derby. That's a big deal," Savannah said.

"I know, right? Only it was a weird day." Jenn shivered. "Best and worst night of my whole life."

"Yours?" Brooke half laughed, but Savannah could tell there wasn't anything funny about what had gone down that night. "You weren't the one he ambushed."

"I'll be right back," Jenn said as she walked behind the last few stragglers leaving the building to lock up for the day.

"She gets freaked out when I talk about it."

"Somebody ambushed you?"

"I'd just moved here. My ex-husband was harassing me so I'd hired Mike to put that to rest. Turned out getting to know Mike put me in more danger than I'd been in before I hired him. Not his fault, though. His wife had been killed by Frank Gotorow and he'd helped put that madman away back then. Only he got out of prison somehow and come back for revenge."

Savannah admired the girl's strength. "You were in the way."

"Or an easier target probably," she said. "He abducted me and held me, half-drugged as bait. Knowing the whole story now, I believe he was trying to re-create what he'd done to Mike's first wife. I was pretty out of it, but still so scared. But I can't even imagine what Mike felt. It hurts my heart to think of that."

"I'm sure it does. That had to be terrifying."

"It was. Had everything not gone exactly according to plan, I might not be sitting here with you today. The governor is giving our sheriff and my Mike an award for their heroism for what they did that night. They risked their lives to save mine."

"I remember it being in the news. It kind of came and hushed really fast, though. I didn't realize that was you. I'm so sorry. Are you doing okay? How do you get over something like that?"

"I'm not sure yet," Brooke admitted.

"Can you imagine the book that would make?" She wasn't even sure where that thought came from, and it really wasn't very sensitive of her to blurt it out like that. The girl had gone through a terrible trauma.

"I already had some big publisher call about that. I won't write about it. Won't give that guy the satisfaction of getting his story in front of every-one. He'd have loved that." Brooke looked over toward Jenn, who was taking her time getting back. "The truth is, the more I talk about it the better I feel, but Jenn gets so freaked out when I do."

"If you need someone to chat with . . . I'm here for a little while. I'd be happy to be your sounding board. And when I'm gone. Call me. Really. We all need someone in our corner to just listen." Savannah felt suddenly close to Brooke.

"Yeah, I'd like to bend your ear about it." She tilted her head toward Jenn, who was saying good-bye to the last couple of people. "She's still more freaked out than me, but then he had me out of it most of the time. She was the one watching and worrying as it all went down."

"I'm so sorry that happened to you. I read all about it in the papers. You just don't expect that kind of thing to happen in this kind of a town, do you?"

"No." Brooke's tension eased a little. "But the bad guy was the only one to die that night, so that has to say something about being in the right place at the right time."

"You've got that right," Savannah said. "I remember when he first went on that spree all those years ago."

Jenn rejoined them at the bar. "Did she tell you how he was living right here in this building?"

"Frank Gotorow?" Savannah asked.

"Yeah," Jenn said with a roll of her eyes. "Don't ask me to choose your friends. I obviously have a knack for sniffing out the crazies."

"Great. So I shouldn't feel honored that you invited me right in and treated me like you've known me my whole life?"

Jenn laughed. "Probably not!"

Brooke laughed at that too. "You're different."

"Well, thank you," Savannah said. "On a brighter note, I love what you've done with this place. It's so peaceful. I swear I could just sit and stare at that mural all day."

Brooke glanced at Jenn. "Not many people know this, but there's a story behind the man who painted those beautiful murals in the locker rooms."

Savannah kept her mouth shut. As hard as it was, she didn't want to say anything that might keep them from talking.

"You saw the one in the ladies' locker room. Great, huh?"

"Amazing."

"Frank Gotorow. The Goto Hell Murderer painted that mural for me." Jenn shook her head. "That one and the one in the men's locker room too. I let him right in. Paid him and let him crash here while he worked on them. He seemed like a quiet, quirky guy. I was so proud to barter that deal."

Savannah saw the shiver go through Brooke.

"You can't be serious. That women's locker room is gorgeous. So peaceful. I've got a fear of heights and I'm ready to book a hot air balloon ride after seeing it. How could someone like him paint something so serene?"

Jenn put her head down on the bar. "I know. I can still hardly believe it. If I hadn't seen him physically do it, I wouldn't believe it. I watched him work though. And he didn't look the least bit evil."

"Oh, but if you'd seen the painting he did where he held me captive you'd know he was nothing short of the spawn of the devil. That stuff was freaky," Brooke said.

"That stuff was alien-like. I can't even think about that." Jenn seemed to try to blank the images from her mind. "It's still hard for me to wrap my head around it." Suddenly, she whipped out from behind the bar. And headed for the locker rooms. "Come. You've got to see the one he did in the men's locker room."

All three girls raced to the back. Jenn gave a courtesy knock. "Coming in. Cover up." She poked her head inside and led them through the door labeled WARRIORS. "All's clear."

The three of them filed inside and stood side by side in front of the mural. Like the other one, this covered every wall space and even a few of the lockers.

Chills climbed right up Savannah's spine. The

199

serene rural setting was painted across the entire wall. Colorful flowers filled a countryside near a small pond where deer drank water so realistic that you just knew it was icy cold. The sky was Carolina blue and extended right on up to the ceiling, where a few clouds floated by.

"Did you just get a shiver?" Brooke asked.

"I did." How had she known?

"I know. Right?" She pointed her finger between herself and Jenn. "Us too. Every time we stand here."

"It's so realistic." Savannah ran her hand up and down her arm to chase the chill. "It's just as beautiful as the one in the ladies' locker room, but there's something different about this one. Or is it just me?"

Both girls agreed. "No. It's not just you," Jenn said.

Savannah stepped closer, reaching toward the wall. "That shiver isn't like the awe you feel in front of a beautiful painting. It's different. I don't know. It's like . . ."

Jenn's voice was steady. "More like it wants to hold you here."

Savannah's words came out as a whisper. "And not let you go." She pulled her fingers back.

"I keep saying I'm going to buy a five-gallon bucket of paint and just paint right over them," Jenn said.

Brooke and Savannah both shook their heads.

"No." Brooke tilted her head. "No. I don't think it's time for that yet."

Jenn walked over to the far end of the room, where a long bench straddled the space in front of the lockers. "He was staying right here in this building. I was sleeping in the same building as he was. I wonder if I'd even locked my doors at night. A million things I've wondered about. He painted the murals and I let him stay here and gave him a couple hundred dollars. I thought it was the best deal ever."

Savannah raised a brow. "Well, you got more than your money's worth."

Jenn swallowed hard. "Yeah, but I almost got my best friend killed in the process."

Brooke shook her head and sat on the bench. "That had absolutely nothing to do with you, Jenn. I've told you that a hundred times. If he hadn't stayed here, it wouldn't have changed a thing. Don't lay that guilt trip on yourself."

Savannah dropped to the bench too. She wanted a story, but she sure didn't expect something like this.

Brooke's mouth curled as if it made her sick to remember that day. "He'd painted every single wall in that little shack where he held me." Brooke pointed to the mural. "The crisp colors are the only thing even remotely similar. The mural he painted there was full of rage." She stared at the mural. "So different."

201

"Is it still there?" Savannah wished she could take back the words.

Both girls looked at each other, then shrugged. "Don't know," Jenn said.

"Probably." Brooke looked to Savannah. "We could see."

Jenn shook her head. "No. We need to leave that place in the past."

Savannah tilted her head. "This is beautiful, but there *is* something unsettling about it. They say there's a fine line between good and evil. Maybe he had multiple personalities."

Brooke agreed. "It takes a sociopath to convince a parole board that he's changed after what he did. Even then, it's amazing he got paroled. Scott's been running that down. Someone did something wrong in that chain of events."

Jenn folded her arms tighter across her chest. "I think that guy wasn't straddling the good and evil lines; I think he was saddled right up on the crazy evil-genius side. Not a speck of good in that one."

"Genius?" Brooke laughed. "If he'd been a genius, I doubt they'd have caught him."

Jenn stared at the painting. "Or maybe . . . he really . . . is . . . two people?"

"Are you okay?" Brooke's voice rose.

Savannah felt the concern in Brooke's question. Jenn's focus seemed to go right through the painting. Had she just crossed the crazy line too?

"Holy . . ." Jenn's mouth hung open.

"What is it?"

"Two people," Jenn said.

"You really think it was two different people? Like he had a twin?" Savannah asked.

"No." Jenn's hand rose to about shoulder height and then she reached. "No. He was definitely just one person. There are two people in this painting. Come look at this. I wasn't going to say anything before, because I thought I'd imagined it. You know, like some post-traumatic something or other, but no . . . This is real. I can see it perfectly clear now." Her gaze never shifted.

Savannah said, "You're kind of freaking me out, Jenn."

Brooke rushed to Jenn's side and stooped to try to get level with where Jenn was staring. "What?"

"I can't tell you."

"Why?" Brooke wrapped an arm around Jenn's shoulders. "It's okay."

"Because if you don't see it . . . you're going to pretend you do just to make me feel okay. Plus you'll think I'm crazy."

"I'm your best friend, Jenn. I know you're crazy."

"Brooke. I'm not kidding."

Savannah wished like heck she'd listened to Scott and kept her nose out of that stupid police blotter comment. Maybe Jenn was the one spreading that rumor. She wished now she'd just stayed home. Being bored waiting for the time to

203

pass seemed a lot better than what she was feeling right now. Because what she was feeling right now . . . she couldn't explain. But she couldn't very well just up and leave now either. She sucked in a breath and walked over to where the girls huddled at the end of the bench.

Brooke spoke softly, trying to soothe her friend's panic. "Fine. I'm looking. It looks the same from here to me. Are you looking at the—"

"No!" Savannah spit the word out like a bitter pill. "It's not the same, Brooke. Jenn, I see two people; it's like there are ghost images in that picture!"

Jenn's face was an odd combination of fear and relief. "Yes! You do see it?"

"I do. Jenn, I see something else." Savannah couldn't believe she hadn't noticed it straight off, because it seemed so clear once you saw it.

"Me too," Jenn said.

"A tombstone with amazingly detailed wreaths around it. Lots of them. Like three deep."

Jenn sucked in an audible gasp and reached her hand toward Savannah without shifting her gaze.

The two girls held hands.

Brooke shifted positions. "I don't see anything. If y'all are playing a trick on me, this isn't funny."

Savannah spoke slowly. "Can you make out the name? I can't make out the name on the headstone. The first letter might be a *B*."

"It better not be my name." Brooke's voice

shook. "Please tell me it's not my name on that grave."

"No. The *B* is not a *B*. I think it's an *S*. It's not you," Jenn said as she turned to Savannah with a look of relief. "Thank God it's not just me seeing it."

Brooke looked aggravated. "I don't know what you two are seeing, but Jenn, how did you even figure this out?"

"I was changing the air diffuser in here. If I change the scents each day, they seem to keep the place smelling fresh instead of like an air freshener. These stinky men exhaust this sucker fast. The first time I only saw the image of the flowers. I thought it was nice. Then, when I saw it again, I saw the rest and I thought maybe it was my imagination because I was tired and I'd been worried about everything we'd been through. Plus when I tried to see it again, I couldn't."

"You can't see it all the time?" Brooke took a step back. "Now you're kind of freaking *me* out. Are we talking like a real ghost here?"

"No. It's not like that. It's in the painting. I'm sure of it. I can see it all the time now that I know what's there. Even from different angles."

Brooke's brows pulled together. "Like those 3-D pictures where you can see two things?"

"Kind of, but not really. It's hard to explain."

Brooke looked determined to rationalize it. "Was it painted underneath the other painting?

Like maybe he started painting something different and painted over it? Why am I the only one who can't see anything?"

"I don't know, but what I do know is that the room was a blank canvas when he got started. I had scrubbed the walls down myself. There was nothing there. I don't think this was an accident. Plus, it seems more like it's on top of the other painting, not underneath it."

"Amazing. Almost scary-talented to be able to do that on purpose." Savannah chewed on her lip. "I remember some artist out near Mount Airy in North Carolina who used to do ghost images in his paintings. Not as subtle as this, but it's been done." Savannah knew exactly what that police blotter message was referring to now. This was it. No question about it. "Jenn, has anyone else noticed this that you know of?"

"Only one person made mention of it, but I thought he was crazy," Jenn said.

"Who?" Brooke asked. "And why didn't you ever tell me?"

Savannah reached for Jenn's hand. "Who saw it?"

"He's this guy that lives down on the creek. Old man. They call him Jelly. I let him shower here."

"Girl, you need to be more careful," Savannah said. "You're just asking for trouble letting strange men into your space . . . alone!"

"No. He's harmless. Really. He's got to be like seventy years old. I saw him when I was walking the jogging path in the park. It was so hot. I wanted him to be able to clean up or cool off, get warm, whatever. It was a small thing I could do for him. He showered here for weeks. Then all of a sudden the day after all that happened, he freaked out on me. Said the place was evil. That it was telling him things he couldn't understand."

"Holy mother of . . ." Brooke had tears in her eyes. "Jenn, you should have told me."

"I didn't want to get the speech. I was just trying to do something nice." Jenn shrugged. "He hasn't been back since. I thought he was talking about the building. Now I think he meant the painting. It makes more sense now."

"Maybe Goto was leaving a message for us of some kind," Jenn said. "I hate to say this out loud, but even though he was a little quiet and odd, he was very nice to me. It's still hard to connect him to all that happened in my mind."

"We should ask him about it," Savannah said.

"You gonna drag out an old Ouija board? Goto died that night," Brooke said.

"Not Goto. I meant I'd ask Jelly what he saw in the painting." Savannah walked to the right corner of the wall. "Did Gotorow sign it?"

"Nope. Didn't sign the one in the other room either."

"Hmm." Savannah turned and faced them. "So no one will know unless you tell them."

"The only other person that knows that Goto

painted them is the sheriff. He asked me to not do anything until he had the whole case wrapped up and paperwork done. I asked him to keep it a secret." Jenn wrapped her arms around herself and moved back from the mural. "Savannah, do you see something in the very far left corner?"

Savannah moved next to Jenn and studied the wall. "Do you see random numbers and letters everywhere? Do you see them?" She held a finger up.

Jenn and Brooke stood silent as Savannah looked at the painting. After a long, quiet moment, she turned to Jenn and said, "There's a child. She's huddled in the corner crying."

"Yes." Jenn looked at Brooke. "I really think there's a story behind all of this."

Savannah felt her chest grow tight. "Do you think it's him as a child?"

"No. I think it's a little girl. The curls. And look at the wrist. There's a little bracelet. It's definitely a little girl."

"I see it now. Yes. You're right." Savannah sucked in a breath. "Wow."

"What are you thinking?" Jenn asked Savannah.

"That we need to figure this out. It's like it was left for us."

"He didn't leave it for me. I can't see a thing." Brooke looked at Savannah and then back to Jenn. "This is between you two. Should we call in Mike and Scott?"

Both Jenn and Savannah answered, "No!"

"Okay, well I don't know what *this* is, but I'm in it with the two of you. But if it seems the least bit dangerous . . . we're telling Scott and Mike."

"Fine." Jenn added, "And Rick. But until then, this is just between the three of us."

Savannah's wheels were spinning like a race car's. Her thoughts practically smoked. This would be one hell of a story to write about.

The beautiful side of a madman.

Maybe she *would* write this story someday. Momma's voice echoed in her mind. *You never know what doors will open up in front of you if you open yourself up to new opportunities and change.*

Of course, that would mean she'd have to be open to opening up. Until now she'd never allowed herself to even think about opening up. Not once since Momma and Dad died. The day of their funeral, it was like her whole life had been zipped up into a hazmat bag. Maybe it was more like a body bag.

Keeping things static in her life, safe, wasn't an accident. It was intentional. She thought she was protecting herself in her predictable and planned life.

Had that been a mistake? Maybe being safe was keeping her from living the life she'd been meant to live.

Chapter SEVEN

On the familiar drive north on I-95, Savannah couldn't stop thinking about the images in that mural. A painting in a painting—it had to mean something. She wished she had the talent to sketch out what she was seeing, but stick people weren't going to cut it, and she wasn't even good at drawing them.

As she recalled the specific images, she used the voice recorder on her iPhone to take note of even the smallest details she'd noticed. It was a staggering amount of information. Especially just going on memory. She couldn't wait to get back and really study it, and then compare it to what Jenn saw.

She stopped by the Hilton Arlington to check in before heading to her apartment to change and then drop off the letters to Evelyn.

As soon as she swung into the parking lot of the hotel, she spotted Scott's baby-blue Thunderbird. It was parked out on the second row, next to the curb, and there was no mistaking it with the vanity tag GR8SCOT.

Nerves raced in her tummy, making her wish she hadn't stopped and gotten those French fries on the way. If she bumped into Scott now, she'd have some explaining to do. He'd probably think she was following him, or worse . . . interested. She sat there debating with herself over what to do.

The front door of the hotel opened, and out walked Scott Calvin.

She dropped down in her seat like she'd just dodged a bullet. Peeking over the steering wheel, she prayed he wouldn't look in her direction. Her blue Mini Cooper stood out less here than it did in Adams Grove, but it wasn't that inconspicuous. She prayed he wouldn't even look in her direction.

He didn't.

She watched until he cleared the parking lot, then let out the breath she'd been holding. She grabbed her purse and jogged inside. With one eye on the front door, she registered and got her room key.

The young man behind the counter was eager to please. "Here you go, Ms. Dey. We have free Internet and complimentary coffee in the morning until nine. The gym—"

"Thank you so much." She snagged the key from his hand and practically ran out the door. Her heart was still pounding when she got to her car. She slung open the door and dropped into the seat in hysterics. That desk clerk probably thought she was a real nut job, or on the run. Nervous, sweating, eyes darting . . . yeah, it couldn't have looked good. If they pulled that security tape for any reason, she'd be at the head of the suspicious character list for sure.

Something about that little race against the clock to avoid Scott had lifted her spirits. She couldn't wipe the smile from her face, nor did she want to. She started her car and headed for the interstate.

She didn't even mind getting stuck in DC traffic, for a change. Instead, she cranked up the radio and sang along. If she was late, she was late. No big deal.

By the time she got to the office, Evelyn had already left for the day. Savannah grabbed a sticky note and wrote a hello and good luck and clipped it to the stack of letters. She had her doubts that Andrew Jones would make it as her replacement, but she was going to stay out of it. If she criticized the poor guy every step of the way, she'd surely never get to leave Advice from Van behind.

The short distance from the office to her apartment took nearly thirty minutes. It was why she usually walked to work. It just wasn't worth the headache of the slow-moving snarl, and she had things to do. Plus she could pick up what she needed from the store each evening. It made for easy shopping that way.

There was nowhere to park on the whole block this afternoon. Ever since the new day spa had opened up around the corner, daytime parking had been a nightmare. She parked the next block over and walked.

The apartment was stuffy from being closed up for the last few days. She cranked the AC down to sixty-eight to get it cooling down and then went to her bedroom and dropped her purse on the bed.

Her closet was jammed with clothes, some still with the tags and others still in the dry cleaner bags. She pushed the hangers to the far left and started whipping through the outfits to find some possibilities.

She laid three dresses out on the bed to choose from for tonight and then tugged a few shirts and jeans from their hangers to pack. Once she'd filled her suitcase with enough to keep her in casual wear for the next few days, she jumped in the shower to get ready.

With her hair in a towel, she tried on all three dresses. The first one was her favorite, but it was bright red and there wasn't one thing subtle about it. If she thought for a second she might get through the night without being noticed, this was not the dress to wear.

The green dress made her eyes light up, but it had gotten wrinkled in the closet and she didn't have time to press it before she left, so she slipped on the simple navy-blue dress. It fit fine and it was understated. A small row of blue-on-blue gem-stones dressed it up without looking too fancy.

Her time was running short. If she was going to make it back to Arlington and to the event on time, she was going to have to hurry. Rather than fuss with her hair, she blew it to a damp-dry and then pulled it into a loose chignon. Lipstick and one tissue blot and she was nearly ready to go.

She slipped on a pair of navy-blue pumps and then stood in front of the full-length mirror that had once been her mother's. Sometimes when she looked at herself it was like looking straight at the memory of her mother. Tonight was one of those times. "Miss you, Momma."

Twisting to the side, and satisfied with the look, she gathered her things to leave.

Part of her wished Scott might get to see her looking like this tonight, but then there was that Cinderella dream that always tested her sensibilities.

Stick to the plan, Van.

Scott hadn't been in the ballroom more than fifteen minutes when someone had scooped him up and shuffled him over to meet some of the guests. If somebody had told him a week ago that he'd be standing here talking to the governor he never would have believed it, but here he was.

It was no secret that there was quite a buzz about how Frank Gotorow had even made parole, and the governor's office was just one of the offices under scrutiny following what had happened in

Adams Grove. Although it hadn't been the intent to kill Frank Gotorow in the process, Scott had to wonder just how relieved some of these high-ranking officials were about how the whole thing went down. At least this way they could pretty much make up whatever story they needed to cover the scandal without worry that Frank Gotorow would leak what had really happened, especially if any special favors had been thrown around as speculated.

It was hard to stand there and take praise for just doing his job. There wasn't an officer or sheriff in the country who wouldn't have done what he'd done to protect his community, or they shouldn't be in the job. Truth was, the crazies tripping into your territory was just a crapshoot. No town, big or small, was safe from that. He'd just gotten the lucky, or not so lucky, draw of Frank Gotorow following Mike Hartman to Adams Grove.

The people he was being introduced to tonight were folks he'd likely never cross paths with again. Big money. Big names. Big egos. Women hung close to their men in their finest clothes, dripping with jewelry like done-up Christmas trees. Senator Macon's daughter was among them, and she had caught his eye as soon as she'd walked up, but he'd talked himself right out of that car crash quick. He was not senator son-in-law material. He didn't want to be under the scrutiny of the state based on every political rant or trend of the time either. That was one risk he wasn't willing to even dabble with.

He'd tired of the idle chitchat thirty minutes ago. He'd never thought he'd be wishing for some rubbery chicken, but if they could just sit down, eat, and get on with this . . . it would suit him just fine.

The place had filled with press. The local television affiliates were even in attendance. Scott wished he hadn't given in and come.

A brunette was taking pictures from across the way. Her hair was pulled up, and her blue dress hung in a simple line that showed a nice curve from waist to hip. Subtle, not showing too much, like some of the girls in the room. He liked it when they left something to his imagination. And his was stirring.

He wondered what Savannah would look like in a sexy dress like that. The girl had her build.

He watched as she talked. Her hands moved in an exaggerated way as she did, and her dress swished from side to side with her movements. Graceful. He could imagine dancing with her. Guiding her across the floor. Holding her in his arms. Maybe he'd get her on the dance floor later. If not, it would just be a night of bland chicken, awards, and a big waste of time as far as he was concerned. Then again, if the time spent here tonight garnered a few extra favors over the next year, his small town could benefit. Reason enough to suck it up.

The senator's daughter interrupted his ogling. "I'm here to show you where your table is, Sheriff. Come with me."

"Thank you." He followed her to the table of honor, where he joined some of the same people he'd already been talking to for the last hour. She hung close for a moment, and he wasn't sure if she had planned to sit at that table or not. "Can I get your chair?"

"Oh, no. I'm sitting over there with my sister and her husband." She pointed to a table and waved. An older version of the woman he was looking at waved back.

He'd seen that look between sisters or girl-friends before. Clearly she'd been put up to connecting with him. He gave the girl a nod. "Well, thank you for the escort."

"You're welcome. I think they'll be serving in about another ten minutes if you still want to mingle. I'd love to talk to you more after the dinner."

"Thank you, but I have to get right on the road after."

"I see." She looked disappointed. "Well, it was really nice to meet you."

He watched the look on her sister's face as she turned to leave. Did women really think guys weren't onto them?

A waiter whisked between him and the gentleman seated to his left, filling the water and tea glasses in front of each of them, and disappeared just as quickly.

By the time Scott turned around, the pretty girl in blue had already moved on.

He scanned the room, but people were still making it to their tables. It was hard to see through the sea of suits. Maybe once everyone was seated, he'd be lucky enough to spot her again.

People were still finding their way to their tables, and the room was crowded, which made it easy for Savannah to blend in. She and Evelyn attended a lot of social events together for GetItNowNews. She was lucky that tonight only a few people stopped her who recognized her from those.

She made a beeline to the bar in the far corner of the room, scanning it for Scott as she did. One thing she'd learned from Evelyn at these things was that most people usually barely entered a room, hanging close to the exits—like they were afraid they wouldn't be able to escape. The key was to get past those throngs of folks blocking the way and make your way to the farthest corners. That's where the real action could be seen.

"I'll have a white wine spritzer," she said to the bartender, then tucked a tip in the jar.

"Hey." The voice came from over her left shoulder.

How could her luck be this bad? Franklin? Already?

Franklin caught her by the elbow. She tugged away as she turned around. He made her skin crawl.

"Thought you were on some kind of hiatus."

And he was always trying to get in her personal business. "Not really. I'm working on some new projects and just taking a few days off. No big deal." It would be just like him to slide in and try to sabotage her chance at the new gig if he knew about it. That was better left unsaid.

He stepped back and gave her a whistle. "Well, you're looking good. I thought I was the only one working this story tonight. What are you doing here?"

"I'm just here as a guest."

"Who's the lucky guy?"

"No one you know. Not from around here. Long story."

"I've got time," he said.

He was always digging around for dirt. He'd be better off with a job at TMZ than with GINN. "I don't."

Franklin trailed her. "There is one recipient that rather surprised me. I'd kind of forgotten about the case. It barely made the headlines. Did you look into the details of the people being honored tonight."

Of course she had done her due diligence, but

that was none of his business. He knew darn well she had; he was just trying to pull her into conversation. "Like I said, I'm just a guest tonight." The one place he couldn't follow her was the ladies' room, and that was exactly where she was headed. Anything to shake him from her tail.

Franklin didn't look convinced, and he wasn't about to be shaken that easily, apparently. "I was talking about the Frank Gotorow case. The bigwigs are probably thankful it happened in that podunk town so no one would hear about it. The actual event barely made the wire. Normally, this would be the kind of crime that would set the nation on its side."

Savannah knew why. Probably because Jack and his sister over at the *County Gazette* didn't want bad news about Frank Gotorow and the Goto Hell Murderer being in their town to get around. Everyone in town knew, and they were having to live with it, but they sure didn't need the whole world to know what was going on in their town. So there was no article to be picked up on the wire. A month ago she'd have been tweeting rants about them for keeping the truth from the people who had a right to know. Now, after meeting Jack and getting a different appreciation for the town of Adams Grove, she could kind of see their point of view.

"Word is, the governor had something to do with the paperwork letting that guy out of jail to begin with. That would look pretty damn bad on his résumé if it got too much press. Guess ol' Barney Fife got lucky and stopped the right guy."

"Don't call him that."

"Who?"

She averted her gaze, then turned back, her words short and terse. "Don't call the sheriff Barney Fife. He's not a bumbling hick." She could feel her temperature rise, and the feeling inside her wasn't the least bit ladylike.

"Come on. You and I both know those small-town gigs don't need the skill of real cops."

"You don't know a thing about Sheriff Scott Calvin or Adams Grove."

"And you're suddenly an expert?" He eyed her in a way that made her regret opening her mouth, but she'd gone too far to shut up now.

"I'm no expert, but you're just spouting off to hear yourself talk. Why don't you try reserving judgment for things you know about?"

"What's up your skirt tonight?"

He had a point. Why was she getting this spun up about a guy she barely knew? Was it really that Franklin just had a way of pushing her buttons, or had Scott wiggled his way into her soft spot somehow? "I'm just saying that you are not an expert on what skills cops or sheriffs have or don't have, and it's unfair for you to bash someone who is clearly deserving of the award they are presenting tonight. If not, why would all these people show up for it?"

"Come on. You know what I mean. Those sheriffs and deputies are just the ones who couldn't get a real gig in a real town."

"You have some nerve." She slugged back her wine spritzer like it was a shot and put the glass on the bar. "I'm not talking to you about this." She turned and started to leave but then spun back on her heel and got right into Franklin's face. "You know what? I do have something to say. Don't you go around passing judgment on people just because of where they're from. You don't know the half of what's going on in those small towns, or anywhere for that matter. You've got that over-inflated ego of yours blown up so big you can't see straight."

"Excuu—"

"And another thing. Just because a small-town cop or sheriff's day isn't filled with record numbers of homicides, assaults, and burglaries does not mean he isn't making a difference in his community."

Franklin looked like he'd had an aha moment. "I got it." He pointed a finger toward her. "Are you here with him?"

"Him who?"

"The guest of honor. Why else would you take up for him like a starving pit bull? You're here with the sheriff."

"Don't be ridiculous." But the way his eyes drifted above and to the left of her made her turn, and when she did, she nearly bumped her nose right into Sheriff Calvin's huge bicep.

"Well said." Scott clapped twice and then looked past Savannah.

Franklin hightailed it across the room, and Savannah looked like she was going to lose her lunch.

She looked up at him. "You heard that?" Her eyes danced in the light.

"I did. I think I may have even given a very similar dissertation one time." He held a finger to his lips. "I was much less eloquent. I think I said something to the effect of 'peepers, perps, and bad guys.' You have a way with words. Maybe you should be a writer." He winked and asked the bartender to make her another drink.

She blushed.

"Thank you," Scott said.

"I was just speaking the truth. That guy is a piece of work. He was talking out of his—"

Scott tipped the bartender and handed her the drink. "Just what are you doing here? Someone send you to fight for my honor?"

Her laugh was light. "Hardly. I told Jack I'd cover the story for him."

"Why didn't you tell me? You could have ridden up with me."

"I wasn't sure how you'd feel about it. I just—"

"It's business."

"Business. Yep." She lifted her phone and thumbed through her messages.

He said, "We might be more alike than I thought."

"Well, don't say that like it's a bad thing."

"I didn't mean it like that."

She looked doubtful. "Uh-huh."

"You never really said what you do for a living up here in northern Virginia. I saw you were talking to quite a few people. Do you know them from work?" Suddenly he wanted to know a lot more about her beyond the fact that she liked to drive fast and had a thing for teapots.

"I told you, I'm a writer."

"I googled you and I didn't see anything published recently, so . . ."

"You googled me?"

He should have kept his mouth shut. "Sorry. Occupational hazard. I'm curious."

"Or just nosy."

"A plus for a detective."

"But you're a sheriff."

"Sheriffs do it all." Sounded like a bad bumper sticker. Firefighters do it in the heat, but sheriffs do it all.

She fiddled with her earring. "You're the big badge guy—the head honcho. You've got people to do that stuff, right?"

"You've got to be kidding me." If he had people to do everything he wouldn't have spent half the day putting himself through the red tape to get into the prison to see Frank Gotorow's cell mate in search of answers. Then again, even if he could task that out, this was something he planned to resolve on his own.

With an odd note of disappointment she said, "No. I mean—"

"This conversation was about you, not me. You know what I do. I'm the sheriff. Apparently you think you've cornered the market on knowledge of a sheriff's duties, although clearly you're mistaken."

She lifted her hands to respond, and then let them fall to her sides. "Then educate me."

"I'd be happy to." Darn if she hadn't done it again. She was good at steering a conversation. "But first you owe me some information."

"I don't really *owe* you anything."

"I didn't mean it like that." He let out a sigh. "Can we call a truce?"

"I'm sorry."

"I didn't even write you the ticket, and by the way I hardly ever do that. So why are you still holding a grudge?"

"I don't know. You just spin me up for some reason."

He knew exactly what she meant. He felt the same frustration. The only thing was that he didn't really know what *that* meant.

"So what exactly do you write?"

"Exactly? I write a lot of different things. It's hard to explain. What's it matter? I mean, really, could you say exactly what you do?"

"I'm responsible for enforcing the law in Holland County."

"So maybe you can, but if you put it like that, I guess I could say I string together words to make a story that has an emotional impact on the reader."

"That doesn't even mean anything."

"It does so. Just as much as enforcing the law does. But you're not like a cop. Someone can't just hire you. The sheriff is an elected position, so that means you have to campaign and all that. There's a lot more to that position than meets the eye, I guess."

"I know."

"Of course you do. Sorry for stating the obvious."

"Probably an occupational hazard."

"Like you being nosy?"

"Touché."

"It's an election year. How does that work?"

"The last couple of terms I've run unopposed, but this year I've got competition."

"Really? It's kind of ballsy for a local to take on the sheriff, isn't it?"

"Some guy from up in the Philly area wants to take a shot at it."

"Think anyone in Adams Grove would ever

vote for a Northerner? Just because he's lived here long enough to claim residency doesn't make him a local."

"You never know."

"I'm sure you'll be fine. You could always go somewhere else and be a cop or run for sheriff there, couldn't you? I mean, you're getting this award and a senator and the governor are here. You have to be pretty good at what you do."

"Thanks, but I don't want to leave Adams Grove. I love my job there. I like helping the people I know and easing change into the day-to-day. It's rewarding."

"Wouldn't it be just as rewarding to put bad guys away in a big city?"

"It's different. And cops don't handle budgets and manage a team like a sheriff does. It's a higher-ranking position than a police officer. I don't mean to sound big headed, but it's important."

"I'm sorry. I just assumed that the cops did the criminal stuff and the sheriff's office did more paperwork and court stuff. I remember court bailiffs came from the sheriff's office."

"Okay, so we're getting nowhere talking about our jobs."

Savannah lifted a brow. "True. New subject?"

"Have you ever been married?"

"That's kind of personal, but fine. Once. High school sweetheart. It ended quickly. You?"

"No. Almost once. City girl. Long relationship until she moved in with me. She hated living in Adams Grove. Ended quickly after that . . . and rather badly."

"Ouch."

"Yeah. I have a knack for picking the wrong girl."

"You must, because after hearing how fabulous you are from your momma, I honestly can't figure out why you'd still be single unless you were gay or something, and that apparently is not the case."

Gay? Or something? He wasn't sure which was worse, but at least she didn't think he was either. The senator's daughter appeared out of nowhere. "Time for dinner," she said. "Would your friend like to join you at your table?"

"Oh, no. That's fine," Savannah said.

"That would be nice. Won't you join me?" asked Scott.

She looked undecided.

"It's okay, isn't it?" he said to the senator's daughter.

"Of course."

He put his arm out to Savannah. "Join me."

She looped her arm through his and followed him to the table.

He leaned down and whispered into her ear. "It's the least I can do, since you fought for my honor tonight."

"It wasn't like I had to climb a water tower and spray paint over a rumor," she said.

She certainly had a quick wit. He liked that.

He held out her chair and she slipped into the seat with the quiet elegance of the morning mist over the Nottoway River. He took the seat next to her just as the waitstaff began placing plates in front of them.

"Chicken. Who'd have guessed?" he whispered.

"Grilled chicken. Says so right here." She lifted a small rectangular card from next to the plate.

Scott poked at the pale chicken on his plate.

Savannah scooched hers to the side of the plate and concentrated on the vegetable medley and rice.

"This is not grilled chicken. I can show you what real grilled chicken is like." He could show her a lot of things.

"I don't eat a whole lot of meat anyway."

"You one of those save-the-animal vegetarian types?"

"No. I figure I can get most of what I need from veggies. Besides, it seems like half the meat doesn't even have any flavor anymore. Trust me, doesn't stop me from chomping on a juicy burger now and again."

"Good to know." He took a bite of the chicken and had to agree that there wasn't much use in eating anything that tasteless.

Savannah giggled.

"What?"

"Your face when you bit into that. Priceless. Hey, at least you didn't have to cook it."

"I don't mind cooking. In fact, I'm a good cook. I darn sure could have done better than this. Jacob's Diner might have the best fried chicken for miles, but I grill the best steaks around. Not a bad chicken either. I'll have you over sometime before you leave town." He watched intently for that wall to go up. He'd grown accustomed to it, but this time instead of tensing up, she relaxed a little. Maybe it was just being on her stomping grounds, but whatever the reason it was nice to see this side of her.

"Thanks. I think I'd like that," she said, clearly surprised that he'd asked her.

"You're on." He hadn't planned it, but now that it was out there, he was already thinking about what a night out, or rather in, might be like with her.

They finished dinner and enjoyed small talk with the others at the table until the governor took the podium to begin the ceremony.

Savannah leaned over to Scott and said, "I'm going to step off to the side to get a few pictures. Good luck."

"Thanks." He watched as she wove between the tables to the edge of the room. She was the girl in blue who had caught his eye earlier, and what he wouldn't do to have her in his arms on the dance floor right now.

He forced himself to turn his attention to the governor, and good thing because he called Scott to the podium.

Thank goodness they didn't expect him to say anything in response to the award. Music began playing from the back of the room, and the press snapped a few pictures. It was a short fanfare. Couples took to the dance floor. He watched Savannah talking with a group of people. Her eyes met his. He'd been staring. His mom would have said it was rude, but he didn't care.

She waved to him, and he gave her a nod. She looked comfortable in the crowd. He watched her excuse herself from the group and begin making her way across the room in his direction.

He couldn't wait to take her out on the dance floor. But then someone else interrupted his little fantasy. "Sheriff Calvin, I'm head of a special task force. I'd like to talk to you about an opportunity."

Scott looked from the man back toward Savannah. "I—" He wanted to say he had plans, but he knew it wasn't a request he could deny.

The man's voice was firm. "It'll just take a few moments of your time. Can you join us in the next room?"

What could he say? They hosted the event. They'd made him the guest of honor. "Of course, yes. Thank you." He turned and mouthed "Sorry," with a shrug to Savannah as the man whisked him away.

• • •

Savannah hung around until most of the people had gone, mostly in hopes that she'd run into Scott again, but she hadn't seen any sign of him once he'd left with the group of prestigious men, including the governor and three guys who had important written all over them. Staying any longer would just look weird, and Franklin was still hanging around. She had no intention of getting into it with him again tonight.

She walked outside. Scott's car was still in the parking lot. Clearly, they'd decided to take advantage of having him in town to talk business. She walked over to her car and got in. It was a short drive to the hotel, but she'd have rather been riding back with Scott.

The night clerk was a different one from the one she'd acted like a nut with earlier this afternoon, thank goodness. She stopped in at the bar and got a diet cola to take up to her room.

She changed out of the dress and got into her pajamas.

A diet drink, her laptop, and pajamas. She wished she'd brought prettier pajamas. If Scott stopped by when he got done, she wasn't going to make a big impression in these PJs.

She forced herself to focus on the story about the award ceremony for the *County Gazette*. It was a short piece, but it read well. "Jack, I think you're going to be happy with this." She grabbed

232

her camera and flipped through the tons of pictures she'd taken. You just never knew what you were going to need. More is better.

She picked her two favorites and e-mailed the article and pictures to herself so she could send them to Jack in the morning after she reread it.

After checking through her e-mails, she shut down the computer and turned off the light, but her mind wouldn't turn off so easily.

She got up and padded to the window. From here she could see the spot where Scott had parked before. Someone else was parked there now, and she didn't see Scott's car in the lot. She stood up on her tiptoes, trying to get a view of the whole parking lot, but there was quite a bit she couldn't see from here.

She pulled the curtains closed and got into bed, thinking about Scott.

It was after three when she finally fell asleep, and with the blackout curtains in the hotel room, she slept until nine o'clock, something she hadn't done in years.

She gathered her things to head back to Adams Grove.

There was no sign of his car in the parking lot when she left either. Maybe he'd gone straight home.

She got on the road feeling tired but reflective. Scott Calvin wasn't the grump she'd pegged him as. The girls were right. He had a quick wit and he was nice. Very nice. All the people at the table at dinner seemed charmed by him, and she was too. He'd sparked her interest, and now she couldn't get him off her mind.

The ride back went by fast, but she didn't risk speeding once she got close to Adams Grove. She stopped at the Walmart to pick up a pack of writable CDs in case that would make it easier for Jack to review the pictures from last night's event. Besides, this way he wouldn't have to know she hadn't used his camera. She'd have had to carry a hobo bag to hulk that sucker around all night, and that would not have gone with her dress.

It was just after noon when she made it back to the apartment in Adams Grove. She'd barely finished transferring the pictures and the article from her computer to the CD when she heard voices in the hallway. Was it her imagination, or was that Scott's voice?

She ran as quietly as she could to the door, but the wood floor snapped and popped under her feet. She peeked out the peephole.

Scott was talking to Mike on the landing.

He turned and rapped on her door. She sucked in a breath and ducked, feeling like she'd just been caught. She could hear her blood pulsing like those bass drums in the parade. Why was she freaking out? It wasn't like he could see her peeking through the peephole.

They were still talking. Her heart pounded so

loud she could barely hear what they were saying on the other side of the door now. She dropped to the floor and crawled back about five steps and then got up and yelled, "Coming."

She opened the door and tried to act surprised. "Hi. I wasn't expecting you."

"You busy?"

"Yes. No. I was just . . ." She swept her hand through her hair. "Come on in. What's up?"

He walked inside. "Looks exactly like it did when Connor lived here."

"Yep. Fully furnished. It's a bargain."

"Compared to northern Virginia, I'm sure it is."

"Yeah. So congratulations again on last night. And thanks for inviting me to join you at your table. I had fun."

"Thanks, but actually I came by to thank *you* for last night."

"Me? I didn't do anything. But come take a look at the pictures. They turned out pretty good."

He followed her over to the table by the window.

She sat down and clicked a few keys, and the pictures popped up on her screen.

He moved in close behind her. Her skin tingled and she could feel his warm breath just over her shoulder.

"Wow, those are good. You've done this before. You make me look pretty good," Scott said.

She smiled, but didn't confirm or deny.

"I couldn't stop thinking about the way you took

up for me . . . for all small-town cops . . . to that guy at the award dinner. I appreciate that."

She turned toward him. Her face just inches from his, and that mouth. Doggone, he had a sexy mouth. "It was nothing. I was just telling it like it was."

"I heard him. I heard your response. Thank you. You didn't have to do that."

"Yes I did. He was being a jerk. Besides, you kind of opened my eyes since I've been here. I'd made some similar assumptions. I guess I was a little bit of a jerk too."

"Well, I did almost give you a ticket." He laid a hand on her shoulder.

"But you didn't." *You could kiss me, though. I'd like that. Plus, my heart is racing. Does that qualify for extra-special attention?*

"And you didn't do that to repay me. You were just being nice. I like that about you."

She licked her lips, her mouth suddenly feeling dry.

"Can I take you to lunch?"

She wanted to have lunch with him. She really did, but she wasn't looking for what he wanted or what his mom wanted him to want. It was all wrong and complicated, and when he learned about her past, he wouldn't understand. She opened her mouth to explain, but her heart was pounding so hard she could barely urge one word out. "I . . ."

He cut her off. "You know, just as a thank-you. To repay you for getting sucked into spending a precious day out of your vacation on that story for our little local paper. It's just lunch."

"It was my pleasure. I got dinner last night. Really, that was payment enough." *No, it wasn't. Why am I fighting this?*

"That wasn't real food."

She laughed out loud. "It was pretty bad."

"Lunch?"

"That depends."

"On what?"

"On if you're still going to make good on treating me to real grilled chicken. Calvin-style. I've got to work on something this afternoon, but if you wanted to barbecue me some of your famous chicken or steak one night, I'm all yours." Her body was wanting a lot more than she was willing to admit, but boy, if she hadn't just laid it all right out there.

"Tonight?"

"I'd love it."

"I'll pick you up."

"I can drive over." Then she could leave if she needed to.

"I'll pick you up at seven."

She sucked in a quick breath. "Okay." *Live a little,* she heard Evelyn say in her mind. No escape route. How bad could it be? He knew she was leaving town soon. They were adults, after all.

They walked to the door together.

He reached for the knob, then stopped and turned, pausing kind of awkwardly.

Was he going to kiss her?

He stepped toward her and she felt herself pull in a breath and hold it, but he didn't come in for a kiss. He gave her arm a gentle squeeze, then walked out, closing the door behind him.

She wasn't sure which was louder, her heart pounding or his footsteps as he descended the steep stairs. She raced over to the window that faced the street. He was already walking down the block

She'd probably have to run to keep up with him, but darned if she wouldn't mind trying.

Chapter EIGHT

Savannah walked over to the couch and plopped back on it like a lazy teenager. Only she wasn't lazy, and she wasn't a teen. But she felt as giddy as one. Dinner with the sheriff.

The grin that stretched across her face pushed her cheeks so high that her bottom lashes tickled them.

Her tummy spun just like it had the first time she ever spoke in front of a group. Nervous. Excited. And not sure whether to hoot or puke.

Her days in Adams Grove were dwindling and everyone knew it, so it wasn't like there was any promise of something serious. She hoped he wouldn't tell his mom, though. It wouldn't do for the nice lady to get her hopes up when there was no chance of it ever being anything long term. Savannah would be leaving in a week to go back to the city, and they'd probably never speak again. That was okay. It could be fun for now.

Even though everyone had told her Scott was a great guy, she hadn't recognized even a hint of it until last night. Not that it wasn't there, but because she'd been very careful to never let herself see anything that might lead her to care too much. About anyone. But since last night, Scott Calvin was all she could think about. Evelyn was always telling her to loosen up and just have a good time. She'd tried yoga, and it wasn't so bad. Maybe a little test drive of the handsome sheriff wouldn't be so bad either.

His great pride in his work made her feel proud for him. She'd been wrong about the small-town cop stuff. She'd made the mistake of generalizing, and she should know better.

Was it the award that had made her look differently at him?

That was silly. She wasn't the type to be impressed by that kind of stuff. But something had changed the way she saw him. Or maybe she'd been holding on to that old protective mode that kept her from seeing any man as a potential partner, and last night there was just enough wine and fun for her to let her guard down. If you didn't care, you couldn't get hurt. So far, she'd gotten through eight years since Momma and Dad died without ever feeling the kind of loss and betrayal her hometown had cast on her. That plan of attack had suited her just fine . . . until now.

A sudden flash of panic hit her and sent her zooming to an upright position.

That first article that she'd e-mailed to Evelyn was not going to go over well for Scott. What if those bigwigs that honored him last night saw it? They were totally in the GINN demographic. He didn't deserve the blast she'd dished out in that article.

Plus, the people of this little hick town might be savvier than she gave them credit for, and if word got out that that article was about their sheriff here in Adams Grove, that could be very bad for him.

A lump stuck right in her throat. She pressed the number for Evelyn on her phone. No answer. She was probably in the sales meeting right now.

"Evelyn. It's me, Van. I need you to pull that article I submitted. I'll send you something new. I got something terribly wrong and I have to fix it. Call me if there's an issue. Thanks."

But there was no telling if or when Evelyn would listen to that message, and the deadline for the issue was looming.

Savannah's stomach gripped the worry like a vise.

She shot off an e-mail to Evelyn and copied the guy in charge of production, just in case. He owed her a favor or two.

Watching the clock, Savannah paced around the room wishing for a phone call, a text, an e-mail. Heck, she'd take a smoke signal . . . anything to let her know that her message had been received.

She sat down at the computer and refreshed her inbox. Nothing. She couldn't waste any more time waiting to hear. She opened up a blank document and started trying to think of a replacement story. Closed her eyes and sat there.

Nothing came. All she could think about was getting a hold of Evelyn.

She clicked back over to the Word document. The cursor blinked at her like a momma shaking her finger at her kid for being bad.

There was no way she was going to relax until she heard from Evelyn. She carried her phone with her to the bedroom and started unpacking the clothes she'd brought back with her. She hung them one by one, sending a little prayer out to the universe for a story idea as she hung each hanger.

Finally, a rattling set of typewriter keys broke the silence.

"Yes!" Savannah shouted as she grabbed her phone. "Finally. Hey, Evelyn."

"Good afternoon, Savannah. Thanks for dropping off those letters for Andrew. I just went through them. They're perfect. This will give us a great jump-start. I'm so sorry I missed you, though. How are things going?"

"Did you get my message? About the article?"

"I did. Honey, that article is fine. Just work on the next one."

"No!" She couldn't let it run the way it was. "I've got a different angle, and one of my facts didn't exactly check out."

"There wasn't much in the way of fact-checking to do on it, Van. It's great, and it's already formatted for production."

"Evelyn, you don't understand. I really need to fix it. If I get it to you by four—same word count—will you replace it? Please?"

Evelyn's pause made Savannah worry. She didn't have even an inkling of an idea of what she was going to write to replace it, but she really had no choice. She'd have to come up with something.

"What's this all about?"

"Please. Just do me this favor."

Savannah heard Evelyn sigh. That wasn't good. She knew that meant she was aggravated. That sound was usually reserved for the pains in the butt at GINN, never her! "I need it by four. You know that's the drop-dead."

"Thank you. I owe you!"

"Yes, you do. How's everything else going?"

Savannah could hear the irritation in Evelyn's tone. "Okay. I'm trying to figure out how to get rid of all these letters you sent over. I might have to go buy a shredder."

"What's the big deal? Just toss them in a trash bag and throw them away. They do have trash cans in that little town, don't they?"

"Of course they do, but this is a lot of letters."

"So it'll make for some interesting reading if they poke through your trash. Big deal."

"We don't want them to know I'm Van."

"Well, technically, you're not anymore."

"I really don't want to have to explain it to anyone. I just have a bad feeling about it, Evelyn."

"What's gotten into you? You've never been a worrier. Maybe that country air is not what you needed after all. You can come on back if you want. I didn't mean to bamboozle you into something that was going to make you crazy. I just thought it would be fun for you."

"The country air is perfect. It's fine. Fun. Everything you wanted it to be. But some of those letters. Evelyn, we've had this conversation before. Half of what those nuts put in those letters should be against the law. It's just bad, and it's mean-spirited. You know they're just going for the shock value."

"You've had no problem doing it for the past two years."

"Well, I'm over it now, and I really don't want

anyone else to know that's how I've been spending my time." She swallowed back the urge to cry. She had been living life in a way that was just like those people she had left behind in Belles Corner. She'd been speculative and judgmental, and made light of things of major importance to others. "It's not who I want to be."

"Settle down, Van."

"I am not going to ruin these people's lives, and I've got to get rid of these letters before someone finds out." Outside her door she heard Connor talking down in the stairwell, and then Mike's voice, just outside her door.

Her heart filled her throat. "Evelyn, I've got to go." She hung up the phone without a good-bye and ran to the door.

Mike was standing at the rail on the landing right outside her door. Had he heard her on the phone with Evelyn? She should have been more careful.

She didn't have much time.

If she was going to get that article rewritten and in to Evelyn by four o'clock, she couldn't worry about Mike or what he may or may not have heard.

There was no time for distractions. She grabbed the laptop from the table in front of the window and took it to the desk in the office.

She pulled up the original article and stripped it down to the details. Only now as she typed, instead of getting even with the Sheriff in her mind, all she could picture was Daphne Calvin with her head slightly cocked to one side, saying, "He's just doing his job, dear."

She'd just been doing hers, but that didn't make her feel any better.

The minutes ticked away, and all she could wrap her head around was that at the time he pulled her over on I-95, it had felt like such a huge deal, a huge injustice. But when you put the incident into perspective, it just was not news. It wasn't even funny.

Sensationalizing the small things had become an art. That's the article she should be writing. But that wouldn't fill the bill for what Evelyn was expecting in this slot . . . today . . . in just fourteen minutes!

Hammering away at the keys, she pulled a story together that would meet Evelyn's expectations, but wouldn't offend Sheriff Calvin or the town of Adams Grove if anyone did happen to pick it up, or make Daphne Calvin think any less of her.

She turned it into a generic view, rather than an exposé on a particular town or person.

She hit Send with three minutes to spare. It may well have been equivalent to a 5K run in the park for the way she was feeling right now. Like she'd sprinted across the finish line . . . with a firebreathing dragon on her heels.

Okay, maybe that was a little dramatic, but still.

She let out a breath and wondered how she'd

get a second wind before Scott picked her up for dinner at seven.

A short nap, a bubble bath in the biggest, deepest claw-foot tub ever, and two hours later she was feeling on top of the world, even a little anxious about her date with the cute sheriff. Or was it a date? She wasn't a hundred percent sure.

She put on jeans and a white blouse. She turned up the sleeves and then wondered if white was just asking for trouble when eating barbecue. She slipped her favorite bangle bracelets on her wrist and then tugged them back off. It was a cookout. She didn't need jewelry. Satisfied that she looked nice but not like she was trying too hard, she plugged the charger into her phone and then texted Evelyn.

Savannah: Thanks for replacing the article. On my way out to dinner.

Evelyn: With the sheriff?

Savannah: How'd you know? You always know everything.

Evelyn: Had a feeling. Have fun. You deserve it.

Not that she needed Evelyn's blessing, but knowing Evelyn seemed to approve made it seem that much more right.

Savannah hadn't felt this excited about any-thing in a long time. She was probably setting herself up for a big fat letdown, something she never allowed herself to do. She was starting to get used to not working at breakneck speed all day every day, even on the weekends. And she was starting to like it.

She paced around the apartment wishing the time would pass a little faster. At about quarter till seven she found herself hanging by the front window, watching for that blue Thunderbird to roll up. She was still looking out the window when a knock came from her door.

The floor creaked beneath her feet as she crossed the room.

It was probably her nosy neighbor again. At least with Scott on his way she wouldn't have to talk to Mike for long. She might even be able to pick his brain a little and figure out whether he'd heard any of her conversation with Evelyn earlier.

She pulled the door open without checking the peephole first, but to her surprise it wasn't Mike, it was Scott. The wine-colored shirt he wore enhanced the gold embers in his eyes. Was that an invitation in those smoldering eyes? Or was she just hoping it was? And just how had he gotten past her vigilant watch from the window?

"You look surprised. Did you forget I was coming?"

"No. Um. You're a couple minutes early. I just assumed it was the guy next door." She tripped over her own feet trying to step back. "Sorry. Come in." She'd been anticipating his arrival and now she was acting like an idiot.

"You already know your neighbor. That's good."

"I do. Well, not like borrow-a-cup-of-sugar know him, but we've met and chatted a few times. Which is kind of funny, since I've lived in my place for over five years and I still don't know any of my neighbors there. One week and I know more neighbors in this town than I do in my own."

"That's a good thing," he said.

No sense telling him that not making friends had been by her own design.

"You ready to go?"

She flattened her palms against her pants. "I think so." She took her phone off the charger and slipped it into the front pocket on her purse. "Let's go."

Scott turned the lock before he pulled the door closed behind them. "After you."

She took the lead down the stairs, suddenly very aware of her backside as he followed behind all the way to the bottom. "Are you parked out front or back?"

"Out front."

She pushed through the door and stepped onto the sidewalk, then turned and gave him a puzzled look. "Did you walk?"

"No."

"Where's your car?"

"Right there." He pointed to a blue Mustang with a black ragtop.

No wonder she hadn't spotted him. She'd

expected him to be driving the Thunderbird, or his sheriff's car.

"Just how many cars do you have?"

"A few. My dad and I worked on them as projects when I was a kid. I guess I never grew out of it." He held the door open for her and she slid into the soft leather seat.

"Are they all blue?"

"This isn't just blue. It's Acapulco blue."

"What was I thinking?" Obviously he wasn't a ROY G BIV kind of guy. "So are they all shades of blue?"

"It's my favorite color."

Visualizing a line of cars a mile long, fender to bumper, in varying shades of blue, she reached for the shoulder belt, but there wasn't anything there.

Scott must've seen her searching as he slid behind the wheel, because he reached across her waist and lifted a shiny buckle with a pony on it. "Lap belts."

"Oh. Gotcha. Like on an airplane. This is a real classic."

"Love the old classic cars." They pulled away from the curb and out onto Main Street. "The new ones are nice, but these old rides are fun to work on and they have style. She's a '67."

"You didn't answer my question. How many cars do you have?"

"More than I need."

So he wasn't ready to share everything. Fine.

She had always thought cops didn't make much money. Maybe his expensive car hobby was subsidized by all those tickets he gave out. Like a sales bonus. But then that was just silly, and he hardly seemed the type to do anything crooked. "Fair enough. How far do you live from town?"

"Not far. Less than a ten-minute drive."

"Not a bad commute. I usually walk to work because it takes longer to drive than to walk it."

He shook his head. "I'd hate to spend so much of my day just waiting in traffic."

"You get used to it."

"It would take a long time to walk anywhere around here."

"It's nice to have everything in walking distance. I mean, I do have to jump on the train once in a while, but it's convenient. A lot of people don't even have their own cars."

"I guess that's perfect for a girl like you."

"Yeah. A girl like me. Not sure what that means, but I'm going to pretend it's a compliment. You might like the city if you gave it a try."

"No. All that sitting in traffic. Waiting in line. And the noise. How do you sleep? Besides, it would cut into my playtime. I work hard, but I play hard too."

"Really? And just how does a sheriff play?" She tapped the gleaming dashboard. "I mean aside from collecting cool old cars."

"She was a hot mess when I got her. Took me a

few years to get her in this shape. You like the Mustang?"

"Like it?" She pulled her lips together. "No."

He looked surprised.

"Are you kidding? I love this car." She ran her hand along the console, then twisted the old knobs on the AM radio. "It's got character. You did a nice job restoring her."

"Thanks. What do you do for fun when you're home in the big city?"

She started to answer, then drew a blank. "Ya know, I work a lot. I don't do a whole lot else anymore."

"Then why bother living in the city? Do you just like to be around that many people, or is it the noise? Wait. I bet it's the shopping."

"No. Actually, I do most of my shopping online. It's like coming home to a Christmas present when there's a package at my door. I like that. I do go to the Nats games once in a while, but no one I know really goes to watch the game, and it's no fun without someone who really loves baseball. The people I know are more interested in sitting in the box seats and gabbing . . . so I really don't do that much either."

"Box seats?"

"A fringe benefit from work." She regretted saying it as soon as she did. She hoped he'd miss the comment and not start digging. "But the shopping online is way more fun anyway."

"Guess you can get just about anything you want online these days."

"I'm keeping the UPS guy in a job. Everything I'm wearing right now, right down to my Victoria's Secrets and the charm on my necklace, came via mail."

"Then why does it matter where you live?"

That made her stop and think. "Well, I never really thought about it like that."

He looked pleased with himself. "Sometimes you have to ask yourself the tough questions."

"Have you seen the architecture in DC? That's pretty awesome to be surrounded by."

"We've got some nice architecture here. Not as much of it. Not as close together, but nice. The building you're staying in was an old bank."

"I know. Connor took me on the tour. That vault is so cool. I'll admit, my first impression of Adams Grove was a good one because I loved the buildings on Main Street. They really grabbed my attention. I loved the way the old is mixed with the new and colorful stuff."

"The people are as colorful as the shops."

Yeah, she knew all about small-town people. "All up in your business, you mean."

"They mean well."

She pushed her hands into her pockets. "Right," she said with a snicker. He could preach that one all day; she knew better.

"No, really. They just want to help."

She cut her eyes toward him.

"Okay. I'll admit. It's annoying sometimes."

She challenged him with a look. "Sometimes?"

"Fine. A lot of the time, but if you keep it in perspective, it's a pretty damn good gift to know you have a whole community of people raising prayers in your favor. And if something happened, they'd all be right there to help pick you back up."

Or pull you down, she thought. When had she become so cynical?

Scott turned into a neighborhood. The mature trees canopied the road. "We have the oldest recorded cypress in Virginia here. Bet you can't say that about your town."

"Can't say that I can."

"She's got a name."

"Who?"

"The tree," Scott said.

"The oldest tree in Virginia has a name? No way."

"Big Mama."

"Now I know that you're just making that up," Savannah said, shaking her head.

"I am not. I'm willing to bet she's proud of that name."

"Somehow I doubt any woman, even a tree, wants to be called big."

"She's reported to be over fifteen hundred years old. She's a hundred and twenty-three feet tall."

"Okay, that is big."

"Over twelve feet around. Google it. I'm telling you, it's true."

She whipped out her phone and started thumbing in words. "Holy cow. Can you take me to see her?"

"I can."

"Is that water behind those houses?" she asked.

"The river."

"Do you have a boat?"

"I do. A pontoon boat and a fishing boat. Do you like the water?"

"Grew up on it."

"Really? I wouldn't have pegged you as the outdoorsy type. If you don't mind the swamp, I can take you to meet Big Mama. She's in a pretty remote area."

"There's probably a lot about me that you wouldn't guess. I'm not afraid of the swamp either." It was easy to feel unafraid with him. It had been a long time since she'd done things like hiking and camping, all those outdoorsy things she used to enjoy with her dad. She'd never actually been in a swamp, but she'd done her share of fly fishing with her daddy. A trek through the swamp in hip waders with Scott Calvin actually had a certain appeal.

"I'm intrigued." He pulled into the driveway. "We're here."

"Nice place." The yard was beautifully manicured, and although the house wasn't fancy, it looked very comfortable, and large for a single guy.

"What did you expect?"

"I don't know. Not this." This was the kind of house you raised a family in. She really wasn't sure how to explain what she'd expected without sounding like a jerk, and for once, her filter seemed to work.

He led her to the side door, unlocked it, and gestured her inside. "After you," he said as he turned on the lights.

"I like the open floor plan," she said.

He laid his keys on the bar.

"I bet that fireplace is nice in the winter. We're not allowed to have a fireplace in my condo. I miss that."

"I sure cuss it while I'm chopping wood in the heat of the summer to get ready for it, but you're right, it sure is great on a cold winter's night."

"Are you a romantic, Scott Calvin?"

He stepped into the kitchen. "Maybe."

"Well, that fireplace is nice, but this kitchen is to die for. Two ovens. Man, you are serious about your cooking. Look at this spread. Is all of this food for just the two of us?" She hoped he wasn't about to surprise her with company. If his mom showed up now, invited, that could bring his appeal score down a notch or two.

"Yep."

"How much do you think I can eat?"

255

"Trust me, when I barbecue, everyone overeats. And I wasn't sure what you liked, so I may have gone a little overboard."

"This could be bad news for my waistline." And where was that filter when she needed it? Why did she have to be a smarty-pants when he was trying to be nice? Wouldn't a simple thank-you have been better? "I'm sorry. I didn't mean it that way. It was really sweet of you to go to all of this trouble."

"If you enjoy it, it'll be worth it."

"What can I help with?"

He picked up a large pan covered in foil and handed it to her. Then he picked up another and led the way. "Follow me."

She followed him through the kitchen and then out the door that led to the patio.

He'd grabbed an apron off a hook by the door as he pushed it open and held it for her. "You can just put that on the table there."

"Your outdoor kitchen is even bigger than my indoor kitchen."

"I just like having the right tools. Mechanic tools, cop tools, fishing tools, cooking tools. Everything in its place."

A man's man. Nothing wrong with that. He made cooking look like man's work. Not a bad idea in her book.

He pulled a black apron over his head. On the front was a caricature that was clearly Scott with an oversized chef's hat on, chasing a cow with a grill fork and his sheriff's badge.

" 'Best Mooin' Marinade'?"

He grinned. "That's me. Told ya I cook the best steak around. Someone had this made for me as proof."

"Can't argue with that, can I?" The guy had confidence, she'd give him that.

"Not really, but chicken is on the menu tonight."

"You're not going to make me hunt down my own dinner, are you?"

"Not a chance." With the punch of one button, the blue flames licked the metal grates of the huge grill. Scott started unwrapping pans. "You just take a seat there at the table while I get this going."

"What are you fixing?"

"We've got fresh corn on the cob, summer squash wrapped in bacon, beans with a topping that will bake up into a cornbread—a little sweet and a little kick—and awesome grilled chicken."

She watched as he placed the chicken on the grill, and then each of the veggies carefully and with very specific placement.

Once everything was searing, Scott stepped over to the outdoor sink and washed up. "Can I get you something to drink?" He stepped back and peered through the glass front of a small refrigerator below the counter. "I've got beer, wine, soda, water, or sweet tea."

"I think I'll stick with sweet tea."

He pulled a bubble-shaped clear glass pitcher out of the refrigerator and served her sweet tea in a frosty mason jar. He had the same.

"Do you get much chance to get out on your boats?"

"I do. I could take you out with me one afternoon."

"I'd love that."

The chicken on the grill was beginning to fill the air with a sweet, smoky aroma. "I'll take you down to the dock after dinner."

"Okay."

"How's the police blotter going for you?"

"A lot better now that you're sending me the file and I don't have to type everything. I turn in another tomorrow."

"That's good," he said. "Bee is old school. Jack's way more savvy than he lets on. Don't let him fool you. But Bee liked things the old way. I don't mind letting her have her way. In some cases, it's just what people get used to and automation isn't always the answer. The paper works, that's good enough for me."

"A good way to think of things." Wouldn't fly back in DC. But if it worked for them, more power to them. "It must be working on me. I even took a yoga class the other day."

"You did? Happy Balance is being very well received. Surprisingly so, considering Jenn isn't from around here."

"She's really nice. I spent some time with her and Brooke the other night. That police blotter entry you had me delete. I think there's something to it."

His reaction wasn't subtle. He sucked in a breath like she'd punched him in the gut.

"There's a mural in the men's locker room," she said.

He turned slowly in her direction. "I've seen it. What were you doing in the men's locker room?"

"I was just commenting on the art. Jenn and Brooke told me I had to see that mural."

"You were snooping."

"I . . ." Heck, she couldn't lie to him. "I was curious."

"I told you to leave that alone."

"No. I think you told me not to include it in the police blotter, and I didn't."

He let out a long sigh.

"I've upset you."

"No." He shook his head and shrugged. "You didn't. The situation does."

"You see the images in that painting too, don't you?"

"I believe Jelly does."

"The homeless guy," she said.

"You know about him too."

Savannah proceeded carefully. He clearly didn't want to talk about this with her. He'd skirted her question entirely, but she had to know. "I don't

259

think everyone does see images in the mural. Jenn and I saw them, but Brooke couldn't see them."

"You have to promise me you won't dig into this."

She couldn't promise that. She wanted to get to the truth. She needed to. It was like that message had come to her and she was meant to help. "Do you know what it means?"

"Not yet." Scott took the food from the grill and placed it on a serving platter. "I'm looking into it, though. Can we talk about that later?"

"Sure. I'm sorry. I didn't realize—"

Scott held up a hand. "You couldn't have known. It's okay. Let's enjoy this meal."

"Let's. It smells delicious."

He served up two plates and handed her one. The dish looked like blue stoneware, but as she took it, prepared for its heft, she was surprised to find that it was light as a feather. "These are so pretty, and I expected them to be heavy."

"A gift from my mom last Christmas. Melamine. Unbreakable too. She's not a big fan of paper plates. I'm not a big fan of stuff that breaks. This fit both of our needs."

"Good gift. I've never seen anything like them. They seriously look like the real thing."

She cut into the chicken and took a bite. "Perfect." A little moan escaped as she sampled the rest of the items on her plate. "You really *are* a good cook." Even the presentation was nice.

"So colorful, and every single thing on this plate is good. I can see why people always overeat when you barbecue."

"Glad you like it."

The mood was lightening up again, and Savannah was relieved she hadn't ruined the whole evening with that talk about the mural. He'd started brooding when she brought it up. Unfortunately for him, that just made her more curious to learn everything about it.

She pushed her plate away from her. "I'm stuffed."

"I'll take that as a compliment." He started stacking plates and pans.

Savannah pushed her chair back and helped.

Scott held the screen door open for her with his foot, and they made quick work of getting everything cleaned up and put away together. "Thanks. I didn't mean to put you to work," Scott said.

"It's always easier with more hands."

"Want to walk down to the dock?"

"I'd love that." She rubbed her stomach. "I could use a walk after that meal."

The slope to the water was steep. He steadied her by taking her hand in his. When they got about twenty feet from the boathouse, a big black Lab came loping up the lawn toward them.

"Hey, Maggie." Scott let go of Savannah's hand and clapped. The dog ran toward them with her tongue lolling to one side. Her tail wagged so hard she looked like she might lose her balance, or lift right off the ground like a helicopter.

Savannah stooped down and scrubbed Maggie's ears. "Such a pretty girl."

By the time Savannah realized Scott had kept walking while she and Maggie got acquainted, he was far enough ahead that they had to run to catch up.

He was already on the dock, toying with a rope on one of the boats.

"Does Maggie ever go out on the boat with you?"

"Oh, yeah. She loves the water. In it, on it, near it . . . you name it. I'm pretty sure that dog has river water running through her veins."

Savannah held her arms out to steady herself on the floating dock. "Love the party boat!"

"The pontoon boat? Yeah. It's fun. Mom likes that one. It's more her speed. She and Dad used to take it out all the time. I got it when he passed on. The fishing boat is my favorite. She'll really scoot."

She cocked her head slightly. Dad would have liked him. "Just like your hot rod cars."

"Yeah, guess so."

"Nothing wrong with that. Especially when you can get out of the tickets." She sat on the dock and pulled off her shoes and socks. When her toes hit the water, she let out a loud gasp that ended in a rather high-pitched squeal. The shock of that water dulled her focus on her dad. Missing him. And part of her wished she could jump right into the river and wash that sorrow away with the current. People said time would make it easier, but it didn't.

He sat down next to her. "The water stays cold in this part of the river."

"It's nice out here," she said, swishing her feet. The water splashing against the bottom of the dock was soothing.

He looked around and then back at her. "Yeah, it is. I'm a little biased, but I love it here."

"I can see why." She lay back on the dock, looking into the night sky. "It's a good place to be."

"It's a great place to be. And quiet," he added.

"Is that your way of telling me to quit talking?"

"No. I'm enjoying your company."

She sat back up. "I wouldn't say it was quiet out here. Don't you hear all of that? The water lapping at the dock. Frogs. Crickets. A couple of neighborhood dogs. I'm not sure what all we've got going on here, but it isn't quiet!"

"Well, it's a natural quiet. No traffic. No jets. No lights. No crime to really speak of."

"It's peaceful." She lifted her chin to the sky and took in a deep breath. "I'll give you that. I feel like I could reach out and touch those stars. Definitely peaceful."

"Fair enough."

"I've enjoyed tonight," she said.

"Me too."

"You were right." She saw the cocky gleam in his eyes. "I mean that you were right that you make an awesome grilled chicken. And those veggies. Do you always cook up that many veggie side dishes, or did you do that just for me?"

"I had a feeling the veggies might be your favorite part."

"You were right, but with cooking like that, I might have meat at every meal."

"Thank you, ma'am. Are you offering me a full-time job?"

"Careful. I might."

"Wait until you try my steak. I'm known for my steaks." He reached over and put his hand on top of hers.

It caught her by surprise. She looked up and made eye contact. "Only if you promise to cook it. I don't like those steaks that seem like they could still be mooing."

"Medium-well it is."

"Is that how you eat yours? Medium-well?"

"Oh, heck no. I like mine still mooing."

"Ick. Make mine well done, please."

"Deal." He pulled in a deep breath. "That means we have another date, right?"

She turned her head, her shoulder lifting nearly to her ear in a self-conscious shrug. *A date? Is that what we've just had?* "Another one?"

"Or a first one," he said. The beginning of a smile played at the corners of his mouth.

She wasn't the only one feeling the connection tonight. She tilted her head back and gazed into his eyes. "Yeah. Yeah, I could totally do that." And more . . . She'd love to see what that mouth felt like on her own, but as quickly as she wished for it, her mind turned to nervousness too. "Next time let me help in the kitchen. I love to cook. Haven't done it in years, so I'm a little rusty, but I'd like that."

He stood and reached his hand toward her to help her up. "Come on. The mosquitoes are buzzing. Let's head back up to the house. Then we can talk about that next date, because I'm looking forward to that."

She looked at his hand, but didn't take it. With not a move to get up, she said, "Me too. Ya know, there's only one thing that would make tonight even better."

"I was going for perfect. I didn't succeed?"

"You were close."

"What's that one thing?"

He was staring at her mouth. His hand was still extended toward her. And the way his mouth moved when he spoke, she knew his kisses would be soft, tender.

He leaned down toward her. If his lips ever touched hers, and his kiss was half as sexy as he was, there'd be no forgetting this night.

Instead, she tucked her feet underneath her and said, "A ride in that cute Mustang with the top down."

He caught her around her wrist just as she got halfway up.

Pulling her the rest of the way up, he brought her tummy to tummy with him, but she began to stumble, off balance.

He caught her. His large hand steadied her at the lower back.

She gasped.

His other hand slid down her arm, leaving a trail of chills as he sought her hand and then wove his fingers between hers.

She tipped her face to his. God, how she wished he would kiss her. For all the silly playfulness, she really wanted him to.

But he didn't. No, he was giving her a taste of her own medicine. Instead, that row of perfect white teeth caught in a smile and he leaned close into her neck.

Her heart pounded, and her eyes closed in anticipation. The scruff on his chin danced in her hair, making it tickle.

Then, he gave her shoulders a squeeze and dropped a gentle kiss on her mouth.

His lips felt perfect against hers. Warm, tender . . . and then he pulled back and said, "Come on. Last one to the car has to pump the gas. Which will be you."

"Me?" She leaped forward. "No! No fair." She pushed past him and ran as fast as she could to the front yard, then jumped into the driver's seat, since it was closest.

Scott slid to a stop at the driver's-side door. "Good Lord, girl. You'd have given Hillcrest Joyful Kixx a run for his money."

"I might be a little competitive," she said between gasps for air. "And out of shape."

"A little? I guess I'll be pumping the gas," he said. "You don't look that fast!"

She laughed so hard her shoulders shook. He dug the keys out of his pocket and tossed them in her lap. "You drive."

"You're going to let me drive this car?" Did he really trust her that much? He loved this car.

"Sure. It's made it this many years. I don't think some lead-footed city girl who drives a Mini Cooper can hurt her."

"Awesome!" She laid her cheek against the steering wheel and placed a gentle hand on the dashboard. "I hope you're ready for this ride, girl," she said, but those words were more for herself than for the car.

"Give me a second to put the top down."

She sat in the driver's seat, feeling extra special as he went through the process to put the ragtop down on the old Ford.

"Not quite as easy to put a top down back in the day, was it?"

"No button to push on this baby, but it's worth it."

He probably knew all the right buttons to push. She reached down and sprung the lever to pull the seat forward. As she stared into the dark night sky, the words just came out. "I'm glad I'm here with you."

"Me too." Scott got into the passenger's seat and reached over and twisted the key in the ignition. "Let's go."

"Where to?"

"I have just the place." Scott pulled one knee up and leaned against the door. She looked beautiful under the moonlight. "Back out and go to the end of the street and then turn left." He rather liked having lost that foot race. It hadn't been the plan, but the view from the passenger seat was certainly to his liking.

She took it slow through the neighborhood and made a left.

"Follow this road around the bend and then turn right. You'll be able to open her up on that road."

"You're giving me an okay to gun the engine?"

"Let her rip."

"You're not going to give me a ticket if I break the law, are you?"

"Try me."

She wiggled her eyebrows as if she was up to the challenge. Once she turned right, she put her foot on the gas and let out a squeal. "This car can roll!"

The wind was whipping her hair in a thousand directions, and he couldn't help laughing at her apparent glee. It was always the little things that meant the most. This little moment wouldn't be one he'd soon forget. If someone had told him a few days ago that this pain-in-the-ass city girl was going to grab his attention and make him want to take days off work, he'd have said that person was crazy. But there'd been something that day when he'd pulled her over. Something that had tugged at him.

Maybe Pearl Clemmons had passed along her matchmaking skills to his mom. This was the first time she'd ever been even close.

Savannah let her foot off the gas and slowed the car to a stop at the edge of the road. "Scott, that was amazing!" She let out a loud whoop. "I *knew* I should've bought the convertible model."

"Girl. There is no way that little car of yours would ever perform like this."

"You don't think it's sporty enough?"

"Or at all! There's nothing that could make that little Mini Cooper of yours a muscle car." He laughed. "I've never been the passenger in this car before. It was cool. You're a good driver. I think you're driving the wrong kind of car."

"Or maybe I'm driving the right kind of car, else you'd be writing me tickets all the time."

"We may have met sooner."

"True. My daddy loved cars. I used to sit outside while he tinkered on them. When I was little he would take my mom and me out every Saturday night for a ride. We would have the windows down, the wind just blowing. I'd come home and it would take, like, an hour for my mom to comb all those snarls out of my hair. It was worth every single teary-eyed tangle. Those rides were pretty awesome."

"You and your dad are close?"

"Oh, yeah. I was a total daddy's girl. Always."

"Was?"

"He died when I was eighteen." She looked down, twisting her hands in her lap. "Both my parents died when I was eighteen."

"I'm sorry. I didn't know."

"I don't talk about it much. I still miss them like crazy."

"I'm sorry." That explained the Kevlar she shielded that heart with. He couldn't even imagine losing a parent at that age. Losing Dad just five years ago had still been one hell of a blow, but at least they'd had a lifetime of memories together.

"Thanks for reminding me just how much I loved those rides."

He reached over and ran his hand along her cheek. "I'm glad I could help you remember some of the good parts."

She lifted her shoulder to his hand. "The best parts."

Her vulnerability was unexpected, but it made him more attracted to her than ever. It's impossible to realize how quickly life can change until it does. He was sure not going to waste any time now, and if spending a few of his evenings with his mom made her happy, it was worth his time to give them to her. He was sure Savannah would understand that. She probably wished she'd had that chance. "Why don't you switch seats with me?"

"Sure."

He got out and walked around, and she slid over the console into the passenger's seat.

Without a word, Scott pulled back out on the road and peeled out, causing the tires to squeal and the car to swerve in its own wake before powering ahead.

Savannah threw her head back, laughing the whole way.

He didn't slow down until they neared Bradford Junction Road.

"That was awesome!" Savannah squealed.

"You like that, huh?"

"Love it!"

"You might like this too." He slowed down and then took his foot off the gas and let the car edge along under the power of just the idle. "There are always a ton of deer out here along this turn, so let's see if we can catch a glimpse of any."

She pulled her feet up in the seat and leaned her arms outside of the door as he slowly drove down the street.

At least a dozen green dots reflected as they neared an open field.

He stopped the car and pointed toward them. "See them?" he whispered. The small herd stood perfectly still with the car lights reflecting in their eyes. The largest one turned and ran for the woods and the rest followed.

"That was so pretty. Did you see the way they hopped across that field? Their white tails were so much longer than I thought they'd be."

He laid a hand next to the gearshift, just inches from her leg, then dropped the shifter into gear and drove back to town.

He pulled the car to the curb in front of Buckham and Baxter. The whole street was quiet and only the glow from the night lights in the residences above the shops was proof that there was anyone else in the world tonight aside from him and Savannah.

He twisted in the driver's seat and hiked his elbow up on the steering wheel. "I had the best time tonight."

"Me too."

He couldn't take his eyes off her. "It was more than I'd ever expected."

She wrinkled her nose and leaned in. "I know

what you mean. It's like we've known each other forever."

"Yeah. Really is."

She shrugged. "Well. I guess this is it. Thanks for a great night."

"I'll walk you up."

"You don't have to do that."

"Oh, yes I do. You've met my mother. She'd have my head if it got around that I wasn't the perfect gentleman. She raised me better than that."

Savannah laughed. "Fine." She reached for the door handle.

"Wait right there."

He jumped out of the car, ran to her side, and opened the door.

She slid out of the seat, and he rested his hand on the small of her back as they walked up to the building and she stepped inside.

She turned to him and stood there for a second. "We're going to do this again. Aren't we?"

"I sure as hell hope so." He almost wished he hadn't sounded that excited. *Don't jinx it, man.*

She dropped her hand into his and they walked upstairs. He'd never taken those stairs so slow, but he didn't want the night to end.

When they got to the landing, she pulled out her key and unlocked the door.

"Thanks again." She leaned her shoulder on the door and it opened slightly, and so did her lips.

He didn't waste a moment. He slid a hand behind her neck and covered her mouth with his. The kiss was slow, and long, and good God he didn't want it to end. He may have been able to hold back before, at his house . . . but there was no holding back now. No playful exit. No bantering.

Her lips responded just as hungrily as his own. She gasped as his hand slid down her bare arm. Soft beneath his fingers.

Could she possibly feel the same way? She had to be feeling the same way. He breathed in her scent. Her hair smelled of honeysuckle or something sweet.

He pulled away.

She looked beautiful standing there, her mouth still damp from his. Her eyes were still closed, but a smile played on her lips. "Nice," she whispered.

He let out a breath and half whispered, "That second date needs to be soon."

"Call me," she mouthed the words, barely audible.

He pushed the door open.

She stepped inside and turned to face him. "Good night."

He pulled the door closed and stayed there for just a moment until he heard her turn the lock.

Each step down the darkened stairway echoed, and suddenly he felt lonelier than he'd ever felt in his life.

Chapter NINE

Scott had been at his desk for more than an hour, but he hadn't gotten the first lick of work done. His mind had been on Savannah since the moment he left her last night.

Leaving her at the door was the hardest thing he'd had to do in a while, and although he wanted to see her again more than anything, now he was in a battle with himself over just how smart—or dumb—that would be.

"Your mom is on line two," a voice came over the intercom.

He punched the button and put her on speaker. "Good morning, Mom."

"How are you this morning?"

"Great. What's up?"

"I heard you had a special date last night."

He snatched the phone from its cradle. "And how exactly did you hear about that?" He glanced at the clock. "Already?"

"It's a small town."

He grunted.

"It's true?" Her voice was full of enthusiasm. Way too much enthusiasm.

"Well, yeah, but—"

"I knew it. That girl is perfect for you. I knew the first day I spoke to her at the artisan center."

"Slow down, Mom."

"You like her, don't you?"

"She's nice."

"I knew it!"

"It was a nice evening, but she lives up in northern Virginia, and she's going home soon. It's not likely anything will come of it." And saying those words out loud had a particularly wounding sting.

"That's only a couple hours away. Y'all could have a long-distance relationship. Famous couples make that work all the time."

"Is this why you called?"

"Isn't it reason enough?"

There was always more to it with her. "Not really."

"Oh, don't be a sourpuss. I just want you to be happy."

Then quit trying to fix me up was what he was thinking, but what came out of his mouth was "Yes, ma'am. I know. I'm in the middle of something. Is there something you needed?"

"Oh, I'm sorry. No, you get back to work. Glad you had a good night. Bye now."

She'd already hung up. Sometimes she was like that. When she was done talking it was like the quarter ran out and *wham,* she was gone.

He put the phone back down and looked at his computer screen.

So it was an itty-bitty lie. He was in the middle

of something; it just wasn't work, as he'd implied. On the screen were the search results on one Savannah Dey. He'd spent the last hour gathering all the information he could about her.

She'd been the belle of Belles Corner in high school. Cheerleader, gymnast, even played softball. People should know that whatever they put out on the Internet could be scooped up by any nosy looker. Today, that was him. Interestingly enough, his little city slicker had grown up in a town about the size of Adams Grove. A little smaller, even.

He'd even found a picture from their local paper. The *Belles Corner Beacon* came out once a week. They had a website too. Adams Grove hadn't even stepped up to that yet. He found a picture in the archives of Savannah standing next to her dad, a big man with a receding hairline and a laughing smile, holding a fifteen-pound bass that they'd caught in a father-daughter tournament on Salem Lake.

Actually, she hadn't been all that easy to find online, but once he found the obituary for her parents, he was able to trace down her hometown and find the old school postings and stuff.

Her parents had died in a car accident. The car overturned, and Savannah was the only survivor. He wondered if that accident had anything to do with her leaving the small town, or if that had been her chosen path all along.

The only tie to her being a writer was a small paper in northern Virginia that got bought out. After that . . . nothing. Maybe she'd been promoted to editor or to a position behind the scenes. Or maybe she really had been working on that novel all this time.

Or maybe she was living off a big, fat inheritance, but then she didn't have that vibe about her. She was a city girl, but not a rich brat. No matter what scenario his brain conjured up, his heart made up an excuse for her.

That was bad news.

This girl had trouble written all over her.

He was way too interested way too fast. It wasn't likely that she'd ever live in a small town like this. If she'd had any interest in that she'd be back in her hometown already. He didn't need to get interested in another girl who wouldn't fit into his lifestyle. Warning flares were shooting off around him like it was the Fourth of July, but he just couldn't help himself. He wanted to know more. Needed to know more.

Deputy Taylor rapped his knuckles on the sheriff's door. "Hey, man."

"Hey, Dan. What's up?"

"Chaz just dropped off tickets for us to get rid of. A couple of the guys got sick and didn't sell their quota of tickets to the annual Ruritan Club Barn Dance. He needs our help. I figured you and your mom were going anyway. That'd be two, unless you already got yours. We each need to sell six."

"That's fine. I hadn't picked up mine yet. I can get rid of them."

Deputy Taylor set the paper-clipped batch of tickets on Scott's desk. "I'm taking mine down to the senior center. Going to let them give them away at bingo."

"Good idea." Scott stood up and pulled out a fold of money from the front of his pants, then counted out ninety dollars. "Give that to Chaz when you see him."

"Sure thing." Deputy Taylor walked out of Scott's office and then came right back in. "Are you going to ask that new girl to go with you?"

Scott jerked his head up.

"Don't look so surprised. It's kind of the talk of the town."

"My mother." His head lolled back. "Got to love her."

"She means well, but there are a lot more tongues wagging than hers. Word is that little DC girl gets her coffee down at Mac's every morning. Mac's been telling folks he thinks it's because she hopes she'll run into you down there, like that first day she hit town. I'm pretty sure Mac may have beat your mom to the punch on this one."

"Mac? What's he know? We were in there once. Just once, and that's before she was even sticking around for a while."

"Must have been some fireworks. Because he's adamant that the girl is going to be the next new resident of our town."

"He's just stirring the pot." Scott thought back to that day. "Those weren't fireworks. That was gunfire. She was still ticked off for me stopping her on I-95."

"Oh yeah. Everyone knows you didn't give her the ticket too. You going soft on us?"

"It wasn't like that." Great. He should have given her the doggone ticket. He never let people out of tickets once he stopped them. Why had she been different? It was that ex-husband-marrying-the-cousin story. Probably wasn't even true. If that didn't take the cake, that flat tire was going to ruin her day anyway. Maybe he *was* going soft, or maybe deep down he'd known there was something special about her right then and there during that traffic stop.

"Fireworks. Gunfire. Hell, call it sparklers, whatever it is . . . other people are noticing it too. Wake up, dude. She's cute. You could do worse. In fact, I've seen you do worse."

Now that was just below the belt. "You too? Whose side are you on?"

"I saw the way you two talked that day she was in here about the police blotter."

"It was work."

"Didn't look like work to me."

Truth was, as much as she could irritate him

and push his buttons, he felt alive when he was around her. And hopeful. Hopeful that he might really have someone around again to cook with, play with, grow old with.

"Ask her to the dance."

"It's probably not her thing." Then again, it was and he knew it. He'd seen her dancing that day at the Cody Tuggle concert. Savannah could move. She might be a city girl now, but there were country roots in her boots.

"You're the best dancer around. If she goes, she may as well get the benefit of our best local talent."

"Then set her up with Derek." Mac's son had way better moves than he ever would. That kid could dance. Only the thought of Savannah in someone else's arms, even on a dance floor, sent a bitter taste to his mouth. "Get out of here."

Deputy Taylor laughed. "I've worn out my welcome. Later, man."

The bumbling Taylor had been a walking catastrophe when he first set foot in Adams Grove. Not because he was a bad cop. He'd come with the highest honors, but he hadn't expected the nuances that a small town added to the job, and it had taken him a while to get his country-town groove on. He was a good guy, and he'd become a great addition to their team. While Adams Grove had taken a while to warm up to the Northern boy, no one considered him a Northerner anymore. Now he was one of their own.

Scott sat at his desk and fanned out the tickets.

"Mom." He dealt two for her. She'd drag some poor sucker from the church.

"Mike and Brooke." New to town, and this would be their first time, plus they were fun to be around.

"Me." He slid his ticket in front of him and stared at the other.

Asking her to dinner had been easy. Why did he feel so nervous about asking her to the dance? He rolled his eyes. *Because everyone in town is already talking. This'll be like pouring gasoline on an open fire.*

He leaned his elbows on the desk and moved the mouse with his finger, which brought his computer screen back to life. That picture of that little girl with her daddy—the ear-to-ear grin and freckles—made him smile. That kiss last night. Now *that* was fireworks.

He grabbed the tickets off the top of his desk, then headed out.

Deputy Taylor was getting into his car when Scott walked out of the station house. "Where you headed?"

Scott almost hated to say it out loud. "Coffee. Mac's."

"Ha, I knew it."

Scott just shook his head and kept walking. Mac's Bakery was a short walk, and if she wasn't there, he'd keep going and see if she was home. Well, not home . . . but in the apartment. She'd only be there another few days. If anything was going to pan out, he'd have to move fast.

And even though he'd set out with the sole intention of tracking her down, when he looked up and saw her barely a block away walking into Mac's, his heart did a flip and landed right in his throat.

His palms went sweaty and he could feel his fingerprints dampening the paper. He shoved the tickets in his pocket and slowed down.

Second thoughts crept in. If he took her to that dance, there'd be no stopping the gossip. Did he care?

He didn't have a choice. If he didn't find a good reason to get her out on another date quickly, she'd be gone, and then all he'd have would be a handful of wonder-ifs.

Scott sucked in a deep breath and swallowed that lump back, forging ahead.

As he reached for the door, Savannah was walking out.

She jumped back, her coffee sloshing out of the lid across her hand.

"Good morning," he said. "I'm sorry. Let me get that." *Smooth,* he thought. He grabbed a handful of napkins off one of the small tables near the door and dabbed at her hand.

"It's fine. It barely spilled." She switched hands

and slapped her damp hand on the rear of her jeans. "See. No harm." She smiled.

"Good to see you." She looked like she belonged in this town. Like she should be walking down this street every single day. Her hair was pulled back in a braid, and with no makeup, she looked even prettier than she had in that fancy dress.

"I was just going to grab some coffee. Want to join me?"

She stopped and turned. "I do."

Scott reached the counter with her on his heels, and Mac placed a large cup of coffee on it in front of him. "Hang on one second." He rushed to the back.

Savannah hopped up on a barstool at the end of the counter and flashed Scott a smile as he walked over to join her.

Mac rushed back out with a plate, and looked panicked when he realized Scott wasn't still in that spot near the register where he'd left him. Mac's face spread into a sugar-sweet grin when he spotted Scott and Savannah sitting at his counter. "Something special to share." He put a cardboard box in front of them and then turned and grabbed two forks. "On the house."

Scott opened the box, and Savannah said, "I am going to have to work out for a week to burn that sucker off."

A thick pastry was spun into a cinnamon twirl covered in sticky icing. "We're going to need a table for this." He picked up her coffee and his, and balanced the box on top. "Come on." He motioned Savannah from the counter to a small two-top by the window. There weren't many seats in the little place, but right under Mac's nose was not the best place for them to chat, since the guy had already run wild with assumptions. Besides, if Savannah turned him down for the dance, he'd just as soon no one else know.

His chair screeched across the tiled floor, and the next sound was a moan from Savannah as she plunged her fork into the pastry. She wasn't shy about taking the first bite.

"Good?"

"Oh, please. You have to ask? We're talking Mac here." She took another bite. "I had such a great time last night."

"So did I. I have something for you."

"What's that?" Her eyes danced. "You're not going to give me a speeding ticket for last night, are you?" She laughed playfully. "I'll citizen's arrest *you* if you do. I saw that speedometer needle buried on Bradford Junction Road."

"Last night stays between the two of us."

"Deal."

He pulled one of the tickets out of his shirt pocket. "I was wondering if you might honor me with your company at the annual barn dance. The Ruritans put it on every year to raise money for their scholarships."

"When is it? You know I've only got the apartment for another week."

It wasn't much time, but he'd enjoy it while it lasted. "The dance is this Saturday night.

"Tomorrow? Yeah. I'll be here."

"Is that a yes?" He prayed it was a yes.

"Yes." She grabbed for the ticket, and he pulled it just from her reach. "All right, wise guy."

"I'll pick you up?"

She cast him a sideways glance. "Like another date? Or a first one."

Why had he said that last night? He had tried to be funny, since she was dodging his every move. Now it just sounded silly. "Does it matter?"

"I don't know. Maybe."

Was she going to say no? "You already said yes to coming."

"So I did. You fixing me dinner before?"

"How about we cook together?"

She peeled a small piece of the cinnamon roll back and popped it into her mouth. "You remembered."

"It was just last night." He picked up the other fork, stabbed the cinnamon roll right in the middle, and dug out the softest, gooiest part.

"True." She watched him put that big hunk of soft pastry in his mouth. "And no fair. You just took the best part."

"You ain't seen the best part yet, Savannah Dey."

"Don't go around bragging unless you can deliver, mister."

Oh, I can deliver. He wasn't sure they were still talking about dinner, and he kind of liked that.

She continued, "You grill those world-famous steaks you keep talking about. I'll get the rest of the stuff together to bring tomorrow."

"Yours will be well done—hot all the way through. Promise." He leaned in closer, rather enjoying the flirting.

The bells on the door sounded and Connor walked into the bakery. "Hey, Scott. Deputy Taylor said you were down here. Hey, Savannah."

"Good morning," she said, straightening back, having not even realized just how physically close to Scott she'd gotten during that flirty war. Things were moving too fast. She had a job to do, and she was getting way too close to Scott. She'd never be able to write those stories Evelyn wanted about the Goto Hell murders and Scott from an unbiased position, but that was her ticket off the Advice from Van column. But she hadn't felt like this . . . Well, she'd never felt like this.

"Everything going okay in the apartment?"

"Fine. Yep. Perfect."

"Good." Connor cuffed Scott on the shoulder. "That strictly enforced speed limit of yours is stirring up trouble for us again."

Scott leaned back in his chair. "It keeps people safe. Fatalities on this stretch of road have been reduced by thirty-two percent since I put that policy in place. It's a good thing."

Savannah piped up. "Do you really know that, or are you just making that number up?"

Connor laughed. "Oh, he knows. He has a freaking chart with the data. He hasn't showed you his chart? He's a little nerdy like that."

Savannah made a mental note of the statistic. She could probably use that in one of the articles. "Nerdy. Well, there's just a whole lot more to you every time I turn around."

Connor nudged her arm. "Stick around. I've got stories that I know he doesn't want you to hear."

"All right, you two. That's enough ganging up on me today. What's going on, Connor?"

"You and I know and appreciate that your stance on speeding has been a good thing, but Adams Grove hit some online paper this morning. Heck, people are even joking about it on Twitter. You're trending."

"I don't think that's a good thing, is it?"

Connor shook his head. "Not in this case. The story has taken on a life of its own."

"It'll pass. That online stuff is fleeting. People will forget about it as soon as someone posts a video about a surfing goat or something."

"It wasn't just a post, Scott. It was on

GetItNowNews.com. And they even threw a few darts directly at you, the sheriff of Adams Grove."

Savannah choked.

"You okay?" Scott turned to her in concern.

She raised a hand and nodded.

Scott patted her on the back. "You sure you're okay?"

"Sure," she eked out.

Connor slid a chair from the next table over. "Do you mind?"

"Of course not," Scott answered.

"Reynolds called me about it this morning wanting to know if there was anything the town could do legally to make them retract it."

"Reynolds? Why's he even worried about it?" Scott put his fork down and leaned back in the chair with his arms folded across his chest.

"Who's Reynolds?" Savannah asked.

"The guy running against me for sheriff this fall," Scott said. "He's probably the reason everyone around here is spun up. He's the one fanning the fire. He probably wrote the damn thing. Have you read the article, Connor?"

"I read it."

"And?"

"It was less than glowing, but there wasn't anything slanderous in it. Mostly generalizations. Definitely not flattering, but . . ."

"Let it go. I don't care about that stuff." Scott's phone rang. "I'm sorry. I've got to take this."

Savannah said, "No problem. I really have to run. I'll see you soon, okay?"

"Yeah. Okay."

Savannah couldn't get out of Mac's quick enough. She raced back to the apartment and slammed the door behind her. Not because of the frustration she felt, but because she couldn't get inside quick enough. She hadn't even heard half of what Scott and Connor had said once Connor had mentioned GINN. Her whole mind had just shut down.

Man, if that article had caused this much of a wake in Adams Grove, the one she'd originally written would have rocked them right out of the boat.

She clenched her teeth. Why hadn't she owned up to it as soon as Connor mentioned the story on GetItNowNews.com? It was only a matter of time before someone connected the dots. It wasn't like Savannah Dey was that common a name. Even though she'd only met a small number of the folks in town, there was no way she'd escape this without someone finding out.

Connor probably already knew. He'd said he'd read the article, but she'd been too afraid to make eye contact with him to see if there was any indication that he'd made the connection between her and the byline. She'd just needed to bolt.

Now it was going to be really awkward.

They'd think she was hiding something. *Well, yeah! Because I am.* The room seemed to spin a little to the left. She sat down and took a deep breath.

Guilt weighed on her.

She hated that she was causing such a stir, although that was quite honestly what Evelyn was paying her to do. It had always seemed like so much fun in the past, but this time was different. This time she had gotten to know the people of the town. Now it seemed wrong. Hurtful. Maybe that's why Evelyn had always preached about not getting to know the subjects of your article personally.

Savannah's moral compass was spinning, and suddenly there were a lot of things that didn't seem quite right. Her mood dipped. When she'd run into Scott this morning, she had been on top of the world; now she wished she could hide under it. She went into the bedroom and crawled underneath the covers.

Only she couldn't sleep this problem away. She pulled the pillow over her head and squeezed her eyes tight, rereading the article in her head.

They were totally overreacting. Maybe this was just that Reynolds guy's way of getting his foot in the door to steal some votes from Scott. He'd look like a hero, if he could get the rumors quieted. Lucky for him, he wasn't the one who started them in the first place.

She climbed back out of bed and turned on her computer.

She went to the online GINN portal. With the tools they had for the staff, she could check the hits on any of her work the paper had published. Statistics showed the website hits by article, ISP, region, right down to the city in some cases. She'd be able to quickly tell just how many people around here had read that article, aside from the Northerner who was determined to take over as sheriff in this town.

Savannah's mood lightened as she pictured some Jersey type and Scott Calvin counting off steps with jingling spurs for a gunfight. "This town ain't big enough for the two of us."

Her money would be on Scott.

She entered her log-in information and mentally prepared herself for much lower numbers than she got on the Advice from Van column. After all, she'd built that following from the ground up and fostered it for two years. This wouldn't have the oomph of the syndication numbers either. Savannah Dey was a brand-new platform. She'd be starting to pay dues all over again, but she could do that. If nothing else, that advice column had given her confidence and experience that could have taken years to get.

The current online issue stats populated on the screen. Out of habit, she drilled down to take a look at the Advice from Van numbers first. They remained steady. That was good. She printed out the page so she could take a closer look later. The printer Connor had on the desk wasn't fast, but it chugged the page slowly out.

It would be interesting to watch the stats as Andrew took over her column. Not that she wished him anything but success, but less success than she'd had would be okay. Once he started picking out the letters himself, there'd probably be a dip.

She took the printout from the paper tray and placed it on the corner of the desk. Then she typed her name in the search bar, but nothing popped up.

"Don't tell me they misspelled my name on my first article." She dropped the *h* from Savannah and tried again. Then spelled *Dey* with an *a* instead of an *e*. Still nothing.

She pulled up the list of all the articles that ran in the day's paper. As she scrolled down through the titles, hers finally caught her eye.

She clicked on the hyperlink, but her article, "Nothing Speedy in a Small Town," was in the Penny for Your Thoughts column.

"What the heck?"

The Penny for Your Thoughts column had been a staple of the paper for years, even before it went digital. No one got a byline for his work there. It was just kind of a hodgepodge of freelance stock articles from the staff reporters. She'd always considered it filler. Someone must have missed a deadline, or late-breaking news had bumped her, for Evelyn to have posted her story there.

She clicked on the stats and was delighted by the numbers. Not only had people clicked on it to read, but it was being shared all over the place on every social media outlet. Connor was right. This sucker was going viral, and there were a lot of hits from this region of Virginia. They must have posted a good stock photo with the story for it to take off like that. There were lots of shares of the image link too.

The image wasn't a stock photo. Instead it was cartoon of a redneck-looking deputy hanging out the window of his cruiser, pointing a blow-dryer toward the oncoming traffic, with the caption "Unable to afford radar, the county keeps drivers in line with a blow-dryer." She laughed out loud. That pretty well summed up how she felt about being stopped that day. No wonder the story was going viral.

She opened the link to the article, and that cinnamon roll from this morning nearly rolled right up her throat.

It wasn't the rewritten story at all.

"Evelyn? How could you . . . ?" She read through it. Start to finish. Word for word. The article in today's paper was the one she'd originally submitted. "Holy shit." She looked to heaven. "Sorry, Momma." Her momma never was one to hear a lady cuss, and it was one rule she'd always remembered—except at moments like this.

Oh yeah, she'd just given Reynolds something better than a hefty campaign donation. She'd given him ammo. She pulled her fist to her mouth. How could she have been so careless? Scott would never forgive her.

She clicked the print icon and watched every ugly word chug out on that little printer.

She dialed Evelyn, but her phone went straight to voicemail. Rather than leave a message, she texted her, while still holding the copy of the article in her shaking hand.

Savannah: Why are you avoiding me? I told you not to run that story.

Nothing.

Savannah: The replacement story was in on time. You said you got it. Was this a mistake?

Nothing.

It was no mistake. Evelyn never missed a step. She pored through every detail of every single thing that went on with GINN, and if there had been a mistake, she'd have been on the phone immediately to explain.

Well, the only saving grace was that she didn't get the byline. At least no one could tie the story to her.

Her gut didn't feel any better knowing that, though. It churned and gurgled. She felt like she'd contracted the flu, but she knew it was what she deserved for that snarky, self-serving story. She'd been mad and she'd taken out her anger in public without giving Scott a chance to tell his side of the story. Not a fair fight.

Scott would be so hurt if he knew she'd written that article about him. Connor probably wouldn't be too pleased either, since he was the one who had led the wolf right into the herd.

Maybe Scott was right and people would forget about it as soon as something else got their attention. Heck, she was ready to start googling to find a video with some viral potential to speed that process up and save herself.

How could this have happened?

Scott was the first guy she'd met in . . . heck, in forever . . . who made her feel good. He challenged her sensibilities and made her feel a little giddy. Made her feel like maybe . . . maybe . . . she could let her guard down. And being with his mom made her miss her own like crazy, but in a really awesome way. She was already feeling like she didn't want to leave this place.

A tear fell to her cheek.

She swept it away. If she started crying, she might never stop.

Savannah tossed the article on the desk and stood there staring at it like it might come to life and jump back across the desk at her. She hadn't cried since she left Belles Corner behind. Hadn't allowed herself. Had barely allowed herself to even think about Momma and Dad. But the tears fell, and they fell hard. She walked into the bathroom in search of tissues. No luck, so she spun off a dozen sheets of toilet paper and blew her nose. She sat on the cool black-and-white tiles and leaned against the wall. Sobbing. Not for this story, which was awful and hurtful, but for every sad thing that had ever happened.

Fear climbed her spine. What if Reynolds won the election because of her? Scott loved that job. This town. It was his whole life. This time Evelyn couldn't soothe her worries. She'd never understand the way Savannah felt. The responsibility of the outcome of that story. Evelyn was focused on sales, and Savannah had delivered a story that fit the bill.

"Momma. What can I do to fix this? Please help me. I need you right now. I miss you so badly."

The sound of a flurry of typewriter keys sounded from the other room.

Anger replaced the sorrow, as she headed for the phone. Savannah stabbed at the answer icon.

Evelyn's voice crooned in that singsong way she had. "Have you cooled down yet?"

"How could you do that to me? And why didn't you warn me?"

"Van, you did submit that story. You know the rules. Once you submit a story, that intellectual property becomes property of GetItN—"

"Don't give me that standard spiel. I've heard

you give it a hundred times to other writers, and we've laughed over drinks about it. I'm not laughing now."

"I'm sorry. It's doing great. I told you it would."

"We're friends. Why would you do that and not tell me?"

"It's business. And look. I was right. People love it. Now when am I going to get the 'Looking for Mr. Feed and Seed' article?"

Savannah felt her lip quiver. She couldn't write that article. She didn't want to write any of them anymore. "I'm not ready."

"You promised me those three articles. I need them."

"I'll come up with something different."

"Don't be ridiculous. You've never missed a deadline. Even when you had the flu and couldn't sit up straight in bed, you came through. Now quit falling in love with that little town, pull up those big-girl panties, and let's get your career rolling. I might remind you too, you're there on my dime."

The words stung. It was a double-edged sword. She'd learned so much from Evelyn, but now she was paying the dues.

She'd been sucked right into that money-over-morals trap.

"I have to go," Savannah said.

"Wait. When will I get that next article?"

"I'm going to have to get back to you on that."

Evelyn's laugh wasn't comforting this time.

"That's fine. I know you won't let me down."

Savannah ended the call and stared at the phone. "Don't be so sure."

She stood and looked at her reflection in the mirror. Her eyes were rimmed in red and her nose was swollen. "Momma? Dad? This isn't who you raised me to be."

It wasn't like she was breaking laws. Sure, there were way worse things, but her mom and dad were good-hearted people, and she had been raised to see the good in things. Why had it been easier to turn her back on that and look for the bad stuff? To make fun of people and do just about anything for the laugh or the money? Maybe because then it wasn't personal. She wasn't living. She was just getting through every day any way that it took to not be that little girl who was the only one to survive that accident. Anything to not feel pain, loss, or love.

A knock on the door surprised her.

She glanced at the time on the phone. She wasn't supposed to meet Daphne for another hour and a half to help at the church. She quickly ran a washcloth under the cold water and dabbed at the tears and got rid of the streaks of mascara, then ran to the door. Maybe Mike had heard her crying. She'd swear it was the radio.

She sniffed back the remaining tears and pasted her best smile on her face, ready to fake it with Mike and get rid of him fast.

"Yoo-hoo." The voice was definitely not male. "You in there, Savannah?"

Had Evelyn sent someone over? There was no way she could have reacted that quickly.

Savannah peeked out the peephole. It was Daphne. Early.

She pulled the door open. "Hi, Daphne. Sorry to keep you waiting. I was just washing my face. Getting ready for tonight."

"I knew I should've called first." She walked right into the apartment. "I can wait."

"You're really early."

She looked sorry. "I wanted to show you something before we went. Do you mind? I can come back later."

Savannah pushed her hair behind one ear and shook her head. "No. Of course not. Could you give me just a couple minutes to finish freshening up?"

"Sure. I'll just sit right here and wait."

Savannah balled her fists and tried to gather her emotions. "Great. You do that. I won't be but a few minutes." She half ran to the bathroom. She did some deep breathing and tried to steady her nerves. There was nothing she could do about that story situation right now. No one knew she'd written the article. All she could do was pray that it fell from the radar quickly.

When she finished she looked in the mirror. "Momma, is this your idea of sending in help? I sure as heck hope so."

Chapter TEN

Savannah walked back out to the living room, where Daphne was sitting on the couch waiting. If she acted happy, no one would know the difference, and she was the queen of acting happy.

"Okay, I'm ready. Sorry that took so long." Savannah grabbed her purse and keys.

Daphne stood up. "No problem at all. I should have called first, but I just got so excited I couldn't help myself."

"Well, now you've got my curiosity up."

"Good. Come on." Daphne took the lead out of the apartment and down the stairs.

"Do you want me to drive?" Savannah asked.

"No. It's nearby. Just follow me." Daphne scurried in such a hurry that it almost looked like she was twerking there for a minute. That thought made Savannah giggle. She took a double skip-hop and caught up with Daphne. "Slow down."

"I'm sorry. I'm just so excited I can hardly contain myself."

"I can see that."

Daphne stopped at the corner and looked both ways, continued up the block, then suddenly stopped.

"What?" Savannah looked around, but they were just standing in the middle of the block.

Daphne pointed across the street. "Look."

A FOR SALE OR LEASE sign was tucked in the corner of the window of one of the storefronts.

Realization struck pretty quickly. "Daphne, are you thinking about the tearoom?"

Daphne turned to Savannah and took both of her hands into her own. "Dear, you have sparked a renewed energy in me. I'd decided I was too old and too darn late to live that dream, but you're right. I can do this on my rules and my timeline and still have what I've always wanted. There's no such thing as waiting too long, and I'm not going to waste one more minute."

Savannah's mood lifted instantly. It was so exciting to see Daphne filled with such joy. She cursed the fact that she'd pretty much wasted all her time in an attempt to somehow dull the pain of losing her parents. How would her life have been different if she hadn't?

"You believed in me." Daphne squeezed her hand. "Savannah, you're so young and full of life. You have no idea what it's like to become old and complacent. I outlived my husband. My son is grown and doesn't need me."

"He loves you very much."

"Oh, I know that, but I'm always meddling in his business. It has to drive him half crazy."

She was right. It probably did, but he didn't really seem to mind.

"You really think I can do this?"

"I do. Yes. I wouldn't joke about something like that."

Daphne plunged her hand into her front pocket and retrieved a single gold key.

Savannah stared at it and then back at Daphne. "You have the key?"

Daphne pulled her lips together, barely able to hold in the excitement. "I do. I couldn't bear to even think about going inside without you. Will you look at it with me?"

"Are you kidding me? I'd be honored!" Savannah was swept up in the excitement.

Daphne's eyes sparkled with life. It was infectious. "Come on. Let's go look!"

The two women crossed the street. Daphne worked the key in the old lock, but wasn't having any luck.

"Here, let me do that for you." Savannah took the key. Daphne's hands were practically shaking. "Calm down, gal. You're going to have a heart attack on me, and I don't know CPR." Savannah worked the key into the lock and lifted the handle. Finally, the old brass mechanism clicked over. She pushed the door open. "You first."

Savannah watched Daphne stride to the center of the room and slowly turn with a little glint of pride and a lot of moxie, not so unlike a magician when he knows he's nailed a trick.

Savannah could just imagine the wheels turning in Daphne's mind, and it didn't take but a moment for Savannah to start picturing the images from those plans Daphne had shared with her—trans-forming the big, dusty space into something elegant and special. "Right here. A long counter. Rich wood with a furniture finish. Right?"

"You remember." Daphne moved through the room with such spirit that for a second there, Savannah thought she might just start twirling in the middle of it. Then she raised a hand and pointed. "One. Two. Three. Tables in these spots. Parties of six?"

Savannah chimed in. "A beautiful display case over here with all of your teapots. You can rotate the services you're using all the time so the room looks different every time someone comes in."

"That would be fun. I love that idea."

"Over here. A computer stand."

Daphne's face went blank.

"Stick with me. An easy iPad app so that people can type in their names and a little note every time they visit. Plus you can record which teas they've tried and their favorites."

"Demographics." Daphne's eyes lit up.

"Yes. Exactly."

"I'm not good with computers."

"You don't have to be. We've got people."

" 'We'?" Daphne sounded so hopeful. "Yes, and just three days a week to start. Maybe forever.

Who knows, but never open on Sundays. That's God's day."

"Of course. People will totally respect that."

"And it will be more special that way." Daphne walked over to a huge wooden staircase. "I wonder if the staircase is in good working condition." She started to take a step.

"Wait," Savannah called out, racing to the woman's side. "Let's not test it without having someone check first. We can look up there later, but if it's usable space you could even rent it out for events without being open."

Daphne clapped her hands. "That's exactly what I was thinking. Especially on the days I'm not open. Franny Markham, she runs the B and B in town, she's been doing some catering on the side. She's a fabulous cook. Everything from scratch, and I'm not just talking Southern dishes. She can whip up those fancy five-star kinds of food too. It's been her dream all along, but the B and B just isn't big enough for a party of any substantial size. I could help her."

"I bet you could partner with Jill over at the artisan center for some things too."

"What a great idea. Jill is always doing fun stuff. We could even let her display some things down here to cross-promote. Franny Markham catered Jill and Garrett's rehearsal dinner. Oh, yes, there would be lots of things we could do."

Savannah looked around. There wasn't a thing

305

left behind to give any hint of what had once been here. "What was in this space before?"

"Jack down at the paper owns it." Daphne sniffed in a breath of air the way she did when she was getting ready to tell a story. Stories that Savannah was quickly learning were rarely short.

"You know he has a sister, but there was also a brother. He passed away two years ago. This was his place. He ran a tax service out of it for the last few years and lived upstairs. They auctioned a lot of his stuff off when he passed, but Jack couldn't part with the building. It's been sitting here empty ever since."

"Two years empty is a long time for an old building."

"This building has been in their family since it was built. The very first issue of the *County Gazette* came from this address. When they moved to the building they're in now, this place became an ice cream shop. There's a kitchen area in the back, but it hasn't been used in a long time. I'm sure it's hard for Jack to let go of it."

"So why are they getting rid of it now?"

Daphne sat on the bottom stair. "They're tired. They need the money. Bee isn't coming back, and she's going to need to buy a place to live in North Carolina."

"She'd gone to help out their grandniece who was having a baby, right?"

"Yes. Anna, bless her heart. She had a difficult pregnancy."

"I'm so sorry. Is the baby okay?"

"Oh, yes." Daphne glanced heavenward. "Thank the Lord for watching over them. The baby is just fine, and so is she. The pregnancy itself had been fine. It just took a real toll on her marriage. They left Adams Grove about three years ago. That family has been through so much."

"What happened?"

"Their daughter was abducted when she was just two years old. It was like she just disintegrated into thin air. No leads. No nothing."

"Oh, my gosh. How does a family get through that kind of trauma?"

"They don't. When Anna got pregnant again it was like a lifeline to her little Christina, but her husband was having no part of it. He packed up and moved out. She hasn't heard one word from him since."

"That's crazy."

"It seems so heartless, but they were so broken . . . just absolutely brokenhearted, broken-spirited when their daughter disappeared. Scott did everything he could to help find that child, but there was just nothing to go on. He had the best people in the state down here helping."

Savannah held her hands to her heart. "It's so sad. Well, I'm glad that Anna had another child. I hope in some way it soothes that heartache just a little."

"Me too, Savannah."

"Were they home when it happened?"

"Actually . . . ," Daphne said, letting the word hang in the air. "The last time they saw her was right here in this building." She pulled her arms up as if to chase a chill. "I'm sure that's part of why Jack has held on to the building. Maybe Anna having the baby made him feel like he might be able to finally let it go."

"I'll keep them in my prayers."

"I knew you would." Daphne's gentle smile sent comfort right down to Savannah's toes.

"Anyway, Jack and Bee are letting go of this building so they can help pay for some of their grandniece's expenses and relieve some of that burden for her. It's a wise decision."

"And perfect timing for you and your tearoom."

"Timeless Tea." Daphne surveyed the room again. "Jack and Bee have worked together forever. She never married, and Jack is so introverted. A man of few words. Which is kind of funny for a man who runs a paper and has accountability for all of the news. But then his daddy and his daddy's daddy had done it, and he was following in those shoes."

"That's kind of sad."

"People can so easily get caught up in the

hurried day-to-day, what-ifs, and have-to-dos that they lose all perspective and forget to live."

Or in just surviving . . . like herself. Only that still wasn't a good excuse.

Daphne seemed to be speaking right to Savannah's heart, but Savannah knew she couldn't possibly know. "I guess their predicament kind of spurred me on with the tearoom too. Since Tom has been gone, I haven't really found a way to live for me. I need to fix that."

"You're an amazing woman." Savannah felt stronger herself just watching the courage and determination of her new friend.

"I love the name Timeless Tea. I knew it was perfect as soon as you said it. I can almost picture the logo with those swirly *T*s."

"Add an awning to the front of the building and it will soften the look. A simple solution."

"Definitely. Plus it will tie in with some of the others here along Main Street. I could ask Mac who did his."

"You could set up special days for mother-daughter teas. Just like my mom did for me. An actual tearoom would be so much cooler than the dining room at home."

"You'll help me. I always wanted a daughter. That would be so much fun."

"Can you imagine all those little girls dressed up for tea? The gloves and everything." Savannah wiggled her fingers. She remembered the first gloves her mother had bought her. "I have pictures from those parties tucked away back home." Maybe it was time to go through some of that stuff.

"Precious."

Savannah walked over to a nook near the window. "You could even post their pictures the following month—to drive repeat business. You know they'd come back to see themselves on the wall."

"You are so full of good ideas. I hope you'll help me."

"Of course I will."

"Even when you leave?"

"Of course." Only for one tiny moment, she'd almost forgotten she would be leaving.

Daphne brightened. "You could still call and talk through things with me on the phone. Or even stop in once in a while. Right?"

"I'd love that, Daphne." The thought hit her in the gut. How could she leave this behind? These people. This place. They gave her a different energy. One that she was beginning to like.

Daphne stood and hugged Savannah. "That's it then. I'm going to do it."

"What did Scott say about it?"

"I haven't told him yet. We can break the news to him together tomorrow night at the dance."

Savannah sucked in a breath. Facing Scott with the whole truth about that article would be hard, but he'd never forgive her if he found out from someone else. She had to tell him.

"But for tonight, we have to get over to the church and get to work."

Savannah dug her keys out of her purse. "Come on. I'll drive. My car's out back of the apartment."

The two of them walked back to the apartment building. Daphne was humming the whole way, and that made Savannah's heart sing.

Daphne looked awkward dipping low to get in the Mini Cooper. She huffed out a breath when she finally plopped into the seat. "Worse than those sporty cars that Scott loves so much. Tiny little car, isn't it?"

"It's good on gas."

"It ought to be. It can't weigh any more than us put together."

Savannah whipped out of the parking spot and pulled up to the stop sign. "Where to?"

Daphne gave her directions one turn at a time. The church was much bigger than she'd expected. The cemetery boasted colorful arrangements like a field of well-spaced wildflowers surrounding tiny buildings.

Dust puffed up around the tiny car as they pulled into the gravel driveway and then over into the paved parking lot on the far side of the building.

A dozen cars were already in the lot.

When they walked inside, it was like a hive of activity with women buzzing about the kitchen,

311

shuffling dishes and sharing ingredients. Daphne introduced Savannah to the other ladies, and then she and Savannah got right down to work on Daphne's famous poppy seed rolls and home-made egg salad.

They hadn't been in that church more than ten minutes when someone brought up the article about Scott.

A stab of guilt buried itself in her chest. All the joy and excitement she and Daphne had just shared was drowned by one dreadful comment.

The room went from a quiet, uplifting hum to a frenzy. Every single person, except Savannah, had an opinion about it, and they weren't holding back.

"No," Daphne shouted about the talk. She waved a wooden spoon over her head like a machete. "No. No. *No.*" Each word got a little louder and a lot firmer. "We will not dignify that online mess with any amount of gossip or energy. We know what's true and real." Daphne tossed the long-handled spoon down into a glass bowl with a clang. "You can't believe everything you see on the Internet. I'm not even on the Internet and I know that. I'm his mother, and if I can see that it's not worth reacting to, then I'd sure bet you can too." Daphne pinched her finger and thumb together and closed a make-believe zipper across her lips. "Zip it."

She didn't say another word. Instead she just

made eye contact with each woman in that room, and suddenly Savannah had a feeling she knew exactly how Scott was raised to be such a good and kind man. This woman had some power.

Savannah fell into bed exhausted on Friday night.

Those ladies at the church were twice her age, but they'd run circles around her. Why Daphne had thought she was too old to run a tearoom was beyond her. After seeing her hustle and choreograph all the goings-on that night, there was no doubt in Savannah's mind that Timeless Tea would be humming on all cylinders in no time.

She'd been so relieved when Daphne took control of that gossip about the article and shut it straight down. She'd sure made a mess of things with that story. How many other pots had she stirred without even knowing it over the last two years?

Momma had certainly sent her a message and a fix in the form of Daphne. Maybe she should have asked for Momma's help a long time ago. Or God's. She'd all but given up on him when he took her parents. It had been so unfair. They'd been such good people. Bringing his word to others. Living a good, caring life. They'd deserved to live on. She'd vowed she'd never put herself in the position to feel that kind of loss again. It had worked, but then she was also shortchanging herself, missing out on that big love that Momma and Daddy had shared. No one she'd ever known had been as in love as her parents.

She fell asleep wrapped in the memories of her parents, and she woke up with her heart aching to feel that level of love. To have someone look at her like Dad used to look at Momma would be incredible. She'd fallen asleep without closing the blinds, and this morning those marigolds in the window box were peeking into her window like they had a job to do.

She raised herself up on one elbow and enjoyed their beauty. "I could be happy with him, Momma. I wish you were here. You'd love him. I know you would." She dropped her head onto her arm and smiled. "I can't keep this secret from him, but I'm so afraid he'll be upset. Help me make this right, Momma."

Her cell phone rang and she swept it off the night table. She answered, half expecting it might be her mom.

"Hi, Savannah. It's Scott."

Gosh, you work fast, Momma. "Hi there."

"I didn't wake you, did I?"

"Oh, goodness, no. I can't sleep in. My body clock won't allow it."

"Good. I'm so sorry our morning got interrupted yesterday with all that mess with Connor."

"No. It was fine. No worries." She sat up and

314

nodded a thank-you to the marigolds for making her morning cheerful. Hearing Scott's voice was the cherry on top.

"Well, we got busy down here. I meant to catch up with you later in the day and it just didn't happen. I'm looking forward to tonight."

"Me too."

"The dance starts at seven thirty. I thought I'd pick you up around five thirty so we'd have plenty of time to cook dinner and eat. Does that still work for you?"

"Absolutely. Why don't you let me drive to your place? It's not that far." Plus, if he was mad when she told him what she'd done, she could leave. This was not going to be easy.

"You know the answer to that. I'll pick you up."

"Of course you will."

"We're going to have a wonderful night. I'll see you in a little while," he said, and he hung up.

Of course we will, she thought. She didn't get the chance to ask what he'd be driving. She was sure it would be a surprise, and that just added to the excitement.

Savannah felt her cheeks tugging from the smile that extended way farther than normal . . . probably all the way to her heart.

"Thank you, Momma." She wasn't about to let Momma down now.

Savannah wandered into the office and cleaned up the desk. She'd let some stacks of things accumulate, and there were still those letters to attend to.

She sat in the chair and pulled the trash can closer to her feet.

Scraps of paper and sticky notes were scattered everywhere. One note read, "Everyone has the same haircut. Cookie Cutter Salon." She crumpled it up and sent it sailing across the room into the trash can.

Another read, "Mailman reading the mail."

Another read, "Dogs groomed at the hair salon?"

Another read, "Grams of fat on the menu."

Another read, "Time warp."

She crumpled each one, then tossed them in the trash too. Those articles would never get written. There was no way she could write them now.

The last one read, "The mural?" She stuck that one right to the top of her laptop.

She went to the kitchen and looked under the sink. There was a brand-new box of great big lawn-and-garden trash bags. She snapped two off the roll and went back to the office to get rid of all the Advice from Van letters that were stacked in the corner of the room.

The two bags were nearly too heavy to carry, so she got a couple more of them and split up the loads into four lighter bags that would be easier to manage down the steep stairs.

It was Saturday and Carolanne and Connor were gone for the weekend.

Savannah went to the window and looked out back. Mike's truck was gone too.

She quickly slipped into a pair of yoga pants and a T-shirt, then wrangled the plastic bags out of her apartment one by one, like a bad guy hauling off dead bodies. She dragged one bag down the stairs, and even though she was in pretty good shape, she was out of breath. Poor George had hulked them all the way up. Bless his heart. She trudged back up and tied the remaining bags extra tight, then, one by one, sent them tumbling down the stairs with one good soccer kick each.

"Way easier!"

Dragging them out to the Dumpster was doable. She'd just finished stuffing the last one in when Mike drove up.

She walked over to her car and scrounged around in the front seat like she was looking for something, but she could feel him watching her.

She clutched a handful of papers in her hand and folded them in half. "How are you today?"

"Good," he said. "You headed out somewhere?"

She shrugged. "Just grabbing some papers to take with me to the . . . library."

"Research?"

"Yeah. You know, half of writing is research." That was totally lame, and now she had to walk somewhere. Stupid.

He nodded. "I guess you would know."

What was that supposed to mean? Okay, she was just being paranoid now. She pushed the car door closed and turned to walk away. "Bye," she said with a wave over her shoulder. Between the anxiety of having to tell Scott the truth tonight the excitement percolating inside to be spending time with him, and Mike's nosiness, she thought she might bust.

"Later."

Only he wasn't going inside. He was still standing there watching her, and that made her feel vulnerable.

She didn't even have her wallet with her, so she couldn't go grab a cup of coffee. Maybe she could stop in and see Jenn, or better yet, she'd go over and see Jack. She'd been so worried about him and all that was going on in his family.

Happy Balance was in the middle of a session. Savannah waved through the glass as she walked by, heading for the *County Gazette* office.

A walk would burn off some of the anxious feeling she had about going out with Scott later too. She power-walked up the block and took the long way around to the *County Gazette* to let Jack know she was thinking about his family and their situation. Momma used to say that prayers were the best gift you could give. Savannah had all but stopped praying when Momma and Daddy died. She had a few saved up over the years. It was time to start giving them.

The metal blind slapped against the door as she walked inside. She made a mental note to buy some stick-on Velcro to quiet that darn thing for Jack. He probably didn't even notice it anymore, but boy did it make her crazy.

"Hi, Jack."

He looked up and smiled. "I don't have anything new for you today."

"I know. Daphne Calvin was telling me that Bee isn't coming back. I wanted to check in with you."

"That was so thoughtful of you. Thank you."

"I'm happy to help out while I'm in town."

"Thank you, Savannah. That means the world to me."

"How's your grandniece doing?"

"Anna and the baby are both doing okay. She had another little girl, ya know. I'd kind of hoped this one would be a boy."

"Someone to carry on in your footsteps." Men were like that.

"No. She's been through so much." He looked too tired to talk about it.

"Daphne told me. I'm so sorry your family went through that."

"We're still going through it. You don't ever recover from something like that. That little angel with the ringlets. Christina was such a happy little girl. Do you know how hard it is to bury an empty casket?"

She swallowed. She'd thought burying her parents was the deepest pain there could be. She wasn't the only one in the world to live through tragedy. How selfish of her to never even consider what others had gone through. "I can't imagine."

"Her husband made us do it. Anna didn't want to. Anna always believed someday she'd see her little girl again. She might still. I don't know. Now that her crumb of a husband up and left her I wish we'd not given in to him on that."

"It's always easier to look back and decide."

"You're right," he said. "I've just been so worried for Anna." The gentle smile on his face looked forced. "I got your e-mail with the article from the event and the pictures. Thank you so much. The article is in today's paper. Have you seen it?"

"You already ran the story?" She would normally have grabbed a paper on her way back from Mac's, but this morning Scott had interrupted her routine. Well, as much of a routine as you could have in such a short time in town.

He passed a fresh copy of the paper her way.

GOVERNOR HONORS
SHERIFF SCOTT CALVIN

Sheriff Scott Calvin, along with Michael Hartman, a licensed private investigator in the Commonwealth of Virginia, were honored last night in Arlington, Virginia.

The Gold Meritorious Safety Award is the highest public service award in the state. Calvin was recognized for stopping Frank Gotorow from reenacting his previous crimes. Gotorow was on the highest level of secure probationary review, and yet was able to infiltrate the Adams Grove community nearly ninety miles away. The Adams Grove Sheriff's Department took actions that saved lives and put to rest an impending threat to the state. Private Investigator, Michael Hartman, was honored for his close work on the case with Sheriff Calvin.

Governor Bill Brock and Senator William Macon were both in attendance as news anchors from ABC7/WJLA-TV served as masters of ceremony for the event held at the Hilton Arlington.

The awards were presented by Senator Macon and Lt. Col. George Forehand of the Virginia State Police.

Clearly, the actions of Sheriff Calvin and Michael Hartman were extraordinary. Sheriff Calvin's keen tactical sense and ability to lead others through an extremely stressful event set him apart from his peers and are a credit to public safety professionals throughout the Commonwealth. Sheriff Calvin's conduct undoubtedly saved the lives of others in what could have been a replay of the Goto Hell murders, which the Commonwealth is still recovering from eight years later. Based on the foregoing, the review committee recommended Sheriff Calvin receive the award for actions of conspicuous heroism that were devoted to the protection of human life in the face of great danger, at the risk of his own life, and beyond the call of duty.

"The front page?" A feeling of pride caused an unexpected swelling of emotion. "Thank you, Jack." He didn't have to put this on the front page. The reason would be for Scott, not for her, but still. It was a pretty cool thing to see her name in big bold letters in the byline. "Can I keep this copy?"

"Sure. You need an extra copy or two?"

"No. Well, yeah. Thanks!"

"You might want to send a copy home to family or something. You did a real good job with that. You can be proud of it." He handed her a stack of six papers. "Is this enough?"

"Plenty. I don't have that many people to share it with. I don't really keep up with my people back home."

A sad look crossed his face. "Miss Savannah, all families seem like a pain at times. Trust me, I know. But that's just because they are part of us, and the apple doesn't fall far from the tree. Isn't that right?"

"Hadn't really thought of it that way before, Jack, but you might have a point."

"I've seen a lot in my years. I know I'm right. Family is everything. Without those ties, you lose who you are."

Aunt Cathy hadn't been there for her after the accident. She'd just shut down completely. Savannah'd never been able to forgive her for that, but now as she'd gotten older, she was beginning to realize that Aunt Cathy had been hurting too. In fact, they'd handled the grief in similar ways: Aunt Cathy shutting down and not leaving her house or talking to anyone, and Savannah leaving town and not ever letting anyone get close. Not so different when she looked back.

"Don't ever let anything come between you and your family. Even if it does, it can always be repaired. Family will bring you through anything. Trust me on this."

She smiled. Her situation was different, but it was nice of him to care enough to share his thoughts on the matter. "That sounds like the voice of experience. I bet things will be different around here without your sister."

"Already are." He leaned forward. "I really appreciate all you're doing for us. I don't know how we're going to keep the paper going now that Bee isn't coming back. I'm thinking about joining her in Carolina. We can do more together. Family should be together, and our grandniece can use our help." He pushed some papers around the desk and sighed. "I don't guess anyone would ever buy this little paper, though. It's a hard decision."

"Gosh, Jack. What would you do?"

"This paper has been our life for a long time, but we're getting old, and you know these papers aren't as relevant as they once were."

"Everyone in this town reads your paper."

He smiled. "That and a quarter will get ya a cup of Mac's coffee." He gave her a wink. "By the way. That article of yours got picked up by several other papers, including that fancy online paper."

"Which fancy online paper?"

"The GetItNowNews one. I'm surprised they picked it up. They're usually just all doom and gloom."

Savannah squirmed. "They aren't *all* doom and gloom."

"Well, mostly. Trust me. I know about doom and gloom. We dished out our share of it for a while. Stirring up trouble sells papers. It's all bad news or complaining. Unfortunately, it's what people seem to want to hear. I guess, in a twisted way, it makes their life feel better."

She'd never really thought of it that way. Did he know that she worked for GINN? There was no way he could possibly know that. Was there?

"I haven't played that game in a long time. In my paper, we focus on the good stuff. I made a conscious decision to do something good. People can see the bad stuff on television. Heck, they're dealing with enough troubles in the day-to-day trying to keep the bills paid. Especially after the plant closed last year. It's tough times here . . . everywhere. I figure if I can tilt the news to the happy side, maybe I can force a little balance."

"You do that intentionally?"

"Of course. Just like they probably do the opposite intentionally in that big online paper. It does sell, for some reason."

"Yeah. I guess it does." Just call her Bad News Van. All she'd written was snarky stuff for the past two years. She was probably one of the worst offenders. Was she bringing people up or just spinning them up . . . and was that really who she wanted to be?

Things looked so different from here in Adams Grove. She leaned against the counter. "So you don't feel any sense of obligation to report all of the news as it comes?"

He laughed. "Not at all. It's not like back in the day when your local paper was your only source of news. People watch television, listen to the radio, and they are on that Internet like it's oxygen from their computers and fancy phones. My job is to keep them informed with what's happening right here in our community. I think it's my job too to make them feel good about where they live, and safe to a certain point."

"Interesting."

"Speaking of local events . . ." Jack reached for a green folder and opened it. He pulled a copy of an ad out and placed it in front of her. "One of our annual fund-raisers is tonight. You should come."

"Do you need me to cover it for the paper?"

"That would be great if you could help, but I'll be there. I can write it up. I just thought you might enjoy something like that. It's always a lot of fun."

"Actually, I'm already planning on going."

His face lit up. "Great. I'll see you there. Are you going with Connor and Carolanne?"

"No," she said.

He raised a brow.

"I'm going with Scott Calvin."

The smile stretched across the bony man's face, making him look a little like a rubber toy being pulled beyond its capacity.

"What's that look for?" Savannah suddenly felt like she was in over her head. Did he know something she didn't?

"Nothing. He's a great guy. Best dancer in town too. All the local girls will be jealous."

"Jack, are you gossiping?" She'd never seen Jack like this. Normally, he was a man of few words.

"No, I'm not gossiping. I'm just sharing local news."

"That is not news."

"Sure it is. You ever looked up 'news' in the Webster's?"

"Can't say that I have."

"Well, I have." He tapped the side of his head. "Got it committed to memory too. News: *A*. A report of recent events. Check. *B*. Previously unknown information. Check. *C*. Something having a specified influence or effect."

"Point taken." Savannah smiled. "Check."

"You're going to have a good time with Scott. I'm glad you're going. I'll be taking pictures, but with you there with the sheriff, you'll be narrowing down my picture opportunities."

"Why is that? I brought back the camera exactly like it was when you gave it to me. I can take some pictures too, if you need my help."

Jack shook his head. "Oh, this has nothing to do with the camera. I usually can fill up a page with pictures of Scott with half the ladies in town. They practically fight over getting to dance with our sheriff."

"They can still dance with him. We're just going as friends."

Jack shook his head. "No. If it was friends, he'd have just told you about it. Ever since his dad died, he takes his momma dancing over at the Moose Lodge in Hale's Vineyard once a month. He's a good son to make the time to do that. Some people drive over there just to watch them dance, but he never takes anyone else. This is special."

"Really? I can't picture him dancing. Couldn't really picture Daphne dancing either."

"Well, I guess you'll have the best seat in the house for it tonight."

"I guess I will." Only she wasn't feeling so good about that. Making all the girls jealous was never a good spot to be in. Maybe she should fake a twisted ankle or something. A yoga injury?

"What else can I do for you this morning?" he asked.

"I was just wondering, do you have your old papers on microfiche or in some kind of an archive?"

He nodded. "Yeah. There was a grant last year. Ms. Huckaby down at the library helped us apply for it. All of our back issues are actually on CD and coded so you can search through them. It's pretty easy to use. Why? Do you need to research something?"

"Yeah. If you don't mind."

Jack stepped down off his stool. It was the first time she'd ever seen him off that stool. The little guy wasn't more than five feet standing. "I'll show you where everything is. You can help yourself. It's the least I can do for all you've done for us."

She followed him back to an office that had wall-to-wall dark pine paneling. She imagined this would be how it felt to be in a coffin. "It's a little gloomy in here."

Jack looked around. "I guess it is. Maybe that's why I never come back here."

"I don't blame you."

He pulled a stepladder from behind the door and climbed it to reach a cabinet. Inside were six boxes of archives. Each was labeled with the years it contained. "You can take some back to your apartment as long as you promise to bring them back."

"That would be great. I'll be careful."

"We have an offsite copy of them, so it's not like it's the only copy, but I know you'll take the right care with them."

"Thanks for trusting in me, Jack."

"That's what neighbors do." He smiled gently. "You belong here in this town, Savannah."

It was so simple for him to say, and so welcoming to hear.

He helped her bag up the years she'd asked about, and she felt empowered armed with that local information and her access to the GINN database. If there was something about Frank Gotorow that would help decipher those images in the mural, she would find it.

She couldn't get back to her apartment fast enough. She sat on the couch and took the top copy off the stack of papers Jack had given her. She'd sent him a couple of pictures to choose from. She was glad that he'd picked her favorite one. Scott looked handsome in it. She tried to picture him two-stepping or shagging, even ballroom dancing, but not one image made its way to her head. She'd just have to wait and see what a good dancer looked like tonight.

But not until after she got to the bottom of what was going on with that mural. She was convinced there was a story there. It could be her big break. This was the kind of story she'd always dreamed of. Her heart raced a little as she thought about digging into the details and pulling the threads that would unravel the cloak of mystery.

She searched through the archives awhile and then made a list of the things she needed to pick up from the store to take to Scott's tonight.

There was a certain amount of excitement about that, and she was looking forward to being in the kitchen with him, although it had been a long time since she'd done any real cooking and she hoped she wouldn't make a fool of herself.

She made the quick trip down to the grocery. On her way back, Jenn was outside on the sidewalk in front of Happy Balance setting up a smoothie specials board.

"Hi, Jenn."

"How've you been, Savannah? I was afraid I'd spooked you off after your last visit and all that talk about the paintings."

"Quite the opposite. I can't stop thinking about it."

"Got time to come in for a smoothie? I'm testing out a couple new flavors this morning."

"Sounds great, but I have some perishables in here."

Jenn glanced at the Piggly Wiggly bags in Savannah's hands. "No problem. Those bags will fit in my fridge."

The two girls walked inside, and once the groceries were safely tucked into the refrigerator, Jenn pulled out a spiral notebook and plopped it on the bar in front of Savannah.

"While I'm mixing up a Banana Balance Blast for you, would you mind looking at the notes I've written up and seeing if there's anything I've missed that you saw, or if you saw anything differently?"

Savannah laughed out loud. "You're not going to believe this." She pulled a notebook and her phone out of her purse. "I made a list too. Mine's on my phone."

"You and I are two of a kind, aren't we?"

"I think we are!" Savannah took a pen from her purse and rewrote her notes, checking off the things that matched up and adding things that she'd remembered that Jenn hadn't listed.

Jenn poured a murky brown smoothie into two glasses and took the chair next to Savannah. "Anything?"

"Maybe. Here," she said, twisting her notebook page toward Jenn and then taking a sip of the drink. "I know this isn't going to sound nice, but this drink is way better than it looks."

"Yeah, the color is a little off-putting, but I refuse to use artificial colors."

"I don't blame you." Savannah marked up the list with some stars and checkmarks. "Okay, here's our combined list."

"Let's go look at the mural together."

They abandoned the smoothies and marched into the men's locker room.

After an hour of staring and lying in different positions around the room, then climbing on the benches and looking again, they'd gathered what they thought might be more information, but the truth was they were both beginning to feel like they were looking too hard.

"I don't know what any of this means," Jenn said.

"It's frustrating. I just wanted to have some inkling of a direction to go in."

Jenn shook her head. "Maybe there is no sense to be made of it."

"I've been doing the police blotter report for the paper. Usually there's not much to it, but last week there was an entry that Scott told me to take out. It was about a homeless guy telling people there was evil in a painting in the yoga studio."

Jenn's eyes widened. "Jelly. I told you about him."

"Right. I bet he sees what we see." Savannah put

the top of her pen in her mouth and bit down on it. "Do you know how to find him?"

"I think so. I mean, it's common knowledge that he stays near the creek off of the jogging path in the park. Rumor has it that he's nuts for jelly-beans, so I'd buy him bags of them from the dollar store. He's really a sweet old man. Do you think we should go talk to him?"

"He mi-might be able to fill in some blanks for us." Savannah stammered a little. "I guess I need to tell you that Scott told me to leave this alone. If he finds out he might be mad." She was treading on thin ice. She'd already kept one secret from him, but this one was different. This story could change her career, set it on a whole new path, and this might even help him too.

Jenn shrugged. "Who cares? It's in my studio. It's my information to deal with."

"I just thought you should know."

"We can go tomorrow. Why don't you come by and take the afternoon class, then when I close up for the day we'll go over to the park?"

Savannah gave her a hug. "I think we're doing the right thing. I don't know why, I just do."

"I know what you mean. I feel it too."

"Well, I've got to run. I'm meeting Scott for dinner before the dance."

Jenn helped Savannah get her groceries together, and Savannah hiked back down the block to her apartment. She was in a great mood.

She had no idea what she was going to do with all this information or where it would take her, but for the first time in her life since her parents died. . . she felt like she belonged to something. And she liked it.

Chapter ELEVEN

She separated the groceries for tonight from what she'd gotten for the rest of her stay and put those items away in the small kitchen. She showered and changed, and just as she put her shoes on, there was a knock at her door. He was right on time, like she knew he would be.

"Coming." She grabbed the bag of groceries and carried them with her.

When she opened the door, Scott pushed forward a small bouquet of wildflowers.

"Thank you." She swapped him her bag for the flowers. "Let me put these in some water real quick, and then I'm ready to go."

He stepped inside and waited.

She came back with the flowers tucked in a nubby white milk-glass vase. "Perfect. This was under the sink." She set them on the table by the window and fluffed them so they fell into a nice rounded arrangement. "I love them."

"I'm glad." He swung the door open again. "Ready?"

She ducked under his arm and out the door. "Waiting on you."

At the bottom of the stairs she waited for him to catch up and lead the way. He opened the door for her and they stepped out.

An old pickup truck was parked at the curb. The shiny chrome sparkled in the sunlight.

"I like it," she said. "And it's not blue."

"Actually, it is."

They walked to the passenger door. "Now that I'm closer I can see it. So blue it looks black, except from the right angle."

He pulled the door open and helped her in, then set her bag on the floorboard next to her feet.

"I like it."

He slammed the door and walked around to the driver's side. "Glad you approve."

"I guess it's a good thing my car is blue or I wouldn't fit in."

"Well, there are a lot of shades of blue. What can I say? I know what I like."

She looked perfectly comfortable riding shotgun in the old truck. Right now, he was liking that.

When they got to his house they both went straight to work on the dishes they'd planned to prepare.

She didn't even ask where things were, just opened cabinets in an instinctive way to find what she needed. He loved how at home she seemed in his kitchen.

"What did you do today?" he asked.

She answered with her back to him. "This and that. Talked to Jack this morning. He might be selling the paper."

"I wondered if that was a possibility. They've been at it a long time."

"It would be a shame for it just to close down, but I think he and his sister are doing the right thing. I heard about the little girl."

Scott nodded. "Yeah. I've followed every lead, the few that there were."

"That would have to be hard, to not be able to solve something like that."

"You have no idea. But let's change the subject. The paper would be missed around here. I really hope someone will take it over and bring it into the twenty-first century." He wondered if she might consider taking it over at the right price.

"Maybe. It would take some work, but you never know."

"Not so different from when I took over the sheriff's department. Everything was still done in triplicate back then. Thought I'd never get it computerized, but things work a lot more smoothly now that it's done."

"Yeah, I'm sure that was a big job. I had to shop for this stuff. Errands. The day flew by."

He went outside to put the steaks on the grill,

and when he came back in, it was so natural to see her standing at the counter with a towel tossed over her shoulder.

"I'm all set. Nothing but to wait now. Can I set the table?" she asked.

"I already set the table outside. It's cool enough under the shade of the tree, I thought it might be nice."

"Great."

Savannah pulled a casserole dish out of the oven and set it on top, and then slid out the muffin tray. One quick stir of a pot on the stovetop and she gave Scott a nod. "I'm ready when the steaks are."

"Mine's done. Yours, however, will take another five minutes."

"Thank goodness," she said. "You remembered."

"Moo," he said playfully.

"We can dish up this stuff in here and let the flies drool from the window."

He nodded and heaped the food on his plate.

They carried the plates outside. Maggie was lying under the table. She looked ready to snag any scraps they might drop.

Savannah sat down and Maggie laid her head on Savannah's knee. Her tail thumped until Savannah patted her head. "I never had a dog growing up, but I always wanted one."

"I've always had a dog. My dad loved little dogs, though." He checked the steaks and then took her plate. "Maggie sure has taken a liking to you."

"Maybe one day I'll have a good girl like you," Savannah cooed as she stroked the dog's head.

Scott scooted her plate in front of her and sat down next to her with his own.

"Looks good." She slid her knife through the center.

Scott watched. Not a sign of pink. It looked perfectly cooked, if he did say so himself.

She took a bite of the steak first. "Scott. You lied." She looked serious, then she laughed. "You aren't just the best barbecuer in Adams Grove; you might just be the best barbecue-griller-guy in the whole nation!" She took another bite and nodded. "Yeah. I've eaten in some of the best steakhouses in DC, and they don't hold a candle to this."

"Thanks."

They ate and shared childhood stories about being on the lake with their dads.

"You're leaving town soon," he said.

"Yeah. The time has flown by."

"You gonna come back so I can take you out on the river?"

She scooted her plate to the center of the table and put her napkin on top of it. "Is it as pretty as the one in that mural at the yoga studio?"

"Savannah?"

"What? I'm just asking. It's beautiful. Come on. You have to admit it."

"Are you dodging my invitation to go fishing?"

"Was that an invitation?"

"Yes."

She pressed her lips together. "Set a date."

He glanced down at his watch. Being in the kitchen together had been easy and the time had flown by.

She glanced at hers too. "I can't believe it's almost time to go," she said.

"I know. That went by quick. I guess I should've picked you up earlier."

It would have had to have been last night, she thought, because being with him was so easy that even then it still wouldn't have been enough time.

"My mom is going to flip over those little apple thingamabobs. I'm glad there are a couple left."

"I had a feeling you'd like those. They were my daddy's favorites. My mom's special apple teacakes. I can make her some."

"She's going to want the recipe."

"I don't know. Family recipes are pretty special. Isn't there a law against sharing them with outsiders?"

"Maybe you could just pretend we're family."

"Or maybe you could persuade me into it."

Was she flirting with him again? Sometimes this sweet little lady turned into a sex kitten right before his eyes—except there wasn't anything kittenish about her; she was more like a puma ready to pounce. Yeah, that more described the feeling she gave him. He knew he should be afraid of the huntress, but she was too damn captivating to run from. He raised a brow. "Sounds interesting."

"Think about it." She got up and cleared the rest of the dishes.

"You can leave that. I'll get it when I get back home tonight."

"Or we can make short work of it right now and you won't have to worry about chores later."

He jumped to his feet and helped her rinse the dishes and put them in the dishwasher. He handed her the foil so she could wrap up the leftovers and put them in the fridge.

"All done."

"See. We're a good team," she said.

"Ready to head over to the dance?"

"Yep. I'm eager to see what all the fuss is about your dancing."

"People are talking?"

"Of course they are. It's a small town. They wouldn't have it any other way. Why do you think I haven't been back home in years?"

"Not once?"

"Nope. If you hadn't stopped me that day, it would have been my first visit back to Belles Corner in eight years."

"Belles Corner. Is that where Southern belles are grown?"

"I guess," she said in an exaggerated Southern drawl. "It's a small town. Not so unlike this."

"So you were just pretending to be a city girl."

"No. I believe you jumped to that conclusion all by yourself without asking. But then I've lived in northern Virginia and DC ever since, so that might make me a city girl."

"How can you stay away from home for so long?"

"It's a long story."

"We have all night."

She hesitated. But this thing with Scott, whatever it was, was going to be something or not. He might as well hear about her baggage. All of it. Because she couldn't separate it from who she was. "Long story short, I was a senior in high school. I'd been drinking. I called my parents to come get me."

"Responsible."

She held her hand up and shook her head. "The accident that killed them happened on our way home. Another car swerved into our lane, and my dad veered to the edge of the road to give him room. Our car must have hit something because we lifted in the air and rolled into the ditch. The other car just kept on going."

"You were in the car."

She nodded.

"I'm sorry that happened to you."

"I was too out of it to even have noticed what

kind of car it was or anything. I was no help at all."

"Did they figure out who was behind the wheel of the other car?"

"No. My dad and I were both thrown from the car. I didn't even get a scratch. Not a one."

"You were lucky."

A black cloud seemed to settle in her eyes. "Everyone says that. I wasn't lucky. I'd have given anything to be the one who died instead of my mom and dad." Her words were steady. Flat. "They didn't deserve that. I was the one who had done something wrong. I deserved to die that day."

"Savannah, your mistakes as a kid . . . they shouldn't drag you down your whole life. Your drinking did not kill your parents. You have to know that by now."

"For a long time they didn't even believe that my dad had swerved to avoid the other car. They even asked if I'd been driving at the time."

"It was an accident."

"It wasn't a mistake. I didn't hit a mailbox, or steal chewing gum."

"That accident wasn't your fault."

"But I was the only one who survived. If I hadn't been drinking that night, none of that would have happened. I'm the one they blame."

"They?"

"Everyone."

"Do they blame you . . . or is it you placing all the blame on yourself?"

"You weren't there. You don't know how people looked at me. The local sheriff was so determined to prove that I'd been behind the wheel of the car that night. I wasn't. I'd called Mom and Dad just like they'd always told me to if I ever drank. I'd never done it before. If I hadn't that night, they'd still be here. That sheriff ruined my life. Everyone in town thought I'd killed them, so I may as well have. Even my own aunt couldn't look at me."

She thought of the little girl crying in that mural . . . she knew what that sorrow felt like.

Savannah looked at her watch. "This is an old story, and I didn't mean to just lay it all on you. I'm a girl with a ton of baggage; you don't want to get involved with this. I'm a hot mess." She tossed her hands up. "Let's just have some fun. Let's go to that dance. You can strut your stuff for me."

"You might be setting yourself up for a disappointment. I'm only good on the grading curve of the men in this town. That's not saying much."

"I'll be the judge of that."

He helped her back into the front seat of the truck, and she scooched right into the middle next to him.

"Savannah, I know it won't change what you've been through, but I want you to know that I'm sorry you went through that. I don't know how I can ease the burden you've carried for so long,

343

but I would like to try. I will if you tell me how."

She held a hand to his cheek. "Thank you, Scott. That's probably the nicest thing anyone has ever said to me."

He started the truck and headed back toward town. They had to pass the bank building on the way, and then just a few minutes later he pulled up in front of the Ruritan Club building. The band was playing loud enough that you could hear a pretty darn good rendition of "Sweet Home Alabama" from the parking lot, even with the windows rolled up.

"Before we go in, can I say one more thing about Belles Corner?"

She smiled. "Sure."

"Savannah, make your peace with what happened. That place. Those people. All of it. It's the past, but you can't erase it. Until you make peace with the past, you won't be able to live your future. That town is your roots, your foundation. Those folks back there are part of your future too. Just think about it."

How many times was she going to hear this lecture, and why was she getting it from every direction from these people she barely knew? She sat quiet for a long moment. "I'll think about it."

He didn't look too hopeful.

She giggled. "I will. I'll think about it. I promise."

"Good. I'll take that," he said, but she wasn't

sure he believed her. Fair enough; she wasn't sure she could really entertain those thoughts anyway. No matter how much, for the first time in years, she thought she wanted to.

Sunset wouldn't happen for quite a while yet, but behind the club there were lights strung across a makeshift dance floor under the sky. Mostly people were nibbling on appetizers from a long buffet table just inside the doors of the Ruritan Club building. A few seniors were slowly scooting around the inside dance floor, where it was cooler out of the sun.

"They always get an early start," Scott said, nodding to the two old couples on the dance floor. "They'll be back home sleeping before the sun goes down."

"That'll be you someday."

"Hope so."

"I hear you take your momma dancing every month."

"People really are telling my secrets, aren't they?"

"Is that a secret?"

"Not really. My mom loves to dance. My dad took her dancing a couple times a month. When he died, I started taking her once a month. She loves it. It's the least I can do to bring her some pleasure, and it's good exercise for a gal her age."

"What kind of dancing? Like ballroom dancing?"

"Lord, no. We two-step. Mom says it's kind of

a shagging two-step. It's fun. I can't spin her, though; she gets dizzy."

"Well, Jack told me that all of the ladies in this town line up to dance with you, so please know it won't bother me at all to just watch you dance all night."

"You're not getting off that easy. I fully intend to take you for a spin around that dance floor."

"What if I get dizzy?"

"Then I'll sweep you off your feet."

She laughed, but the truth was he already *had* swept her off her feet. She knew it before he even said those words, but hearing him say it just made it more real. And scary as all get out.

As nervous as she felt about dancing with him, she didn't even care if she looked like a fool if it meant he'd be holding her in his arms.

It was wall-to-wall people, and there were kids in strollers and a couple granny types with walkers. It wasn't what she'd expected at all. Too bad she and Scott had just eaten, because there were tables full of homemade goodies lined up at each end of the hall.

"Yooo-hooo," Daphne called from across the room. She stuck her arm in the air, waving it like she should be shaking a pom-pom. She wore a mother-of-the-groom kind of grin, almost down-right teary-eyed.

Savannah knew that woman was jumping to a thousand conclusions way too early. Even though she'd thought Daphne had been off her rocker in the beginning when she'd tried to hook the two of them up, she hadn't been wrong about the two of them. But the secrets between Savannah and Scott, Savannah's secrets, were too big for even a mother's love as big as Daphne's to ease the trouble they could bring.

Scott and Savannah grabbed a couple of drinks and joined the others listening to music outside, where the band was set up.

As the sun went down, most of the families and the seniors began to leave. "The real fun starts now," Scott said.

The band started playing "You Know Me Better Than That" by George Strait.

"Excuse me," Scott said. He waved a hand to his momma and she headed straight toward him.

He took her by the hand and they eased into a two-step that was good enough to be on *Dancing with the Stars*, at least. It was obvious that they'd done it a million times before.

When the song ended everyone clapped. Savannah stuck her fingers between her teeth and gave out a whistle. Maybe Scott was right; your roots are your roots, and hers had a little redneck in them.

She watched as they headed back toward her, but then Brooke and Mike stopped Scott short. They spoke for just a moment and then Brooke walked off. Mike continued to talk to Scott, and that gave Savannah a nervous feeling.

Scott was stopped by at least three more people before he made it back to her, and she quickly realized that the sheriff was one popular guy in Adams Grove.

"You ready to dance with me yet?"

She held Scott's gaze. "I think I need another drink before I'm brave enough to follow that act."

"Oh, come on. It's just for fun."

A brunette walked over. "Can I steal your date for just one quick dance? My husband only does slow dances, and then he just rocks back and forth and spins in a circle. It's not pretty."

"Absolutely." Savannah could just picture that action. "Go on."

Scott looked uncertain. "You sure?"

"Yes, yes. Go on." She watched as they danced. Not as good as he was with his mom; he looked fine, but his partner was stomping a little like she'd rather be clogging. Savannah cursed herself for sounding like a mean girl. She was in no position to judge. No telling just how silly she was going to look. Scott held the girl at a respectable distance. Maybe she could get him to do a slow dance with her instead.

She walked over to the bar and got a beer for Scott and a sweet tea for herself while he was on the dance floor.

When he walked back over she handed him the beer.

"Thanks." He slugged it back and set it on a

table nearby. "Okay, your waiting time is up. Come on."

He pulled her onto the dance floor.

Reluctant, she let him guide her. "I don't know how to do this. It's been a million years."

"That's not true. I saw you dancing at the Cody Tuggle concert. Besides, it's like riding a bike."

"I need training wheels."

"I'm your training wheels." He pulled her into his arms, much closer than he'd held that other girl. "And your horn. And the little streamers on the handlebars."

And my kickstand, she thought.

He was right; by the time they'd two-stepped halfway around the dance area, the lights had begun to twinkle against the sky and she was following his lead like they'd been dancing together for years.

"Thought you said you didn't know how to do this. Fibber."

The word stuck her like a fork in the arm. She had to either tell him tonight, or plan to hit the road and never look back. Neither option was appealing. "You're a good lead."

"We'll see."

He looked like he was up to no good, and she had a feeling she was going to regret that remark.

He lifted his arm and guided her into a reverse and then a spin.

"Fun!" She tossed her head back and laughed.

"All you need is a hat and some boots."

He recognized the first few chords of "A Better Man" by Clint Black.

Savannah started to head off the dance floor.

"Oh, no." He grabbed her hand and tugged her back in. "This song is all you."

They danced the entire song and then she began to walk off the floor again, and he followed her only to lead her off to the side near one of the cook sheds they used at the pork festival. He stepped on the seat of a picnic table and turned to sit. He patted the seat next to him. "Come here."

She followed his lead and sat, leaving about a foot between them.

He scooted closer.

"Remember that day I stopped you?"

"How could I forget it?"

"You said I looked familiar. I said something smart-assed back, but I want you to know that I had a feeling about you too. I couldn't get you off my mind. Even remembered your name when I saw you sitting outside of Mac's Bakery on the parade route that day."

"You did?" She felt like Rudolph the Red-Nosed Reindeer when he realized Clarice liked him, only she was more like the reindeer that had made fun of Rudolph in the first place. Could he ever forgive her?

"I did."

"I'm glad." She'd felt that connection that day. If she'd had any idea it would lead to this, she'd have had a whole different attitude about that traffic stop.

He lifted his hand under her chin and tipped her mouth to his.

Everything inside her unraveled.

She welcomed the slow, thoughtful move. He dropped soft, gentle kisses on her lips, and she caught each one. Then, he pulled her into his arms and dropped two kisses in the crook of her neck that sent a thrilling chill right through her body.

"You are something else, Savannah Dey."

She dipped her head forward into his chest. "You keep me totally off balance, and I like it. A lot." Her heart was racing and she could see her own chest rise and fall with each breath she took. She'd never felt this way about anyone. She couldn't afford to be distracted by romantic notions. She couldn't fall in love. It wasn't the plan.

"I won't let you fall."

And there it was again, like he'd read her mind.

He lifted her face to his and kissed her again. Even more gently this time. "Think anybody would miss us if we left?"

She shook her head. "No one's going to miss me."

"I don't care if they miss me. Come on." He

stepped to the ground and helped her down from the table. "Your place or mine?"

"Mine's closer," she said.

"I was thinking the same thing."

There wasn't one single car on the road. Everyone must have been home already or still at the dance, so the ride to her building didn't take but four minutes, but it might as well have been an hour. The ride was quiet. Neither of them said a word.

He put his hand on hers, and didn't lift it until he'd needed it to park behind her apartment and take the key from the ignition.

She jumped out of the car feeling so nervous she wasn't sure if she was even going to be able to walk. He caught her from behind as she opened the back door of the building and kissed her on the neck.

The kiss was feverish, like those kisses in the movies that always look so hungry. Now she knew what that felt like.

That didn't make things any easier.

When he let go of her, she let him wrap his hand around hers and they climbed the stairs.

As she retrieved the key from her purse, he took it from her and worked it in the door.

"After you," he said.

"Thanks." She stepped inside and reached for the wall, but he pushed his fingers between hers and held them. "Don't bother." He kissed her again, full on the mouth. She heard herself moan in response to his touch.

"Do you want some—"

"I'm not that patient." He stepped her back toward the wall, one hand on each side of her. "All I want is you."

She initiated the kiss. It was easier than words. These kisses weren't sweet or soft like those at the club. No, these were hungry, and her heart was pounding so hard she could hear her own heartbeat.

He pressed closer. His hands running the length of her sides to her hips. His body against hers.

She welcomed the frenzied feeling. The burn, the dizziness. It was unexpected in the most delicious way.

He scooped her into his arms in one motion. "Which way?"

She laughed out loud, but pointed toward the bedroom, only he must have misread her because they ended up in her office. At this point she didn't even care.

He set her down on the huge wooden desk and pushed the papers to the side. He had her shirt off in one easy movement, and laid her back against the cool wood.

Hot kisses ran the length of her as he slowly removed the rest of her clothes. She couldn't help but press against him from the need building inside her. The world fell away and there was nothing but him and her and power. The muscles in his arms flexed as he outlined her form with his strong hands.

His clothes hit the floor, and every single touch set her body ablaze like nothing she'd ever even imagined.

Making love was an act of the heart, not just a physical act. Something she'd never experienced until tonight. And in his arms she felt not only satisfied, but safe.

He hugged her and then sat down in the desk chair. "Come here."

She suddenly felt self-conscious about being naked and stepped behind the chair, draping her arms around his neck. Then kissed him on the shoulder. His skin was salty from the sweat. Hers probably was too. It was going to be really hard to work at this desk tomorrow.

She started laughing.

"It's not nice to laugh when a guy is naked."

That made her laugh harder. "I'm sorry. I just don't even know how we ended up in here. My bedroom is across the hall."

"Me either, but I'm not complaining." He spun the chair around and kissed her again.

"I'm pretty sure I'm going to have a bruise on my tailbone."

"I can make that better," he said, pulling her into the chair.

"Promises, promises."

He tapped his finger on the tip of her nose. "I know this is happening fast, but I want you to know I'll never break a promise to you."

She sucked in a breath and then smiled. "I know that, even if you do make me feel off balance."

"You're not going to fall."

Savannah knew he was wrong. She already was falling. Falling in love, and that realization scared her. She stood up. "I'm going to get us something to drink."

"That would be great."

She pulled her shirt back on and rounded up her panties. She stepped one leg and then the other into them, feeling self-conscious with him watching, but in a nice way.

Her bare feet slapped against the wooden floor as she went to the kitchen and made two glasses of ice water for them.

She carried both glasses, enjoying the tinkling sound of the ice cubes as she moved toward the office where Scott had turned on the light.

Scott pulled his belt through the buckle and pushed his feet into his shoes.

"What's the matter?" Her eyes darted from the desk to where her pants still lay on the floor behind him, to the papers clenched in his hand. The printouts from GetItNowNews. The stats. The article.

"You did this?" He shook the papers in the air.

355

She looked like a squirrel in the middle of the road, undecided as to whether to go forward or back. "I?"

"Don't." Across the desk, where they'd just made love, crinkled sticky notes were pressed out. His tone forbade any further argument.

She stepped forward and put the two glasses down on the credenza near the door.

His words came out like darts. Sharp and pointed. "You were never working on a novel."

"I—" She looked like she was gasping for her last breath.

"This is all just a big-ass joke to you, isn't it? Well, this is my life. My career. You made fun of our life in this town." The betrayal he felt was impossible to put into words.

One by one he swept those sticky notes and scraps of papers to the center and began reading each one. "Mailman reading the mail. That's a crime, darlin'. Everyone has the same haircut. Cookie Cutter Salon. Who are you to judge? Looking for Mr. Feed and Seed. Seriously? Time warp? Well if you ask me these are gifts. Not problems." He swept them all off of the desk in one motion. "This community doesn't need the likes of you."

"Wait." She flinched as if he'd slapped her. "No. Scott."

But he wasn't going to listen to excuses. All he wanted was to get the hell out of here.

"Please. I can explain. I didn't even know you when I wrote that."

He spun around, his eyes narrowing. "Do you think that makes it better?"

"I'm sorry. You have every right to be angry." She rushed toward him.

He held his arm out, keeping her back. "Damn right, I'm angry. I don't need your permission for that. You're not who I thought you were."

"I'm sorry. I told you I was a mess—"

"You sure weren't lying about that."

Her voice shook. "I was going to tell you."

"When?"

"Tonight, but then it was so nice. The kisses. I—"

"It's all a big game to you. That article was mean-spirited. This is my life."

"I know. I'm so sorry. I wasn't thinking—"

"It wasn't bad enough you dragged me through the dirt, but it really hurts to think you reeled my mom in too. What? Did you just need more dirt on me?"

"It's not like that." Her knees went slack, and she wished she could undo what was happening. "I think the world of your mother." She placed her hands over her eyes. "And you. I think the world of you too." She heaved in a breath and dropped her hands. "Please forgive me."

"No. Mike was right to warn me. Not only did you write that article that slammed me, but he told me that you're the one who writes that Advice from Van column."

Her mouth dropped open.

He leaned toward her. "Do you know what people think about that column? It's not very flattering, especially for a lady."

She lowered her head. "Please don't tell anyone that was me."

"Yeah. I'd be embarrassed too. What kind of uncaring kook are you?"

"It's not like you think, Scott. Please stop. I was going to tell you, but—"

"You had plenty of chances to tell me if you'd wanted to. I asked you a dozen times about your work. You dodged every opportunity like a rodeo clown."

"I wanted to tell you, but I was afraid. I was doing my job. I never intended to write that column. It was all this crazy April Fool's joke. Only it went viral and the money rolled in and the joke was on me. Really. You have to believe me. I was just trying to live my best life. I never meant to hurt anyone."

"No. No, Savannah. You are not living your best life. You're hiding from it. You run from anything the least bit hard. You should have at least owned up to that article."

"I was afraid you would walk away from me."

He turned his back on her and headed to the door. He heard her pleading from behind him.

"Like this. Like right now. Please, Scott, I'm not hiding anymore. Please believe me."

She cared. It stung. She wasn't the woman he'd made her out to be. What had made him think this time would be any different? Talk about fools.

He jerked the front door open. "You're still hiding, Savannah. You're keeping your life safe . . . and small . . . and you don't even realize what you've done here. If you knew what living your best life meant, you wouldn't have stayed the hell away from your family back in Belles Corner. You had a bad turn, I get it, but do you think you were the only one affected by their deaths? No. Death affects a whole community."

"I didn't mean—"

"Stop it. You are bad news, girl." His jaw tensed. He closed his eyes and put his hand up to stop her. "Just. Stop."

When Scott stepped onto the landing, he found Mike staring into the apartment through the open door. He must have heard the ruckus.

Scott shook his head. Mike may have warned him, but the last thing he needed right now was a told-you-so.

"That's what I was trying to tell you, man. Sorry."

"Not as sorry as I am," Scott said, taking the stairs two at a time. When he threw his truck in gear, the tires squealed against the pavement.

Chapter TWELVE

Savannah stared out the window into the dark night, wishing Scott would call, or come back, but all she got was more sad and tired. He'd never forgive her. What she'd done was an attack not only on him, but on his people. His community. The ultimate betrayal. At sunrise she crawled into bed emotionally drained. She didn't bother getting up, instead staying tucked under the covers torturing herself with the instant replay in her mind the rest of the day.

She'd done it to herself.

She should have told him when she'd had the chance. He might not have understood, but then she wouldn't have fallen for him either. It would have been early enough that things would have stopped before they ever started, and that would've been for the best.

She turned over and hugged her pillow.

Or maybe not. It had felt good to have feelings like that. For the first time in her life, she understood the look in Momma's eyes when she watched Daddy. She'd felt it.

But it wasn't meant to be. Must not have been, or it wouldn't have turned out this way.

She'd thought she'd been brought to Adams

Grove for a reason. After getting to know Scott, and his mother, she'd begun to believe that her trip here was fate. Destiny. That finally she was finding a home for her heart. How would she ever make it up to him, to everyone in this special town?

Maybe the whole reason she'd landed in Adams Grove wasn't Scott Calvin, or his mom and her teashop. Maybe it had been that mural and the possibility of solving a heartbreak the community had suffered long ago—still suffered.

Once word got around that she'd written that article about Scott, everyone would be mad at her. "Now what?"

She didn't have any desire to go back to DC, which was what she should do. It was where her apartment and her job were, after all.

And she'd promised Daphne she'd help with the tearoom. She didn't want to let Daphne down.

Once Scott told his mother what Savannah had done, Daphne wouldn't want her help, though.

He didn't want to listen to her reasons; no one else would either. What was it about small towns that hated her? She just couldn't survive them.

She closed her eyes and chased the thoughts away, praying she could dream of something better or maybe nothing at all.

She pulled the sheet up over her head and went to sleep.

When she woke up the next morning she felt

so empty that she didn't bother to get up and brush her teeth. Didn't bother to even go get coffee. Even her stomach growling couldn't convince her to get out of bed.

She twisted and turned under the covers for an hour, but rest wasn't going to come.

She got out of bed and went into the kitchen. She was out of sugar.

"Great. Can't really borrow a cup from my neighbor." She could hardly go down to Mac's and get a cup either. What if she ran into Scott?

She went into her room and packed all of her things. There was really no sense in staying now.

With her overnight bag over her shoulder and her laptop bag hanging by her side, she locked the apartment and headed downstairs. She wondered if Connor had already heard about everything. She twisted the key in the palm of her hand. At the last minute, she decided not to give Connor the key. She could mail it back rather than face him.

All of her bags just barely made it in the car between what she'd packed for the wedding and the additional stuff she'd picked up for her extended stay. She'd carried down the boxes of CDs from Jack too. She'd have to overnight those back to him. The back hatch just barely closed, but everything fit. Well, the physical baggage anyway. She had more emotional baggage than she could fit on an aircraft carrier.

She headed out of town and got up on the interstate heading north. She drove past three exits before she realized she wasn't headed where she really needed to go.

Three hours later she was in Belles Corner.

She drove past the house she grew up in. A new family lived there now. There was a Barbie Jeep in the side yard and a Frisbee stuck in the gutter of the roof. The irises Momma had planted on the side of the house where her bedroom had been had grown tall. Their blooms would be so beautiful before long.

Momma always had flowers in the house. She'd cut them fresh from the garden and place them in tall vases in nearly every room, even one in each bedroom, all summer long. Savannah had always loved the way those delicate petals of the irises hung over like a colorful waterfall.

She took a right. It had been way too long since she'd come back to visit her parents graves, but things hadn't changed much. The cemetery should be only a couple of miles away. A cocktail of shame and sorrow whirled in her gut. There would be flowers; she'd seen to that with the money they'd set aside for her. It was the only thing she could really bring herself to ever spend it on.

The local florist let her pay for flowers six months at a time and arranged the delivery and placement for her. She'd kept fresh flowers on the graves, but she'd never made the trip back once she left town. That would have been more than she could bear.

She wasn't quite sure what was drawing her here now, except that Scott's words had stung. And what he said mattered to her. She had no idea if she'd find answers here, but she knew she wouldn't find them by hiding from what had happened.

The cemetery was much smaller than she'd remembered. She slowly pulled her car through the arched, scrolled gates and inched her way through the grounds. Nothing seemed familiar until she spotted the small cement bench with the cherub perched on it. She'd forgotten about that.

When she had still lived here in Belles Corner, she'd come every day until the headstone had been made and delivered. She'd sit on that little bench, trying to stay connected to her parents. To anything. Sometimes she'd sit right on the ground and just lean back as if that angelic cherub was on her shoulder telling her she'd be okay. Not that she believed it. That stone cherub had been the only thing that had brought her any peace during that time. Maybe that's what she was hoping for today.

She got out of the car and walked over to the bench. The ringlets of curls atop the cherub's sweet face reminded her of the image in that mural. That poor little girl.

Her parents' headstone was clean and well cared

for. The flowers on the top were just as she'd ordered them.

Roses because it was June.

For as long as she could remember, Daddy had sent Momma the flower of the month. By the time Savannah was ten she could recite the whole list by memory. It seemed only fitting to carry on that tradition with these flowers, even if she'd never come to see them.

Next week would have been Momma's birthday. Dad would bring her one single red rose on that day.

"Happy birthday, Momma."

She stooped in front of the headstone and closed her eyes. "I'm so sorry."

Her hands shook as she swept a tear from her face. "I've made such a mess of things. I've run. I've tried to forget. I've done so many things wrong. You wouldn't be proud of me."

A breeze kicked up, pushing her hair back from her face. She opened her eyes to an ominous sky.

Light raindrops began to spatter on the grass around her.

"I wish I could start over. I wish I could turn back the clock and never have called you that night."

Large, heavy drops started to fall. The flowers in the arrangement parted. She tugged a single rose from it and twisted it in her fingers. The rain felt cool compared to the hot air.

When she'd made that call home, asking her momma to come get her because she was drunk, her mother hadn't had one unkind word to say. She didn't preach. She didn't complain. She'd simply told Savannah to stay right where she was, that she'd be on her way.

When the car pulled up and her dad was driving, she'd been scared to death, but they'd told her they were proud of her for doing the right thing and thanked her for calling.

She'd been so out of it when the headlights of the oncoming car nearly blinded them that the whole thing seemed to happen in slow motion. Still did even in her memory today. She hadn't realized that she'd been thrown from the vehicle until the sheriff's flashlight was in her eyes. Red and blue lights were bouncing off everything and she couldn't focus on a thing. She'd been tangled in the brush along the roadside. They'd taken her to the hospital in the ambulance, and when she woke up the next morning she'd learned that the dream she'd thought she'd been having wasn't a dream at all. The car accident was real. She'd been the only survivor.

Her tears mixed with the cool raindrops.

She stepped back to the little bench and sat, placing the rose in the cherub's hands. "Save this one for Momma's birthday."

She leaned forward, her elbows on her knees, and prayed.

The rain was coming down hard now and between it and her tears, she couldn't focus on a thing. She closed her eyes and covered her face with her hands, satisfied to just be here.

"Savannah?"

She jerked her head up, frightened by the sound of her name. A familiar sound. *Momma?*

The silhouette of a woman in a raincoat carrying an umbrella negotiated the puddled lawn toward her.

"Savannah? Is that you?"

"Aunt Cathy?"

"Oh, Savannah."

Savannah stood and her aunt pulled her into her arms. "Oh, honey. I prayed you'd be back one day. Look at you. My goodness, you are the spitting image of your mother."

Savannah gulped back the tears that fell uncontrollably now.

"My sweet Savannah. How I've missed you. I love you so much."

"I'm so sorry."

"Stop that. What are you doing sitting out here in the rain? Have you been here long?"

"I don't know."

"Come." Aunt Cathy took her hand. "Let me get you home."

Home? Savannah didn't even know where home was anymore.

She let her aunt corral her to her car, leaving the

blue Mini Cooper behind. Savannah huddled in the car, shivering. The rain pounded so loudly that there was no way you could carry on a conversation, and that was just as well.

A few minutes later, her aunt pulled into the driveway of a small white house.

"You don't live at the farmhouse anymore?"

"No, honey. Not since your uncle Johnny died."

Savannah felt like her lungs had just deflated. She tried to catch a breath, but she couldn't utter a word.

"You didn't know?" Aunt Cathy closed her eyes.

Savannah shook her head.

"I'm sorry, honey. I sent a letter to you when he got sick. When I didn't hear back I just assumed it was too painful for you."

"I didn't get the letter." She choked on the words. "Sick? What happened? When?"

"Let's get you into some dry clothes first." Aunt Cathy held the umbrella over them as they ran for the front porch of the little house.

The furniture was the same. Aunt Cathy looked tired.

Savannah stood dripping in the entryway.

Aunt Cathy disappeared down the hall and then came back with a pair of pink pajamas and a bathrobe. "Get out of those wet clothes. I'll toss them in the dryer for you."

She quickly peeled out of the soaking clothes and walked back out. Aunt Cathy took the wet clothes from her and headed for the laundry room.

Savannah trod behind her. "Thank you." Savannah hugged the robe around her. "I'm so sorry I've never come back."

"Don't apologize."

"What happened to Uncle Johnny?"

Aunt Cathy sat back in the chair. She looked older now. Still beautiful, but older and so tired. "It's been almost four years now, Savannah. I sold the farm about six months after he died. It was just too much for me. I couldn't bear to not keep it up the way he had. He loved that place so much."

"I remember."

"He got pneumonia, and a few weeks later they did a chest X-ray when he wasn't getting better. He had stage four cancer. It was so advanced he didn't make it much longer. We didn't even go through any treatments before he was gone."

"I didn't know. I'm so sorry I wasn't here for you." Savannah picked up a silver frame from the end table that held a picture of her aunt and uncle from years ago. "Are you okay?"

"I am." She smiled gently. "Really. If he had to die, I'm glad it was fast. You know your uncle would have hated to be sick."

Savannah remembered all the things her dad and Uncle Johnny used to do together. "He and Dad both loved the outdoors."

"Sure did. Johnny missed your dad. I still miss them both."

"Me too. I still hate myself for what happened."

"Savannah, please tell me you are not still carrying around that guilt. We've been through that a million times. It was not your fault."

"Sheriff Pittman sure didn't hold back his opinion on that. Everyone in town looked at me different after that."

"Pittman was an ass. He was taking out his grief the only way he knew how. He needed to blame someone for your mother's death. He'd always loved her. Did you know that he was the first guy your mother ever went out with?"

"Sheriff Pittman?"

"Yes."

"No way. He was old. And fat."

"Well, he wasn't always old and fat. In school he was right good-looking. On the football team. He was older than us, but boy, did he love your mom."

Savannah sat there, stunned. It was hard to imagine her mother in any way except as a mom. Her mom, and with her dad.

"The whole town blamed me."

"No, Savannah, you blamed you. Yeah, the sheriff fanned the fire there for a while, but no one else bought into his theory. Besides, it was kind of his job to be sure he knew what happened." Aunt Cathy swallowed back a tear and then hugged Savannah. "I'm so happy to see you. I've prayed and prayed for this day."

"I've made so many mistakes, Aunt Cathy. I was such a burden on you."

"Honey, you were never a burden. I was torn apart losing your mother. She wasn't only my sister, but my very best friend. I wish I'd been stronger for you. We all made mistakes."

"Not like mine. I make big, unfixable mistakes."

"There's nothing that can't be fixed. I've got some things of your mom and dad's put away for you." She smiled gently. "You don't have to take them now. Or ever, if you don't want to, but I wanted them to be here for you when you were ready."

"Thank you."

"How's your job?"

Savannah looked to the ceiling. "If you'd asked me that two weeks ago, I would've said awesome."

"What happened to change that?"

"I met a guy."

"And he messed up your job? That doesn't bode well."

"No. It wasn't like that. He opened my eyes to a whole lot of things. Actually, I met him the day I was on my way here for the wedding."

"The day you got stuck in that town."

"Yes. I've been there ever since."

Aunt Cathy raised a brow. "Must have been one heckuva parade."

Savannah laughed. "You could say that."

371

"Your mom would have loved to know that you were working at the paper. Did you know she used to write when she was a young girl?"

"She was always journaling. I remember stacks and stacks of little notebooks always being around."

"She wanted to be a writer, but after she had you all she wanted was to be a mom. She loved you so much."

"She gave that up for me?"

"She didn't see it as giving anything up. She loved being a mother."

"She was a wonderful mom." Savannah sniffled back the tears. "I miss her so much."

"It's okay. Let it out."

The tears came again, hot and fast. "I'm sorry I left like I did. I never meant to hurt anyone."

"We all knew you were hurting. Everyone has to grieve in their own time and own way. We all understood, but don't let those memories keep you away forever. Your mom and dad loved this town. We love you. Not living here doesn't change that."

"Really?"

"Yes, Savannah. You're in our prayers no matter where you are." Her aunt got up and went to an old chest in the corner of the room. She pulled out a stack of church bulletins and handed them to Savannah. "Look. Read the back. The prayer list."

Savannah flipped over the tan paper and read

the list. Then she fanned through the large stack of Sundays in her hand. Her name was on every single one of them.

"Family is not a place. It's not stuff. It's what's important in here." Aunt Cathy patted her hand to her chest and then clenched it into a fist. "It's what's in your heart that matters."

"My heart is broken."

"You'll find love one day and it will heal."

"I'm afraid to love like that."

"Don't be. It's beautiful. Yes, it hurts like heck when you lose it, but Savannah, it's not worth it to live and not love fully. Don't cheat yourself. Your mom and dad loved each other like no two people I've ever known. I'll be honest, it was a blessing they died together that night. I don't think either could have lived without the other." She reached for Savannah's hands. "And honey, I wouldn't have traded even the bad days with your uncle Johnny to spare the sorrow I've felt since he died. Trust me. Love is so much bigger than sadness."

Savannah felt the sorrow of losing Scott, and she hadn't even had him, really.

"I pray you will find that person who makes your heart race, makes anything seem possible. It's real, Savannah. I know you're skeptical . . . but you're still young. I promise you it's out there. Find it."

"What if I already found it?"

Her eyes lit up. "That's great."

"No. I've screwed that up too. Aunt Cathy, I betrayed a trust. I did some things I'm not proud of."

"Honey. Who hasn't? You fix it. Apologize. But words aren't enough. Show your love. Say it and prove it. If it's right and true, it is not gone. Unfortunately, sometimes the ones we hurt the most are the ones we love, but that's the beauty of love. It mends anything."

"You really believe that?"

"Completely." Aunt Cathy jumped up to get Savannah's clothes from the dryer. "Here you go, kiddo."

Savannah laughed. "I used to love it when you called me that."

"Are you going to stick around?"

Savannah nodded. "Yeah. I think I am."

"You have to stay with me. I've got plenty of room. Don't say a word unless it's yes. I'm going to go make us some tea." She practically skipped out of the room, and it wasn't but a short moment later that Aunt Cathy carried in a tray with a tea service on it.

"Is that Mom's tea service?"

"It is, honey." She set it on the table. "I've saved so many things for you."

"I don't deserve them."

"Stop that. It's the past. You weren't to blame then, and you're not now. The only thing you are to blame for now is not living the life God has given you. Do not waste that gift. It's precious."

That struck a chord with her.

"When do you have to be back at your job in DC?"

Savannah took in a deep breath. "I think I might not go back to that job."

"What will you do?"

"I have no idea, but I've got skills that are transferable and I still have the insurance money set aside." She'd let most of that money from her parents' estate sit in that account all this time. Somehow it felt wrong to use it, and the insurance had been a large amount that she didn't feel worthy of taking. So she'd only used it to make sure the flowers and graves were well tended and figured one day the right use of it would come to her.

"What makes you want to leave that job?"

"I'm not proud of what I'm doing there. I think there's something more important I can do with my life."

"Then you should. Take a chance. What's the worst thing that could happen?"

"Whatever it is, it can't be worse than what's already happened."

"You're a bright girl. You're just like my sister. She'd be so proud of you. You will always be fine. I promise you that."

Savannah sipped her tea, only half listening to Aunt Cathy prattle on about what everyone in town had been doing since she'd been gone. All she could hear was her mother's voice saying, "Never think you know God's plan," and Aunt Cathy saying that real love could mend anything.

She set her teacup down. "Aunt Cathy, I know I just got here, but would you be terribly upset if I left?"

"So soon?" She looked panicked. "Did I say some—"

"No. No. You didn't say anything wrong. You said something right. I'm going to go back to Adams Grove and I'm going to tell that special someone how I feel."

A smile spread across Aunt Cathy's face, and her eyes twinkled with the joy that Savannah had once seen so often in her eyes. Cathy raised her hands to her heart. "You love him."

"I never knew what falling in love felt like until I met Scott."

"Then fight for him, honey." Aunt Cathy pushed a fist in the air and then clapped her hands. It reminded Savannah of her junior high days, when Aunt Cathy would help them at cheerleading practice. "Go. Absolutely. I'll be here when you're ready. And you bring that man back with you. Come on. I'll take you to get your car."

Savannah wrapped her arms around Aunt Cathy's neck. "I love you. Thank you for being here for me today."

"I don't know what made me drive to the

cemetery this morning when I did. Something was telling me to get there, and I just followed that message. I was stunned to see you there."

"I've been talking to Momma the last couple of days. I've never really done that."

"I think I felt that." Aunt Cathy stood and waved Savannah from her chair. "Go. Get dressed."

Savannah ran to the bathroom and changed back into her clothes, still warm from the dryer. Her heart was pounding so fast that she was nearly panting when she stepped back into the living room where Aunt Cathy was already standing with her keys in hand.

Aunt Cathy gave her an encouraging smile and the two walked silently to her car. When they pulled up next to Savannah's car, Aunt Cathy put a gentle hand on Savannah's cheek. "You drive careful and you call me if you need me to come get you."

Savannah felt fear crawl inside her. Those words were meant to be supportive but they carried the heavy weight of déjà vu of the very worst kind for her.

"Don't," Aunt Cathy said. "I know exactly what you're thinking, but if you need me, don't you dare hesitate to call. Your call had nothing to do with what happened. I promise you that, Savannah."

Savannah climbed out of the car and then turned back around. "After all this time. Me being

away. Not calling. You would really do that for
me, wouldn't you?"

Her aunt looked surprised. "Of course. We're
family."

Chapter THIRTEEN

On the ride back to Adams Grove, Savannah felt
unsure of how things would go, but she felt
darn certain she was doing the right thing.

She turned the radio down and dialed Evelyn.

"Hi, Evelyn."

"You still owe me some stories, young lady."

"I know." She swallowed hard. "Evelyn, things
are changing."

"What does that mean?"

"For starters, you won't believe where I've been."

"Not in Adams Grove?"

"No. Belles Corner."

Evelyn's voice changed from business to that
tone she used when they were just talking as
friends. "Not surprised at all." Savannah could
hear Evelyn's chair squeak. Speakerphone. Even
this was on speakerphone. "I'm kind of surprised
it's taken you this long. But sometimes you
have to heal before you can see things clearly.
How'd it go?"

"It was a great visit."

"I'm glad for you."

"I can't believe how much I've missed out on."

"You haven't missed a thing, gal. You just weren't ready until now."

Savannah knew Evelyn was right.

Evelyn picked up the phone. "Dear, I'm so glad you went. It's a good thing for you, but what on earth happened that made you go there now?"

"Something someone said."

"The handsome sheriff?"

She hesitated, but only for a moment. "Yes."

"You like him." It wasn't a question.

Savannah nodded. "I do, Evelyn. In fact, I've fallen in love with him."

"Now *that* surprises me."

"Surprised the heck out of me too, but I've made some mistakes. Some big ones. I've been so busy thinking about the bad stuff that happened, I'd kind of forgotten all the good times I had growing up. I'd forgotten how Momma and Dad loved each other so much too. I want that kind of love." Savannah took the next exit and pulled into a gas station parking lot.

"You should have it. Just like my dear husband. Nothing compares to a love like that." Evelyn cleared her throat. "You on your way back?"

"No. I'm calling to . . . This isn't easy, Evelyn." Savannah took in a deep breath and pictured Daphne, and Scott, and Jack, and Aunt Cathy, and she knew no matter what, no matter if Scott didn't forgive her, there was a different life waiting for her somewhere. "I want to give my notice."

"Your notice? I told you I'd let you out of the Advice from Van column. If this is about those articles, we can find something new."

"It's not just that. Evelyn, you have been an amazing mentor and the best friend in the world, but I think I'm going to try something brand new."

"Savannah. You know I'd be on your side no matter what, but you could still work for GINN from Adams Grove. I'd be flexible."

The familiarity of what she'd known the past couple of years was tempting, but she wanted more. She'd had a taste of it. It was clear now. "I won't have time."

"Why not?"

And until that moment she wasn't even sure exactly what that all meant, but it came to her at that moment and it felt right. "I'm going to buy their local newspaper, and I'm going to help a friend open a tearoom."

"You what?"

"Yep. I'm going for it. Like my aunt Cathy said, what's the worst thing that can happen?"

"You'll make it a success, Van. You're a bright young lady. I'm very proud of you. And that Aunt Cathy of yours, she sounds like a smart lady."

"So much like Momma. It was so great to see her." She thought of Scott's mom. She'd love Aunt Cathy. "I won't leave you high and dry.

I'll give you whatever kind of notice you need."

"Honey, you don't owe me a thing. I'm thrilled for you, and I want to buy the first ads from you once you take over that little paper."

"You don't have to do that."

"I want to do it, and it'll be a write-off."

"It's always business for you."

"Van . . . it wasn't always business. Before my husband died, things were so different. You and I have been there for each other, both learning to live without the most important people in our lives. I couldn't have done it without you. I've been busy for the same reasons you have. Only I think you're young enough to have a second chance."

"You never seemed the least bit fragile. I was a hot mess."

Her voice softened. "I'm just older. Wiser. Trust me, you'll do the same for someone someday."

"I'm so thankful for our friendship. I don't want that to change."

"It won't." Her voice garnered that corporate strength again. "Now you get your business plan pulled together, and if you need any advice, I'm right here for you, even if you just might end up being my biggest competition."

"Somehow I doubt that."

"I don't. You're an amazing woman. You've got a good intuition about you. You're going to do amazing things no matter what the scale, and don't go thinking just because you're in a small town it changes how important it is."

Now, why hadn't she realized that before? She'd learned that lesson just recently watching Scott and understanding that although his commitment and achievements were different, they were surely not any less valuable.

An important message.

"Good luck, my dear. I'll cover you for a three-month severance. Consider yourself fired . . . in the very nicest of ways. I've got to run, dear. You knock 'em dead."

Savannah only hoped that somehow she'd patch things up with Scott. If she didn't, moving to Adams Grove wouldn't be an option, because he was the very best part.

She took the exit off I-95 toward Adams Grove.

Her palms were sweating. "Please let me say the right thing to make this all work out."

She drove straight to the *County Gazette* first. If she struck that deal with Jack first, it would be harder for her to chicken out of the rest of her plan.

Jack had no idea she'd even been out of town, so he thought she was there to pick up the stuff for the police blotter.

He gave her a smile and grabbed the folder from its designated spot. "Here you go, Savannah."

"Thanks, Jack." She felt nervous even asking

about it now, but she needed to know. "I have a question for you."

"Sure. What's up?"

"Were you serious about selling the paper?"

He straightened. "It depends. I won't sell it to just anyone. Are you interested?"

"I think I might be. Would you consider selling it to me?"

He smiled, then his smile faded. "I know you work for GINN."

"Oh, Jack. I'm sorry I didn't tell you. I've done so many things wrong. It was me that wrote that article about Scott Calvin in the Penny for Your Thoughts column."

"I know," he said with a thoughtful nod. "I might seem old-school and out of touch, but I still have a lifetime of contacts in this business. I'm pretty well connected."

"I'm so embarrassed. And I'm sorry. So sorry. I quit that job today."

"It's okay. You're growing. You're finding you. It's a process." He paused and looked her right in the eye. "Would you keep the tone that I've set? I like knowing that I provide a good service to these people."

Savannah nodded. "I would. I completely respect what you do and why you do it."

"I'll make you a deal you won't be able to refuse."

He trusted her, and she'd never let him down.

Maybe things would go her way yet. She held up a finger. "You hold that thought. I'm working on something. Don't you let anyone else make an offer without talking to me first. We got a deal?"

Jack nodded. "We sure do."

She walked out of the newspaper, reminding herself that the first thing she'd do would be to fix that blasted blind so it wouldn't slap against the door every time she went in or out of the place.

She got in her car and let the air conditioning wash over her face. The cool air felt good against her skin. She raised one sweaty palm to the air stream and then the other. "That was the easy part."

Driving down Main Street, she pulled along the curb across from the building Daphne was planning to buy from Jack's family. She could picture the awnings and a bright coat of paint. Lettering across the window and maybe even twinkle lights. Why not? They looked great in the Floral and Hardy window that was just at the end of the block. She'd be close enough to walk from the paper to the tearoom without breaking a sweat on a warm day.

She wondered if Scott had told Daphne what had happened.

She hoped not. It would be hard for Daphne to forgive her for hurting Scott.

The Mini Cooper was tiny enough to park just

about anywhere. She pulled back onto the street and turned right toward the sheriff's station. Worried Scott might refuse to see her if he saw her coming, she parked at the far end of the building and walked around.

She went inside to find Deputy Taylor in the front office. "Hi, Savannah."

It was a relief that he seemed happy to see her. "Hi. Is Scott in his office?"

"Sure is. Go on back."

"Thanks." There was no way the deputy knew what had happened. He'd been too nice.

She walked down the hall and then stopped short of Scott's office door. A moment of panic filled her body with a flood of adrenaline that made her want to run the other way. Then, just as quickly, she recalled being in his arms and feeling safer than she'd ever felt in her life.

She stepped quietly into his doorway, watching him work until he looked up.

He didn't say a word. Just leaned back in his chair.

"I'm sorry," she said.

He put his pen on the desk. "It doesn't matter."

His voice was flat. He was still mad. He had every right to be.

She straightened. "It does matter. It matters to me."

"What do you want?"

She stepped inside and closed the door behind

her. He looked unhappy about that. He opened his mouth, but she jumped in. "Wait," she said. "Don't say anything yet."

She sat down. "Scott, I love you. I really didn't mean for all this to happen."

"Savannah—" He stood up.

"Wait. Please just let me get this out. That first day . . . when we met . . ."

"When I stopped you for speeding."

"Yeah . . . that day. I asked you if we'd met."

"I remember."

"I meant it. I wasn't playing you. There was something about you that felt familiar. Something about you that sparked with me. That connection was there for a reason. It was meant to be. You felt it too."

He sat back down.

"I never meant to hurt you."

"It wasn't meant to be. You don't have to apologize."

"I can't change what happened, but I really wish you could forgive me."

"It's not all your fault, Savannah, or Van, or whoever you are. I pick the wrong women. I always have. It's me."

"That's just it. You didn't pick the wrong girl. I'm the right girl. I know I am." A flicker of apprehension coursed through her.

"No. I've been down this road before. Too many times. You really kind of did me a favor.

Even if I did forgive you, you'd just leave eventually." His shoulders hunched forward as he leaned his elbows on the desk.

She answered quickly, over her pounding heart. "No. Scott. Seriously, I could live here. I love this town. I love the people. I love your momma. I want to be with you, and I want to be a part of this community. You make me a better me. Don't you see that?" She feared if she stopped talking he would just say no again and she didn't want to hear it. Couldn't bear it. "Please believe me."

"People shouldn't have to change to be in a relationship. That's a recipe for disaster. Savannah, you'll always be special."

"I'm not changing. I'm finding who I am. I want to move here. I gave my notice at GetItNowNews. I want to buy the *Gazette* from Jack. I just talked to him about it. The only thing that will stop me is you. Please give me a chance."

He stared at her for a long moment. "Move here if you like, but don't do it because of me." He stood and turned his back to her. "Do it because it's what you want."

"You don't want me?"

She heard him exhale. Without turning to face her, he said, "I didn't say that."

"But?" Savannah sat there in disbelief. She knew she'd hurt Scott, but she'd really expected he'd forgive her. If you love someone—really love them—there's nothing you can't get through.

Right? Maybe he hadn't felt what she'd felt after all.

Scott shook his head. "I'm sorry, but this heart of mine isn't up to this again."

It was like a dagger through her heart. What more was there to say?

She couldn't make him love her. Her lips quivered. "I wanted you to know how I feel. You've changed me. Made me aware of so many things. I went home to Belles Corner. I'm making peace back there. You're the best thing that's happened to me in eight years."

She headed for the door, then stopped. "Thank you."

She walked out and went straight to her car. Her mind was so consumed with thought that she was blind to what was around her, or if she'd even passed anyone on the street. She revved the engine on her little blue car. Scott's favorite color.

She drove over to the bank building and parked next to Mike's truck. It was hard to be mad at him; after all, he was only looking out for his friend. It just sucked that it had to be at her expense.

All she'd ever done was hurt everyone she'd ever loved.

Letting people down. It's what she excelled at.

She climbed the stairs to the apartment, and Mike walked out on the landing. "Hey." He looked awkward. "Sorry."

"It's okay, Mike. It's not your fault. I know you were just looking out for Scott."

"Yeah. Brooke said I should have kept my mouth shut."

How she wished she'd told him that before he told Scott, but then it would have all come out eventually. It was just a matter of time. It wasn't Mike's fault. "Mike, I love him. I really do."

"Then how could you make fun of him like that? His job means so much to him."

"I'm sorry." Even the words didn't sound like enough to her anymore. "I know that just saying I'm sorry doesn't make it okay, but I'd written that before I got to know him. It was my job." She lifted her clenched hands as she spoke. "I'm not proud of myself. I'd never stopped to consider the impact my responses had on the faceless people targeted with those sharp words. That's the kind of stories GINN runs, though." She lowered her eyes, not even able to look his way. "I'm sorry I ever wrote for them. It's been a raw lesson for me."

"Wrote?"

"I quit my job this morning."

"Well, then maybe something good has come of it."

"I guess. Also means I have to give up my apartment. Or sign a lease. It was a corporate apartment."

"Maybe you could stay here," he said. "I know Brooke and Jenn would like that."

A raw and different kind of grief consumed her. "I'm sorry I hurt your friend. I'm sorry I put you in that position."

"I believe you. I kind of wish I'd kept my mouth shut, to tell you the truth. Brooke and Jenn were so excited about the prospect of you maybe even moving here. Brooke said you'd fit right in."

"He'll never forgive me. You should have seen his face."

"I thought I was helping." His lips pulled into a thin line. "I can tell you this. He's crazy about you. He's hurting right now. Talk to him."

"I tried. That's where I just was. He can't forgive me."

"He can. Just give him time. Guys can be as hardheaded as you girls sometimes. If you really love him, don't stop trying. He'll come around."

She didn't think there was enough time in the world. "I'm going to go lay down."

"Sorry."

She closed the door behind her and stood there until she heard Mike walk down the stairs. Thank goodness she hadn't given the key back to Connor. She plopped down on the couch and stared at the ceiling. She counted the old tin ceiling tiles until she fell asleep.

A loud rap woke her from a dead sleep. She sat up on the couch, and it came again. Three loud, heavy knocks on the door.

She ran to the door, praying it was Scott. Had he changed his mind?

When she swung the door open it was Brooke and Mike.

"I told her you were sleeping," Mike said.

Brooke opened her arms and gave Savannah a hug. "It's going to work out."

"It's not. He'll never forgive me."

"Don't be a fool. It's totally meant to be. I saw y'all on the dance floor this weekend. He is totally smitten with you."

Savannah had thought so too, and the feeling was mutual.

Brooke pointed inside. "Can we come in for a second?"

"Yeah. Sure." She stepped aside, and they came in and sat on the couch. "I don't have anything to offer you."

"That's fine. It won't take but a minute. I was down at the paper placing the ads for summer camp and Jack said that you had stopped by earlier this morning and said you might buy the paper."

"I did. I can't very well do that now."

"Why not?" Brooke rolled her eyes. "Okay, so doofus here shouldn't have opened his mouth so that nature could take its course, but it'll work out. Besides, Daphne is about to bust a seam about the new tearoom. She'd be devastated if you didn't stay. And Jenn and I"—she gave an inconspicuous nod toward Mike—"we're dying to work on that little project with you."

Savannah had been so consumed with her thoughts about Scott that she'd put the mural on the back burner, and that needed to be dealt with. She really was making a mess out of everything. "I wish it had worked out differently, but I think I've just burned that bridge. And it's the only way in and out of this town."

"Not the only way," Brooke said.

"Well, we've got an idea," Mike said. "Will you give me a chance to make this right?"

Savannah wasn't sure she had the energy to even try.

"Mike has a good idea," Brooke said. "And while he's figuring that all out, you need to get yourself pulled together and we'll spend some time down at Happy Balance. Jenn has something on that smoothie bar to fix any problem that ails you. I'm sure she has a broken heart remedy in her recipe box."

How could people who barely knew her be so important in her life all of a sudden?

"You can do it, Savannah," Brooke reassured her. "It's going to be okay. You in?"

"Okay. Yeah, what harm can it do?" Savannah sucked in a deep breath. "Thanks, y'all."

Mike headed for the door. "Well, I kind of think I owe you on this one. I've got some work to do."

He left, and Brooke waited until she heard him start down the stairs. "While you were gone, Jenn and I think we've made some progress. Go get dressed. We need your help."

Chapter FOURTEEN

Savannah and Brooke racewalked all the way down the street to Happy Balance.

Jenn sprang out through the front door and ran to meet them at the corner, giving Savannah a hug. "You've got to stick around. We need you, girl!"

She hugged Jenn back. Savannah felt welcome here. Like Brooke and Jenn were true friends. "Brooke said you made some progress."

"I think so. Come on!" Jenn led the way back to the studio. "Only I don't know what we do with it next." She turned the lock with a click and then led them up the back stairs to her apartment.

Brooke spoke as they climbed the stairs. "So, I can't see whatever it is that y'all are seeing, but I am an awesome puzzle girl. So when Jenn was writing down all the letters and numbers she saw, I started trying to put them together."

"Good idea." Savannah felt better not focusing on her own problems.

"Then," Brooke said, "I took a picture of the

mural and printed it out poster size down at the office."

Jenn opened the door and held it for them as Brooke kept talking.

"Oh, my gosh." Savannah started toward the kitchen. The whole wall was covered in enlarged copies of the pictures they'd taken of the murals downstairs, and dotted with colorful sticky notes indicating every little detail they knew so far. "This is genius."

"I know, right?" Jenn handed a marker to Savannah, and one to Brooke. "It's like our own game of Clue."

"Or an episode of *Castle*," Savannah said.

"Isn't that guy adorable?" Brooke said.

"Totally. I love Rick Castle's boyish charm on that show," Savannah said.

"And we were so happy when him and Beckett got together, pretty much like we wish you and Scott would." Brooke snapped the cap off her marker. "And we're going to fix that too."

"Ugh. Let's not talk about that right now. Okay, so what do we have?" Savannah focused on the wall.

Jenn ran down all the images.

"Little girl crying. Ringlets. Bracelet. Skinned knee. Can't really tell how old she is."

Savannah nodded and added, "And the headstone with all those gorgeous flowers. So many. Can you read it?"

"No," Jenn said. "I don't think it says anything, but there were a bunch of letters in the flowers. Brooke put some words together. Goto. Christ. Learns. Weak. Sinners. Avoid. Way. Rile. Only they don't seem to mean anything."

Savannah stared at the paper. "You can't see the images in this photocopy. Can we go down to the locker room?"

"Sure," Jenn said.

"Let's take the picture with us." Brooke peeled the tape back from the corners and carried the papers with them. "It's all I've got. I don't have superpowers like y'all."

"Real funny." Jenn led the way.

When they reached the locker room, Brooke hung the picture on the mirror.

Savannah stood in front of the mural, looking at the images. Then she looked back at the poster and then sat down on the floor, scanning the entire mural again. "Jenn?"

"What?"

"Look up there, where the creek trails off." Savannah walked closer, pointing out the exact spot where she saw what looked like a door.

"How did I miss that before? It's a door. Just beyond those flowers. See it?"

"Yeah. Yeah, that's what I see. There are numbers on the door. Four seven something?"

Jenn nodded. "I think it's four seven zero five three."

"Hold on a sec," Brooke said. She took her marker and checked off the numbers four, seven, five, zero, and three on her notepad. "Yep, they're all here."

"An address?"

Savannah tilted her head. "I'm going to run home and get my computer. I've got an idea."

"I've got a computer," Jenn said.

"Yeah, but I need mine, and I have something else that I think will help. It won't take me long. Hang tight."

"We'll be right here."

Savannah laid her marker on the bench and jogged back to the apartment. She swept up her laptop, went to her car and dug out the CDs that she'd borrowed from Jack, and then ran back to Happy Balance.

Jenn and Brooke were sitting at the smoothie bar when she came back in.

Savannah could barely talk, she was so winded. "There was a little girl who went missing a few years back."

Jenn ran to her side. "Do you think this message is something about that? Do you think Frank Gotorow did something to that little girl?"

"I don't think so. His victims were always women. Never children." She started her computer. "Brooke. The little girl's name was Christina. Rework those letters." She clicked a few keys and turned her attention to Jenn. "Can you see if you can find an online GIS for this town?"

"What the heck is a GIS?" Jenn asked.

Brooke chimed in. "Geographic information system. Basically it's an online map of all the properties and owners in an area. We use them all the time down at the extension office."

"Right," Savannah said. "Can you see if there's one for Adams Grove and track any address that starts with 47 or 53?"

Savannah started searching the CD for articles about the missing child. There were several. No doubt Jack and Bee had done everything in their power to get the word out. For a moment, she thought they should stop and call Scott, but he'd told her to stay out of this, and there was no sense in making things even worse between them . . . if that was even possible. If they found anything at all, she promised herself they'd bring him into the loop.

"Anything, Savannah?" Jenn was typing on her computer. "I'm not seeing anything here. We'll have to go down to the courthouse."

"Wait a second. The little girl, Christina, her birthdate is April seventh."

"Four seven. It's not an address." Brooke clapped her hands. "This is about her."

"Y'all. She was abducted on May third." Savannah stopped typing. "It says here that she was abducted on May third, three years ago, from her uncle's place of business. No one heard a sound. It was like she'd just disappeared."

"How sad." Brooke rewrote all the letters on individual pages of sticky paper and started rearranging them.

"It was Jack's grandniece's little girl. He was just telling me about it. They never found her."

"She could be alive," Jenn said.

"Or at least they could have closure." Brooke kept moving the letters around.

Jenn pressed her hands to her heart. "Brooke. That's awful."

"I'm just trying to be realistic here."

Jenn tsked. "Well, stop it."

"We have to tell Scott," Savannah said. "He told me to leave this alone. But even if he hates me, I have to tell him."

The front door of the yoga studio opened, and Brooke scrambled to move the giant printout behind the counter.

"Sorry. I must've forgotten to lock it when I came in," Savannah said.

Mike made his way through the space. "I figured y'all would be here."

Brooke walked over and gave him a kiss. "Hey, honey. What's up?"

"I need y'all to come with me," he said.

"Now?" Savannah needed to talk to Scott.

"Yes, now. We're going to Daphne's new shop." Mike started toward the door. "Come on."

"Oh, Lordy. Daphne knows? I can't face her."

"It was use Daphne or call in a fake crime, and that's against the law. Let's just give it a try." Mike put his hand on her shoulder. "Trust me. Scott's mom is one of your biggest fans. Plus she's the only person who is kick-ass enough to tell Scott to wake up and smell the coffee. Trust me. We've all done stupid stuff in love before. Daphne is going to get Scott down to her building. It's step one."

Brooke tucked the papers behind the smoothie bar. "This can wait. We need to talk to Scott."

Mike nodded. "And if this plan works, that's exactly what you'll be doing."

Savannah followed along, but she wasn't sure this was a good idea.

"Should we tell Mike?" she whispered to Brooke.

"Just hang tight."

When they reached the front door of the tearoom, Savannah closed her eyes and prayed she wouldn't retch right here on the doorstep. "I can't do this."

They shuffled her inside under protest.

"Oh, Savannah. I heard what happened." Daphne pulled her into her arms and rocked her. "Honey, we all do something we regret in our lifetime, especially when it comes to love."

"I'm one big fat walking mess," Savannah said. "I hurt everyone I love."

"That is not true." She pulled a paper towel from a roll sitting on a table. "Here, dry those tears. We're fixing this. That pigheaded son of mine can't get out of his own way sometimes when it comes to affairs of the heart."

"I already went and talked to him this morning, Daphne. He doesn't want to forgive me."

"Like heck he doesn't. I know my boy, and I saw you two together. I knew the minute I met you that you were going to be a permanent fixture in Adams Grove. I'll steer him in the right direction."

"I don't think he wants to be steered."

Daphne laughed. "Not a man on God's green earth does, dear; the trick is doing it so they have no idea." She gave her a theatrical wink. "I've got lots of years of experience doing that. Stick with me."

A sick feeling twisted in Savannah's gut.

"We don't have much time." Daphne looked to Mike. "Okay, you know what to do."

Mike nodded and left.

Brooke took Savannah by the hand. "Come on. You and I are going to wait back here until Daphne gives us the signal."

Scott had just slugged back the last of a tall glass of iced tea and pushed his plate away when Mike walked into Jacob's Diner.

"Hey, Mike," Scott said.

"There you are. I've been trying to track you down."

"What's up?"

"I had no idea your mom was buying the old building up on Main Street."

"She's not."

"That's not what Brooke said. I was just walking down the street and your mom was up on a ladder in there. I went in to see what the heck she was up to, and she said she's opening a tearoom."

"She hasn't mentioned a word about it to me. Which is fine, but why the heck was she up on a ladder?"

Mike lifted his shoulders. "My darn dad is the same way. Always getting into one thing or another. They think they're still forty or something."

Scott stood and pulled a fold of money from his front pocket. He peeled off the bills and tossed them on the table. "I guess I better get down there and see what's going on."

"Yeah. I figured you'd want to know."

"Thanks, man. I appreciate that."

Mike followed him outside. "Hey, Scott. I'm really sorry about that stuff with Savannah. She's a nice lady. I'm sure it'll work out."

Scott just shook his head. "Don't worry about it, man." The last thing he intended to do was have any more conversations about Savannah with anyone.

He marched down the block to the old building, and sure enough, there was his mother up in the display window with newspaper and some Windex.

Staring at her from outside the window, he gave her a what-the-heck-are-you-doing look.

She waved and smiled. "Hey, son!"

He went inside and she scurried down the ladder. He rushed to her side and spotted her to the ground. "You're gonna break your fool neck climbing that thing."

"Oh, stop. I'm just fine."

"Mom, you can't do this stuff by yourself. What is this about you buying this place?"

"I know. I was going to tell you the other night at the dance, but then you and Savannah left in a hurry." She nudged him with her elbow. "I love that girl."

So do I, he thought, *but that's not going to happen.*

"I'm opening my tearoom. I'm finally going to do it. I'm calling it Timeless Tea."

As pissed as he was that she'd gone and done something like this without even a mention to him, he was excited for her. She'd had that dream as many years as he could remember back. It wouldn't be a bad thing to get those kazillion teapots out of the dining room either.

"That's a perfect name." He nodded. "I like it."

"Savannah came up with it. She said she's going to help me some."

Just the mention of her name made him feel like he was being wrapped in a cocoon of anguish. "Mom, maybe you shouldn't count on her help."

"Why not? She's amazing. I knew you two would hit it off." Joy bubbled in her laugh and shone in her eyes. How could he tell her the truth?

He stood there, but his mouth wouldn't move.

"What is it?" she asked. "I know you like her. I saw the way you looked at her the other night. Am I wrong?"

Scott shook his head. "Mom. Don't push."

"Are you saying you don't like her?"

"I didn't say that."

Daphne dropped the bottle of cleaner, and it splashed across the floor when it hit the ground. She backed up against the ladder, knocking it over, too. "Oh, my goodness. I can't believe I just knocked that over," Daphne said, rushing forward to clean it up.

Scott picked up the ladder and righted it. "That's exactly why you don't need to be in here alone."

"I'm not alone," Daphne said. "Brooke is here somewhere. Brooke?"

"Look who I found," Brooke said.

Scott turned around and saw Savannah standing next to Brooke.

"Hi, dear. How lovely to see you." Daphne hugged Savannah and then grabbed Brooke by the arm. "Brooke, come look at this outside. I think I might need to get you to help me with it."

403

They practically ran outside and Savannah stood there, not five feet away from Scott.

He turned and looked behind him. His mother and Brooke stood right in front of the door, talking but intently watching.

"It wasn't my idea," Savannah said. Her voice sounded tired.

His teeth clenched. Why did his mom insist on butting in? She had no idea what was going on here. He found it hard to even speak to Savannah. "My mom will stop at about nothing when she thinks she's right."

"I think she's right too." Savannah nervously moistened her lips. "I want her to be right so badly." Her faint smile held a hint of sadness.

"Are you buying the paper?"

Savannah lowered her eyes. She looked so fragile today, so unlike the strong, feisty girl he'd been spending time with. "Scott, I love this town, the people. But mostly it's you that makes me want to be here. I love you."

"Don't . . ." He looked away.

"I can't not love you. It's too late."

He shook his head.

"I don't blame you if you can't forgive me. I'm so sorry I made such a mess of things. It just all happened so fast. I didn't mean to hurt you."

He steadied his breath and turned back to look her in the eye. "What will you do?"

"Does it even matter?" She stared at him,

hoping, wishing that he'd take her in his arms and tell her it would be okay, but he didn't move. "I quit my job. My apartment was tied to my job. If I go back, I guess I'll have to sign a new lease." She looked at him, held his gaze for a long moment.

He stared at her. It was hard to separate the emotions he was feeling. He was mad as hell, hurt, and sad. He loved her too, but they were polar opposites in so many ways.

"I guess I should leave." She lifted her chin. "I have a lease to renew."

He nodded. "I guess you should."

She stepped past him. He could just barely hear her say good-bye as she passed by.

That good-bye felt like a bullet.

He heard the door close, but he couldn't move. Standing in that spot, he felt so much and absolutely nothing at all.

"Don't be a fool, Scott Calvin."

His mother's voice rang like the echo of that bullet ricocheting around the room.

She stepped forward with her hands on her hips. "If there's one thing I know, it's you. Don't let your pigheaded pride keep you from what you really want. Trust me, pride will get you absolutely nowhere when it comes to love."

He didn't respond. How could he?

"What else can I even say? Figure this out, son." She slammed the door behind her and he stood there by himself in the dark, empty building.

Daphne ran out into the street. "Please don't leave, Savannah. He'll come around. I know he will."

Savannah stopped and turned. Scott's back was to the door. "Thanks for trying."

Brooke ran over to Savannah's side. "I'm so sorry. I thought he'd come around."

"He will. You'll see." Daphne scrubbed her hands across her eyes. "It's so infuriating. It will work out. You'll be here working on the paper. He'll have to get used to the idea. Please don't leave," she pleaded.

"I think I better tell Jack that I can't buy the paper." Savannah stopped and turned to Daphne. "I really made a mess of things, but I want you to know that my friendship with you was sincere. Every moment of it. I'd like to at least call and check in on you."

"I hope you will."

"I will. I can promise you that, Daphne."

Brook and Daphne didn't say another word as they walked to Savannah's car.

Savannah reached for Brooke's hand. "Please tell Scott everything. Hand it all over to him. Don't waste another moment."

Brooke nodded.

When she got in her car, Savannah knew she should go see Jack, but she just couldn't bear to talk about it right now. She'd left his CDs in

Happy Balance too. She'd have to get that worked out. Another day, though. It would have to be another day.

She got on the interstate and headed north. She headed back to the only place she belonged right now, and really she didn't even belong there anymore.

The traffic was horrendous, but she didn't even care. She felt numb to the world and everything around her. She'd already quit her job, and she really didn't regret it. She'd figure something else out.

The whole ride back to northern Virginia, that look on Scott's face haunted her. He was so hurt. So disappointed. Why hadn't she told him when she had the chance? She knew better than to lie.

It would have been hard to tell him. He would have been mad, but to keep hiding it . . . it was wrong, and she couldn't blame him for not forgiving her.

Evelyn's ringtone sounded from her purse.

She dug her phone out and stuck it on speaker since she was still navigating the traffic.

"How did it go?" Evelyn asked.

"It didn't."

"He'll come around."

"He won't, but that's okay. Not everything we want or wish for is meant to be."

"You've softened, Van. It's a good thing. You

deserve change and a new chance. You're going to see that it will all work out for you."

"I think I want to un-quit."

"I fired you, remember?"

"Only because I quit."

"Well, I'm not letting you come back. You need to open up yourself to this change. It's time, honey."

"He doesn't want me."

"Okay, well if it's not him, it's someone or something. Take some time. You're going to find a new path."

"I've held on to some things for a long time. I made mistakes."

Evelyn's laugh filled the car. "My goodness, I think you're growing up."

"You're not mad that I'm leaving?"

"I'm disappointed. Of course. You're making me money hand over fist, but Van . . . my sweet Savannah, you are my friend. When you came to me green as a tree frog, you had the most desperate look in those beautiful eyes. It nearly broke my heart. I've watched you grow into a confident woman. You're smart. You're good-hearted. It's time for a change. You're ready. I know that you are."

"You've been so wonderful. How will I ever thank you?"

"Just because your life is changing a little does not mean we won't always be friends. You just keep me in the loop. And you keep doing a few articles freelance for me. Never burn a bridge . . . especially one that can help pay the bills."

"I definitely learned that from you a long time ago."

"You love him. He'll come around."

"Scott? That's not going to happen. Forget about that."

"Easy to say. You won't."

"I'll have to."

"No. Just give him a little time, but not too much. The more time you let go by, the more he gets used to the idea that you're gone. If you want my advice, I say get your fanny down there to Adams Grove and stay there until he gives in."

"I'll think about it, but I'm beat. For now, I'm just going to go to my apartment and try to get used to the idea of a new life. Until the lease runs out."

Evelyn's voice lost its soft tone and now it sounded like all business. "Now you listen up. Stop that 'woe is me' stuff. This is going to all work out. Trust your heart and don't give in."

When Savannah got to her apartment, rather than unpack, she walked around, assessing what she'd need to move. No job. No corporate apartment. There wasn't even anything here she was too attached to. Whatever was in her future, it wasn't going to be here.

She still needed to be sure all of that information from the mural got to Scott.

"One more thing I've done wrong." She knew she should have told him right then and there. He was going to be furious. Or maybe not. Maybe he'd just figure she was a complete mess, and he was right.

Savannah picked up her phone and googled the phone number to Happy Balance.

There was no answer, so she left a message. "Hey, Jenn. It's Savannah. Did you get with Scott about the mural? He'll know what to do. Give me a call and keep me posted, okay?" She left her phone number and then she dialed Aunt Cathy's number.

She got her voicemail too. "Hi, Aunt Cathy, it's me, Savannah. I thought I'd come back down in the next day or two and stay for a while. Can you help me find a place? Give me a call when you get a chance." She tossed her phone in her purse.

Tomorrow would be a better day.

She climbed into bed fully clothed and didn't even care that her shoes were on the bed.

When she woke up the next morning, she made a pot of coffee only to realize that the industrial-strength creamer had curdled while she was away. She slammed through the cabinets and refrigerator, frustrated by it, and everything in her life.

She was a wrinkled mess, but that didn't matter. She pulled a brush through her hair and brushed her teeth, then grabbed her keys and headed down the block to get a cup of coffee and something to eat.

Despite the sunshine, it felt gloomy. No one nodded or said hello this morning as she went down the street. Somehow the little café she'd been coming to forever seemed bland and unexciting. She missed the smell of Mac's sinful treats.

She ordered coffee—not the swanky latte that she used to get, but a regular coffee with cream and sugar. Two cups, of course. One for now, to get the motor going, and a second to enjoy.

She sure hoped this feeling would subside once she got back to Belles Corner to visit with Aunt Cathy.

Chapter FIFTEEN

Scott sat in his car waiting. Surveillance was his strong suit. A lot of people weren't patient enough for the task. He sipped his coffee. The subject had entered the apartment building about ten minutes ago.

It was easy to blend in with so many cars on the road.

Timing was still critical, though. He knew that.

He took the elevator to the fourth floor and stood in front of apartment 4E. He'd served hundreds and hundreds of warrants over the years, but today he planned to not only deliver this paper, but stay and see that it was followed to the letter.

He pulled an envelope from his shirt pocket and slipped out the trifolded paper inside.

Raising his hand to knock, his heart thrummed so loudly he wondered if he even needed to bother to knock. He took a breath. Noticing a stream of light from under the door, he stooped and slipped the paper underneath.

He let out a slow breath, trying to calm himself, then knocked and waited for a response.

Quick footsteps from inside the apartment came closer, then stopped short.

Savannah stopped and picked up the slip of paper someone had slid beneath the door. Probably another menu or political something or other.

She unfolded the white paper as she headed back into the living room, but the first two words made her stop.

Dear Van,

She glanced back toward the door and then at the letter and read on.

What advice do you give to a man who has met the woman of his dreams, but needs a second chance? She's his perfect match in every way. After being apart from her for just a few days, he knows that he will love her always and in all ways.

She's getting ready to renew her lease on an apartment that is hours away from him, and he wants her back.

Savannah walked over to the door and looked out the peephole. Scott was leaning against the wall across the hall. It sent her pulse spinning. Another look and she could see he hadn't slept much the last couple of days either. He looked like hell. Why did that make her feel a little hopeful? She bit down on her lower lip, stepped away from the door, and read on.

Do you have any advice on how they could make a long-distance relationship work? Or better yet, advice on how to get her to reconsider moving closer where I can hold her in my arms again night after night?

Okay, I'm that guy. I want that second chance . . . with you . . . and I have a better lease for you to consider. I'd even let you add your blue car to my cool collection and drive me around with the top down in the Mustang at all hours of the night over the speed limit, because I am just that crazy in love with you. I'll even burn perfectly good meat if that's the way you want it.

    Let me be your April Fool forever.
    Signed,
    Desperate(ly in love)

She took in a deep breath. It was unexpected. It was perfect.

He knocked on the door with the back of his knuckle and hoped this was going to work.
    She opened the door still clinging to the letter, but he couldn't read the expression on her face. He'd hoped for a smile.
    His voice cracked. "I'm sorry. I don't care about the past. Can we try this again?"
    She looked hesitant.
    "I want you to come back to Adams Grove. There are a lot of people already missing you there . . . especially me. If you could live there . . . in that little town . . . you could make me the happiest guy around."
    "I wasn't there that long."
    "You made a big impact," he said. "On more than just me."
    She smiled. "I feel inspired there, and I really am going to write a book someday."
    "I'm sorry I accused you of lying about the book. That wasn't fair."

"It's okay. We both said things that weren't nice. At least you didn't put yours in a newspaper."

"Doesn't make it any better. There's something else I need to tell you," he said.

His serious tone scared her a little. "It doesn't matter." Do I even want to know?

"This matters. I don't know if Brooke and Jenn have come to you yet, but that information you put together. On the mural I told you to leave alone—"

"I don't take direction well."

"No kidding, but in this case, I'm thankful. You were right. Those clues tie to the little girl, Christina, who went missing."

"Is it good news?"

"Uh-huh. You're a good detective too. Those letters that Brooke put together? They also formed a sentence once you gave her the name Christina."

"Really?"

"Yep. It said 'Christina is alive. Gardeners lawyer knows too.'"

"That doesn't make any sense. Who is the gardener?"

"Frank Gotorow's cell mate. His last name was Gardener. I met with him that day we went to the award ceremony in northern Virginia."

"You already knew?"

"No. I was looking for information on Gotorow; that's why I wanted to talk to his cell mate. I thought he might shed some light. Until Jenn and

Brooke brought all this to me, Jelly was the only one who had come to me about the mural. Poor guy was worried to death about it. He might be a bit on the peculiar side, but the man has a good heart and he knew there was something important in it."

"The clues were easy to miss. Brooke never could see them."

"I didn't see half what y'all did. I don't know how long it would have taken for me to put this together without your help."

Savannah's mouth was dry, making it hard to swallow. "I know I was overstepping boundaries. I hope you're not mad."

"Mad? I'm thankful you didn't listen to me. You might also like to know that the person leaving all the poetry on the doors around town was Jelly. I'd figured that much out."

"I didn't see that coming. I figured it was some kid on a poetic journey," Savannah said. "I was way off on that one. But the murals, they just begged for my attention. I couldn't stop."

"Thank goodness for that. It wasn't until y'all brought me those missing pieces that I realized the clues in the murals were tied to the crime that Gotorow's cell mate committed. Not Gotorow. It must have been part of the reason Gotorow ended up in Adams Grove. I've been working that case to find little Christina for three years. When Brooke and Jenn came to me with all of those notes and images y'all had worked on, everything fell right into place."

"Oh, my . . . Scott, is Christina really alive?"

"Yes. Thanks to you, she'll be reunited with her mother."

"Is she okay?"

"Yeah. Gardener snatched her and sold her for private adoption to his lawyer to pay for his services."

"His lawyer?"

"Well, he was disbarred last year for an unrelated incident, but yes. That's how Gardener paid his lawyer. Not only will we reunite Christina with her mother, but the trail for that lawyer has unlocked several other potential cases. You brought peace to Adams Grove, Savannah, and to a lot of other families."

"That's why the image of the door was beyond the garden. Gardener was the doorway to the information." She spoke a silent *Wow*. "I feel bad for the people who have to give those children up now. Three years? Did they have her the whole time? I'm sure they had no idea."

"No. They had no idea. They are as much victims here as the parents, but I have a feeling all parties will be amicable about keeping those connections. Jack is with Christina right now. The people who had adopted her are upset, but they're not stalling at all."

"Thank goodness."

"Thank you," he said. He took her hand. "Savannah, Jack's kind of counting on you taking over the paper too. Like right now."

"How do you feel about that?"

"It's nothing short of a miracle. For Christina. For us. I want to try this again. Can you?"

"I think so. Scott, you remind me of the good things I left behind, and you make me feel safe from the bad things. Momma would have adored you, and my dad would have been your best buddy. Cars, boats, and all. The bad news is . . ." Savannah raised the letter in front of her. "I can't answer this letter."

His heart dropped. She wasn't going to come back. It was over. He'd missed his opportunity, and damn if he couldn't ever get this love stuff right. He let out a breath. "I understand." He took a short step back.

"No. I don't think you do."

His hopes cautiously grew. "What do you mean?"

"I told you I quit that job. Us not getting together didn't change that. There's some guy downtown that answers these letters right now, and quite frankly I don't think he's going to give you the right advice."

"Are you saying . . .?"

"I'm saying, let's do this."

"That's not bad news. That's headline news. You know better than to bury the lead."

"The good kind of news. Worthy of the *Gazette*."

"You should still buy that paper. If it doesn't work out for some reason for us, that town loves you. You belong in Adams Grove."

"You really think so?"

"I do."

"I'm going to make my life in your town, Sheriff. I'm going to buy that paper from Jack, and we better get busy because I think we have a campaign to get started."

He stepped slowly toward her, and she walked right into his arms. "I've got some news for you, Savannah Dey."

"Uh-oh. Is it good or bad?"

"Depends on how you look at it." He held her close, resting his cheek on hers and whispered into her ear, "I have no intention of ever letting you get away again."

Acknowledgments

I'm so thankful to all of you for sharing my love for the small homespun community of Adams Grove. Like old friends, you welcome each story into your heart, and you've made my journey such a blessed one.

A special thank-you to my amazing Montlake family—the publishing team and the authors—who were so helpful as I pulled myself together after the passing of my husband earlier this year. Your support meant so much to me, and I'm honored to be a part of such an innovative and creative group of people. You continually push me to new limits and make me a better writer.

To Pam, a tour de force when it comes to organizing and getting it done. You not only kept me on my feet during the most difficult times of my life, but camped out with me as I finished this book in the middle of moving and retiring from a sixteen-year career to pursue my dream of becoming a full-time writer. You never doubted that I could make it all happen in this amazing year of change, and I would never let you down. Thank you for being such a special friend. You truly inspire me to be a better me. Quit being so perfect!

To my amazing author friends, especially (in alphabetical order because I know how competitive all y'all are!) Kelsey Browning, Grace Greene, Tonya Kappes, and Tracy March, thank you for sharing your time and brilliance brainstorming new stories, titles, and marketing ideas, and for all the motivation and cheerleading as we kept on moving forward! This job ain't for sissies. Hugs and happy writing.

Mom, Dad, and Greta—I love you so much. You are the reason I have the confidence to pursue this dream. Thank you for the best gift of all: unconditional love.

About the Author

Nancy Naigle writes love stories from the crossroads of small town and suspense. *Barbecue and Bad News* is the sixth novel in her contemporary romance series set in Adams Grove. When she isn't writing, she enjoys antiquing, cooking, and spa days with her friends.

A native of Virginia, Nancy now calls North Carolina home.

Center Point Large Print
600 Brooks Road / PO Box 1
Thorndike, ME 04986-0001 USA

(207) 568-3717

US & Canada:
1 800 929-9108
www.centerpointlargeprint.com

2/17

DATE DUE

MAR 1 4 2017		
JUL 1 8 2017		
SEP 0 5 2017		
8- 02-24		
Barrett Hrs		
10 - 13-21		
		PRINTED IN U.S.A.